Happy Birthday Mom 2006

THE
Kingdom
AND THE
Crown
VOLUME TWO

COME
UNTO ME

Love,
Cheryl

GERALD N. LUND

COME UNTO ME

SHADOW MOUNTAIN®

© 2001 Gerald N. Lund

First printing in hardbound 2001
First printing in paperbound 2006

Visit us at shadowmountain.com

Library of Congress Cataloging-in-Publication Data

Lund, Gerald N.
  Come unto me / Gerald N. Lund.
    p.   cm. — (The kingdom and the crown; v. 2)
  ISBN 1-57008-714-8 (hardbound : alk. paper)
  ISBN-10 1-59038-668-X (paperbound)
  ISBN-13 978-1-59038-668-2 (paperbound)
1. Bible. N. T.—History of Biblical events—Fiction. 2. Jesus Christ—Fiction.
  I. Title. II. Series: Lund, Gerald N. Kingdom and the crown; v. 2.

PS3562.U485 C66 2001
813'.54—dc21   2001004747

Printed in the United States of America
Banta, Menasha, WI
10   9   8   7   6   5   4   3   2   1

PREFACE

In the preface to volume one, *Fishers of Men*, I noted some of the challenges associated with attempting to write an "accurate" historical novel set in the times of the New Testament world. These included such issues as:

- The many different versions of the Bible and which one to use when citing the words of Jesus.
- The date of Christ's birth and whether to use the Jewish or Roman calendar.
- Dealing with the multiple languages that were part of the cultural life of the period—Hebrew, Aramaic, Latin, and Greek.
- The proper pronunciation of various names.
- Dealing with the name of God and other religious traditions.
- Supplying specific details required for a novel that are not given in the scriptural record.

I did not feel it necessary to repeat that information here. I suggest that readers concerned about such issues may want to review the earlier preface before reading *Come unto Me*.

Once again, chapter notes are provided in many cases to help clarify historical, linguistic, or cultural information or to explain why I, as an author, chose to treat the material as I did.

It has been a gratifying and rewarding experience to once again immerse myself in the life and times of Jesus. I owe a great debt to the numerous scholars, both living and dead, who through a lifetime of study made it possible for that immersion to take place.

I also offer the deepest thanks to the staff at Shadow Mountain for their enormous contribution to this project. Jana Erickson and Cory Maxwell are not only consummate professionals, but they have become dear and treasured friends. Sheri Dew's unflagging support has been significant in bringing this work to a wide market of readers. Jay Parry's thoughtful and meticulous (but never intrusive) editing has strengthened the book in countless ways. Simon Dewey, whose cover paintings become treasured pieces of art in their own right, has also contributed significantly to the overall project.

My daughters, Cynthia Dobson and Julie Stoddard, not only read the manuscript and made suggestions, but they also undertook the tedious and enormous task of cataloguing the thousands of details (character descriptions, geographical locations, scriptural references, and so forth) that I need to keep straight while writing a multivolume series. Though never seen by the reader, their work has influenced almost every page. Shawn Stringham, friend for a good share of our lifetimes, is a thoughtful and, more importantly, an honest, perceptive reader and critic, and I thank her for her willingness to read and make suggestions for improving the manuscript.

Above all, I offer thanks to my wife, Lynn. She is always my first reader and most valued text evaluator. Readers of this series and previous works have largely been spared the pain of laboring through tortured passages or weak characterizations because of Lynn's editorial contribution. I value her insights and wisdom, and more critically, I value her love for the Savior and his teachings that makes her insist that I try to "get it right." Our companionship, now approaching forty rich and wonderful years, has been the most significant influence in my life, and words seem terribly inadequate to thank her for that.

My hope for all readers, whether they agree with my portrayal and depiction of the Savior and his disciples or not, is that this work will stimulate in them a desire to answer for themselves the question that Jesus asked: "What think ye of Christ? whose son is he?" (Matthew 22:42).

Alpine, Utah
July 2001

SYNOPSIS OF
VOLUME ONE

Fishers of Men opened as Marcus Quadratus Didius, a tribune in the Roman legions, comes to the family of David ben Joseph, a wealthy merchant from Capernaum. The Holy Land has been under the total and often brutal rule of the Roman Empire for almost a century. The corrupt system of Roman tax collection encourages corruption, and David ben Joseph has gone to Damascus to try to raise money to pay an exorbitant assessment. His wife, Deborah, is already deeply embittered against the Romans. When she was fifteen years old, her family was caught up in a rebellion against Rome. Several, including her father, were killed, and her mother died in the months following as they were forced to hide through the winter in the mountains. This hatred for everything Roman has been passed on to her son, Simeon, twenty-one, who leads a band of "Zealots." When Marcus Didius learns that the family does not have the money for their taxes, he refuses to accept their pleas for additional time and tries to arrest them. Simeon resists and is nearly killed. David, his father, returns barely in time to rescue his wife and daughter from being sold into slavery. It is against this backdrop of violence and injustice that the story unfolds.

As a young man some thirty years before, David ben Joseph was in the shepherd fields of Bethlehem. He saw the angels and heard the glorious announcement that the Messiah had been born. So when word comes to the Galilee that a man named John the Baptist claims to be the forerunner for the Messiah and has designated a carpenter from Nazareth as that Messiah, David is anxious to learn more. Then Jesus comes to Capernaum and calls David's partners in the fishing business as followers—Simon Peter and his brother, Andrew. David decides to investigate further. He is convinced almost immediately that Jesus is the Christ, or the promised Messiah, and soon is able to convince the rest of his family—all except for Simeon. Simeon finds the teachings of Jesus highly offensive. Loving your enemies and turning the other cheek seems antithetical to all the true Deliverer would stand for. Simeon's refusal to follow Jesus alienates Simeon from his family.

However, in time, Simeon cannot help being drawn to Jesus by the simple impact of his teachings and the increasing evidence of his remarkable power. After watching Jesus instantly and completely restore a man's twisted and withered hand and then feed five thousand people with five small loaves of bread and two fish, Simeon can no longer say that Jesus is an ordinary man. This realization does not bring Simeon peace, however. Now he is torn between his old loyalties to the Zealots and his desire to become a follower of Jesus of Nazareth.

Mordechai ben Uzziel is one of the richest and most powerful men in Jerusalem. An aristocratic Sadducee and member of the Great Council there, he is anxious to make accommodation with Rome in order to maintain peace and protect the base of power he and the other Jewish leaders hold. His eighteen-year-old daughter, Miriam, is pampered, coddled, and accustomed to a life of comfort and luxury. But she is also filled with a strange sense of unrest. She sees that her father's religion consists mostly of outward trappings, and she searches for deeper meaning in life. On a trip to the Galilee, she and her father are rescued from the hands of a vicious bandit, Moshe Ya'abin, by Simeon and his band of Zealots. Though Miriam feels a great sense of obligation to Simeon for this, her father does not. Because the Zealots threaten war with Rome, Mordechai sets up an intricate plot with Pontius Pilate, the Roman governor of Judea, to draw the Zealots into a trap.

As the story unfolds, Miriam also comes in contact with Jesus of Nazareth. She is on the Temple Mount when he drives out the money-changers. Later she watches him deal compassionately with a woman taken in adultery. Though she knows little about him, she determines to learn more. To her surprise, her father is furious when he hears of her desire and forbids any further contact.

Then Miriam accidentally learns of her father's plan to draw the Zealots into the trap. A seemingly isolated wagon train of arms will be sent to decoy the Zealots into the Joknean Pass; then waiting Roman legionnaires will swoop down and kill them. Knowing that Simeon and the others who saved her life will most likely die, Miriam decides she cannot simply stand by. She goes to the Galilee and tells Simeon everything.

This puts Simeon in a terrible dilemma. Just prior to Miriam's coming, Simeon had told his band of men that he would not lead them in the raid against the Romans. Because of his commitment to follow Jesus, he has decided he must turn from his life of violence. But when he learns of Mordechai's treachery and the danger to his men, there is no choice. He and his father ride to the Joknean Pass. Ironically, in order to stop a massacre, Simeon has to save the Romans, led by Tribune Marcus Didius, the very man who epitomizes all that Simeon once hated. Driven by a desire to do what is right, Simeon intervenes and saves the Roman column, but in doing so, one of his men is killed, and another, Yehuda, his closest friend and second-in-command, is captured.

The book closes as, in an agony of conscience, Simeon realizes that his commitment to be a disciple of Jesus has come only at a terrible price to those who trusted in him.

LIST OF MAJOR CHARACTERS

The Household of David ben Joseph, Merchant of Capernaum

   David: Simeon's father, 46[1]

   Deborah bat Benjamin of Sepphoris: Simeon's mother, 44

   Simeon: Second son of David and Deborah, ardent Zealot, 21

   Ephraim: Simeon's older brother, married to Rachel, 25

   Rachel: Ephraim's wife, 22

   Leah: Simeon's sister, 15

   Joseph: Simeon's youngest brother, 10

   Esther: David and Deborah's granddaughter, daughter of Ephraim and Rachel, 4

   Boaz: David and Deborah's grandson, son of Ephraim and Rachel, almost 2

   Aaron of Sepphoris: Deborah's brother, Simeon's uncle, a dedicated Pharisee, 39

The Household of Mordechai ben Uzziel of Jerusalem

   Mordechai: Miriam's father; leader of the Sadducees, member of the Great Sanhedrin of Jerusalem, 42

   Miriam bat Mordechai ben Uzziel: Mordechai's only daughter, 18

   Livia of Alexandria: Miriam's servant and friend, 20

   Drusus Alexander Carlottus: Livia's brother who was sold into slavery, 17

   Ezra of Joppa: Sandal maker, married to Lilly, 30

   Lilly: cousin to Miriam's deceased mother, Ezra's wife, 28

---

[1]Ages are given as of A.D. 30.

The Household of Yehuda of Beth Neelah

    Yehuda: Simeon's friend and partner in the Zealot movement, a farmer, 24

    Shana: Yehuda's sister, 17

Other Prominent Characters

    Jesus of Nazareth: Carpenter and teacher, 30

    Mary of Nazareth: Mother of Jesus[2]

    Marcus Quadratus Didius: Roman tribune, 25

    Cornelia Alberatus Didius: Marcus's mother

    Sextus Rubrius: Roman centurion, about 50

    Moshe ben Ya'abin: Bandit and thief

    Eliab: Ya'abin's chief captain

    Pontius Pilate: Procurator of Judea

    Azariah the Pharisee: Leader of the Jerusalem group and titular head of the Pharisees, 50

    Simon Peter: Fisherman, one of the Twelve Apostles called by Jesus

    Andrew: Simon Peter's brother, one of the Twelve

    James and John: Sons of Zebedee, partners in fishing with Peter and Andrew; both apostles

    Matthew Levi: A publican in Capernaum; called to follow Jesus, also one of the Twelve

    Luke, the Physician: A disciple of Jesus in Capernaum

    Amram the Pharisee: Leader of the Pharisees in Capernaum, about 50

    Joseph of Arimathea: A wealthy member of the Great Sanhedrin in Jerusalem, a secret follower of Jesus

    Mary Magdalene: A follower of Jesus from Magdala on the Sea of Galilee, from whom Jesus cast out seven devils

    Martha, Mary, and Lazarus of Bethany: A family close to Jesus with whom he sometimes stayed while in the Jerusalem area

---

[2]Ages for actual Bible characters are not given here since they are not known (other than the age of Jesus), though suggestions about their age may be included in the novel itself.

GLOSSARY

NOTE: Some terms which are used only once and are defined in the text are not included here.

Abba (AH-bah)—Diminutive of *Ahv*, father; thus "Papa," or "Daddy."

bath or *bat* (BAHT)—Daughter, or daughter of, e.g., Miriam bat Mordechai, or Miriam, daughter of Mordechai.

ben (BEN)—Son, or son of, as in Simeon ben David or Simeon, son of David. An Aramaic translation of *ben* is *bar*, as in Peter's name, Simon Bar-jona, or Simon, son of Jonah (Matthew 16:17), and *bar mitzvah*.

Beth (BAIT; commonly pronounced as BETH among English speakers)— House of, e.g., *Bethlehem,* House of Bread; *Bethel,* the House of God.

boker tov (BOH-kur TOHV)—Literally "good day"; used like "hello."

Eema (EE-mah)—Diminutive of *Eem*, mother; thus "Mama," or "Mommy."

goyim (goy-EEM)—Gentiles, literally in Hebrew, "nations," a word used for anyone not of the house of Israel, or in modern times, one who is not a Jew; singular is *goy.*

matzos (MAHT-zos)—Unleavened bread, especially that used during the Feast of Unleavened Bread and with the Passover meal.

menorah (commonly, men-ORE-rah, but also men-ore-RAH)—A candlestick; usually refers to the sacred, seven-branched candlestick used in the tabernacle of Moses and later in the temples.

mezuzah (meh-ZOO-sah)—Literally, in Hebrew, "doorpost"; the small wood or metal container with scriptural passages inside fixed to the doorposts and gates of observant Jewish homes in response to the command in Deuteronomy 6:9.

pater familias (PAY-tur FAH-MILL-ee-us)—The "Father of the family"; suggests his absolute authority over his wife and children.

Pesach (pe-SOCK)—The Hebrew name for Passover.

praetorium (pree-TOR-ee-um)—Official residence of the Roman governor or procurator or other high government official.

publicani (poo-blee-KHAN-ee)—Latin for "public servant"; the publicans of the New Testament were hired by Romans to serve as the tax assessors and collectors in local districts.

Sanhedrin (san-HED-rin)—The ruling council in various towns and cities; the Great Sanhedrin in Jerusalem was the supreme governing body of the Jews at this time.

seder (SAY-dur)—From the Hebrew word for "order." The Passover meal is often called *seder*; there the various prescribed foods are laid out in a specific order.

Shabbat (sha-BAHT)—Hebrew name for the Lord's day; the source of our word *Sabbath*.

shalom (shaw-LOWM)—"Peace," used as a greeting and a farewell.

Sh'ma (SH-MAH)—Literally "hear!" the opening word of Deuteronomy 6:4; the name for the most sacred prayer of the Jews.

Talmud (TALL-mood)—A collection of sacred writings and commentaries written by learned rabbis and Hebrew scholars of the Torah over many generations.

Torah (TORE-ah)—The writings of Moses; the first five books of the current Old Testament.

Via Maris (VEE-ah MAR-ees)—The Way of the Sea; famous highway following the eastern Mediterranean coastline from Egypt to Syria.

Via Sacra (VEE-ah SAHK-rah)—The Sacred Way; main street of the Roman city center, or Roman Forum.

Pronunciation Guide for Names

Readers may wish to use the common English pronunciations for names that have come to modern times, such as David. The Hebrew pronunciation is for those who wish to say them as they may have been spoken at the time of the Savior. Any such pronunciation guide must be viewed as speculative, however; we simply do not know for certain how Hebrew names were pronounced in antiquity.

Abraham—In Hebrew, ahv-rah-HAM
Anna—ahn-AH

Azariah—ah-zeh-RAI-ah

Bethlehem—English, BETH-leh-hem; Hebrew, BAIT lech-EM

Beth Neelah—BAIT nee-LAH

Bethsaida—English, BETH-say-dah; Hebrew, BAIT sah-EE-dah

Caesarea—see-zar-EE-ah

Capernaum—English, ka-PUR-neh-um; Hebrew, kah-fur-NAY-hum

Chorazin—khor-ah-ZEEN

Daniel—dan-YELL

David—dah-VEED

Deborah—deh-vor-AH

Ephraim—ee-FRAI-eem

Esther—es-TAHR

Eve—hah-VAH

Galilee—English, GAL-leh-lee; Hebrew, gah-LEEL or gah-lee-YAH

Ha'keedohn—ha-kee-DOHN

James—Same as Jacob, or yah-ah-KOHV in Hebrew

Jerusalem—ye-roosh-ah-LAI-eem

Jesus—Hebrew form of the name is Yeshua (yesh-oo-AH), which is the same as the Old Testament *Joshua*; Greek form is hee-AY-soos.

John—Hebrew form of the name is Johanan (yo-HAH-nahn).

Joknean Pass—yohk-NEE-an

Joseph—yo-SEPH

Leah—lay-AH

Miriam—meer-YAM

Mordechai—mor-deh-KAI

Moshe Ya'abin—mohw-SHEH ya-ah-BEEN

Mount Hermon—hur-MOHN

Mount Tabor—English, TAY-bur; Hebrew, tah-BOHR

Ptolemais—TOHL-eh-mays

Rachel—rah-KHEL

Samuel—shmoo-EL

Sepphoris—seh-PHOR-us

Shana—SHAW-nah

Simeon—shee-MOHN

Simon—see-MOHN

Yehuda—yeh-HOO-dah; other forms, Judah or Judas

CHAPTER 1

I

CAPERNAUM, IN THE GALILEE

16 JUNE, A.D. 30

"Archers! Take your marks!"

The bull voice of Yehuda roared in the darkness, almost drowned out by the clash of swords and the shouts of terrorized men coming from the battle raging below.

In perfect synchronization, the two dozen or so Zealots of the band of Ha'keedohn the Javelin notched their shafts to the string, pulled back the bows until the feathers caressed their cheeks, and squinted carefully as they picked out their targets below them in the light of the half-moon. Yehuda dropped his arm and shouted. "Three!" Two dozen shafts shot away.

Below them, on the narrow road that snaked its way through the Joknean Pass, men screamed or gave a soft cry of surprise as they crumpled and fell. Simeon felt a rush of exultation. It was going to work. Moshe Ya'abin was on the run.

Suddenly, though, everything seemed to slow to half-speed.

Yehuda's voice echoed hollowly, as if he were shouting from inside a cistern. "One!" The hands began to raise towards the quivers on their backs, but slowly. Too slowly! Simeon gaped in horror. The quivers were empty! There were no arrows to loose. Dark shapes were swarming up the hill at them, howling, their faces twisted with fury. In the lead, Ya'abin swung an enormous sword, his lips drawn back in a hideous grimace.

Simeon stiffened as everything changed. In a fleeting instant, the bowmen were gone, the attackers had disappeared. All was black. The silence was eerie. What was happening? Where—? Then his heart seized up, and an icy breath blew across his neck. A ghostly figure began to materialize out of the darkness. Simeon tried to lunge upward, panic squeezing at his chest, but he was tied to the earth. His fingers dug into his palms. It couldn't be! Not—

But it was! It was Daniel. Yehuda's younger brother staggered toward him, his face whiter than the driven snow, his hands clutching at his stomach. Something inside Simeon's head warned him not to look, shouted at him not to look, but he couldn't stop himself. His eyes dropped. Daniel was clutching at an enormous arrow protruding from his body. It was longer than a man's bow, almost longer than Daniel's entire body.

Simeon shrank back as the apparition came towards him, larger, looming ever larger. He could not take his eyes from Daniel's face. It was twisted with pain, the features barely recognizable. His eyes were huge, questioning, betrayed.

Simeon tried to turn away, unable to look any more, but Daniel's hand shot out and jerked him around, leaving a smear of blood across Simeon's tunic. "Why, Simeon?" The voice echoed as if it came from a huge drum. *Why? Why? Why?*

Simeon sat up with a jerk, eyes wild. He was bathed in sweat, and he was gasping frantically. Then with a flood of relief he realized he was not in the Joknean Pass. He was not with Yehuda and Daniel. He was in his bed. He was in his father's house in Capernaum.

He fell back on the bed. It had come again, but it was just a dream.

And yet—. His shoulders slumped and he put his hands over his face, the chills still coursing through his body. "Oh, Daniel!" he whispered. "I am so sorry."

II

JOPPA, ON THE COASTAL PLAINS OF JUDEA

About seventy-five miles to the southeast of Capernaum, in a small seaside house in the town of Joppa, Miriam, daughter of Mordechai ben Uzziel of Jerusalem, moaned softly. Reaching up, she rubbed at her eyes, pressing gently against the lids, trying to ease the weariness that lay behind them. Why? Why couldn't she sleep? She could not remember when she had last felt so totally, utterly spent. Yet her mind would not rest. Her thoughts were like a chariot wheel thrown off in full flight.

She sat up and looked around. In the soft moonlight coming through the window, she could see Livia's still form on the smaller bed in the corner, her honey-blond hair a splash of pale gold. They had not returned here to the house of Ezra the Sandalmaker until about two hours after sundown. Lilly, Ezra's wife and Miriam's cousin, had fixed them a quick supper; then they had all gone to bed. Livia fell asleep almost instantly and now slept deeply. How Miriam envied her. Miriam had not so much as dozed off in that time, not even for a moment.

Moving carefully so as not to make any sound, she slipped quietly off the bed and padded to the window. The shutters were open to catch the breeze off the sea. She leaned out, resting her elbows on the sill, and breathed deeply. The moon was low in the sky, making a silvery ribbon across the surface of the water. She could hear the soft lapping of the waves on the sand below her. The sound soothed and relaxed her. This was the Great Sea, or the "internal sea," the *Mare Internum*, as the Romans named it, or the *Mediterranean*, the Sea-in-the-Middle-of-the-Land. She liked that last name. It seemed to fit it best.

Miriam lowered her head and rested it on her arms. What danger had she brought upon this simple household? Unlike her father's side of the family, Ezra and Lilly were neither rich nor powerful. Lilly was Miriam's mother's cousin. Childless, she and Ezra lived simply but comfortably here on the coast. It was a good location for a sandal-maker. Joppa was on the *Via Maris*, the Way of the Sea, the great Roman road that led from Egypt into Syria. Miriam didn't see them a great deal, but regarded Lilly, who was ten years older than she was, as more like an aunt than a cousin.

When Miriam had overheard her father and Marcus laying out the plot to trap the Zealots at the Joknean Pass, she hadn't known what to do. Then she had decided to come to Ezra for help. It said a lot about both of them that neither Ezra nor Lilly hesitated. With his wife's encouragement, Ezra took Miriam and Livia to Capernaum so Miriam could warn Simeon. Now Miriam realized that if her father ever learned of what they'd done, she would not be the only one in serious trouble. Her father was a powerful man, both financially and politically. She suspected that he would wreak his revenge on Ezra in more ways than one.

But she was struggling with deeper issues that concerned her even more than that. Even before coming to maturity, Miriam had realized that her father was not a deeply religious man. Oh, the outer trappings were there. The Sadducees cloaked themselves in the robes of righteousness, but Miriam came to realize early on that what they really worshiped was power. Power lay even behind the drive for wealth.

Miriam had grown up in a life of unbridled luxury. Her father was one of the richest men in the country, and she had been coddled, pampered, and spoiled. Her friends, who came from similarly wealthy households, never questioned their wealth. In their eyes, this was their rightful place in life. So why couldn't she just accept it? As she entered her teen years, she found the question more and more troubling. She would walk through the markets of Jerusalem's inner city, see the squalor and the poverty, see the children who had so little of the world's abundance, and she would wonder. What divine plan put her where she was and them where they were? If she could have pointed to some deep sacrifice she had made or some act of supreme effort, then she might have been more comfortable with her status. But she couldn't. She had done nothing to merit it. And knowing that she loved her circumstances—loved the luxurious home in the upper city, loved being able to choose her clothing from exotic fabrics from across the empire, loved the scented baths and the mysterious perfumes—only deepened her guilt.

Miriam's mother had died when she was six, so Miriam was not sure if she had gotten this inner sensitivity, this natural sense of injustice, from her or not. It certainly hadn't come from her father. She had once asked him about the obvious unfairness of life, wondering if it was from God or simply some blind chance. He responded with a derisive laugh. Fate? Divine intervention? What about effort and natural talent and a willingness to work? The poor were poor because they were lazy. They were satisfied with their hovels and their uncomplicated lives. It wasn't injustice at all. Life actually was infinitely just.

The answer hadn't satisfied her. For one thing, she knew that it wasn't totally true. Especially for her. Virtually nothing she enjoyed was due to her own labors. Even her beauty. She knew that she was uncommonly lovely. Her long dark hair would glow like something liquid and alive after her bath. Her skin was almost without flaw. Her dark, wide-set eyes reflected intelligence and sensitivity. Her body was slender and graceful.

What all this privilege did for her was create a vague discomfort, a never-ending feeling of unease. It was more than guilt. For reasons she could not explain, she was filled with a deep spiritual hunger. The religion of her father was not satisfactory. For a brief time she thought perhaps Pharisaism might fill her void, but she quickly turned away from its stifling obsession with minutia. Through the influence of her father's position, she was able to obtain her own copy of the Torah and other scriptures. She went through a period where she devoured those scriptural writings—the five books of Moses, the historical books, the prophetic writings. That helped, but did not totally satisfy.

And then Jesus had come into her life. And therein lay her sorrow. Her father utterly rejected the idea that Jesus might be the Messiah. When she tried to speak with him about it, she found an implacable coldness in him that almost frightened her. He had forbidden her to even speak the name of Jesus.

The pain squeezed in around her heart. Was her joy, only so recently found, to be crushed? Must she choose between Jesus and her father? In a few days, Miriam would be back in Jerusalem. In spite of his failings, she loved her father deeply. What would she say to him? She carried two terrible secrets in her heart now. First, *she* had been the one to betray him. She could barely fathom what he might do if he learned that piece of knowledge. Her second secret had even greater implications. She believed in Jesus. Her time in Capernaum with Simeon's family had convinced her. She wanted to become one of Jesus' followers. Somehow, instinctively, she knew this would affect her relationship with her father even more profoundly than her betrayal.

With that thought, unable to bear the piercing sadness that swept through her, she left the window and threw herself down on the bed.

She closed her eyes, trying to smother the thoughts long enough to get to sleep.

III

CAPERNAUM

Simeon slipped away from his father's house while it was still dark, going carefully through the gate so as not to awaken anyone. It would be another hour before the villagers on the streets began to stir. He walked swiftly down to the seashore, found a place beneath some willows where he was half-hidden in the shadows, and sat down to wait. He wasn't very hopeful. Peter, Andrew, James, and John still fished occasionally to provide for their families, but not on a regular basis. As four of the Twelve Apostles Jesus had chosen, they had little time to pursue their former occupations.

Half an hour later, he heard voices floating to him across the water and could see the dark shapes of the boat against the lightening eastern sky. He stood, hoping that his luck would hold. Ten minutes later his wait was rewarded when he heard Peter's booming voice directing Andrew to steer the boat into shore. Simeon moved down to the water's edge to meet them.

IV

ON THE SHORES OF THE SEA OF GALILEE

"How much have you spoken of this to your father and mother?"
Simeon shrugged.

"That much, eh?" Peter snorted, giving him a baleful look. They
had finished sorting and cleaning the fish. The fish destined for the
markets were in buckets of water; the others had been tossed back into
the lake. It had been a good night for fishing. There would be money
for the two families this day. Peter and Andrew began to spread their
nets out to dry in the morning sun.

"You know my father," Simeon began. "Believing in Jesus came as
easy to him as fishing does to you two."

"Yes, it did," Andrew agreed. "Part of that was because of the experience he had with the shepherds in Bethlehem thirty years ago."

"I know," Simeon said.

"And part of it," Peter added, "is that your father just has a believing heart."

"Exactly my point," Simeon answered. "With Mother, it came a
little harder, but once she was convinced, there has never been any
looking back."

Both brothers stopped what they were doing and gave him a pointed
look. "Are *you* looking back, Simeon?" Peter finally asked softly.

"Oh, no," he said, surprised that they had taken it that way. "It's
just that—" He sat back on his heels, watching them work as he
sought for the right words. He had a lot of confidence in these two
men. They had been his father's partners in business since he was a
boy, and they were more like older brothers to him. Peter, the younger
of the two, was just a few years older than Simeon, but shoulder-length

hair and a thick, luxuriant beard made him look older than that. Peter had a quick sense of humor, a droll way of pricking at you if you got a little too pompous or took yourself too seriously. His eyes were a clear blue with tiny flecks of green.

The resemblance between him and Andrew was not that strong. Andrew's hair and beard were darker in color and finer in texture than Peter's. Andrew was three years older than Peter, which was often reflected in a more thoughtful and deliberate approach to life. Both showed the results of a lifetime of pulling in nets from the sea, with strong, muscular bodies and powerful hands, but Peter was shorter and more stocky and Andrew's hands were enormous. It always fascinated Simeon how they could be so large and yet as nimble as a woman's.

"How long have you two been partners with my father now?" he asked.

"Seven years and a few months," Andrew said. "I was eighteen. Peter was fifteen."

"So I would have been about eleven then. Which means you've known me for a long time."

"We knew you even before we became partners," Andrew noted. "I can remember you when you were still a minnow."

Simeon chuckled at that image. "Then you know how deeply ingrained into my system the whole Zealot movement is. From the time I was little, Mother would tell me the story of her family, of the beginnings of the Zealot movement, and how my grandparents died. I don't ever remember her consciously telling me that I should become a Zealot myself. I don't even think she asked me to be the one to revenge those terrible evils, but her stories filled me with such anger and indignation that I could hardly stand it."

"I remember," Andrew said somberly. "By the time you were ten, you were determined to overthrow the entire Roman empire by yourself. Your father used to threaten to tie you down when any Romans came to town so you wouldn't run up and punch one of them in the nose."

Simeon smiled. "I remember that, too."

"And now that you've decided to become a follower of Jesus, you don't know what to do. Is that it?" Peter said, glancing at the buckets of fish. They would soon have to be off if they were to keep them fresh.

Nodding, Simeon went on. "Unfortunately, holding on to my temper has never been my strongest attribute. When I see something that I feel is wrong, I feel like *I* have to be the one to make it right." He reached up and pulled back his tunic, revealing the long white scar across his chest. "Of course, that's how I got this."

Andrew was somber now. "I remember that day very clearly. Young Joseph came to our house looking for help. Peter and I were among the first ones to find you there in the courtyard."

"You're very lucky to be alive," Peter murmured, staring at the scar.

"I know. But that's what I mean. Since I was a boy, something inside of me just won't let me leave things alone."

A slow grin split Peter's thick, dark beard. "Your mother told me there were . . . what? sixteen soldiers standing around you that day?" When Simeon nodded, Peter shook his head in disbelief. "I can understand impulsive. I have the same failing myself. But whipping out your dagger and jumping the commanding officer?" The grin broadened. "I've caught fish with more brains than that."

Simeon laughed in spite of himself. "I come here looking for sympathy, and this is what I get? Thanks, Peter."

Andrew was smiling too, but his eyes were probing Simeon's face. "Is that really why you came?" he asked. "For sympathy?"

The smile died. "No, not really."

"Then what?"

"I came looking for counsel."

"Now, that we give freely," Peter said.

"And it's usually worth exactly what it costs you," Andrew noted dryly.

Simeon barely heard him. "Do you remember the day you and I talked, Peter? The day Jesus fed the five thousand?"

"I do. You looked like you had been struck by lightning."

"I may as well have been. I watched five loaves and two fishes go from person to person, from mouth to mouth, never being depleted, and in fact coming back with more than there was to begin with. Being struck by lightning barely describes what I felt that day."

"Then I suggested you go to Nazareth and talk to Jesus' mother," Peter said.

"And I did." He sighed. "And nothing has been the same since."

Peter was filled with satisfaction. "It is good to know that occasionally I am in tune with the Spirit of God."

"When I left Nazareth, everything had changed. I had changed. I could not disbelieve her. I couldn't. There was no question about it. That was when I went to Beth Neelah and told Yehuda I could no longer lead them into battle. If Jesus was truly the Son of God, it changed everything for me."

"And then came the Joknean Pass," Peter said quietly, finally understanding why Simeon had come.

"Yes, and then came the Joknean Pass." He began to rub at his eyes. "So much for all my determination to change. It was the same old me up there. I thought I was trying to do what Jesus would have me do, but I went charging off, sure I could be a disciple of Jesus *and* save the world."

"You may not have saved the world," Andrew said slowly, "but you saved many lives that night, Simeon. What you did was right."

"Was it? Then why is Daniel dead? And why are Yehuda and Samuel and Barak in prison awaiting crucifixion. If I was so right, why did everything turn out so wrong?" He looked at the two brothers in turn, the anguish twisting his face.

Peter had finished with the net now. He watched Simeon closely, his eyes thoughtful. "Is that the real question you want to ask, Simeon?

Do you really want to know why things happened as they did, or are you here to see if we can help you decide what to do now?"

Simeon slowly nodded. Peter might be just a few years older than Simeon, and he might be impulsive and playful and quick of wit, but something had happened to him since he had started developing into the Lord's chief apostle. He was more thoughtful, more pensive, more . . . Simeon sought for the right word. More wise.

"Yes," he finally said. "I guess it is. Three of my friends are in prison awaiting execution because of me. Do I just turn my back on them? Is that what Jesus would expect of me? Or do I revert to my old ways? The old Simeon wouldn't be sitting here agonizing about it. He'd be out doing something by now. Mount an attack on Caesarea. Batter down the walls and free them all. Or maybe I would kidnap some prominent Roman and trade him for the three prisoners. Instead, I sit here like a bird hopping back and forth on a branch, too timid to fly but knowing I can't just sit there either."

Peter was suddenly determined. "Come. This is not a question we can answer for you. Come to my house and you can ask Jesus for yourself."

V

CAPERNAUM

By the time they took the buckets of fish to the waiting fish-mongers, the sun was well up in the sky. Jesus had long since gone from Peter's house when they arrived. Anna told them that he had wanted some time to himself and was going up into the hills above

Capernaum. The disappointment left a sharp taste in Simeon's mouth. But Peter only smiled and patted his shoulder. "Come, come," he said. "Jesus rarely gets away by himself. Someone always sees him and that's that. I'll wager my best fishing net that we'll find him either still in town or not far away."

He was right. They found Jesus on the north side of the main synagogue of Capernaum, standing in the shade provided by the building. There wasn't a large crowd yet, but more people were coming even as Peter and Simeon approached. Simeon wasn't surprised to see some of his family there as well. His mother was there with Leah, his sister who was almost sixteen, and Rachel, Ephraim's wife and Simeon's sister-in-law. Rachel had her two children, Esther and Boaz, with her. The five of them were just beyond Jesus. They waved when they saw Simeon with Peter. Simeon smiled back at them, but made no move to go to them. Instead, he and Peter moved over to join others of the Twelve— James and John, Nathanael, Matthew the publican, Bartholomew.

"What's happening?" Peter asked John in a whisper as they came up.

John shrugged. "Jesus is mostly asking and answering questions." He looked at Simeon. "Your uncle was here a little while ago."

"Uncle Aaron?"

"Yes. He and Amram and several other Pharisees were challenging Jesus about his unwillingness to keep all the rules of the Sabbath."

"Did my mother see him?" Simeon wondered.

"Yes." It was Bartholomew who answered now. "But Aaron would barely speak to her. It was almost like he was embarrassed to be seen with her."

"That's my Uncle Aaron," Simeon said grimly. "Since the family was baptized, he's been convinced they've ransomed their souls to the devil."

But he didn't really want to think about Uncle Aaron. Moving slightly so he had a clear line of sight to where the Master was standing, Simeon tried to gauge if he might be able to get the Master apart for a few moments. It didn't look very promising, and he wasn't going to ask his questions with everyone looking on. He turned to Peter. "This isn't the time to ask him anything."

But Peter was not about to let him get away with that. "Come with me," he said, grabbing Simeon's wrist. "This is important."

"Not with all these people around," Simeon demurred. "Maybe later."

Peter looked at him sharply. "A while ago, you seemed very anxious for an answer."

"I was, but—"

"Then let's go." When Simeon still held back, Peter turned and called in a loud voice, "Master?"

The group immediately went quiet, and those in closest stepped back to see who had spoken. The Master's eyes fell on Peter, and Jesus gave him a brief smile. "*Boker tov*, Peter. And how was the catch last night?"

"Very good, Master. Thank you." He glanced at Simeon. "There is a question here."

"Peter!" Simeon hissed. "Not now."

"Yes?" Jesus said.

Peter smiled triumphantly, stepping back as he gestured for Simeon to proceed. Simeon stepped forward, his face burning. Everyone was watching him now. He especially noted his mother's quizzical look. He had no desire to try to explain everything, so he decided to couch his question in a more general way. "Master, living the life of a disciple raises many questions about practical matters. How does one do this or how does one do that and still act in compliance with what you have taught us? Obviously, you cannot address every possible variation, but do you have some general counsel on what it means to follow you?"

The Lord's expression was thoughtful. "Were you perchance with us out in the fields on the day that I spoke of the Bread of Life?"

Simeon hesitated. That didn't sound familiar. Then Peter answered for him. "No, Lord. Simeon was at the Joknean Pass that day."

Jesus nodded. "On that day I spoke somewhat of how one comes to truly know me and become my disciple. Perhaps Peter can share that with you some time. But you should know that when I finished that day, there were many who had said that they were my disciples who were offended and went back. They have walked no more with me from that time on."

Simeon's face flamed. Did Jesus think that he was asking these questions because he, too, doubted? "I would not go away, Lord. I wish only to better understand what it means to be a true disciple."

Jesus pushed his way forward. The people stepped back to make way for him. But he did not come all the way to Simeon. He stopped when he was more in the center of the crowd. Then, in that way that Simeon had noticed was his habit, his head moved slowly back and forth, his eyes touching each person so they would know he spoke to each of them.

"If any person would come to me, and does not love me more than his father and mother, his wife and his children, his brethren and sisters, yea, and his own life also, he cannot be my disciple."

Those words caused a soft exclamation from all around him. Simeon was not sure but what he had been one of those to gasp a little. Not even family could come between you and Jesus?

Now the wide, expressive eyes turned and fixed on Simeon. "And whosoever does not bear his cross, and come after me, cannot be my disciple."

That sent a slight shudder up Simeon's spine. To bear one's cross was an idiomatic expression taken from the horrors of crucifixion. It was a most fiendish way to die. To bear one's cross meant to accept whatever duty rested upon you, even if it cost your life.

Jesus let his eyes move about again. "Which of you, intending to build a tower, would not sit down first, and count the cost, whether he has sufficient to finish it? If not, perhaps after he has laid the foundation, he will not be able to finish it. Then all that behold it will begin to mock him, saying, 'This man began to build and was not able to finish.' "

Simeon found himself nodding. That was easy enough to understand. One of the fundamental principles of good merchandising was to calculate the costs of doing business *before* you contracted to take the business.

Then it hit him. *Is that what I did? I said that I accepted Jesus. Had I really counted the cost of that decision?*

Jesus paused, giving everyone a chance to digest his words. Finally he went on. "So likewise, whosoever he be of you that forsakes not all that he has, he cannot be my disciple."

He paused once more, then quietly, looking directly at Simeon, he said, "He that has ears to hear, let him hear."

Simeon felt his head swirling. And what did that mean? What did it mean in terms of his specific question? Could he try to free Yehuda? Could he take specific action even if that action required violence? What could he do without offending Jesus or going contrary to his teachings?

But he couldn't bring himself to ask any of those questions. "Thank you, Master," Simeon mumbled, looking more confused than satisfied.

At his side, Peter nudged him. "So is that your answer?"

"I—I'm sure it is. I'm just not sure what it means."

"Nor am I. So ask him straight out. He knows about what happened at the pass. He knows about Yehuda. Ask him what to do."

Simeon stared at his friend. "I'm not sure I should."

"Why not?"

Simeon just shook his head, suddenly forlorn.

"Lord?"

They turned as someone off to their left called out. It was a man of about Andrew's age. Jesus had turned about as well. "Yes?"

"I will follow you whithersoever you go, but first allow me to go and bury my father."

No one was surprised by that comment. The man had not left his dead father to come to hear Jesus. Again this was a common saying, an idiom. To "bury your father" meant that your parents were aging and needed care until they died. It could be years before that obligation was fulfilled.

"Let the dead bury the dead," Jesus responded, "but you go and preach the kingdom of God."

The man gave a look of shock, then outright irritation; then he turned away, muttering to himself. Immediately a second man stepped forward. "Lord, I would follow thee," he said, "but first let me return to my home and bid those who are there farewell."

Suddenly Simeon saw it, and it stabbed him like a spear in the side. Both men had said it. Was that his line too? *I would follow thee, Lord, but first . . .* The shame came then, hot and powerful. I would follow thee, Lord, but first tell me how to solve my problem. I would follow thee, Lord, but first take away my pain. I would follow thee, Lord, but first I have to free Yehuda.

Jesus took a deep breath, then spoke very plainly to all around him. "No man having put his hand to the plow and looking back, is fit for the kingdom of God."

Simeon didn't move. The scene around him seemed to dissolve. The words echoed like distant thunder in his mind. Somewhere, as though afar off, he saw the man who had asked the last question also turn and walk away, his head down.

Finally Simeon turned to Peter. "*That* is my answer," he whispered.

"It is?" Peter said in surprise.

"Yes."

"What? I don't understand."

"Neither do I, but I put my hand to the plow the day I talked to Mary in Nazareth. How can I turn my back on that?"

18

Before Peter could answer, Simeon started to walk away. "Will you tell my mother that I won't be home until supper? I need some time by myself."

CHAPTER NOTES

The teachings of Jesus on discipleship come from three different sources. The Bread of Life sermon is in John 6. It is in the final verses that we are told that the doctrine Jesus taught on that occasion caused some former disciples to turn away from him. Luke 14:25–35 contains the parables of counting the cost. The accounts of people volunteering to follow Jesus, then making excuses, and his concluding statement about putting one's hand to the plow, come from an earlier chapter (Luke 9:61–62), but is included here to round out Jesus' teachings on this subject.

CHAPTER 2

I

JOPPA
16 JUNE, A.D. 30

Miriam did not lift her head. She kept her eyes fixed on the simple midday meal of bread, barley broth, cucumbers, and olives. "Ezra?"

She felt both his and Lilly's gaze upon her.

"I want to go to Caesarea."

If a catapult stone had come crashing through the window at that moment, it could hardly have created a greater shock. Lilly drew in a sharp breath. Ezra's hands dropped to the table with a heavy clunk. "Caesarea?" Livia gasped.

"Yes." She tapped the sheet of papyrus on the table in front of them. It was a letter from her father to Ezra, come while she and Livia and Ezra had been in the north. Ironically, though he had no idea that Miriam was in Joppa, Mordechai had written to Ezra from Alexandria and asked him to forward the letter on to Miriam in Jerusalem. His plans had changed somewhat, he said. He had to make some other stops and would be delayed at least another week in his return. "Since Father will not be back yet, there is no rush for us to get back to Jerusalem. I know you need to spend some time in the sandal shop, so Livia and I will go." She ignored the looks she was getting and rushed on. "I know the Roman tribune there. First, I will find out if Yehuda is still alive—and may God be willing that he is. If he is, I will tell Marcus how Yehuda once saved the life of my father and me. I will offer whatever money the Romans require as ransom for his freedom."

Ezra was aghast. Lilly's face was pale as a piece of muslin.

"He will listen to me," she went on doggedly. "I won't reveal anything about what I know."

"If the Romans suspect that you have any association with the Zealots—" Lilly stopped, too horrified to finish.

"That is folly, Miriam," Ezra broke in sharply. "Utter folly."

"This whole situation was created by my father. There would never have been anyone at the Joknean Pass if he hadn't set it up. I have to do something."

Ezra shook his head, still clearly shocked at the idea. "We spent an extra two days in Ptolemais so no one would connect us with the events at the pass. That's also why we bypassed Caesarea completely. We could not take the chance that someone might see you coming from the north. And now you want to just walk in to a Roman officer and start asking about Yehuda?"

"I have to know if Yehuda is already dead," Miriam said stubbornly. "If not, then I have to try to save him."

He took a deep breath, fighting for patience. "I understand what you're feeling, Miriam, but—" He threw up his hands. "And what will you say when the tribune asks how you happen to know about Yehuda?"

Her mouth opened, then shut again. Earlier that morning, she had finally fallen asleep just before dawn when she had figured out this course of action and had found a small measure of peace. She realized now that her mind had been so spent that she had not thought through all of the implications. "I'll tell him that . . . " Her voice trailed off. What?

"Yes, word is out down here about the clash," Ezra went on. "But there are no details. Certainly not the names of actual prisoners."

Lilly's breath exploded softly. "Think, Miriam! The Romans are not stupid. They must be furious about what happened up there. Instead of a major victory, they came away looking like fools. If there is even a breath of suspicion that you know something, they'll not hesitate to use any necessary means to make you tell them. Not even your father's influence will save you."

Miriam could only nod. She had thought about that, but she felt she had to do *something*. "All right," she finally whispered.

Ezra sagged back, the tension leaving his face. Lilly smiled wanly. Livia gave her mistress a quick but fervent hug.

"Miriam," Lilly said after a few moments of silence, "the Lord has not seen fit to open my womb. As much as we would love to have children, it seems that is not to be our lot."

Miriam turned to her, surprised by this sudden turn in the conversation.

"You are the closest thing I have to a child of my own."

Miriam was touched. It was true, especially after Miriam's mother had died.

"When you came to us the other day to ask for help, we knew that you were putting yourself in danger. But we also knew that you were right. What your father did was a terrible thing, and you intervening to stop it was the right thing to do. But I can't allow you to do anything more." Her voice was trembling slightly with emotion. "If something were to happen to you . . . " She looked away.

Miriam surrendered. "It was a foolish idea. I'm sorry." But she thought of big, gentle, bearish Yehuda and felt a great desolation.

Greatly relieved, yet understanding her feelings, Ezra decided to change the subject. "While you and Livia were still sleeping this morning, I told Lilly everything." He paused for a moment. "I told her all about Jesus, including everything Simeon's family told us about him."

Miriam was surprised. She looked at Lilly. "And?"

"I want to meet him," she answered without hesitation.

"And I as well," Ezra added.

"We want to see him and hear him for ourselves," Lilly said.

"Wonderful." Miriam was deeply pleased. "So do Livia and I. However, Jesus seems to spend most of his time in the Galilee. I don't know when he'll come to Jerusalem again."

"When he does," her cousin replied, "send word immediately, and we'll come."

"Father can't know," Miriam said. "I'm sorry that I have to hide things from him, but he'll forbid me to see Jesus."

Ezra considered that. It was contrary to his nature to be a party to her going against her father's will, but he had thought this out when she had first come down from Jerusalem. The problem here was not Miriam. The problem was her father. She was of age. He had no right to tell her what she could and could not believe, and he certainly had no right to use her as a dupe in carrying out something truly evil. Finally, he nodded somberly. "We'll be careful when we come up to Jerusalem. He doesn't need to know."

II

CAPERNAUM

At the sound of the front door opening, Deborah pushed aside the preparations for the evening meal and walked swiftly into the entryway. David was there at the open door. He reached up and touched the *mezuzah* on the side of the frame, then stepped inside, bending down to remove his sandals. Deborah's face fell. "No Simeon?"

He shook his head. "Haven't seen him all day."

"Peter told me he might be late. Shall we wait supper?" she asked.

Again he shook his head. "If he's out looking for answers, there's no telling how long he'll be."

He came forward, took her hand, and moved with her back into the kitchen. Leah was there, sitting beside Joseph. She started to rise, her face eager; then, seeing David was alone, she fell back in disappointment. "No Simeon?" she asked.

David laughed softly. "Did you know you grow more like your mother every day?" He bent down and kissed the top of her head.

He turned and laid a hand on Joseph's shoulder. "And how are you, Son?"

"Fine, *Abba*." Though Joseph was nearly eleven now and no longer considered a child, he still used the intimate diminutive for *Ahv* or father. He also called his mother *Eema*—Mama—instead of *Eem*—Mother.

"Simeon will be along soon enough," Deborah said. "Come, Joseph, you are doing too much talking and not enough work." Since their baptism, David and Deborah had determined to reduce their dependence on the household servants they had hired. This was partly so they could teach their children to work and partly to free up funds so they could contribute more to help Jesus. Joseph was still getting used to the new arrangement.

Joseph frowned and started breaking off the tips of the beans that were before him. "I'll wager he's got a plan," he said, his eyes shining with excitement. His hands stopped again and began making arcs in the air, using a bean pod as a miniature sword. "He'll ride into that prison and take Yehuda out from under the noses of those old

Romans." He slashed downward, striking a fatal blow. "No one can stop Ha'keedohn."

Deborah smiled at his fervor. Who but a worshipful boy saw the world in such simple terms? "The beans, please," she prodded gently.

"Don't be suggesting that to Simeon," Leah said, chiding her brother's fantasizing.

"Don't be suggesting what to Simeon?" came a voice from the hallway.

"Simeon!" Joseph leaped up and darted to his brother. "Did you decide what to do, Simeon? Did you?"

"Joseph!" David said firmly. "Would you let Simeon come in before you start pestering him?"

"We're going to have supper first," Deborah said, observing with some concern the deep lines on her older son's face. "Then if Simeon wants to talk, he can." She shot Joseph a warning look. "But if he doesn't, then we're not going to keep pressing him, are we, Joseph?"

Joseph's crestfallen look was so forlorn that Simeon laughed heartily. He reached out and mussed up Joseph's hair. "Maybe I'll just send you to Caesarea. The Romans would throw themselves into the sea at the sight of a warrior as fierce as you."

"Aw," Joseph said, knowing he was being teased.

The amusement on Simeon's face melted away. "Actually, no. I don't know yet what I'm going to do." He looked at his father. "Yehuda and Samuel might already be dead. Pilate may choose not to wait a month to—"

"But they're not!" Joseph shouted in exultation.

Simeon whirled to look at him. "What?"

"Yes," Deborah said excitedly. "Sextus Rubrius came by this afternoon."

David was as surprised at that as his son. "Sextus came here?" he exclaimed.

Deborah went to Simeon and took his hands, her face filled with happiness. "Sextus received a dispatch from Caesarea today. The executions have been postponed until fall."

"Really?" Simeon nearly shouted it.

"Yes," Deborah said squeezing his hands.

He was ecstatic. "That changes everything. Did Sextus know when in the fall?"

"There is evidently some Roman festival in September—*Ludi Romani*, or something like that."

"Yes, in Latin, *ludicum* means a public show, or game. *Ludi Romani*, or the Roman Games, is a huge festival held to celebrate some ancient Roman victory." His mind was working furiously. He had made it a priority to understand everything he could about the Romans—how they thought, lived, fought, and played. "It's held in the latter part of September. And Pilate wants to save them for that?"

"That is what Sextus said. Vitellius, the legate of Syria, Pilate's direct superior, often comes down for the festival and Sextus thinks Pilate may want to make a public example of the prisoners then."

Simeon half-closed his eyes. "Then there is time."

Deborah didn't want to raise his hopes too high. "That was what the letter said, but Sextus said to warn you that Pilate is still in a rage over his losses at the pass. He could change his mind at any time."

"But they're alive," Simeon breathed. "That is what I needed to know. They're still alive. That is a great burden off my mind."

Joseph tugged on Simeon's tunic. "What are you going to do, Simeon?"

"Joseph," his mother warned.

The narrow shoulders fell. "Oh, Mama, it's all right if Simeon tells me. I won't tell anyone."

"I can't tell you because I don't know." Simeon slipped an arm around his brother's shoulder and moved him gently toward the table. He picked up one long bean pod and handed it to Joseph, then got one for himself. He snapped off the ends and tossed it in the bowl. When he looked up again, he saw his parents watching him with sorrowful eyes.

"So you didn't get an answer?" Deborah asked quietly.

He took another bean and broke it into pieces before he shook his head. "I went over what Jesus said today again and again in my mind. It made sense when I heard it, but I can't figure out exactly how to apply it."

"Then maybe . . . " She sighed, then went and sat down beside him, putting one arm around his waist.

Simeon looked at her, seeing the wrinkles at the corners of her eyes and the slightly pinched look around her mouth. How much of that was from him? he wondered. She had always sent him off on his forays with the Zealots with a brave smile and an encouraging wave. Was this what it had cost her? He reached up and stroked her hair, noting that there seemed to be more gray than before. "It will be all right, Mother. I'll just move ahead. I have one possible idea, but . . . " He shrugged.

Joseph pounced on that like a chicken on a bug. "What, Simeon? What is it?"

"Joseph?" David came in sternly. "Would you like to finish all the beans by yourself, *and* clean up the dishes after supper?"

Joseph fell back, crestfallen. "I think we need the servants here more than every few days."

Simeon nudged him, picking up another bean. "You'd better get going," he warned.

His mother was still thinking about what Simeon had said about Jesus. "Well, you are at least doing one thing he said. You're not rushing into something. You're counting the costs, as Jesus put it."

"The costs to me, or the costs to Yehuda?" Simeon asked darkly. "If I had known the cost of my choices, I would never have tried to save the Romans up there," he said, his voice clipped and sharp.

"Really?" David said softly.

"Yes, really!" came the tart reply. "And now I have to do something, and do it quickly. Disciple or not, I can't let Yehuda die. I can't. I put him there."

Everyone knew he was thinking about Daniel, but no one expressed that.

"I have gone over every possibility. There are several things I can do, but then I stop and wonder. Will that violate my commitment to Jesus? Will that go against what I now know to be true?" He blew out his breath in disgust. "Yehuda's right about that, at least. He said that since I started listening to Jesus, I can't make up my mind about anything anymore."

Leah finally spoke up, torn by the anguish she saw on Simeon's face. "You just have to trust your feelings, Simeon. I know you've been praying about it. Well, when the answer comes, you'll feel that it is right."

"Oh, Leah," he sighed. "How I wish faith came as easily to me as it does to you."

They sat there for several moments, the dinner forgotten by all except Joseph, who was breaking beans as quickly as his hands could pick them up.

"I have one idea that's been forming the last little while," Simeon said, looking at his father. "I want to think about it some more. It's not ideal."

"Which means it's dangerous," his mother murmured.

He turned to her sharply. "I have to do something. Yehuda would, for me."

"I know that, Son," Deborah said. "And I won't try to stop you. But you can't ask me not to worry."

"I know, I'm sorry." He looked at David. "Father, I'm sorry that I have been of no help to you these past two weeks," he said. "But if I decide this idea is what needs to happen, I will have to be gone some more. Probably several days again."

David nodded gravely. Then after a moment, he said, "Will you need money?"

Simeon smiled gratefully, a little ashamed for his previous outburst. "Yes, I will. Thank you."

Leah came around behind Simeon and put her arms around his neck. She laid her head against his. "Don't go unless it feels right," she whispered.

"I won't."

"We're praying for you too, Simeon."

"I know, Leah. Thank you."

III

CAPERNAUM

17 JUNE, A.D. 30

It was still a quarter of an hour before the first light of dawn when Simeon slipped quietly out of his father's house, not wanting to awaken his family. He padded swiftly across the spacious courtyard and stepped out into the street. Only then did he set down the leather bag filled with his belongings and bend down to put his sandals on. Peering up and down in the darkness, listening intently, he finally moved away, noting that at this hour he had the street completely to himself.

As he moved past the house of Ephraim, his oldest brother, Simeon didn't even glance at the barred door. His mind was fixed on what he had to do now, and nothing else broke through. Ten minutes later, he surveyed the heavy wooden gate across from where he stood.

His eyes briefly swept upward, taking the measure of the house, or at least what part of it he could see over the walls.

Making sure he was still alone, Simeon walked swiftly across the street, then raised his hand and rapped sharply on the gate. He noted that the planks were thick and tightly joined. The hinges were large and made of thick iron. He guessed that the bar securing it on the inside was equally impressive. The house might be Jewish, but the gate was designed by someone who knew he was an enemy in a Jewish state.

In a moment the door opened. It caught him by surprise. He had heard no footsteps. No lamps had shone in the upper windows.

"Yes?" And then the servant's eyes widened slightly, and Simeon guessed that he had recognized him even in the darkness.

He decided that there was no point in withholding his name, as he had planned to do. "Simeon ben David requesting an audience with Sextus Rubrius." He hesitated for a moment. "I know the hour is early but—"

"It would be a rare day when the rising sun found my master in his bed," the man said sardonically. He stepped back and opened the door widely enough to allow Simeon to step inside. Immediately he pushed the door shut again and let the bar drop with a solid thud. "This way, please."

He followed the man inside the house to a spacious entry. "Please wait here."

Simeon nodded and set down his valise as the servant ran lightly up the stairs. A minute later he heard footsteps. Sextus Rubrius appeared. He was fully dressed and held a cane. He gave a brief nod; then he started down, holding onto the railing and heavily favoring one leg. Rightly so, Simeon thought. It had been only a week since Rubrius had taken one of Moshe Ya'abin's arrows in the upper thigh at the Joknean Pass.

"*Shalom*, Simeon ben David," Sextus Rubrius said in Aramaic. If he was surprised to see his visitor, it did not show on his craggy face.

"And peace to you, Sextus Rubrius. I apologize for coming at this hour, but I am leaving for a time and needed to see you."

Sextus waved a hand. When he reached the bottom of the stairs, he motioned toward one of the doors, but Simeon shook his head. "I can't stay long."

Sextus nodded. Simeon couldn't help but see the contrast between the two of them. The centurion was close to Simeon's father's age, perhaps a few years older—around fifty. He had probably spent thirty or more years as a legionnaire. Those years showed on his face and in his body. He was built like an ox—solid, steady, deliberate in his motions. His hair, thick and showing streaks of gray, was short-cropped. The hands were not overly large but were strong and thickly veined. His features showed the weathering of a man who spent his life out of doors. Like most Romans, he was clean shaven. Simeon guessed that he had already shaved—or been shaved—that morning, for there was no hint of stubble on his face.

Simeon, who had celebrated his twenty-first birthday in December, was not even half the other man's age. Though more slender than Sextus, Simeon had spent a lifetime working in the warehouses of his father—stacking bags of wheat, moving casks of salted fish, heaving bales of hides onto carts, rolling the great jars of wine back and forth—and his body was also tightly muscled. Unlike most of his fellow countrymen, Simeon was clean-shaven too. Some years earlier he had chosen that as a way to pass himself off as a Roman if ever the need arose. Now he was accustomed to it and preferred it to the hot, heavy beards most of his countrymen wore.

Simeon started a little as he realized the Roman was waiting for him to speak. "My mother told me of your visit to our house yesterday. I wanted to thank you for that."

Sextus made another dismissive wave of his hand. "You saved my life. I told you that if there was any way I could help you, I would do so."

Simeon saw that while he spoke easily, the Roman's eyes were watchful, curious.

Simeon cleared his throat. "How much chance is there that Pilate will change his mind and crucify the prisoners before the festival?"

There was a moment of hesitation, then, "Not much, but it is possible. I've never seen the governor in such a state of mind. I thought he was going to crucify every one of them on the spot."

"Will there be a trial?"

Sextus shook his head. "There is no question of their guilt, and they are not Roman citizens."

"And only Roman citizens have any rights under the law," Simeon said, softly bitter.

Rubrius said nothing. There was no need to. It was not something he created. It was not something he could change.

"Does Pilate know that it was Yehuda and my men who helped save your column from even greater disaster?"

Sextus gave a brief bob of his head. "I told Marcus Didius and the governor that. It made no difference to Pilate."

"Of course not." He pushed those thoughts aside. "I would ask some questions of you, Sextus Rubrius."

There was a curt nod. "Pilate may overlook who saved us that night, but I have not forgotten."

"I do not wish to place you in a position where you would betray your country or violate your oath as a soldier."

Another slight inclination of his head. "Thank you. Violation of the *sacramentum*, the oath every legionnaire swears to the emperor, is punishable by death. I would not go against that even if I feared no discovery."

"If I ask things that would push you over the line of treason, please know that I have no wish to offend, nor will I expect you to answer."

"I shall be the judge of that, but thank you for your concern."

"Did you hear that two others of my men besides Yehuda of Beth Neelah were captured?"

"Two?" Rubrius clearly had not heard that.

"Yes. One is named Barak. One is called Samuel. All three of them are of Beth Neelah."

"I thought all the rest of the captives belonged to Ya'abin's band."

"I wish it were so." Simeon began to pace back and forth in the entryway, deep in thought. "Is there any chance the sentence will be changed? Could they be sold as slaves, for example?"

Rubrius, watching Simeon's movements with his eyes, slowly shook his head. "It's possible, but not likely. Not in this case. Pilate has somewhat of a political problem. His brilliant plan to wipe out the Zealots nearly caused a great disaster. Executing the prisoners while Vitellius is here could somewhat soften Pilate's problem."

"I understand." Simeon had hoped for a sentence of slavery, but had not expected it. Freeing someone from a gang of slaves, or even after they had been sold, would be relatively easy. Even if they had to go to Rome or some other province, it could be done. Now he looked at Rubrius fully, his eyes hooded. "Will they be tortured?"

One eyebrow lifted slowly.

"Pilate surely will want to find out who betrayed him."

"Ah," came the reply. It was obvious that Sextus was bothered at what appeared to be an accusation of barbarism. But to get the needed information—? He nodded slowly and spoke more directly. "Yes, torture is possible."

"They don't know anything," Simeon said shortly.

"What's that?" the centurion said.

"Yehuda and the rest of the band have no idea of how I knew of your plans. No one knows except for my father and me."

"And you want me to pass that on to Tribune Didius?" Sextus asked softly.

Simeon instantly saw his mistake. "If you can't without bringing suspicion on yourself, I understand. But perhaps you could send word of an informant or something. My men don't know, Sextus. You have my word on that."

"Let me think about it."

Simeon nodded, grateful for even that much. "Where are Yehuda and the others right now?"

Sextus was surprised by what he thought was an obvious question. "In Caesarea."

"I know that. Where specifically? Are they being held inside the Praetorium?"

Rubrius nodded, understanding now. "Yes, in the Praetorium. Have you ever been to Caesarea?"

"Several times," Simeon grunted, "but obviously not into the governor's palace."

"You have to understand. The Praetorium is not a single building but a whole complex. The palace is the largest, of course, but there are barracks, shops, storage sheds." He stopped for a moment. "There is also the prison. That's where they are being held."

"Is it a separate building?"

"Yes, in the northeast corner." Then, guessing why Simeon would ask such a question, he went on with studied deliberation. "The cells themselves are underground. Heavily guarded. A full cohort would have difficulty breaking in."

Simeon went right on ignorning Sextus's warning. "But it isn't part of the barracks, or anything like that? I mean, it's separate from everything else? You don't have to go through other buildings to get to it?"

Sextus Rubrius began to massage his leg gingerly, no longer looking at Simeon. "It is a separate building. What I have told you is common knowledge in Caesarea, Simeon, son of David. You could find that information for yourself by asking almost anyone in the city. But I cannot say more. I cannot tell you the number of soldiers there or how the prison is guarded. That would cross the line of which you spoke."

"I understand. I was not going to ask anything more about those specifics."

"Thank you."

"I do have one last question. I do not think it compromises you."

"Then I shall answer as best I can."

Simeon's eyes grew distant. "It is the Roman way to take those accused of capital crimes and crucify them outside the walls of the city, generally near a main thoroughfare." He couldn't keep the anger from creeping into his voice. "Supposedly, it serves as an effective deterrent to those who are tempted to challenge Rome." He finally met the older man's eyes. "Will that be the case in Caesarea?"

Rubrius once again was thoughtful, his mind clearly considering not only whether it was appropriate for him to answer, but also what lay behind the question in Simeon's mind. He sighed. "Perhaps, but you can't be sure. If the governor decides to make the executions part of the games, they will likely happen in the hippodrome, where the chariot races take place."

"I understand, but it is also possible that they could be crucified outside the walls?"

"Yes."

When Simeon merely nodded, Sextus raised his head slightly. "Simeon—" Sextus reached up and rubbed at his chin. "It would be the greatest folly to try a rescue, even outside the walls. Your men and Ya'abin's—the prisoners—are rebels. Everyone knows they have many allies. There will be hundreds of soldiers. I have been told to bring my garrison to Caesarea for the games. Others will come as well. Pilate made the mistake of underestimating the capabilities of the Zealots once. He is not fool enough to do it twice."

Simeon feigned surprise. "Who would be mad enough to think otherwise?" he asked innocently.

Sextus gave him a searching look but said nothing.

"*Todah raba*. Many thanks." Simeon reached down and picked up his valise.

The two of them stood there for a time, eyes not meeting. Finally, Rubrius broke the silence. "Loyalty to a friend is a noble thing, Simeon, and I commend you for it. But not even Yehuda would expect you to throw yourself into an abyss in a pointless attempt to save him."

Simeon laughed softly and without humor. "Who would be mad enough to think otherwise?" he asked again.

CHAPTER NOTES

The *mezuzah* is mentioned in this chapter. In observant Jewish homes a small metal or wood container holding scriptural passages on pieces of parchment was attached to the door frame. This was in response to the injunction in Deuteronomy 6:9.

The *Praetorium* takes it name from *Praetor*, meaning a magistrate, commander, or governor. In the field of battle, the *praetorium* was the general's tent. It was also used as the title for the governor's place of residence, denoting a grand palace or complex (see Collins, 274; Fallows, 3:1365).

CHAPTER 3

A LIVING DOG IS BETTER THAN A DEAD LION.
—*Ecclesiastes 9:4*

I

DAMASCUS, PROVINCE OF SYRIA
18 JUNE, A.D. 30

Simeon had been to Damascus several times before with his father. Sitting squarely on the King's Highway, which came up from Arabia and major east-west trade routes, Damascus was an important center for trade, and David ben Joseph maintained a small office there to oversee his interests. Each time they came they stayed in the merchant's quarter not far from the southern gate, which opened onto the King's Highway. However, this time Simeon was staying completely away from his normal places; in fact, the place where he was now was vastly different from anywhere he had been before.

Damascus had been a city of note when Abraham walked the earth nearly two thousand years before. Back then, Jerusalem had been little more than a collection of huts occupied by Canaanites. Damascus was a completely Oriental city, a city of the East. Simeon imagined that this was what the cities of Arabia must be like. Its markets spread across huge blocks of space, making Jerusalem's markets pale in comparison. Narrow, twisting streets sprouted off in every direction, defying any sense of order or comprehension. He had been walking steadily for more than half an hour, and all he did was burrow deeper and deeper into the city.

Simeon knew that if his young guide should decide to disappear, he would be hopelessly lost. And probably in danger as well. Simeon was dressed as a Roman of the patrician class, which automatically signified comfort and wealth. Covetous dark eyes peered out from shuttered windows or through cracks in doors as they passed. People called out from windows and doorways, offering this service or that product at an unbelievable price. When he didn't respond to their halting Latin, they tried Greek, then Aramaic and other tongues he didn't understand. He suspected that if he had been alone, he would have been accosted long before now.

The boy—who could have been aged anywhere between twelve and sixteen—looked back over his shoulder. "You keep up, Excellency. Bad place to get lost." His Latin was broken and spoken haltingly.

"Really?" Simeon said, feigning innocent surprise. He had made the fifty-some miles from Capernaum to Damascus in two days, arriving just a few hours after sundown. He was tired, but not too tired to get right to work on the reason he had come.

The boy only grinned and turned another corner, pushing ever deeper into this quarter of the city. The lad was the third guide to lead Simeon. Each time, Simeon had repeated the password he had been given and dropped a small stack of coins into the outstretched palms. It could have been an elaborate ruse meant to take his money, but he sensed it was not. There was a seriousness of purpose that let him know he was moving ever closer to the man he needed to see. All the precautions were fine with Simeon. It greatly bolstered his confidence. It meant no Romans were going to drop in while he was transacting his business with the man whose real name he did not know—nor would he ever.

Finally, the boy stopped before a low door. It was a two-story house, with all of its windows shuttered. The upper walls seemed to bulge outward, as though the building had to see what was below it in the street. The moon was up, but in these narrow streets little light filtered down to ground level. Simeon sensed that the place was filthy.

Again the hand came out. Simeon had the coins ready and handed them to the boy. As they clinked softly, the boy nodded. He didn't need to count. The worth of money was always determined by its weight, and Simeon suspected this boy could judge the worth of what was in his hand within half a *denarii*.

There was a brief flash of movement; then the boy was at the door. He rapped once, hesitated, rapped again twice more, more sharply this time, and stepped back. Simeon heard sounds of movement from inside. The boy called out softly, then turned and walked away. "I'll take you back when you are ready," he said without looking back.

After a moment, the door opened. For an instant, Simeon was illuminated in the flickering light of a small, hand-held lamp. The man's head jerked sharply and Simeon followed him inside. There was a solid thunk as the door was barred behind them.

Turning slowly, Simeon surveyed the room in the dim light. It was bare except for two wooden stools and a rough-hewn table in one corner. A tunic hung on a peg behind the door. So this was not where the man did his work. Again, that little piece of information reduced Simeon's anxiety. If the authorities broke into this place, they would find nothing.

"Well?" the man said abruptly. His beard was heavy and his eyes suspicious. He spoke in Latin. Good, Simeon thought. He had accepted Simeon as a Roman without question.

Knowing that no small talk was expected and would actually send the man's suspicions rising, Simeon plunged in. "I am in need of eight complete uniforms for a regular legionnaire, and one for an officer, preferably a tribune."

If the man was surprised, his eyes did not show it. Simeon couldn't see his mouth in the tangle of beard. "Delivered to where?"

Simeon thought for a moment. He obviously couldn't go staggering through the streets with piles of Roman uniforms stacked in his arms. "At the inn near the south gate. It is called the Jackal's Lair." That was not the inn where he had taken his lodging, but it was close at hand.

The man nodded curtly. "I know of it." A moment's pause. "A hundred *denarii* for each legionnaire—that includes sandals, shield, sword—everything."

Simeon had tried to anticipate what the uniforms would cost him. He had already exchanged his money to the Latin coinage. The Hebrew shekel was worth four *denarii*, so it would cost twenty-five shekels per uniform. That was steep, but not exorbitant. His father had given him the equivalent of about three thousand *denarii*. "Go on."

"The tribune's is much more difficult. Half again for that."

"And they will be completely authentic?"

"Totally."

That was nine hundred fifty *denarii*. "Make it seven hundred for the lot," Simoen said firmly.

The man's head jerked back and forth quickly. "Nine hundred, and that is only because you order so many."

Simeon frowned. He was really in no mood to bargain, but he didn't want the man to think he was too eager. Besides, it was the way of his people. "It isn't every day you get an order of this size. Eight hundred."

Stubborn resolve hardened the features. "Nine hundred. That is my last offer."

"I'll tell you what," Simeon said, as if he had a sudden idea. "I will need a cart. I have some distance to travel. One thousand for everything."

"A cart?" the man said. He pulled at his beard. "What about a horse?"

"I have a horse. Also, I will need a bill showing that these uniforms are destined for one of the Roman garrisons—let's say Ptolemais, on the coast. I don't want any customs officials getting suspicious and confiscating them."

The man sniffed contemptuously. "Do you think I know nothing about my work? A cart will not be easy," he said, trying to look dubious. But his eyes had already given him away. A thousand *denarii* did not often walk through his door. "Twelve hundred."

Simeon just raised one eyebrow.

"Eleven hundred, and that is my final offer."

"Nine hundred, and that is *my* final offer."

There was an unctuous smile. "All right, Excellency. A thousand *denarii*, and may you be cursed for taking food out of the mouth of my children."

Simeon just chuckled. This was how it was done. This man was probably in his fifties. If he had any children at all, the youngest was probably Simeon's age or older. "Agreed."

"There is one more thing," Simeon added.

Both hands flew up. "No, sire, the price is set."

"This would be additional." He reached within his tunic and withdrew a roll of parchment. "I was told that you can create official Roman documents of high quality."

There was no expression in the beady eyes. "Civil or military?"

"Military."

"Depending on the level required, the cost can be very steep. It is a great risk for me."

"I understand." Simeon was not inclined to bargain on this part. He handed the scroll over and waited patiently while the man unrolled it, and quickly read it.

In spite of his attempts to mask his feelings, the man's eyes registered shock. "Oi," he cried when he finished. "Are you mad?"

"Can you do it?"

"The governor of Judea? Why not just ask for the signature of the Emperor?"

"The governor will be sufficient. Can you do it?"

The greed was almost naked now in the dim light. "You are a man of very good fortune, Excellency. I just happen to have an authentic copy of the governor's official seal. Five hundred *denarii* more."

It was clear the man expected Simeon to gasp at that, but he didn't flinch. "How soon?" was all he said.

The man's eyes narrowed. "I assume you came to me because you were told I am the best."

"Yes."

"Something this important must be done very carefully. Give me a week."

"I cannot wait a week. Two days and I'll give you the full five hundred."

He waved the parchment at Simeon. "And this is what you want the document to say?"

"Yes."

"You *are* mad, you know."

"So I've been told."

To Simeon's surprise, there was admiration in the dark eyes now. "But it will work. With what only Rashah is able to prepare for you, you can march straight into that prison at Caesarea and bring out whomever or whatever you wish."

Simeon was satisfied. "That's what I wanted to hear." He reached for his purse. "Half now, the other half when the goods are delivered to the Jackal's Lair?"

"Done."

II

Ezra, Miriam, and Livia left Joppa early on the morning of the fourth day after their return from the Galilee. Joppa was on the sea-coast, about thirty miles west and slightly north of Jerusalem. They left at dawn in order to reach the capital by nightfall. By midday, they were well up the Beth-Horon pass, and the Great Sea had long since passed from their view. Had they been able to see that far, they would have seen a small ship about a mile offshore. It flew the flag of Tyre and moved slowly northward, already well past Joppa.

This wasn't one of the massive, big-bellied Roman grain ships that made the run between Alexandria and Rome. The *Astarte* was a much smaller ship, not even a hundred feet long. Named for the ancient goddess of the Phoenicians (whom the Greeks had embraced and renamed Aphrodite, goddess of love), it had one large square mainsail and two smaller triangular sails to help it maneuver. Its draft was shallow so it could put in at even the smallest ports. It made its passage in an endless repetition up and down the eastern coast of the Mediterranean between Alexandria in Egypt and Seleucia in northern Syria, carrying a few passengers who slept on the deck and anything and everything someone was willing to pay to have shipped to the next port.

Usually the voyage from Alexandria to Caesarea, a distance of about three hundred miles, took about five days, depending on the amount of cargo to be loaded. It had cost Mordechai ben Uzziel of Jerusalem a hefty sum to convince the owner-captain of the vessel to forgo his usual route and sail directly to Caesarea. Mordechai had already been delayed in Alexandria longer than he wished, and he didn't have the patience for the usual methodical trip.

On the morning of departure, it had taken another hundred shekels to hold the captain to his original plan. The sacrifice, required before any ship could sail, had gone off well. The soothsayer—a horrid woman with long, black fingernails and hair that was like a rat's nest— had seen no bad omens in the sheep's entrails, and so the captain had given orders to cast off. Then, just as Mordechai's manservant was stowing his things in the captain's cabin, the steersman appeared, a look of horror on his face, to announce that he had dreamed of a black goat the previous night.

The whole body of superstitions that were prevalent among sailors so vexed Mordechai that he had barely been able to contain his temper. The pre-sailing sacrifice had to be just right. The day of the week and month had to be fortuitous. If a raven happened to light in the rigging, that was bad. If someone sneezed while walking up the gangplank, some kind of trouble was in store. On the other hand, if someone sneezed to the right during the sacrifice of the sheep, that was good. But dreams were especially worrisome omens. To dream of wild boars meant there would be violent storms. Bulls were the same—but if they gored someone, then shipwreck was imminent. Goats meant large waves or bad weather, and if they were black goats, it would be particularly bad. As long as the weather was good, no one was allowed to cut his nails or his hair. If the weather turned bad, then nail clippings and locks of hair were tossed into the sea to appease the *daemons*, or spirits that ruled the great deep. There were a few good omens as well, but Mordechai had learned they were not nearly so numerous as the bad ones.

Disgusted, Mordechai had pointed out to the captain that every year the province of Judea went into six months of virtual drought from late spring to early fall. There would be no storms. To get rain even in the highlands of the Galilee or around Jerusalem was very unusual at this season. Later, he wondered if the captain didn't know all this already, and had used the occasion to squeeze additional money from his wealthy passenger. Gratefully, greed was a more powerful driver than superstition, and they had finally cast off only an hour or so later than originally planned.

This was their fourth day at sea. Now, less than a day from his destination, Mordechai was at the end of his patience. He paced the decks, stopping occasionally to peer through the haze at the land that slipped slowly past them. He had recognized Joppa about an hour before—he had even been able to pick out the home of Ezra and Lilly, his wife's cousin. Joppa was about thirty miles south of Caesarea, so if all went well, they would dock tomorrow a little before sunset.

He felt the familiar surge of excitement mixed with nervousness. Had things gone off as he and Marcus had so meticulously planned? Was Pilate finally satisfied that the members of the Sanhedrin really were anxious to keep their relationship with Rome positive?

He wiped at his brow with a scarf. The sun was hot, and Mordechai ben Uzziel was a big man. He had spent far too many nights in front of sumptuous tables and too many days riding around Jerusalem in a litter or by carriage. He didn't mind. A little girth, especially when covered by robes made in Jerusalem's finest tailor shops, bespoke wealth and prestige. He cultivated that image by keeping his thinning hair and adequate beard—both graying now—immaculately trimmed. He even had his personal manservant trim his heavy eyebrows each week so he would not appear to be one who let things go unnoticed.

"Sire?"

He turned as his servant approached him.

"The sun is getting very hot, sire. I have put up the covering near the captain's chair. The captain asked me to convey his good pleasure if you should join him there."

Mordechai bit back a muttered retort about the captain being a crass fool, and simply shook his head. "Tell the captain that I have much to sort out in my mind before we reach Caesarea tomorrow." He glanced upward. He was already in the shade of the main sail. "If the heat becomes unbearable, I shall retire to the cabin. Otherwise, I would prefer to walk about for a while."

"Yes, sire." He bowed and quickly backed away.

III

CAESAREA, CAPITAL OF THE PROVINCE OF JUDEA
21 JUNE, A.D. 30

When Marcus Quadratus Didius, senior Roman tribune in the province of Judea, entered the small marbled room, he saw instantly that Pilate was in a foul mood. That wasn't terribly surprising. Pilate had been in a bad temper ever since they had returned from the Joknean Pass almost a fortnight before. Even though it could have been much worse—they had lost only four wagons out of the more than forty and had recovered all but two bars of the gold—the disaster lay in the opportunity lost. Had things gone as planned, the Zealot movement, and with it the number one danger to Rome in this province, would have been eliminated once and for all. Instead, their enemies had only been emboldened the more.

So far, the governor did not hold Marcus responsible, but knowing how mercurial his commander's temper could be, Marcus was anxious not to displease him. And that would be difficult tonight.

"Have you seen him?"

Marcus didn't have to ask who "him" was, though the question came out of nowhere.

"Briefly. The centurion on duty had me come down to the gate and confirm Mordechai's identity. I took him to his room."

"Did he ask you how things went?"

Marcus shook his head. "Mordechai is far too shrewd to violate protocol. I could tell he is very anxious to know, but he will wait and learn it from you."

The governor's face, lean and weathered by too many days in the sun and too many years of political life, tightened even more. The dark gray eyes glittered with anger. "And you're still convinced that he had nothing to do with the betrayal?"

"Absolutely," Marcus responded without hesitation. "I think when Mordechai hears what happened, you'll see it on his face. It is going to be a bitter blow for him as well. The last thing the Sanhedrin wants is war with Rome, and the Zealots are the greatest threat to peace."

"You'd better be right. If I find out that he had anything to do with this, even if he was only careless about those he told, I'll march him naked through the streets of Jerusalem at the point of the spear. I don't care who he is or how rich he may be."

Marcus said nothing. This was just Pilate blowing off his anger.

The governor suddenly slammed the flat of his hand against the polished marble armrest on his chair. "By the gods! Who betrayed us? I want to know!"

"I don't know. Not yet." Marcus spoke grimly. "But I lost almost thirty good men that night. I will find out."

"And you're convinced that rebel Jew knows nothing?"

"Yehuda of Beth Neelah?" Marcus hesitated. This ground was no more than a thin crust over a seething volcano. "Oh, he knows a great deal, but I am convinced he doesn't know how Simeon—the one they call Ha'keedohn, or the Javelin—"

"I speak Aramaic, Marcus," Pilate snapped. "Don't patronize me."

"Sorry, sire, that was not my intent. Anyway, I'm convinced that this Yehuda doesn't know how Simeon learned of our plans. In fact, I received a dispatch from our centurion in Capernaum. He says one of our informants swears that no one but this Simeon knows who our betrayer is."

Seeing Pilate's frown deepen, Marcus went on hastily. "We put the man on the rack for an hour today and got very little."

There was a grunt which could have meant anything.

"This Jew is no coward. He refuses to say anything that would compromise his followers, but he feels he was betrayed that night too. He has nothing to gain by holding back, and so far everything he's told us fits with what we've learned from the other prisoners."

He paused, watching the governor closely. Pilate at least was listening.

"Anyway, according to this Yehuda, Simeon had decided not to participate in the ambush."

Pilate stirred impatiently. "And all because of this fanatic from—" Pilate waved a hand.

"From Nazareth. Yes. I find it hard to believe, but evidently Simeon of Capernaum has decided Jesus is a man of God. Jesus teaches peace and love and submission, including submission to your enemies."

Pilate gave a sarcastic grunt. "Maybe we ought to hire the Nazarene to preach for us."

Marcus smiled and went on. "Perhaps. Anyway, Yehuda says Simeon was supposedly out of the game. Then this someone, whoever it was, brought information to Simeon about our plans. That's when he rode out to the pass and tried to stop what was happening, to save his own men from being caught and killed."

Pilate stirred and Marcus stopped again, but the governor waved him to continue.

"It was Simeon who came up with the compromise solution—we lay down our arms, and we would get safe escort through the pass."

"And then Ya'abin pulled a double-cross."

Marcus's brows furrowed deeply. "Yes. And since Simeon had given me his word that we would have safe passage, that's when he intervened in our behalf."

"And you believe that?" Pilate said in a mocking voice. "The man you once almost killed saved your life because of some oath?"

Marcus shrugged. He was still trying to reconcile that in his own mind, and yet the evidence seemed pretty conclusive.

"If I hadn't decided to ride up the pass to meet you two hours earlier than we had previously planned, it would have been far worse."

Marcus nodded. "Yes. And Jupiter be praised for that, sire. You saved the day."

That seemed to mollify Pilate slightly, though it was obvious he was still brooding about it all. "And still nothing on Ya'abin?"

Marcus's face hardened. "Not yet. I've got a full cohort, almost six hundred men, searching the wilderness of Judea. I've sent word to the garrisons at Jerash and Machaerus to be on the alert as well, in case he slips across the river." His voice was cold. "He's one I very much want to get my hands on."

"I still think massaging this Yehuda's tongue with a hot iron before we crucify him might loosen his memory a little," Pilate grumbled, returning to the subject of their prisoner.

Marcus didn't think he was serious, but nodded quickly. "If that is your wish, sire, we can carry it out tonight."

He wearily shook his head. "No, no. If Sextus Rubrius says this Yehuda doesn't know and you're convinced as well, I'll accept that. I want the prisoner's screams unimpeded when we bring him out at the games. Then he will learn what it means to fight against Rome."

Just then there was a soft knock at the door.

"Open!" Pilate barked.

The door opened and a slave clad in a white tunic bowed his way into the room. "Dinner is ready, Excellency."

"It's about time. Is the Jew there yet?"

"Yes, sire. Mordechai of Jerusalem is in the dining room awaiting your arrival."

"Did you tell my wife to handle the other guests?"

"Yes, sire. She will be in the north vestibule. You will be undisturbed."

Pilate muttered something under his breath that Marcus didn't catch. The slave couldn't have heard it either, but he took it for what it was and left quickly. The governor got to his feet. "All right, Marcus. Let's go hear what your Mordechai has to say about all this."

IV

Pilate barely waited for the food to be served and the slaves to leave again before he turned to Mordechai. "So," he said bluntly, "I suppose you've come for a report."

Mordechai nodded. If he was surprised by the sudden coldness in the governor, he gave no sign. "I haven't been back to Jerusalem yet. I sailed straight here from Alexandria."

Pilate speared a piece of roasted quail breast with his knife and popped it into his mouth. "Tell him, Marcus."

After almost five full days aboard ship, Mordechai should have been delighted to finally have a decent meal set before him, especially one as sumptuous as this. But any thoughts of food were quickly dispelled as Marcus began to speak. He started at the point where the column of wagons from Damascus had reached Capernaum. Mordechai listened, his face grave but attentive. By the time Marcus described the arrival of Simeon and his father, and the fact that they obviously knew everything about the trap, Mordechai's features were a flaming purple. That quickly turned to a deep, ashen gray as Marcus told of Ya'abin's treachery, of the fierce but brief battle in the midst of the pass, of the triumph turned into debacle.

Pilate did not interrupt the narration. He ate lazily while Marcus talked, his eyes never leaving the Sadducee's face. When Marcus finally stopped and sat back, Pilate was convinced. Mordechai ben Uzziel had no complicity in the events of the previous week. Not even the most consummate actor could have feigned such emotions.

Finished, Marcus picked up a cluster of grapes and began to eat them as Pilate took over now. "Understand clearly, Mordechai, we do not think that you had any part in this treachery. But think, man! Who else knew the details of our plan? Who could have betrayed us?"

"Marcus and me and you," came the almost instant reply.

"No one else?" Pilate sneered skeptically.

"Several knew small parts of it," Mordechai said firmly, "but no one knew everything." His mind was working furiously even as he spoke. Then Mordechai snapped his fingers. "Someone must have seen your soldiers as they were moving into position."

Marcus was shaking his head before he finished. "I have talked with each of the commanders. They were not discovered. They were very careful."

"Just because they didn't see anyone," Mordechai retorted, the frustration making his voice harsher than he intended, "doesn't mean they weren't seen."

"True, and I thought of that," Marcus said calmly. "But if that were it, things would have developed much differently. The same thing is true if Simeon or someone else merely suspected it was a trap." He tossed the grapes aside contemptuously. "No. They *knew*. Simeon knew every detail, even down to our plan to feign a wheel breakdown at the mouth of the pass."

"But how?" Mordechai cried. "I took every precaution. Marcus, you and I even met out in the garden that night, remember? And it was late. I didn't want to risk even having the servants see you there."

"I remember."

"Ya'abin?" Mordechai said, groping, still clearly shaken to the core.

"He would be capable of it," Marcus agreed, "but no. He nearly got caught in the trap as well. If he hadn't decided to try to massacre us, we would have had him and all of his men."

That brought Mordechai back to a thought that had come to him while Marcus had spoken. "And it was Simeon's band who intervened and saved you?"

"Saved us!" Marcus exploded. "We lost twenty-eight men." Then the integrity which his father had so deeply ingrained in him and his brother surfaced. "But yes," he admitted, "if he hadn't come, it would have been much worse."

"That's what I still can't understand," Pilate grunted. "Why would a Zealot fight to save a Roman column? You would expect that they would have thrown in with Ya'abin."

Mordechai had already come up with the answer in his own mind. "For the oath's sake."

As before, Pilate brushed that aside with a flick of his hand, but Marcus was nodding. "That's what this Yehuda said too. Simeon and his father did swear to me that if we laid down our arms, they would see that we were allowed safe passage."

"An oath is a very sacred thing to us," Mordechai said. "More binding than a written contract. Did they actually use the word oath?"

Marcus thought for a moment, then his head bobbed. "Yes. And Sextus, my centurion, says that David ben Joseph of Capernaum is a man of high integrity."

Mordechai was nodding. "Then hatred or not, they would be duty bound to protect you. Knowing Simeon, it must have galled him terribly to have done it."

Marcus held out his arm, showing a long white scar. "Especially since it was me. He and I carry tokens of each other's affection."

Mordechai looked puzzled at that, but Pilate broke in harshly. He didn't care about the who or the why or the how of Marcus's deliverance. He wanted answers. "What about your daughter? You had her write up this report on your conversation with the two rebels. Did you tell her any more than that?"

Stiffening, Mordechai turned slowly to face the governor. "I am not a fool, Pontius Pilate. I had Miriam sit in on my meeting with those two and keep a record of it in order to bolster their confidence in what I was offering them. But aside from that, do you think I would put my only daughter at risk?" He forced himself to speak less critically. "I'm telling you, no one except the three of us knew all the pieces of this puzzle. No one!"

Now the Roman governor's face was like the face of a frozen waterfall. "Someone did, and we're going to find out who." He swung on Marcus. "Simeon and his father know who it is. Send word to Sextus. I want the two of them arrested and brought in immediately. One night in the dungeon with them, and we'll know everything we want to know. Then we'll crucify them along with the three we already have."

Marcus blanched a little. "Sire, I—Do you think that is wise?"

Pilate's brows lowered dangerously. It was one thing to question a direct command. It was something else to suggest the commander was a fool for issuing it.

Marcus rushed on. "The whole of the Galilee is in turmoil over what happened. We are understandably angered because we were betrayed, but think of it from the point of view of the Zealots. They thought they were on the verge of getting forty wagons filled with arms and a fortune in gold. Instead, they were nearly caught in a very clever trap set by us for them." He glanced at Mordechai, looking for support. "They were betrayed as well. If we are angry, they must be boiling."

To Mordechai's credit, he saw instantly what was going on between the governor and his chief officer, and Mordechai sided with the tribune. Pilate wanted revenge, as did Marcus, but not at the risk of open battle. "Marcus is right, Excellency. If you go into Capernaum and take Simeon, you could have full-scale war on your hands."

Pilate muttered something and flung down a piece of meat without tasting it.

"We must be wise and bide our time," Mordechai suggested, choosing his words carefully. "We have lost an important opportunity to destroy the Zealots. We must search for ways to undo the damage this loss has brought to us. We will find another way to defang these fanatics."

Marcus, gratified by Mordechai's support, started again. "I would like to put this Simeon on the rack or under the lash as much as you would, sire, but if we act hastily, we may bring about the very thing we are trying to prevent."

For a long moment, Pilate considered that. Marcus watched him closely, taking hope. Pilate had a violent temper and absolutely no tolerance for being shamed, but he was also shrewd and cunning. You didn't keep the office of governor in a province as difficult to administer as Judea by being stupid.

Finally Pilate nodded. "All right, we shall let things ride as they are." Then more sharply, he spoke to Mordechai. "When you return to Jerusalem, I expect that you will look into this and see if you can learn what went wrong."

"Most assuredly, sire," Mordechai answered.

"In the meantime, rest up tonight. Tomorrow we shall talk about what we can do to eliminate the Zealots, to recoup at least something from this disaster."

"Sire?" Mordechai's face had turned grim.

"Yes?"

"With your leave, I would like permission to depart for Jerusalem first thing in the morning."

That caught the other two by surprise. "Tomorrow?" Marcus said. "But you've just arrived."

"I know. But if the Zealots know of my part in this whole thing, there's going to be a lot of hate aimed in my direction." He shook his head, his face dark. "And Moshe Ya'abin is still free. Remember, I am the one who drew him into this. He is a man who will not stop until he is avenged." He suddenly seemed very tired and old. "Miriam is alone in Jerusalem. I pray God that it is not already too late."

Marcus leaned forward. "Sire, with your permission, I would like to escort Mordechai to Jerusalem and provide him with protection. If we leave early tomorrow, we can be there the day after tomorrow."

"Of course," Pilate said.

"Thank you." Mordechai's mind, always gifted at seeing the larger picture, was racing now. "Under the circumstances, once I have rejoined Miriam, it would be best if we left Jerusalem for a time. That will give you time to catch Ya'abin and let the Galileans cool off."

Pilate was nodding gravely. Even the Romans couldn't guarantee this man's safety if there was a determined attempt to assassinate him. Then the governor suddenly brightened. "Some time ago, we talked about sending you to Rome to meet the emperor, to put forth the cause of your Great Sanhedrin. Perhaps now would be a good time to do that."

Startled for a moment, Mordechai stared at the governor, then began to nod thoughtfully. His mind had already considered, then rejected, the various possibilities—Alexandria, Damascus, Antioch. There were several places where he had business interests and would be warmly welcomed, but none of them was outside the reach of a determined enemy. But Rome!

He made up his mind. "Thank you, Excellency. As usual, your mind is much quicker than mine. That is the solution. I could take Miriam with me, I assume."

Pleased, Pilate stood up. "Of course. And Marcus has been here almost a year now. I think he would welcome a chance to take a brief leave of absence and see his family again."

Marcus was as surprised at that as Mordechai was.

"To say nothing of escorting your beautiful daughter," Pilate hooted lasciviously. "Agreed, Marcus?"

Dazed, Marcus stood up as well, as did Mordechai. "Yes, sire," he murmured. "It would be an honor."

The governor turned back to Mordechai. "A delegation is planning to sail from here in about four weeks. Could you be ready that soon?"

Mordechai was also reeling a little from the swiftness of this development, but his answer was quick. "I will have to get my affairs in order, but that should give me sufficient time." Then he had another thought. "I can protect myself for four weeks." He smiled thinly at Marcus. "I appreciate the escort to the city, but once there it wouldn't do for me to be seen in Jerusalem with a permanent Roman bodyguard. I'll hire extra protection. But I worry about Miriam. Could Marcus bring her back with him to Caesarea? She would be safe here until we leave."

"But of course," Pilate said expansively. He liked the idea of being the deliverer—and also of putting Mordechai ben Uzziel in his debt. "But of course."

CHAPTER NOTES

The details on ancient ships and sailing come from Casson, 66, 155–57.

In ancient Israel, each town or city with more than a hundred and twenty persons had a local ruling body. These were called the lesser Sanhedrin, or councils. They consisted of twenty-three members and were empowered to deal with lesser disputes and violations of the law. In Jerusalem, the Great Sanhedrin was the supreme Jewish authority. It consisted of seventy members selected from among the eminent priests and other religious and political rulers. The high priest was typically designated as the president or chief of this council (Fallows, 3:1522–23). In the time of Jesus, the Great Sanhedrin operated under authority of the Roman government, and while given a lot of autonomy, ultimately had to answer to the procurator or governor of the province.

CHAPTER 4

I

IN THE WILDERNESS OF JUDEA
21 JUNE, A.D. 30

The man who was the subject of conversation around the table of Pontius Pilate that night was actually not posing much of a threat to anyone in Jerusalem at the moment. Moshe Ya'abin and what was left of his band were still licking their wounds.

Ya'abin had taken fifty-six men north with him to the Galilee. He had lost thirty-five of them at the battle of the Joknean Pass. If the reports from the coast were correct, a dozen of those had been captured and were now awaiting execution in Caesarea. How many of the rest the Romans had killed that night and how many had been lost as they scattered wildly in the darkness was not clear. Two had just returned the night before—tired, filthy, and greatly relieved to be back with their comrades. Ya'abin guessed that others who had escaped may have decided that life with the Desert Fox was neither as safe nor as profitable as they had been led to believe. He would be surprised to see any more limp back in.

They were camped in a large limestone cave near the head of one of the endless narrow canyons that honeycombed the wilderness of Judea. The Dead Sea lay about five miles to their east. This cave was likely one of the same caves that King David used when he was on the run from King Saul a thousand years before. If it was, that held little interest for Ya'abin. The past meant nothing. All that mattered was the present, because the present directly determined the future.

They were here because it was an excellent place to hide. The springs of Ein Gedi, which emptied into the Dead Sea, were within walking distance of their camp. The cave was high up the steep canyon wall, and with sentries posted no one could approach within a mile without being seen. Though he was not overly worried about the Roman patrols that fruitlessly scoured the countryside looking for them, Ya'abin was wary nevertheless. He had men following their movements and reporting at the end of each day.

At the moment, with full darkness upon the country, most of his band were already stretched out for the night, rolling out what rugs or blankets they had on the thick dirt of the cave floor. In the day, the temperature in the wilderness of Judea rose to the point where it felt like it could melt a man's flesh, but at night it was chilly enough to require a covering to stay warm.

Ya'abin and his chief lieutenant, Eliab of Adullam, were bent over a small, smokeless fire, talking in low tones, assessing their situation. That afternoon, Eliab and four others had raided a shepherd's encampment a few miles to the south, getting away with two sheep, a young goat, a brick of goat's cheese, and four loaves of bread. It had been sorely needed, but with about twenty mouths to feed it would be gone in another day, maybe two. This desolate part of Judea provided a perfect place to disappear but little to sustain a band of men on the run.

Eliab rubbed at his beard, dusty and stiff with sweat. "Maybe we should go to Beersheba. Split up for a time. Rest the horses. Maybe kidnap a fat merchantman or shopkeeper and get some money. But we wouldn't let the Romans know it's us. Let them think we've given up and scattered. We'll hope eventually they'll give up the search."

Ya'abin looked at his second-in-command for a long, searing moment, his eyes flickering ominously in the firelight. Ya'abin's face was long, its narrowness accentuated by the pointed beard. On reduced rations, his face had become gaunt, the cheeks starting to hollow. It only added to the feeling of menace. "So run with the wind?" he sneered. "Is that what you're saying, Eliab?"

Eliab started to fumble. His leader had never been an easy man to please, but in these last few days he had become as one demented. "No, Moshe, I'm not saying we give up. Just maybe let some of the heat die down. You're the most wanted man in Judea at the moment. You can get your revenge later. Right now we've got our hands full just surviving."

There was a soft hoot of disgust. "Why don't you go back to that shepherd's camp and see if they'll let you sleep with the old women tonight."

Eliab blanched. "That's not fair! I've always stood by you."

"Then stand by me now!" Ya'abin shouted. Around them several heads came up, startled by the explosion.

Swallowing hard, Eliab nodded. "What do you want to do?"

The man they called the Fox of the Desert sat back, rubbing his hands on his robe. "We'll cross over the River Jordan into Moab. Hit some of the incense caravans moving up the King's Highway. There is a lot of profit in incense."

Eliab was nodding even before he finished. It wasn't the safest solution, but it was something. The Romans weren't scouring the highlands of Moab on the east side of the Dead Sea.

"What we need is two or three stunning successes so that men will beg to join us. Maybe we'll hit some of the custom houses. We lost our chance for Roman gold the other night. Well, we'll take it from somewhere else."

"I can see that," Eliab said, not daring to challenge Ya'abin further.

"Go through the men. Find out who has a contact in Jerusalem we can trust."

As quickly as his hopes had risen, they were dashed again. "Jerusalem?"

"That snake Mordechai betrayed us, Eliab." His voice was a soft hiss. "I have a score to settle with Ha'keedohn as well, but the Galilean will have to wait until we're stronger. It was Mordechai who lured us into the trap. It was Mordechai who thought he could outfox the Fox. If word gets out that he made fools of us, then we are lost." His voice rose sharply. "So get me someone who has contacts in Jerusalem."

Eliab fought back a sigh. "All right, Moshe."

The ferret face of the bandit twisted wickedly. "Where is the closest Roman patrol?"

Eliab stared for a moment. "It is—" He bit his lower lip. "It is camped on a ridge about four miles north of here."

"Get the men up. We'll hit them before dawn." He grinned maliciously. "Let's give the Roman dogs a memorable farewell before we head east."

"Moshe, you know they'll be in a secure camp. That's the Roman way."

"All the better," he said with relish. "Pilate needs to know that Moshe Ya'abin has not been run to ground."

II

The village of Beth Neelah was mostly in darkness as Simeon slipped through the narrow, dirt streets. If he saw movement ahead of him, he stopped, shrinking back into the shadows until the other person passed by.

He hesitated momentarily as he passed the stone house that was the home of Yehuda and Daniel and Shana. Now only Shana would be there. A deep sadness overwhelmed him as he stared at the lamplight in the window. The image of Shana's eyes—haunted, betrayed, filled with bitterness—would stay with him for a very long time. Finally, he moved on, not looking back.

Near the northern edge of the village was an ample house set amid rows of grapevines. He stopped, listened for a moment, then moved silently through the opening in the rock wall. At the front door, he paused for a moment, took a quick breath, then softly knocked.

From inside he heard a child's voice, then the scraping of a chair or bench across the floor. A moment later, the door opened and a young woman of about Simeon's age stood in the light. She looked up, then fell back a step, her eyes springing wide with surprise.

"*Erev tov*, Judith."

"Simeon. I—" Now her eyes were wary, almost suspicious.

"Is Issachar at home?"

Her head turned involuntarily as Simeon heard the sound of movement behind her. If that sound hadn't already given her away, Simeon wasn't sure if she would have answered him truthfully or not.

A figure stepped up behind her, not much taller than she was. His hair was full and his beard thick. "*Erev tov*, Simeon."

"Good evening, Issachar." Issachar's face was in shadow—the light was directly behind him and Simeon could not read the expression on the Zealot's face. Shadow or not, there was no mistaking the coolness in both husband and wife. "May I speak with you?"

The woman turned anxiously, but Issachar didn't respond. "Of course," he finally said. Then to her: "We won't be long." He stepped out, shutting the door behind him. As they moved down the row between the grapevines, Simeon saw a form at the window, watching them go. Finally they stopped, deep in the shadow of a large sycamore tree. Issachar was obviously not going to speak first.

The temptation to try to explain it all—what had happened, how things had developed, and what went wrong—rose up in Simeon again, but he shook his head. "I have a question to ask you, Issachar. It is important that you answer honestly. Too many things now stand between us not to speak freely."

"I hold no grudge for what happened at the Joknean," Issachar replied. "We know the risks—all of us—and go into battle prepared for the worst."

"But?" Simeon prompted, sensing there was more.

"But Yehuda told us that once the night was over, he would explain to us why you were no longer leading us in battle. Unfortunately, Yehuda . . . " He looked away.

"Unfortunately," Simeon finished for him, "Yehuda didn't come back."

"Nor Daniel," the man said softly.

Simeon said nothing.

After almost a full minute, Issachar looked squarely at him. "So there is no explanation from you, either?" His voice was filled with soft bitterness. "No reason why we risked our lives to save the very men we had come to kill?"

"Perhaps someday we can sit down and I will explain everything. Tonight, I must speak of other things. Will you hear me out?"

"I have always had the greatest admiration and respect for you as a man, Simeon, and for you as Ha'keedohn, my leader." There was an implied, "until now," but he didn't say it. "I am listening."

"Thank you." Simeon paused, deciding how best to start, then plunged. "Do you think you could convince the men to follow me one last time?"

There was a long questioning look. "To kill Romans or to protect them?" he finally said.

Simeon flinched at the barb, but only said, "To free Yehuda and the others."

He saw Issachar straighten and knew he had his full attention now. "How soon? They are to be executed in a few days."

"The execution has been postponed, perhaps even until September."

"You know that for certain?"

"Yes. It comes from an unquestionable source." .

"May the Lord be praised for his mercy." Issachar savored the news for a moment; then, "Have you told this to Shana?"

Simeon gave a brief shake of his head. "No. You may tell her as soon as we are through. But I would prefer that she doesn't learn how you came by this knowledge."

"I'm sorry about the betrothal, Simeon," Issachar said. His tone was considerably warmer now. "She is stricken beyond grief. Perhaps with time . . . " He shrugged.

Not answering that, Simeon went on. "Are there any in our band who speak Latin?"

Issachar cocked his head. "Latin?" He thought a moment. "All of us know a few words, of course, but Yehuda was the only one besides yourself who could converse at all."

"It doesn't matter. It would be helpful, but it is not required." He sighed. "I will need eight others besides myself who are willing to put themselves at great risk."

"Only eight?" Issachar was no fool. There were nearly two dozen in their band.

Simeon spoke quickly, telling Issachar of his plan, of his trip to Damascus and of his return that very day with the equipment they needed. "We'll take everyone to Caesarea, but only eight will actually go into the city with me. That constitutes two squads of four, or what the Romans call a *quaternion*. If we came with less, it would look suspicious. More puts too many at risk."

"And you plan to just walk right into the prison and . . . " He couldn't finish. The shock seemed to choke off his voice.

"We could try it without the uniforms," came the dry reply. "We could tell them we're just looking around."

Issachar moved over to the tree and leaned heavily against it. "This is crazy, Simeon. It's like sticking your head into the jaws of the crocodile, then slapping it across the face to see if it is paying attention."

Simeon laughed shortly. "I was thinking it's more like stepping off a cliff without a rope, but I like your analogy better." Then he too grew quite serious. "Yehuda, Samuel, and Barak face execution because I asked them to stand by me in keeping my oath to the Romans. Would you have me just wring my hands and hope the governor changes his mind?"

"No, of course not, but—"

"I know the risks, Issachar. I've thought of little else. But unless you see a way to raise a thousand men and lead a full-scale assault on Caesarea, I don't see any other alternative. And we don't have forever. The governor could change his mind at any time about when to execute them."

The wind sighed in the treetop above them as Issachar stared at the ground for a long time. Then at last his head came up again. "How soon?"

"I came straight here from Damascus. I have to take the uniforms down to Capernaum, where I will hide them. Then I would like to make a trip to Caesarea on my own, to reconnoiter the Praetorium. We'll also want a day or two to practice looking and acting like Romans. Say about two to three weeks."

"All right." Issachar pushed away from the tree, looking out into the night. "I'll tell the men."

"Will they do it?"

"As I said, we all have great respect for you and normally would follow you anywhere."

"But?" Simeon pressed again, knowing there was nothing about this circumstance that was normal.

"But I think the first thing you'd better do when you return is tell us everything. You owe us that."

"Yes, I do. And I will." He straightened. "I'll return a few days before the actual time so we can start training. We'll talk then." He reached out and grasped the other man's hand. "Thank you, Issachar. Thank you for listening."

As Simeon started away, moving in the opposite direction from the house, Issachar called out softly. "Are you sure I can't tell Shana you were here? If she knows you are trying to free Yehuda, it could change everything."

"Can it change the fact that Daniel is dead?" came the low reply. Then, without waiting for Issachar's response, Simeon disappeared into the darkness.

III

Ephraim visibly jerked when Simeon stepped into view. He jumped to his feet, completely astonished. "How did *you* get here?"

"How do I always get here?" Simeon said with a chuckle. "I came through the door."

"But—" Ephraim turned and looked at the main door to the warehouse, which was behind him. "I've been sitting right here all afternoon."

Simeon's grin broadened. "The *back* door."

"Oh." His face relaxed. "You and that back door. You're the only one who ever uses it."

"That's good," Simeon said cheerfully. The back wall of their main warehouse butted up against the outer wall of Capernaum. There was a small metal door through the wall that few people knew was still operative.

"Does Mother know you're back?"

He shook his head, looking around. "Are you the only one here?"

"Yes. There was only a little left to do, so I told Father and Leah to go home, I'd finish up."

"Have you been out to hear Jesus?"

"No," Ephraim said. "The Master's been teaching in Bethsaida and Chorazin the last couple of days. By the way, Mother asked Rachel and me and the children to come over for supper tonight."

"Great!" Simeon hesitated; then, much more serious, he asked, "Do you have a minute?"

"Sure." Ephraim sat down again, pointing to an empty stool.

"No. There's something I need to show you."

"Where?"

"In the back corner of the warehouse."

IV

For several long seconds, Ephraim just stared. Finally he turned back to look at his younger brother, deep alarm on his face. "What are these, Simeon?"

"Roman uniforms."

"I know that," he retorted. "*Whose* are they?"

"Mine."

"Yours! What do you mean, yours?"

"I need to leave them here for a few days, Ephraim. I don't think anyone will notice them back here in the corner, but I couldn't take a chance. I need you to make sure they remain undisturbed."

Ephraim was four years older than Simeon and had always been the solid one, the steady one, the one who loved working at the warehouse and keeping the books. He was most like their father in both temperament and spirit. That was why Simeon had decided that Ephraim would be the one he would tell—the only one he would tell. "Would you like to sit down?" he suggested.

Ephraim shook his head, still staring at the crate of uniforms. "What are you doing, Simeon?"

Simeon withdrew the folded parchment carefully from his tunic and held it out. Ephraim took it, examining the red wax that sealed the edge. It was stamped in the center with an official-looking seal. Finally, he looked up. "What is this?"

"A letter." Simeon decided the time for playing the innocent little boy was over. "The seal is that of Pontius Pilate."

Ephraim's head came around slowly. "Pilate?" He looked at the stamps more closely. "What does it say?"

"I'd let you read it," Simeon said, "but obviously if we open it, that will spoil everything." And so he told him. Simeon had drafted the original to give to the forger and had read this copy carefully twice before it was sealed. He could quote it almost word for word.

As Simeon spoke, Ephraim groped his way to the nearest bale of wool and collapsed onto it.

Simeon laughed softly. "I told you to sit down."

"You're going to . . . " He couldn't finish it.

"I am," Simeon said simply. "You have to give me your word that you won't tell Mother and Father. At least not until after it's underway."

"You can't, Simeon! This is insane!"

"Can't you think of another word? That one has already been taken. In fact, several times."

"What are you thinking?" Ephraim cried, not amused in any way. "Who is going to—"

Simeon cut in smoothly. "I went to Beth Neelah night before last. My men are going with me."

"Did you tell them what you planned?"

"I did."

"All of it?"

"They know it all, and they're still willing."

Ephraim set the parchment down, then dropped his head in his hands. "Oh, Simeon! Simeon! What have you done?"

Simeon's lips compressed into a tight line and his eyes hardened. "I've done *something*, Ephraim. Maybe it isn't the best thing. Maybe it's not insane. Maybe it's just plain stupid. But I least I've done *something*. And it feels good."

68

V

"Rachel, you stay here and visit for a time. Simeon and I will put the children to bed."

Simeon looked at his brother, raising an eyebrow. The evening meal had been cleared away and the family visited comfortably on the rooftop, enjoying the cool of the evening. Ephraim ignored the startled look.

"Hooray!" Boaz shouted.

"Are you sure?" Rachel said.

"Yes." Ephraim shot Simeon a glance that said, "Please!"

"Uh, . . . sure," Simeon said quickly. "That would be nice. I haven't been able to see these two for a while."

Esther watched him, her expression unreadable. He smiled at her. "Is that all right with you, Esther?"

"Will you tell me a story?"

"Of course. What story would you like?"

A tiny smile appeared. "Queen Esther."

Simeon reached out and brought her into his arms. "Why doesn't that surprise me?"

Ephraim laughed. "But I told you that story last night, Esther."

"Uncle Simeon tells it better," she said with a matter-of-fact tone of voice.

That brought a burst of laughter from the family. Simeon put his hands on his hips, mimicking Esther's favorite stance. "So there, Papa," he said to Ephraim. "See what happens when you don't add a little embellishment?"

"I want a story! I want a story." Boaz was hopping up and down.

"Can I tell you a story?" Ephraim asked, pretending to be hurt.

Boaz stopped, the two-year-old face screwing up, obviously torn. Then his shoulders slumped. "I guess."

"There you go," Simeon said proudly. "There's just no competing with their favorite uncle."

"I'll come too," Joseph said, getting to his feet.

Ephraim swung around, a little too quickly. "No, Joseph." He forced a smile. "That's all right. We'll be fine."

David had started to get up too, but at that he sank back down in his chair. "Not tonight, Son," he said to Joseph. "We'll stay here."

"But Papa!"

Deborah had been watching this interchange between her two oldest children with interest. By mutual consent, no one had asked Simeon where he had been for the past several days or what he had been doing. But Simeon and Ephraim had come from the warehouse together, and there had been a studied casualness between them all through supper. "Joseph?"

He turned.

"Your father is right. We'll stay here and visit."

Ephraim gave her a grateful look, then went to her and kissed her on the cheek. He gave Leah a hug, then kissed his wife as well. "Take your time," he said softly.

Rachel gave him a strange look, but nodded.

"Come on," Simeon said to the two youngest in the family. "First one in their night clothes gets the first story."

VI

Reaching out with his fingertips, Simeon gently pushed a strand of black hair away from Esther's face. She didn't move. He bent down and kissed her on the forehead, pulling the light blanket up around her neck. Then he moved to Boaz and did the same. Together he and Ephraim backed out of the bedroom.

"Those are two precious little ones you have there, Brother," Simeon said huskily, surprised by the sudden emotion in him.

"I know. And they love you dearly, Simeon. You need to have some of your own." He got that far before he caught himself. "Oh, I'm sorry."

Simeon waved it away. "It's all right. My betrothal seems like something from a different life."

Ephraim only nodded. They moved into the main room of the house and sat down. Simeon leaned back. "All right, I'm braced," he said with resignation. "What did you want to talk about?"

Ephraim laughed. "Am I that transparent?"

"No more than a cup of water."

"I am going with you."

Whatever Simeon had braced himself for, this wasn't it.

"I am. I've thought about it all night. I'm going."

"No, Ephraim." Simeon felt like he had been struck from behind. "I told you, it's already been decided."

"Yes, it has, and I'm going."

Simeon was on his feet. "Don't be ridiculous. You can't go."

"Why not?"

"Because of Rachel. And those two in there." He sat down again, rubbing his hands through his hair. "Look, Ephraim, I may have made it sound like this is going to be a stroll along the seashore, but I know full well the risks. I won't put both of us in danger."

"That's interesting," Ephraim said, musing. "Let's see. I don't know all of those men from Beth Neelah, but I do know some. Tell me about Issachar. Is he one of them?"

Simeon flinched. How had he guessed Issachar's name, of all of them?

"Well, is he?"

"Yes."

"If I remember right, he's married, isn't he?"

Simeon nodded, guessing what was coming.

"Children?"

"Two."

There was an incredulous look. "Only two? Well, that explains it then. And I've got how many?" He pretended to be calculating. "All right, with so many children of my own, I see why you think I shouldn't go."

"Ephraim, I—" He took a deep, pain-filled breath.

"And what about Joshua? He's betrothed, isn't he?" The sarcasm was light but unmistakable. "Well, as long as he's not married. Let's see, who else? Oh, yes. There's Ezekiel, but then I suppose his wife and four children won't mind—"

"All right!" Simeon snapped. "You've made your point. But you are not going."

"Why not!" Ephraim snapped right back.

"Because you are my brother." His voice fell to an agonized whisper as he gestured toward the bedroom. "I can't take away their father."

"Yes, I am your brother, Simeon, and I want you to listen to me. I know you have to do something about Yehuda. I don't want to try to talk you out of that. But this is not the way."

"Then give me another!" Simeon cried.

"I can't! I don't know what you should do. I only know this is not right." He got up and came to stand before Simeon. "Look," he said, pleading now. "You are torn with guilt because Daniel is dead and Yehuda and two other men are in prison. You lost Shana because of what happened that night. I understand all that. But what you did was the right thing, Simeon." He grabbed him by the shoulders and shook him gently. "It was. You know it was. But what if something goes wrong now? It won't be just Shana you have to face anymore. It will be eight other wives or who knows how many children."

Simeon stared at the floor. "Don't you think I've thought about that? Yehuda is their neighbor, their cousin, their comrade. They know the risks. I know the risks."

"Do you know the exact protocol for getting a prisoner released?" He overrode any answer. "Do you know if the guards are required to confirm the governor's signature?"

Simeon just shook his head. "You give me something better, and I'll do it in a minute."

"You've got to count the cost, Simeon. Isn't that what Jesus told you? And counting the cost includes counting the consequences."

"You've been talking to Father," Simeon said dully, all life gone from him now.

"Yes. Actually this family has talked about little else since you left. And prayed about little else." He dropped to one knee, lowering himself enough to look into Simeon's face. "Go ask Jesus again, Simeon."

Simeon felt a burst of pain. "Don't you get it, Ephraim? He's not going to answer me. He gave me some general principles, but it is up to me to work out what that means. He is not going to tell me specifically what to do. That is not his way."

"Then lets *us* talk about it. Let's make it a family question. There has got to be something better than this."

Simeon jerked free. "*No!*" He raised a clenched fist and shook it at him. "You promised you wouldn't say anything, Ephraim."

"And I won't. Not unless you tell me I can."

Simeon dropped back. "We can make it work." His voice was low and filled with pain. "I'm praying that we can make it work."

Moving back to his chair, Ephraim sat down again, knowing that he was losing. "How soon do you go?"

"I've got some things I have to do here first. That will take a couple of days. Then I'm going to Caesarea. I need to get into the Praetorium and see the layout for myself."

Ephraim just shook his head in disbelief. "I know you can pass for a Roman just about anywhere, but what are you going to do if you happen to bump into that tribune? Isn't that where he's stationed? Will you just nod and wave and pass on by and hope he doesn't notice?"

"If you think you're asking me things I haven't already asked myself, you disappoint me."

"Will you at least not decide yet? Keep looking for answers. We'll go and hear Jesus again. He should be back tomorrow. Maybe if Peter talks to him, Jesus will be more specific."

Simeon shrugged. There was no hope in him.

"Two days. Will you give it at least two more days?"

Simeon got wearily to his feet. "Thank you, Ephraim." He came over and put his arms around him. "Thank you for caring."

They held each other, both awkward in the depth of the moment. "Will you at least think about it?" Ephraim finally asked. "Just for two more days?"

Simeon nodded, too tired to fight any longer.

CHAPTER 5

FORTUNE FAVORS THE BOLD.

—*Virgil, Aeneid, x.284*

I

JERUSALEM

25 JUNE, A.D. 30

"Miriam! Wake up!" Livia reached over and shook her vigorously. "Wake up!"

With a soft moan, Miriam cracked one eye open. "Livia?" Then confirming who it was, she swatted at her. "Go away!"

Livia grabbed her hands and half-dragged her to a sitting position. "Miriam! You've got to wake up. Your father is home!"

Miriam started to fall back, but then Livia's words registered. She sat up fully. "Papa?"

"Yes, he's home. He came in late last night."

"But . . . " She was confused. She had been up until nearly midnight; now as she looked out, she saw the sun was up.

Livia sat down by her. "He was in Caesarea." Her eyes were wide and touched with fear. "The tribune is with him."

That brought Miriam to stiff attention. "What? Marcus?"

Livia nodded quickly. "What if they know about—" Her mouth pinched. "Oh, Miriam!"

Miriam reached out and took her servant by the shoulders and steadied her. "Everything is fine, Livia. I'm sure that Father just went there to get a report."

"He wants to see you right away."

She swung her feet over the edge of the bed. "Did you tell him I was asleep?"

"Levi told him." Levi was her father's chief servant. "Levi came and awakened me."

One hand came up unconsciously to pull at the tangle of her dark hair. "And Marcus is here?" Miriam asked again.

"Yes. He's waiting downstairs with your father."

Miriam stood swiftly, her mind finally fully functioning. "Tell them it will take me a few minutes to get dressed."

"Yes, Miriam."

As Livia started for the door, Miriam called to her. "Livia?"

She turned.

"There is nothing wrong," she said firmly. "We just went to visit Lilly and Ezra while Father was gone. He knows I hate to be alone in this huge house. Everything will be all right."

Livia nodded gravely and managed a wan smile. "I hope you are right."

II

At the door of the library, Livia gave Miriam's hand a quick squeeze, then left her. This was not a meeting for servants. Miriam entered the luxuriously furnished room, then stopped dead. Ezra was seated there, but no one else was in the room.

"I thought you went back to Joppa," she cried, her knees suddenly weak with gratitude. If Ezra was here to stand with her it would be all right.

He smiled. "I had a few things to do here in Jerusalem." He glanced quickly at the door. "I thought it might be well if I were here when your father returned."

"Oh yes, thank you."

They turned at the sound of footsteps in the hall. The door opened and her father walked in. She ran to him and put her arms around him, kissing him soundly on the cheek. In spite of all that had happened, she was very glad to see him. "This is a nice surprise," she said.

"I thought it might be." He hugged her tightly for a moment— holding her for just a moment or two longer than normal—and kissed her back. "It is so good to see you, Miriam."

"And you, Papa. Did your business go well in Alexandria?"

He frowned. "Yes, very well."

"I suppose Levi told you that Livia and I have been in Joppa while you were gone." She smiled brightly at her cousin's husband. "Ezra was kind enough to bring us back here."

Her father half turned. "I am very grateful for that. Very grateful."

That was not what she had expected. She was braced for questions about why she had gone to Joppa and stayed so long. Miriam looked more closely at her father. "Are you all right, Papa? You look very tired."

"I am. We traveled until late, then rose early to come on into the city."

Miriam looked around. "Livia said that Marcus came with you."

"He did. He left a few minutes ago to take his men over to the Antonia Fortress. He needs to return to Caesarea first thing tomorrow morning. He and his men need some rest."

To her surprise, Miriam felt both relief and disappointment. She had steeled herself for the meeting, prepared to put on an innocent face in front of her father and Marcus. Yet she realized now that she had been a little excited to see Marcus again too.

Her father took her by the arm, guiding her toward the empty chair beside Ezra. As she sat down, Mordechai went behind the large table and took his chair. In that position, the light from the large window illuminated his face fully. She drew in a breath. This was more than weariness she saw. The lines around his eyes were deep. His mouth was pinched and drawn. He looked suddenly much older than he actually was.

"Father, what's wrong?"

His shoulders lifted and fell as he took in a deep breath, then let it out slowly. "Miriam, I have something to say. I want you to listen carefully and not interrupt until I am through." He glanced at Ezra. "I'm glad you're here to hear this too. It will save me writing a letter to you."

A little shiver ran through Miriam's body. She had never seen her father quite so somber. Did Pilate know after all? Simeon had sworn that no one else knew of her involvement, not even Yehuda. But what if Pilate had somehow learned of her role in all of this?

He began then, and in a moment immense relief swept through her. As he told her of the events at the Joknean Pass it became immediately clear that he had no inkling of her role in those events. She fought to keep her face calm. He didn't know!

What he told them was only a partial version of what had actually happened, of course. The fact that the whole thing was actually an elaborate ruse concocted by her father in cooperation with the Romans was not even hinted at.

A rush of bitterness welled up inside her again. She had been one of his game pieces, pushed about the board to further his own ends. She forced herself to listen intently, pretending growing astonishment, as did Ezra. There were a few surprises. It came as a great relief to hear that Yehuda and his two followers had not been executed yet, and they would not be for several more months. She hadn't known that more than two dozen Roman soldiers had been killed by Ya'abin's treachery. Pilate must be in a fury over that.

As her father continued, Miriam only half listened. A new thought had sprung into her mind. Did she dare approach him about paying a ransom for Yehuda and having him freed? Going to Caesarea and asking Marcus to help would have been foolhardy. She accepted that now. But her father owed a debt to Simeon and Yehuda as much as Miriam did. She wouldn't have to give anything away.

Then suddenly, her father's words jolted her back to awareness. She shook her head, throwing off her other thoughts. "Rome?" she blurted.

He laughed softly. "I thought that might get your attention."

"Rome! What did you say about going to Rome?"

There was impatience in his eyes. "Where were you, Daughter? This is serious."

She was half-stammering now. "I was thinking about Yehuda and that day that he and Simeon came into our camp and saved us from Ya'abin."

He shook his head in exasperation. "Miriam. We are in danger. I don't want to frighten you unnecessarily, but we have to face reality." He glanced at Ezra, who had not said a word through all of this. "You see it, don't you?"

"I do," he said soberly. Then Ezra looked at her, and there was silent warning in his eyes. "If what we know about this Ya'abin is even half-true, Miriam, there is great danger."

"Danger?" she finally managed, realizing that she sounded like a slow child.

Her father threw up his hands and rocked back. "Good heavens, Miriam, have you not heard a word?" He shot to his feet, leaning over the table, his voice hard. "Moshe Ya'abin is out there somewhere. Marcus learned this morning that he attacked the maniple of soldiers out looking for him. Came in at night. Eight men were killed and the camp set afire."

That was enough to get her full attention. If Ya'abin was strong enough to hit a Roman camp, then . . .

"I'm the one who sent him to the Joknean. He knows now it was a trap to try to catch him. He's going to be looking for revenge, Miriam, and it won't be just me that he comes after. I'm sorry. It's not a pleasant prospect, but that's what we are facing."

He looked at Ezra. "I don't think he'll bother you and Lilly. I doubt he even knows that I have relatives in Joppa. But I want you to be especially careful as well."

Ezra nodded, then turned to Miriam. "Your father is right. You can't stay here. Not until Ya'abin is caught."

She sat back, staring fixedly at her father's face. "Rome? You want me to go to Rome?"

"Yes," he said, pleased to see that she was finally with him again. "With me. And Pilate is going to send Marcus back with us too."

Finally he smiled, looking again at Ezra. "I knew she'd be speechless." Then he rushed on, speaking to her again. "We've talked about it before, Miriam. You said you liked the idea. It's just going to be sooner than we thought."

He saw that she was still a little staggered by it all.

"I've thought about other alternatives—Alexandria, Antioch, Damascus. But Ya'abin could still find us there." He took a quick breath. "And it's not just Ya'abin. The Zealots are going to think I'm the one who betrayed them."

But you are *the one who betrayed them!* Fortunately, her lips were pressed tightly together and she had shouted the words only in her mind. But he was right. Her mind was working now. Ya'abin wouldn't be the only one bent on getting revenge, and the Zealots had been known to penetrate even the loftiest halls of Jerusalem. She felt as if she couldn't breathe. Only one word finally came out, and that was a strained whisper. "When?"

"Four weeks." He was all business again. "There are some things I must do before I can leave, but I dare not leave you here even for that long. I want you to go back to Caesarea with Marcus tomorrow. You'll be safe there until we sail. I'll come as quickly as possible."

It was the second numbing blow in as many minutes. "Caesarea? No, Father."

His face went instantly hard. "Miriam, don't fight me on this. I can't be worrying about you while I'm trying to get my affairs in order."

Without realizing it, she was on her feet. "Not Caesarea. Hire guards for the house. If need be, Livia and I will not go out until Ya'abin is caught." Even as she said it, she realized how foolish she sounded. "Please, Papa. Four weeks in the palace with Pilate and his wife and a bunch of Romans . . . I can't."

"You can!" Mordechai roared, startling both her and Ezra. "This is not a game we're caught in, Miriam. We are talking about our lives. Now that's the end of it."

She dropped back into the chair, sick at heart. "Rome?" She looked up, her face stricken. "For how long?"

"Probably a year. Maybe longer. Pilate has troops out in the wilderness of Judea looking for Ya'abin. Until he's caught, we can't return."

She laughed, nearly hysterical. "The wilderness of Judea? It could take five years for the Romans to find anyone there, clumsy as they are."

Mordechai glared at her. Then he remembered something. There was a soft plop as a folded piece of parchment landed on the table in front of her. "Marcus asked that I give you this."

Completely taken aback, she picked it up. It was folded, but not sealed. She opened it, eyes widening in amazement as she read the neatly written Latin.

From Tribune Marcus Quadratus Didius of Caesarea. To Miriam, daughter of Mordechai ben Uzziel of Jerusalem. Warmest salutations and respect.

It is with pleasure that I inform you that just a few days previous, I received correspondence from the "slave hunter" that you and I discussed some weeks ago. He reports success in trying to locate the younger brother of your servant girl, Livia. Said brother, one Drusus Alexander Carlottus, was taken to Silicia four years ago and sold as a household slave. Since then, he seems to have been sold to one of the many patrician families who live in or around Rome. By now your father has told you of his plan for you to accompany him to Rome. The governor has graciously asked me to serve as your escort, which allows me to see my own family as well. It will give me the welcome opportunity to serve as your guide in my city—a pleasant turn of affairs in my eyes.

While there, it would be possible for us to pursue the search for Livia's brother more vigorously, something difficult to do from such a distance as this. I would consider it an honor if you would allow me to continue to assist you in this regard.

At the bottom was a stamped seal with his name within it.

More dazed than before, she looked up at her father. "Do you know what this says?"

He nodded. A brief frown clouded his features. "I must say, Miriam, that I was disappointed that you would undertake such a query without my knowledge, but—"

"I will do everything I can to help Livia find her brother again, Father. Please don't try to stop me on that."

He reached across and took her hand. "I didn't say I was going to try to stop you, only that I wish you had said something." The corners of his mouth softened. "Actually, I think it is quite commendable. I have no objection." He paused momentarily. "It gives you a reason to seriously consider Rome."

So *that* was why he had waited to give her the letter. She half-closed her eyes. She was nearly nineteen now. She was of age. He could not force her to go. Yet the power of the family in their religion was almost irresistible. "Honor your father and mother," had thundered from Mount Sinai along with the nine other commandments. And with all of that, there was still the very real problem of Moshe Ya'abin and the Zealots. She wasn't naive enough to believe she would be safe. Ya'abin had been stopped short of having his way with Miriam once before. She shuddered at the thought of what he might do this time.

She cocked her head as a thought sprang into her mind. "Livia would go with us?"

He nodded immediately. "Of course."

"As my sister?"

He reared back, anger flashing in his eyes. "That is not up for discussion, Miriam. I told you that before. I have not objected to the fact that you no longer treat her as a servant, but no, there will be no adoption."

Her jaw set. "If I go to Rome, it will be with Livia as my adopted sister, Father."

"You would bargain with me like I was buying melons in the marketplace?" he roared. And yet, to her surprise, she saw a touch of admiration in his eyes. She knew that he liked her fire, her streak of independence.

"I am not bargaining, Father," she replied calmly. "If you wish me to go to Rome with you, then I will adopt Livia and go with her as my sister. You don't have to do it. I'll see to it that she has no claim on your means. I'll pay for everything out of my own funds." She folded her arms and calmly met his glare. "That is my condition, Father."

He rose and began to pace, stopping every three or four steps to mutter something at her. Finally, he nodded. "You show me that you'll go to Rome and follow my counsel; then we'll talk about it."

She felt a burst of exultation. It was more than she had hoped for. "All right, Papa."

"But you both will start packing immediately. Think in terms of what you'll need for a year. Marcus will return for you and Livia at sunrise tomorrow."

She shook her head firmly. "No, Papa. I will go to Rome, but not Caesarea." She rushed on as he spun around, his face darkening. "I can't bear the thoughts of being there alone. I don't know anyone. Their food is not in accordance with the Law."

He was astonished. "Since when did you get to be a Pharisee?"

She went right on. "Making conversation with Pilate's wife for all that time?" Her eyes locked with his, no compromise or surrender in them now. "I won't, Papa. Lock me and Livia in the house if you must, but I won't go to Caesarea until I go with you."

"You will do what I say!" His voice rocked her back. His cheeks were touched with spots of red and his eyes were flaming.

"No, Papa," she murmured. "Not in this. I will not."

Ezra got to his feet, stepping between the two before a greater eruption took place. "May I speak, Mordechai?"

The older man half turned. "Yes, yes," he said impatiently. "What is it?"

"I have another solution that perhaps both of you may find acceptable."

Miriam turned in surprise. Mordechai also gave him his full attention now. "Go on."

He swallowed quickly, clearly nervous about interfering. "For some time now, I have been talking about making a trip to Gaulanitis. As you know, the area of the Golan Heights, what the Romans now call Gaulanitis, is a center for much cattle. My supplier of leather goods, a man by the name of Simon the Tanner, has been unhappy with the quality of the hides he has been receiving from the merchants lately." He held out his hands in a gesture of frustration. "I don't need to tell you that a sandalmaker, such as myself, depends heavily on the quality of leather he can purchase."

Miriam turned, scarcely believing what she was hearing. Gaulanitis was the area directly northeast of the Sea of Galilee. He was suggesting that they go back to the Galilee!

Mordechai was clearly intrigued as well. "Go on," he said again.

"Suppose I were to take Miriam and Livia back to Joppa with me early tomorrow morning, before it's light. I can put a covering on my carriage. We could hide them until we are well out of the city. It will be night when we arrive in Joppa, so no one will know that Miriam and Livia have returned with me. The next morning, Lilly and I shall leave for Gaulanitis."

He smiled finally, gaining confidence even as he spoke. "It will take us about two weeks to do our business up north. And, of course, we would have to return by way of Caesarea. We could bring the two of them there to you on whatever day you specify."

Mordechai looked dubious, but Miriam practically leaped on Ezra's proposal. "Oh, yes, Papa. That would answer your concern and get me away from Jerusalem until we leave."

"*No one* will know where they are," Ezra emphasized.

"Please, Papa! Don't make me go to Caesarea. I will hate every minute of it."

To her amazed joy, her father pursed his lips. He was considering it. "You are sure no one in Joppa would know they are with you?" he asked Ezra

"Who is to know?" Ezra said smoothly. "When I return, I will be 'alone.' When Lilly and I leave, we will be 'alone.' Send their baggage with this Roman. Let people think Miriam has gone to Caesarea. That will give us even greater secrecy."

Miriam was holding her breath. Ezra's boldness was breathtaking. It was all she could do to keep from throwing her arms around his neck and knocking him off his feet.

For a long moment, a moment that seemed to stretch on for an eternity, her father stared out the window. One hand came up and he pulled at his lip, the tiredness now showing in every aspect of his demeanor. Then he turned at last to his daughter, his face stern. "If I let you go with Ezra, will you give me your word that you will do exactly what he and Lilly tell you to do? That you will stay with them at all times? You won't be running off on your own? You have to promise me, Miriam."

Tears welled up in her eyes. This man had used her for his own purposes and that had cut deeply, but he still loved her. He was greatly concerned about her safety. "Yes, Papa," she whispered. "You have my word. I will be good." She went to him and slipped her arms around him. "And you must promise me that you will be careful, too."

He nodded, trying not to show that he was touched as well. He turned to Ezra. "It shall be as you say. Thank you."

III

CAPERNAUM

In the end, it was easier for Simeon to go with the family than to try to give them his reasons for not going. Ephraim had been true to his word and had not even hinted at what had happened at the warehouse between him and Simeon. But Simeon's parents knew he was struggling to decide what to do about Yehuda. They knew he had gone to Damascus to work out some kind of solution. Since he had not volunteered any information, they had not pushed him for it. So their answer was to go to Jesus. They hoped he would say something that might help Simeon. None of that was expressed, of course, but it was clearly known to all.

David closed the warehouses for the day—an indication of his silent concern for what was going on in Simeon's life—and the whole family left together after breakfast. Jesus was back in Capernaum and had been seen near the house of Peter and Anna.

They didn't get very far in that direction. As they started up the street on which Peter lived, heavy throngs blocked their way. "Come," David said, taking Deborah by the hand. "Let's go around. Maybe we can get closer if we go in the back way."

Simeon was carrying Esther on his shoulders. As he turned to follow his father, she grabbed his head with both hands and turned it firmly back. "There's Jesus," she said.

He smiled up at his niece. "Yes, Esther. Pampa is going to take us to him."

Satisfied, she settled back again. "Jesus likes me," she said as they turned away and started down a narrow alley.

"I know he does," Simeon said, touched by the joy in her voice. "He knows what a special little girl you are."

"I'm not little," she shot right back.

Simeon nodded, fighting to keep his face sober. "You're right, Esther. Sorry. I keep forgetting that you are four and a half years old now." Seeing that she was satisfied with that, he added, "You are like Queen Esther. She was very beautiful and very brave. That's why you like that story so much, isn't it?"

She made an emphatic bob with her head. Esther was a happy child, but quite sober in her demeanor. To win a smile from her took special effort, and even then her smiles were generally reserved only for those closest to her. But now, as Simeon looked up to see her reaction, a full smile lit up her face. "Yes," she said contentedly. "My name is Esther, too."

They all laughed at that and Rachel reached up and touched her daughter's cheek. "Yes, it is, Esther. You are our little queen."

There was a regal sniff. "*I'm not little!*"

Simeon felt a tug on his tunic and looked down. Boaz was walking beside David, holding his grandfather's hand. He had turned two years old in April. "I brave too," he said. His hair was black, his eyes like two pieces of ebony.

"Yes, you are," Simeon said, smiling down at him. "Boaz is also a wonderful name. He was a handsome man who lived many years ago. He married a beautiful woman named Ruth."

"I handsome," he said happily.

Again all the family laughed. Rachel looked a little embarrassed. "My children don't lack confidence, do they."

"I think it's wonderful," Deborah said. "It's not pride. They're not old enough for that. They just know that they are loved, and that makes them feel they are of worth." She reached out and touched Rachel's sleeve. "It says a lot about what kind of parents you and Ephraim are."

His talk with Ephraim the night before had left Simeon filled with dejection and agonizing all over again. So this was like an elixir to him. He had always loved his family and been close to them, but it was like he was seeing them all with new eyes now. It felt good. Very good.

They worked their way down the alley, took another route around the main square of Capernaum, then started back down another way. Simeon's father had been right. The crowds were still thronging the streets, but the majority of them were coming from the other direction. As they approached, Simeon saw Jesus in the very thickest part of the crowd. The Twelve were standing back, listening but ready to move in if the people pressed in too tightly.

John, the youngest member of the Twelve, saw David's family coming. He waved and started towards them. The younger of Zebedee's two sons, John was about Simeon's age. Because of the partnership of James and John with Simeon's father, John and Simeon had always been good friends. As John approached, Simeon let Esther down to stand beside her mother.

"*Shalom*, David. *Shalom*, Deborah," John said. "I thought you might come." He spoke quickly to the others, bending down solemnly to shake the hands of Boaz and Esther. Then he turned and looked back toward the crowd. "Jesus is just answering questions at the moment. He hasn't started formally teaching as yet."

Peter and Andrew and James had now seen the family too and also came over to join them. As they approached, John looked directly at Simeon. "And how is everything with you?"

"All right." This was not the place to raise his concerns.

The other three apostles joined them before more could be said. They, too, shook hands all around. When he came to Simeon, Peter held his grip for several seconds. "Well?" he said, giving him a searching look.

Simeon shrugged. "I've made some decisions." He looked at Ephraim and then away again. "Whether they are the right ones or not, who can say?"

The stocky fisherman gave him a quizzical look, but only nodded. Sensing that the apostles had come specifically to see how Simeon was doing, Deborah turned to the others. "Let's go closer," she said. She took Esther and Boaz by the hand and started away.

Ephraim took the hint for what it was. He stepped up beside Rachel. "I'm coming too."

Leah was disappointed, obviously hoping to learn more about what Simeon was up to. Clearly she wanted to linger, but Ephraim took her arm and the six of them moved away. Only David stayed beside his son.

"So?" Peter asked again. "What have you decided to do?"

Simeon just shook his head. "I thought I had a solution, but Ephraim has put some doubts in my mind about it."

David wanted to ask more about that—obviously something had happened between his two sons when they went over to put the children to bed the night before—but he decided against it. He would let Simeon tell him what he wished, when he wished.

"Why don't you tell Jesus what you've decided and ask him if it is the right thing to do?" John queried.

Simeon shook his head. "I'm not sure I'm ready for that. Actually, the more I think about it, the more foolish it sounds, even to me."

"And you wouldn't want Jesus to think you are foolish, would you?" Peter's eyes mocked him a little. Then, before Simeon could answer, Peter turned and looked toward the crowd. "Look there," he said. "Since the feeding of the five thousand, the multitudes come in ever greater numbers. We worry about the Master. He never has time to himself. There is always something or someone. And yet he won't turn them away. He is always willing to stay a little longer, answer their questions, listen to their problems." He peered intently at Simeon. "He answers *all* their questions, Simeon, whether they are foolish or not."

James was nodding. James was closer to Peter's age, about twenty-four, and of a much more serious nature than his younger brother. Now his eyes were grave. "There isn't a day goes by that one of us doesn't say something foolish to the Lord. Sometimes he just smiles. Mostly he uses those opportunities to teach us."

"And that isn't always a comfortable thing," Andrew agreed. "Jesus has this remarkable ability to see beneath the surface of things, to point out something you've never thought of. It can be pretty humbling."

"Maybe he *will* tell you that you are wrong," John said, prodding Simeon verbally now. "Is that what you're afraid of?"

Simeon thought about that for a moment, then shook his head. "Actually, that would be a relief. At least then I would know one way or the other."

"So, let's go ask him," Peter said, ever the one to want to keep things moving along.

Simeon just shook his head. "Not today. I need more time to think about it." He felt the discouragement wash over him again. "What I once thought was an idea born of inspiration is starting to look more and more like it came from desperation. And yet . . . " He thought of

Yehuda languishing in a cell in Caesarea. "I need more time to think about it."

Peter turned to his brother. "He is afraid of seeming the fool. Tell him, Andrew. Tell him what you were saying to the rest of us last night after Jesus went to bed."

Andrew was immediately pensive. "I was just thinking that sometimes being with Jesus is really discouraging."

Both David and Simeon were surprised by that, and Andrew went on quickly to explain. "Do you know why? Because being with him is like having someone hold up a lamp inside you so you can see what you really are. And that is not always a flattering thing."

"We often feel like children," Peter said somberly. "Jesus is constantly teaching us. Correcting us. Expanding our perspective." He gave a crooked little smile. "Holding up our humanity alongside his divinity. Like Andrew says, sometimes it can be pretty humbling."

This turn in the conversation had piqued Simeon's curiosity. He didn't want to admit it, but Peter was right. The fear of looking foolish was partly what was holding him back. The more he thought about his scheme with the Roman uniforms and the letter from Pilate, the more crazy it seemed. More and more it seemed like desperation was what was driving him. "Like what?" he finally said. "Give me an example."

John laughed softly. "We could give you a dozen examples. But here is one I still cringe about every time I remember it." He looked at David now as well as Simeon. "Do you remember the name that Jesus has given to James and me?"

Simeon was blank, and David seemed equally puzzled.

"*Boanerges.*"

"Ah," David said. "That's right. The Sons of Thunder."

Simeon looked puzzled. He had not heard this name before.

Peter chuckled richly. "It is kind of hard to think of these two being like a clap of thunder, isn't it. They are so docile. So eventempered. Nothing fiery or stubborn about them."

John eyed Peter sardonically. "Shall we talk about others among us who might be stubborn and impetuous and . . . "

"Get on with your story," Peter growled good-naturedly.

John turned back to Simeon "I only point out our name so that you will better appreciate what happened on this day. We were on our way to Jerusalem for Passover. Instead of going by way of the Jordan Valley, we took the Way of the Patriarchs, the road that leads right through Samaria to Jerusalem."

He shook his head. "That alone is a lesson. Jesus doesn't seem too concerned about being 'corrupted' by contact with the Samaritans, as so many of the rest of us are. So anyway, as we were passing through Samaria, Jesus sent a couple of our group ahead to arrange for food and lodging for the night. They went to the nearest Samaritan village."

His eyes took on a distant look. "As you know, it's not just us Jews who have deep feelings against the Samaritans. The Samaritans have some pretty strong feelings against Jews, too. So when the people there saw we were Galileans and knew we were headed to Jerusalem for Passover, they refused to let us even come into the village, let alone give us food or lodging." His mouth tightened. "They were not going to let some group of Jews take advantage of them."

To Simeon's surprise, John's face colored slightly. He also noted that James was staring at the ground, clearly ashamed of what was about to be said. "We were all furious. It would have been affront enough if some of our own people had turned us away. But these were Samaritans! How dare they insult the Son of God?"

Simeon suppressed a grin. He could see that John was starting to fume all over again with the memory. Son of Thunder was an appropriate name for this man. "So what did you do?" he asked.

James came in now, his voice low with pain. "Well, Jesus has taught us on several occasions that if we had enough faith we could even move mountains."

"Yes."

"And one of our favorite stories of faith has always been of the prophet Elijah."

As the implication of that sunk in, David nearly choked. "You didn't?"

"We did," John said. "We took him aside. 'Lord,' we said, 'wilt thou have us call down fire from heaven to consume them as Elijah did when he destroyed the priests of Baal?' There was a faint but sad smile. "That seemed like an appropriate punishment for their impertinence."

Any humor in the four men was gone. They were all very somber now. Peter was shaking his head. "It may have been these two who said it, but we were all thinking it would be a way to teach these heathens a lesson about whom they had just rejected."

"And what did Jesus say?" Simeon asked quietly.

"Well, he obviously was not pleased," John said. "But he wasn't angry, really. It was more like the question had saddened him deeply."

James spoke again. "I'll never forget his eyes when he looked at us. 'Do you not know what manner of spirit you are of?' he asked. That question still hurts. Then he added very softly, 'The Son of Man is not come to destroy men's lives but to save them.'"

Andrew finished the story. "That was all he said. Jesus had us go to another village and nothing more was said about the incident."

"No one likes to look the fool, Simeon," Peter said, "especially in front of the Master. But you won't be alone if that's what happens. And no one in our group will be pointing fingers at you, I can promise you that."

Simeon sighed. He knew they were right, but he was still torn. If he stepped away from his plan, what did that mean for Yehuda and Barak and Samuel? Somehow, he instinctively knew that Jesus wasn't going to solve this for him. He could get counsel, perhaps, but not a step-by-step plan.

"Do you know what it really comes down to?" Andrew asked, and Simeon saw that he was speaking directly to him. He shook his head.

"Do you remember the day when he gave that sermon on the hillside above Tabgha?"

Simeon nodded. It was the day he had stomped away in a huff because of Jesus' teachings about love and forgiveness. It was not one of his finer moments.

"You had left by then, but Jesus said something that sums it all up. He said, 'Be ye therefore perfect, even as your Father in Heaven is perfect.' That's what he's about, Simeon. He's trying to teach us what that means. He's trying to help us become more like him and the Father. Isn't that what being a disciple really means?"

Simeon began to nod. "Yes, I suppose it does."

"Then if this plan of yours is not in harmony with God's will, wouldn't it be best to know that as soon as possible?"

Simeon didn't answer, and Peter finally nudged him. "He's got you, Simeon, and you know it. It's all right to say, 'You are right, Andrew.'"

Simeon smiled then, ruefully and sheepishly, but it was genuine. "You are right, Andrew. Let's go speak with Jesus."

John clapped him on the shoulder and turned him so that they faced the crowd some distance away. "Just remember, it couldn't be any worse than wanting to call down fire from heaven to wipe out a whole village."

Just then, someone behind them called out Peter's name. They all turned. An older man in long, ornate robes was coming at a swift walk, waving one arm. "Peter! Peter, son of Jonas."

David frowned. It was Absalom the publican, one of Capernaum's leading tax collectors. Capernaum sat astride a major Roman road between the coast and Damascus, so it had its share of levy stations and tax collectors. The myriad of assessments fell into two categories— customs, or a tax on merchandise, and tribute, or taxes on persons and property. With the natural encouragement for corruption built into the

Roman system of *publicani*, or local tax collectors, the publicans in Capernaum were all wealthy and powerful men. Absalom was one of those who had most profited from his position, alienating many of his countrymen in the process. His elaborately embroidered robes and expensive sandals testified to the extent of his extortion. It had been Absalom who had assessed the exorbitant charges on David's household the previous fall, which had brought the Romans to the home of David ben Joseph and nearly led to Simeon's death and the capture of Deborah and Leah. The thought of that day still left David cold. He and Absalom had not spoken since.

The publican saw who was with Peter and glowered briefly at David. Then, with a toss of his head, he ignored the rest of them. "Peter, I have a question for you."

Peter had also sobered at the sight of this man. "Yes? What is it?"

"Does not your master pay the tribute money?"

Peter's eyes registered surprise. "Of course. Why do you ask?"

"Because I have no record that he has paid." It was said with a triumphant sneer. Obviously Absalom did not like Jesus and his rising popularity.

Peter was taken aback, as were the others. Absalom was not talking about Roman taxes here. The "tribute money" had reference to the half-shekel tax expected of every adult male in Israel. The tax went to support the maintenance of the temple in Jerusalem. It wasn't much on an individual basis—about the equivalent of a day's wages for a laboring man—but it brought enormous revenues into the temple coffers. That was one of the reasons the Sadducees in Jerusalem contracted with local publicans to make sure all eligible males paid the tax. It was the base of the Sadducees' enormous wealth and influence.

By law, the tribute money was due prior to Passover in the month of Adar, which covered parts of the Roman months of March and April. Since it was now June, that meant the payment was three months late. If Jesus had truly not paid it by now, then he was liable to a fine or even arrest. Simeon could almost see that thought flit across Peter's face.

"Well?" Absalom demanded. "Is he going to pay or not?"

"Yes," Peter said, turning away. "Of course."

John stepped forward to stand beside his fellow apostle and longtime fishing partner. He turned his back to shut out the publican. "Peter," he said in a low voice. "You cannot speak for the Master in these matters."

"It's the law," Peter retorted, still smarting from Absalom's insolent manner.

John's voice lowered even further. "Jesus has no money of his own. You know that. He owns nothing but the clothes he wears. We carry the only money we have."

"We'll take it out of the bag if we have to," Peter said back.

Simeon's father had told the family that the Twelve kept a leather purse, which they called "the bag," in which they kept their funds. They used those funds to buy bread or fill their other needs while out preaching in the villages. Though his father had never spoken of it, Simeon suspected that he contributed to "the bag" from time to time.

Simeon moved forward a little. "Peter. We can help."

Absalom heard that and shook his finger at them. "This is supposed to come from each individual. Yes, you can satisfy his obligation, but it says a lot about your Master if he refuses to pay the tax himself."

Peter turned slowly, his face darkening. "This conversation is between us, Absalom. As long as you get your money, it is not your affair."

The publican stepped back in the face of Peter's glowering look. "That is true." He smiled maliciously. "But I shall be happy to spread the word that Jesus won't pay the temple tax."

Without further consultation with his brethren, Peter said, "I will speak with Jesus and bring the money to you."

"I shall expect it before the end of the day," came the cold reply. Absalom turned sharply, his long robes billowing, and stalked away.

David was thoughtful. "As Simeon says, Peter, we will gladly help. But I will be surprised if Jesus has not paid it, perhaps while you were in Jerusalem for Passover."

Peter didn't look so sure. He moved forward, and the others fell in behind him. "Make way please," Peter called as they approached the assembled throngs. "We have a matter to bring before the Master."

Deborah and the rest of the family had seen them coming and moved over to join David and Simeon. The crowd pulled back, and Peter stepped forward to face Jesus. Jesus acknowledged him with a nod, then smiled at David. "*Shalom*, David ben Joseph."

"And peace to you, Master."

Now the gentle eyes came to rest on Simeon. There seemed to be a touch of surprise in seeing him. "*Shalom* to you, Simeon ben David."

"*Shalom*, Jesus," Simeon said gravely.

"I was told you were away—" there was a moment's pause—"on business."

Startled, Simeon nodded. "I was. I returned just yesterday."

"And things are well with you?"

There was something in his eyes that made Simeon look away. "In most respects, yes," he mumbled. "Thank you."

Jesus nodded briefly, then looked at Peter. "Yes," he said. "What is it, Peter?"

"Absalom the Publican just accosted us, Master."

"Oh?"

"He said you had not paid the tribute money this year. He asked if you were going to."

There was a murmur of surprise from the crowd. Jesus seemed not to notice. His eyes were fixed on Peter. "And what did you answer him?"

Peter's face flushed as he realized that perhaps he had acted too hastily. "I—I told him that you would, if you had not already."

For several seconds, Jesus looked calmly on the fisherman, making Peter's color only deepen. Then he spoke. "I would ask you a question, Simon Peter."

"Say on, Master."

"Of whom do the kings of the earth take tribute? Of strangers or of their own children?"

Clearly puzzled by the odd question, Peter hesitated. But it was not a difficult problem. "Of strangers, Lord."

"Then are not the children free?"

"Yes."

Simeon found himself nodding too. It would be a strange thing for a king to levy a tax on his own family. But what did this have to do with—. He straightened as the answer came with the clarity of a flash of lightning. Mary, the mother of Jesus, had told Simeon that Jesus was the Son of God, not the son of her husband, Joseph. The implications of that simple statement still left Simeon a little breathless. Now the impact of what Jesus was saying took on new meaning. He was the *Son*. He was the child of the greatest King of all!

Then Simeon had a second thought. He remembered Miriam had told them about the day Jesus had driven the moneychangers from the temple. "You have made my Father's house a den of thieves." *My Father's house!* The temple was God's house, his palace, his castle. And Jesus was the Son. He owed no tribute money. It was such a remarkable thought that for a moment Simeon was unaware of what was going on around him.

Jesus was waiting, but Peter no longer looked at him. He had dropped his head, clearly chagrined for speaking in behalf of the Master without his authorization. A soft smile stole across the face of Jesus. He reached out and laid a hand on Peter's shoulder, finally bringing Peter's head up. "Notwithstanding all of that, Peter, lest we should offend them, go get one of your fishing lines. Cast a hook into the sea and take the first fish that comes out."

Peter just stared blankly at the Master. Jesus wanted him to go fishing?

"Yes, Peter." The gentle smile deepened. "Open its mouth and there you shall find a piece of money—a *stater*."

Simeon heard himself gasp. A *stater* was a coin equivalent to four *denarii*, or one full shekel, exactly twice the amount needed for the tribute money. In a fish's mouth?

"Take that," Jesus went on calmly, "and give unto the assessors for me and thee."

Peter was speechless. He was a fisherman. Over a lifetime, he had caught thousands upon thousands of fish. How could such a thing be?

Jesus nodded, watching his disciple with gentle patience. Then he motioned with one hand in the direction of the lake. "Go and see."

IV

ON THE SHORES OF THE SEA OF GALILEE, NEAR CAPERNAUM

"Easy! Easy!" John was on his knees on the dock, peering down into the water where the fishing line disappeared. It was taut as a bow-string. "Don't let him get away."

"Thank you, John," Peter grunted. "Being as new at this fishing business as I am, I appreciate your help."

Andrew, who carried a long pole with a net on one end, stood over John, poised for action. The others on the dock—a small crowd had gathered in addition to James, David, and Simeon—pressed forward, anxious to see as well. Peter's brow was wrinkled in concentration. He held a short length of stick in one hand and guided the line with the other. His body bobbed and weaved as he played the fish carefully, pulling back to draw the fish in, then rapidly winding the line as he leaned forward and let the line go momentarily slack. This was not taking a lot of strength on Peter's part. The fish was not a big one. Judging from the tension on the line, it was probably not much more than a handspan—not a major battle, but in light of their expectations, one that Peter had never fought more carefully.

"There it is," Andrew cried. "Steady!" He bent over, shoving the net into the water. Everyone leaned forward as well, as if controlled by the same mind. Then a cry of triumph went up as Andrew jerked back. "Got him!"

He swung around, lifting the net to show the fish flapping violently inside it.

"You did it," someone behind Simeon cried, but he barely heard. He and his father were standing just behind Peter and quickly moved forward as Peter, Andrew, James, and John all surrounded the net.

By mutual consent, the others let Peter take the lead now. He laid the stick and the line down, then reached inside the net. The fish was still flipping and jerking violently. After two tries, Peter got both hands around the squirming wet body. He pulled the fish clear, and Andrew let the net fall to the dock.

There was a collective moment where everyone drew in a breath; then, with a deft movement, Peter pried the fish's mouth open, ignoring the line that protruded from it. There was a sharp gasp. A flash of gold gleamed in the sunlight.

Eyes wide and filled with wonder, Peter held up one hand. Between his fingers was a single gold *stater*, as shining and new as if it had come from the mold just moments before. Then he dropped the coin into a fold of his tunic, carefully removed the hook from the mouth of the fish and tossed the fish back into the water. He looked around at the astonished crowd. "Come," he said, his voice still filled with awe. "I need to visit Absalom the Publican."

CHAPTER NOTES

Though we are not told specifically why Jesus called James and John *Boanerges*, or the Sons of Thunder (see Mark 3:17), most scholars assume it was because they were dynamic and bold in their approach to life. The experience with the Samaritan village seems to bear out that characterization (see Luke 9:51–56). We are told that it was James and John specifically who asked if they might call down the fire and who received the rebuke from Jesus.

The call to be perfect is found in Matthew 5:48.

The account of the miracle of the coin in the mouth of the fish is found in Matthew 17:24–27. Obviously the author has supplied some details not found in the scriptural account. It is interesting that Matthew, who was himself a publican before his call to the apostleship, is the only one of the gospel writers to include this event.

There is a species of fish unique to the Sea of Galilee, somewhat like a perch, which is very popular among the locals in Israel and with tourists as well. It is now called "St. Peter's fish," deriving its name from this miracle.

The system for collecting taxes used by the Romans through agents called *publicani* or publicians was described more fully in volume 1, *Fishers of Men* (see Prologue, and notes for chapter 18).

CHAPTER 6

IT IS I; BE NOT AFRAID.

—*John 6:20*

I

CAPERNAUM
25 JUNE, A.D. 30

By the time they found Absalom and triumphantly gave him the coin, then returned to Peter's house, Jesus was no longer there. Anna, Peter's wife, told her husband that the crowds had grown so large that Jesus had moved to the outskirts of the town where there was more room. She also told David and Simeon that their family had gone home to give the children their midday meal. Peter, Andrew, James, and John immediately set out to rejoin Jesus and share the news of what had happened on the dock. All four of the apostles encouraged Simeon to come with them, but he demurred. Now, more than ever, he needed time to think before he spoke with Jesus, so he and his father decided to go home and rejoin the family.

As they walked along the streets of Capernaum, neither spoke. Simeon was grateful for the time to think. The wonder of what had happened still lay heavily upon him. It left him almost dizzy to think about how Jesus had known the fish would be there and would be the first to hit Peter's hook. And for some reason, each time he thought of that, he came back to his problem with Yehuda and the others. There was a lesson in all of this, but he wasn't yet sure exactly what it was.

II

The family ate their midday meal together at David's house; then Ephraim and Rachel took Esther and Boaz home for a nap. Since this day was one of those when the servants did not come in, they began to clear away the food and the dishes. Then a loud knock came on the courtyard gate. Leah was closest, so she went quickly over and opened it. To their surprise, it was Peter who stepped through.

After greeting each of them, and declining Deborah's invitation to share in what was left of their meal, Peter grew very somber. "There has been some bad news this afternoon."

David stepped forward. "Bad news?"

"Yes, from Judea."

Deborah motioned them to the benches and chairs where they had been sitting. "Tell us." Peter sat down, showing a deep tiredness in his eyes. "Some of the disciples from Judea came up today. There is word of John the Baptist."

David sat down slowly. "Yes?" John was still in one of King Herod's prisons for condemning Herod's marriage to Herodias, his brother's wife.

Peter rubbed his hands over his eyes; then his fingers moved up and began to massage his temples. "John is dead."

"No!" Several cried out at once.

Peter seemed not to hear for a moment, then finally looked up. "Even though at one point Herod announced he was going to execute

John, he didn't dare follow through with it. John was so popular with the people the king was afraid it would trigger an uprising."

"So what happened?" Deborah asked.

"A week ago, it was Herod's birthday. They held a great feast in his honor. The reports are that as part of the celebration, Herodias had her daughter dance for the king."

"Go on," David said, feeling sick at heart, sensing what was coming.

"Herodias hated John, of course. She tried several times to persuade Herod to have him killed for criticizing her." He let out a long breath. "They say her daughter is very beautiful. I suppose it was a very seductive and provocative dance. Herod, who was probably completely drunk by then, was so enchanted he brought the girl forward and announced she could ask anything she wanted. He swore with an oath that he would grant it to her."

"He must have been very drunk to make a promise like that," Simeon said in disgust.

"The girl, whose name is Salome, went immediately to her mother. She was thrilled, I'm sure, with the king's offer. Salome asked her mother for advice on what to request."

Peter's eyes were haunted now. "Herodias told her to ask the king for the head of John the Baptist on a charger."

Deborah paled.

"Oh, no!" David moaned.

Peter nodded grimly. "Herod was shocked. I guess all the court was. But he had given his word."

"How awful!" Deborah cried. "How utterly awful."

Peter lowered his gaze. He and Andrew had been among some of the first of John the Baptist's followers. It was John who had pointed Jesus out to them one day, saying, "Behold the Lamb of God." The shock and grief were evident on his face.

Peter took a deep breath, then looked up. "Actually, I didn't come just for that." He looked at Simeon. "When Jesus heard the news, he went off by himself to pray."

"He must be filled with terrible sorrow," Deborah said.

"Yes," Peter answered. "It came as a real blow to him." Then, still speaking to Simeon, he went on. "Jesus asked if we would take a ship across the lake and meet him over beyond Bethsaida after nightfall. It will be just me and Andrew and James and John. If you came with us, we could talk some more while we wait for Jesus."

Simeon hesitated. He wasn't ready. He had barely had a moment to think about things. This wouldn't be the time to bother Jesus, but Peter made a good listener and gave good counsel. He nodded. "All right. Thank you for thinking of me, Peter."

Peter turned to Simeon's father. "David, you are welcome to come as well."

There was a moment's hesitation. Clearly his father would have liked that as much as Simeon, but David looked at Deborah. Something passed between them, though there was nothing said; then David shook his head. "No. I had better see to things here."

Simeon felt a rush of relief. He still planned to tell his father everything, but it would be easier not to have him listening as Simeon struggled with what to tell Jesus. He turned to Peter. "How soon are you leaving?"

"As soon as I return to the boat. Andrew, James, and John are getting it ready now."

Simeon got to his feet. "Then we'd better go."

Deborah got up quickly and went to her son. She gave him a fierce hug. "Don't be afraid to tell Jesus what is in your heart, Simeon," she whispered. "Let him help you."

He kissed her on the cheek. "I will, Mother."

III

NEAR GERGESA, ON THE EASTERN SHORE OF THE SEA OF GALILEE

"Have you given much thought to what happened today, Simeon?"

Simeon turned his head to look at Peter. They were stretched out on a thick patch of grass not far from the water's edge. The boat they had come across in rode at anchor a few feet away, its stern to them as it swung in the stiff westerly breeze coming off the lake. At the moment they were alone on the eastern shore of the Sea of Galilee. Andrew, James, and John had gone into Gergesa, about a mile from where they were anchored, to buy some bread. Simeon also suspected they had arranged it so Simeon could have Peter to himself. "About the coin, you mean?"

"Yes."

"What about it?"

Peter was looking up at the cloudless sky, now a deep purple as the last of the daylight faded away. "As we were saying this morning, Jesus never does anything without purpose. He's always teaching us."

"Hmm." Simeon had been totally amazed to see the coin in the fish's mouth, but he hadn't thought about it as a teaching moment. "Like what?"

"Think about it. Think about what happened, and *how* it happened. Is there anything that strikes you as odd?"

Simeon laughed aloud. "To put a line in the water and pull out a fish with a gold *stater* in its mouth? No, I don't think that's odd at all."

Peter chuckled too. "Sorry. Let me rephrase that. That's not what I was talking about. Think about the rest of it. Or better yet, think what Jesus could have done instead."

"I'm still not sure what you mean."

"We had enough money in the bag to pay the tax, Simeon," he said slowly. "And Jesus knew that. We had gone over our funds this morning."

"You had?"

"Yes. Also, you and David had offered to give the required amount to us. There were probably a dozen others there this morning who would have gladly paid it. So why do it the way he did? What was he trying to teach us? To teach me?"

"Well, what he said about the children not owing tribute, that really hit me hard. It was a subtle but powerful reminder of who he is. He is the Son of God, the heir of the king. By rights, he doesn't owe anything."

"Yes, I came to the same conclusion." Peter sat up now, looking down earnestly at Simeon. "But that lesson was given verbally. Once he had taught us the principle, why not just get a coin from the bag? Or ask someone if they would donate it for him?"

For a long time Simeon didn't answer, his mind probing at the possibilities. Finally he began to nod. "Maybe it was a reminder that Jesus doesn't depend on us to meet his needs. And it was certainly a reminder of his miraculous powers."

Peter shook his head slowly. "I've been thinking about it all afternoon. Even though I never doubted that Jesus knew what he was talking about, it was still a shock when I pried that fish's jaws open and there it was. It gave me the chills."

"How in the world did that coin ever get in the fish's mouth?" Simeon wondered.

"Oh, that's not too hard to explain," Peter answered. "It would be very unusual, but it's not impossible. Let's say someone on one of the many boats on the lake has a coin in his tunic. Somehow it falls overboard. The coin is bright and shiny. The sun catches it in the water and a fish strikes at it, thinking it is a worm or a bug. It is too big for the fish to swallow; hence, it stays in his mouth."

A little surprised to hear him explain it away so easily, Simeon gave him a strange look.

Peter chuckled. "No, Simeon. What is incredible is this: how did Jesus know there was a fish out there with a coin in its mouth? How did he know that fish would be where I threw in the line? And exactly when?" His smile faded away. "The real miracle is not that the fish had a coin in its mouth. The miracle is that Jesus knew everything about it."

"Yes," Simeon echoed. "Yes, that's it."

"So, again I ask you. What are we supposed to learn from all this?"

"That Jesus is the Son of God."

"We already knew that," came the blunt retort. "What else?"

Again the silence stretched on for several seconds. It was Peter who finally broke it. "Think about this. When Absalom came, I was worried about the predicament Jesus might be in." There was a soft explosion of self-derision. "Kind of ironic, isn't it. Just this morning we were talking about how often we feel foolish as we deal with Jesus. Well, here's another great example. Peter, the unlearned, imperfect, impetuous Galilean fisherman, is going to step in and solve a problem for the Son of God."

Now Simeon sat up too, seeing finally what Peter was seeing. And he began to understand why Peter was so determined that Simeon should see it too.

"Jesus could have just told me all of that straight out," Peter went on. "That's not his way. He wants us to think about things. He wants us to discover things for ourselves."

"So," Simeon said, pouncing on that opening, "is that what's going to happen if I ask him what I should do about Yehuda? Is he going to let me discover for myself what I'm doing wrong?"

"Here's something to think about." Peter shook his head. "No, two things."

"What?"

"You haven't decided that it's all up to Simeon, have you? Strong, courageous, impetuous Simeon isn't going to try to fix things that God doesn't know how to fix, is he? He wouldn't be as foolish as his good friend and mentor, Peter the fisherman, would he?"

"I—"

"Second item for consideration. Have you wondered if it might be that I was not the only one there today that Jesus was trying to teach?"

IV

By the time the other three apostles returned to where Simeon and Peter waited, it was dark. The wind, out of the west and stiff to begin with, had swung around so that it now came out of the northwest and had strengthened considerably. Peter stood at the edge of the water, head back, as though sniffing the wind to discern its intention. At the sound of voices, he turned.

"Ho, Andrew? Did you get the bread?"

The approaching figure held up a bulging cloth bag. "Yes."

"Then we must be off. The wind is contrary. It's going to take some doing to make our way toward Bethsaida."

James came over to stand beside Peter. "I agree. We had better eat on the boat."

"Where are we supposed to meet Jesus?" Simeon asked.

John moved forward as well. "Somewhere between here and Bethsaida." Then he laughed at the dubious look on Simeon's face. There was no moon as yet and it was very dark. Even when the moon did come up it would be no more than a bare crescent, surely not yielding enough light to see a person who was any distance away. "We'll light the fishing lamp," he explained, "and stay within hailing distance of the shore. Actually, it's more a question of Jesus finding us than of us finding him."

Simeon relaxed a little. Most fishermen on the Sea of Galilee had a pole near the bow on which they hung an oil lamp enclosed in glass. The light would not only attract the fish to the surface but help the fishermen see them when they did come up, so they could cast their nets in that direction. That was one of the reasons the best fishing was at night.

"We'll have to keep a sharp ear," James said. "The wind will be blowing toward shore and it will be hard to hear him."

Peter was already wading out to grab the anchor line. "Come, brethren," he called to the rest of them. "Let's get underway."

V

ON THE SEA OF GALILEE
26 JUNE, A.D. 30

Simeon clutched the side of the boat tightly, letting his body roll with the pitching and yawing of the craft. He had quickly learned that trying to brace himself too stiffly only made things worse. He thought he had been out enough with the fishermen over his lifetime that his stomach could take anything, but he was growing close to being sick. He looked up and saw Peter grinning at him in the yellow light of the lamp that bobbed and danced from the long pole at the bow. James and Andrew were at the center of the boat, swinging the long oars up and forward, then dropping them into the water and pulling back with all their strength. In the light of the lamp, Simeon could see that their faces were streaked with sweat in spite of the stiff wind that had turned almost cold now. Behind Simeon, John manned the rudder. He peered through the darkness to where there was supposed to be a shoreline.

"Is this as bad as that night when Jesus stilled the storm?" Simeon called.

Peter threw back his head and laughed. "About half as bad, I would say."

"Not even that," James amended.

Simeon groaned. What must that night have been like? Tonight, the boat would lift as each wave passed beneath it, rising higher and higher. Then it would plunge downward, sending Simeon's stomach into his throat. The waves were high enough that some were cresting into whitecaps. When they did, the wind caught the spray and flung it against their faces. Simeon was soaked, cold, and very, very tired.

Simeon had long ago given up trying to tell if they were making progress. As Peter had so casually described it, the wind "was contrary." They had to keep the bow at an angle to the wind, and even then it would have blown them back if it weren't for the rowing. He wasn't sure how long it would be before dawn came, but there was no hint of it yet. He was certain that they were well into the fourth watch of the night, so they had been at this grueling battle now for six or seven hours.

For a time, just after they had put out, he had watched a solitary light—probably from a fisherman's hut—slide slowly past them, barely a speck in the darkness. It was greatly disheartening to see how slowly it fell away. Now there was nothing. The moon was up, but it offered little illumination. Simeon just hoped John could make out the darker shape of land, because he certainly couldn't. Bethsaida was supposedly just five or six miles from Gergesa. So why couldn't they see any lights?

Despairing, he tapped James on the shoulder. "My turn."

James nodded, lifted the oar and slid out from beneath it. Simeon slipped into his place. "Jesus has probably given up on us by now," he said to Andrew, who sat beside him now.

Andrew gave a quick, emphatic shake of his head. "He'll see our light."

"But what if we don't hear him when he shouts?"

John leaned forward. "Peter's got the ears of a rabbit," he said. "He can tell down to half a dozen cubits how close we are to shore."

That was comforting. But Simeon was still worried. It was so black. With no lights to serve as a reference point, what if they ran aground?

Andrew nudged Simeon mischievously. "That's why we let Peter stand up there while the rest of us do all the work."

"I heard that," Peter growled.

Simeon chuckled. It built his confidence to know that while they were all working very hard to keep the boat moving forward, none of these men, who made their living from the sea, seemed overly anxious about the situation. Simeon remembered that on the night when Jesus had stilled the storm, Peter had admitted they had all been terrified and despaired of their lives.

"My turn at the oars, Andrew," John said.

They too changed places, and Andrew moved back to take the rudder.

As the two settled into their new positions, Peter gave a low cry. He wrapped one arm around the lamp pole and leaned forward, wiping the spray from his eyes. "Something ahead," he shouted, pointing with the other arm.

Simeon saw John stiffen and felt his own stomach lurch. Had they miscalculated? Were they closer to shore than they thought? There were places where there were rocks out in the water. They weren't moving fast enough to be in mortal danger, but a rock could still punch a hole in the side and sink them.

"It's another boat!" Andrew exclaimed.

They were all peering into the faint circle of light cast by the bobbing lamp. And then Simeon saw it too. He froze, the oar forgotten, an icy chill sweeping over him. It was pale white, barely entering the circle of light, but it was not the sail of a boat. It wasn't nearly large enough for that. It—he swallowed hard, swiping at his eyes. It looked like—goose bumps were popping out all over him. It looked like—it was! It was a man!

Simeon heard John gasp beside him. Then, at that moment, a wave lifted the boat's bow, blocking their view of the apparition; then the nose dropped, slamming them downward again. The boat leaped forward ten or fifteen feet. When it leveled again, the circle of light caught the figure fully. It was no more than thirty or forty paces away now and growing more visible with every moment.

Simeon wasn't sure if his body had turned to fire or ice. Every nerve was tingling. His neck was bowed as he leaned forward, unable to believe his eyes. The ghostly image was walking steadily toward them. Walking . . . He wiped at his eyes with the back of his arm. Walking *on the water!*

Simeon cried out. He fell back, cracking his knee against the oarlock.

At the bow, Peter dropped to his knees, scrambling backwards, one hand up to ward off the terrifying sight before him. "It's a spirit!" he cried. "Turn the boat! Turn the boat!"

But even as they lunged for the boom of the sail, a sound came to them, whipped partially away by the wind. "Peter!"

The fisherman stopped, his jaw slack.

"Peter! It is I. Be not afraid."

"Master?" It was torn from Peter's throat in a hoarse exclamation of shock and terror. He got to his feet, leaning forward, peering into the night.

The figure kept coming, walking as confidently as though it were a mountain and not a hundred fathoms of water beneath his feet.

"It is Jesus!" Simeon wasn't sure whether it was James or John or

Andrew who had uttered that. Wave after wave of chills were coursing through his body.

Peter was fully on his feet now. He lifted one hand and steadied the oil lamp, tipping it slightly to throw the circle of light further out. It *was* Jesus. He wore the usual long robe with a hood, but the hood was on his shoulders now. The wind whipped his hair and sent the skirts of his robe billowing. Simeon's eyes dropped. He could see the sandals on Jesus' feet. He saw that the bottom of his robe was darker, wet from the water boiling around him.

"Be of good cheer," came the voice again. "It is I, brethren. Be not afraid."

They were all on their feet now, each frozen in whatever position they had taken. No one spoke. Perhaps they couldn't have even if they chose to. Utter astonishment had struck them dumb.

Then Peter released the lamp and took a hesitant step forward. "Master?" He reached the bow and, gripping the rail with both hands, leaned out. "Master, if it be thou, bid me come unto thee on the water."

Simeon gaped at his friend.

Jesus' answer came in one word. Simple, and yet beyond comprehension. "Come!" he said.

Peter turned to look back at his companions, his eyes both exultant and anxious. Without another word, he swung one leg over the railing, then lowered his body down the side. The other four were all on their feet now. Rudder and oars were still clasped tight in their grip, but their movements to keep the boat facing into the waves was automatic. The wind, the waves, the sea were all but forgotten as they stared in astonishment as Peter dropped from their sight.

Then he appeared again, just ahead of the bow. He stood on the surface of the water, his head moving back and forth as he looked nervously at the ship, then forward to where Jesus had stopped and awaited him. With eyes as wide as the hawsers that held the oars, and with a childlike grin splitting the beard that was plastered to his face, Peter looked up at his brethren for one moment. He stood alone!

Turning his face directly into the wind, he started away, walking across the surface of the turbulent water. He moved slowly, gingerly, as if he were walking through a bed of glass. But move he did. Five feet, then ten. He was completely away from the boat now. One hand was outstretched, as though he were a child taking his first steps toward an encouraging parent.

It was if time had been suspended. Simeon felt as though he were another person, outside of his body, watching something unbelievably incredible taking place, as if in a dream. The two figures moved slowly toward each other. Jesus was close enough now that they could see that he, too, was smiling. He reached out a hand, beckoning Peter closer.

As they drew to within ten paces of each other, John grabbed at Simeon's sleeve. A wave was coming toward them from the right. It was a huge swell, and it started to crest as it approached the two figures. It was as high as a man and would certainly swamp the two men before it.

"Peter! Watch out!" It was Andrew who shouted. He pointed.

Peter turned, then went rigid with fear. His arms flailed as he tried to keep his balance. His body rose sharply, then fell away again as the wave passed beneath him. And then, to the horror of those watching, Peter began to drop. It didn't happen in an instant, but in two or three seconds, his feet disappeared, then his knees, and the water reached his waist. He was sinking!

"Master, I perish!" Peter screamed. "Oh, Lord, save me!"

Jesus was only three steps away now. He lunged forward and caught Peter's hand. Instantly, the sinking stopped. Jesus drew his chief apostle up again, as though he were lifting something no heavier than a feather duster from the floor. In a moment, Peter was on the surface again, trembling violently as he clutched at the Master's hand.

"O ye of little faith," came the gentle rebuke. "Wherefore did you doubt?"

Peter was too shocked to answer. Taking him by the elbow, Jesus brought him back to the boat. Four pairs of eager hands were there to help them both climb in.

As they straightened, all of them staring at the Master in wonder, Simeon looked around, suddenly realizing that something else had changed. He nudged Andrew. "The wind has stopped."

And so it had. The sail hung limply from the yardarm. The sea, which just moments before had been a rolling, pitching, undulating surface, was now as flat as a tabletop.

All eyes turned back to Jesus. He watched them steadily, calm and unruffled. Then Peter dropped to one knee, his tunic still dripping water on the deck. He touched the edge of Jesus' robe, bowing his head, in awed astonishment. "Master," he whispered, "truly thou art the Son of God."

VI

The first light of dawn silhouetted the eastern highlands as the boat moved slowly toward the pier where, less than twenty-four hours earlier, Peter's hook had drawn in a fish from the water. No one spoke, nor had they since Jesus had asked for a straw mat and laid it out near the bow, and then had gone immediately to sleep. Andrew stood just beyond the sleeping figure, guiding them in to the pier with quick motions of his hand. James and John were at the oars, Peter at the rudder. The surface of the lake was now as smooth as a sandy beach. Simeon sat on a coil of rope, leaning back against the side of the boat, his eyes closed.

"So, Simeon," Peter said softly.

He opened his eyes and turned to look up at the burly fisherman. He knew what the question was going to be.

"Would you like to have some time with Jesus before we go home?"

Simeon shook his head.

One eyebrow lifted questioningly. "So what are you going to do?"

"Well, I know now for sure what I'm *not* going to do. I'm not going to trust in my own wisdom to solve this problem." He exhaled slowly. "As for what I *am* going to do. I haven't the slightest notion. Go home and think about things for a long time."

Andrew spoke then, without taking his eyes off the approaching pier. "I think it's safe to say we are all going to do that, my friend."

CHAPTER NOTES

John the Baptist's death is recorded in Matthew 14:3–12 and Mark 6:17–29.

Three of the gospel writers record the incident of Jesus walking on the sea (see Matthew 14:22–33; Mark 6:47–51; John 6:15–21), though only Matthew records the story of Peter's attempt to do the same.

We do know that fishing boats used oil lamps on poles while fishing at night. Whether it was this that allowed the disciples to see Jesus approaching them on the water, or whether there was a moon out that night, the scriptural record does not say. Having been on the Sea of Galilee at night when there is no moon, the author can testify to how black the night can be, so there had to be some source of light for them to see Jesus approaching.

The scriptural accounts do not specifically talk about a large wave that frightened Peter, only that when he "saw the wind, boistrous, he was afraid" (Matthew 14:30). Other small details were furnished by the author but are in harmony with the Gospel accounts.

CHAPTER 7

THE FINING POT IS FOR SILVER, AND THE FURNACE FOR GOLD:
BUT THE LORD TRIETH THE HEARTS.

—*Proverbs 17:3*

I

CAPERNAUM
29 JUNE, A.D. 30

When the centurion came out from his house into the small court-yard, Simeon stood up immediately. "*Shalom*, Sextus Rubrius."

"*Shalom*, Simeon ben David."

"Thank you for giving me audience."

Sextus gave him a sharp look, a reminder once again of his commitment to help Simeon in any way he could in return for Simeon's saving his life.

"I have just returned from the highlands of the Galilee." Beth Neelah, to be exact, he thought to himself, though he did not say that to Sextus. Simeon idly wondered what Sextus would say if he knew about the uniforms and the forged document, knew that they would not be used now. He had gone to the village and told Issachar that the plan was off. He would not risk the lives of eight men on something so tenuous. He had never planned to say anything to Sextus about his plan. That would have strained the bonds of loyalty and duty too far. "My visit today has to do with our former conversation. I wanted you to know that I have no plans to break my friends out of the prison at Caesarea."

Sextus's expression was typically inscrutable, but Simeon thought he saw a momentary relief in his eyes. "I am still determined to free my friends, but I am looking for other alternatives."

"I commend you for your wisdom. The other plan would have failed. Worse, it would have been a disaster for you."

Something in the way he said it caught Simeon's attention. This wasn't just a prediction—it was a flat statement of reality. "Why do you say that?"

The leathered features remained expressionless, but there was a mixture of amusement and admiration in his eyes. "We got a report from Damascus a few days back that a handsome young Roman had purchased eight uniforms and a forged document with the governor's seal asking for the release of three prisoners being held at Caesarea." Now the smile almost reached his mouth. "It wasn't too difficult to decide who that might be."

A cold sweat had suddenly broken out all over Simeon's body. "Did they—?"

"No. The informant did not have a name or know where this person was from. Nevertheless, all garrisons have been alerted and told to be on the lookout."

Simeon was astounded. So Rashah the forger had taken Simeon's fifteen hundred *denarii*, then turned around and sold the information to the Romans. A lucrative business, indeed. Suddenly his knees felt weak. He and Issachar and the others would have marched into Caesarea, right into their waiting arms.

Though tempted to feign his innocence, Simeon knew there was no point in it. It would be an insult to Sextus's intelligence. "Well," he finally said, rather lamely, "I had already decided it wasn't a very smart idea."

"I'm glad to hear that. It was clever, but . . . "

"I think the word everyone likes is *insane*." There was a brief, grim smile. "But I have not given up on freeing my friends. So I have more questions. I hate to keep imposing on your good will."

"Say on," the Roman said evenly.

"First, has there been any change of plans for the date of execution?"

"No."

"Good. Second. While I was in the highlands of the Galilee, there were reports of your soldiers scouring the forests around the Joknean Pass."

Sextus was momentarily startled, then quickly wary. "Well," he said slowly, "they were not actually soldiers from my garrison, but yes."

"Are they looking for gold?" Then he shook his head. "No, don't answer that. You don't have to. We know that Ya'abin loaded the stolen bars of gold on horses. We know also that he had to leave most, if not all of it behind, in order to save his own skin. Since your soldiers are asking about stray horses, I assume that at least one horse was not found."

Sextus's head moved just slightly, confirming the accuracy of Simeon's information.

"Can you tell me how much was lost?"

The heavy, dark brows furrowed slightly. This was pushing the line, and Sextus understood very clearly that if his commanders ever found out he was even conversing with this Jew, his career in the military would be ended—if not worse. On the other hand, Sextus Rubrius was standing here today because Simeon had once crossed a line of his own that night at the Joknean Pass.

"Two bars," he finally said. "The last horse was found only a few days ago. Each horse carried four bars. However, this horse's saddlebags had torn open—probably as the animal galloped through the forest in panic—and only one of the bars was still there. They found a second bar by following the back trail as far as they could." He smiled faintly.

"Perhaps a few years from now, some fortunate peasant out gathering acorns will find himself suddenly very rich."

Simeon barely heard him. "And these bars are of one talent each?"

"Yes."

No wonder Pilate was furious, Simeon thought. A talent—especially a talent of gold—was a significant fortune. The gold talent weighed about forty-six pounds and was worth three thousand shekels. His father always liked to calculate the worth of things based on that "most important of all commodities," human labor. The typical wage for a day laborer was half a shekel. Thus, a talent could purchase six thousand days of man labor! That was not quite twenty years if you hired a man every day but the Sabbath.

Rumor had it that Pilate had been given ten talents of gold by the legate of Syria to finance his military operations in Judea and carry out some construction projects within the city. In actuality, Pilate was using some of the money to continue construction of the aqueduct bringing water from Mount Carmel to Caesarea. The loss of two talents would be a crippling blow to whatever he was doing.

Simeon hesitated, knowing what this next question could mean. "Finally, it is common gossip among our people that the governor has been known to take—" he almost used another word, but caught himself in time—"*consideration* from the people in return for a prisoner's freedom. Is that true, to your knowledge?"

The eyes of Sextus had narrowed to a squint. "You want to know if Pilate can be bribed?" he said bluntly.

"That is such an indelicate word," Simeon answered smoothly. "Let me put it another way. Suppose someone were to find those last two bars of gold. Would it really be a bribe if they were simply returned to their rightful owner? And might it not be possible that the governor would feel sufficient gratitude to respond with some kind of favor in return?"

Sextus hadn't moved. His facial expression was like stone. "Has someone found the two missing bars?"

Simeon was going to dodge that, then decided with what Sextus was doing for him, he couldn't. "No." Then he went on quickly. "But gold is gold. Does it really matter if it came from Syria or not?"

Sextus studied Simeon's face; then finally he nodded. "It might work."

"Do you think so?" Simeon said eagerly.

"Two talents is a great deal of money." He cocked his head to one side. "The freedom of your friends would mean that much to you?"

"Yes. Especially if I could secure it without putting others at risk."

"Perhaps I could serve as arbitrator for you. I could tell Pilate that someone has come to me with an offer and see if I could set up an exchange."

Simeon was shaking his head before Sextus finished. He realized that Sextus was already pushing dangerously close to the line of treason as it was. He knew the name of the man who had purchased Roman uniforms, he knew what he planned to do with them, and yet he was saying nothing to his superiors. "You've done more than enough, Sextus. And I am deeply grateful."

There was a brief incline of his head.

"I'm not even sure yet if that's what I want to do, but this information will help me decide."

"It will have to be carefully done."

"In what sense?"

Sextus spoke carefully. "Pilate has requested Vitellius to replace the two talents that were lost. If the legate learns that the gold has been recovered, my assumption is that the replacement will not be sent."

"Ah," Simeon said slowly, seeing exactly what Sextus was suggesting. "So the more quietly it can be done, the better?"

The Roman shrugged, pleased that he didn't have to say more.

II

"Oh, Simeon," Deborah exclaimed. "It makes me sick to even think about it. You would have walked right into a trap."

He reached out and took his mother's hand. "No sicker than it made me when Sextus told me." Three days before, after his experience on the boat with Peter and the others, he had told his family everything about his previous plan; now he was telling them what he had learned since. He looked over at Ephraim. "Thank you, brother, for not letting me go blithely on my way. In Beth Neelah yesterday, after I told the others the plan was off, Issachar's wife actually smiled at me when I said goodbye to them. Before, she would barely meet my eyes." A shadow passed across his face. "Can you imagine how terrible I would feel to lose eight more men?"

"Not eight," David said quietly. "Nine."

No one said anything at that. It was deeply sobering. Just the four of them were sitting on the flat roof of their home in the cool of the evening. Leah and Joseph were over with Rachel and the children.

"You are very fortunate," his father went on. "If you hadn't left Damascus immediately after taking delivery of the uniforms, you would very likely have gone back to the inn where you were staying to find soldiers waiting for you."

Simeon nodded, absently fingering the scar across his chest. He had thought all of that through as well. "And if I hadn't driven all that night, staying completely off the main roads, they could have found me that next day. I'm sure they put patrols out."

"The Lord was watching over you," Deborah said, giving Simeon's hand a gentle squeeze.

"I'm not sure why. Maybe he takes special mercy on the stupid."

Ephraim poked at his brother's shoulder. "I don't think I ever said your plan was stupid. Actually, it was brilliant, but it was terribly risky."

"I think the word you used was *insane*," Simeon noted. Ephraim had never lived the life of excitement and action that his younger brother had, and he was clearly fascinated with all that had happened.

"So what now?" Ephraim asked.

"Well, thus far the execution date hasn't changed, so that still gives us a little time." He looked directly at his father. "I have never thought about anything so long and so hard as I have this, nor have I ever prayed for anything as fervently."

"And?" David said, sensing that Simeon had more to say.

"After I left Sextus this morning, I spent all day in the hills." He sighed. "I am sorry that I have been of no use to you in the business of late, Father. You and Ephraim have been left to do it all." He frowned. "Not that I have ever been around enough to be heavily involved."

His mother was watching him closely. "That doesn't matter, Simeon. What matters is that you find an answer." She hesitated, but only for a moment. "Did you find an answer?"

"Yes." A great sense of peace was on him now. "Finally."

"We're listening," David said softly.

Simeon plunged in, eager to lay it out for them. "The other day, after seeing Peter pull in that fish with the coin in its mouth, then watching Jesus come to us on the water, Peter asked me what lessons we were supposed to learn from all of that."

"Yes," David said. "We talked of these things yesterday."

"Jesus is the Messiah," Ephraim said. "He is the Son of God. What greater lesson is there than that?"

"Well, Peter and Andrew and the others taught me an important principle. Jesus typically uses his remarkable powers to help people—to cure disease or return sight or cleanse leprosy. But sometimes he does things as a way of teaching. Think about those two miracles for a moment. Neither was directly beneficial to someone in need—at least not in any physical need."

"That's true," Deborah agreed. "I hadn't thought of that. So what have you learned?"

"First, that I've been trying to solve this by myself. Like Peter assuming Jesus needed his help to solve the problem with the tribute money, I thought I had to solve this whole thing myself. I decided that I couldn't go to the Lord about Yehuda. It was my mistake that sent them there and—"

He raised his hand to cut off his father's protest. "I know. I was trying to do the right thing, but it was my mistake, nevertheless. So I felt like I had to work this out by myself, with my own resources. That's when I came up with this—" he glanced at Ephraim—"*insane* idea about the uniforms." He remembered Issachar's metaphor. "It was kind of like putting your head in a crocodile's mouth, then slapping its face to see if it notices."

"Fortunately, the Lord was kind enough to intervene before I could make another terrible mistake. And that brings me to the second lesson. When Peter started to sink in the water and Jesus pulled him up again, Jesus asked him a question. 'O ye of little faith,' he said, 'wherefore did you doubt?'"

Deborah shook her head in wonder. "I can't imagine who wouldn't have doubted at that point. Standing on water and suddenly you start to sink."

"That's true. But as I thought about it, I decided that Jesus was also saying to me, 'O ye of little faith, why do you doubt that God can help you? Where is your trust in me and in God? Why don't you show more faith?'"

He looked from face to face, seeing the love in their eyes. "So I have come up with another plan. This time I'm not going to put anyone at risk except myself. I'm going to try to demonstrate some faith and put my trust completely in the Lord."

There were somber nods from all three of them at that.

Simeon swallowed quickly, and went on. "The only bad thing is that it will be much more expensive."

"How much more expensive?" Ephraim asked.

"Two talents."

Ephraim gave a low exclamation. His mother's face registered shock. His father finally, with a forced lightness, asked, "Only two?"

"I don't expect you to come up with it, Father. Since you have given both Ephraim and me part of our inheritance to invest in trade and merchandising of our own, I plan to liquidate those assets and take my share of the inheritance now."

David dismissed that with a wave of his hand. "We can talk about that later. Tell us what you are thinking."

So he did. He told them about the lost gold. He told them about the aqueduct project and Pilate's desperate need for funds. He told them what Sextus said about keeping the offer under the table so Pilate could directly benefit by the recovery of the gold. It was at that point that he stopped because Ephraim was shaking his head. "What?"

"This is the answer you got today?"

"Yes."

"I don't think it's right."

"Why not?"

"You're talking about bribing a government official, Simeon. Oh, I know the Romans are corrupt and that is the normal way of doing business, but surely the Lord would not approve of such a thing. If you asked Jesus, what do you think he would say?"

Stung and feeling terribly deflated, Simeon tried to hold his temper. "It's not a bribe, Ephraim. It's returning what Pilate lost. In return for that favor, he grants us a favor."

"It's a bribe," Ephraim said stubbornly. "Paint it any color you want, shape it to look like whatever you wish, but that doesn't change things. You are offering him a bribe."

"You sound just like Uncle Aaron," Simeon shot back. "Since when did you become a Pharisee and start counting the hairs on the back of a flea?"

"You haven't found Pilate's gold," Ephraim shot right back. "If you had, maybe it would be different. But you're talking about a bribe, and rolling it in honey just makes it easier for you to swallow."

David broke in quickly. "We can discuss the issue of the money later, Ephraim. Let Simeon finish."

"Pilate doesn't care about the life of Yehuda one way or another," Simeon said, clearly still defensive. "He knows that my men were actually trying to save his troops, but that counts for nothing with him. He's just using Yehuda to divert attention from himself for the disaster he and Mordechai created with all their scheming. The gold will just give him a way to release them and save his pride."

"I'll have to think about that," Deborah said slowly. "I have some questions about whether it is right too, but there's a greater issue for me. Pilate knows by now that someone betrayed the whole plan to you. I'm sure he would like very much to get his hands on whoever that was. What's to stop him from taking the gold and then taking you too, so he can force you to tell him everything?"

"I know it sounds crazy—insane, if you will—but that's where faith comes in. I've worked out a way to protect myself against any double-dealing, but ultimately I've got to trust that if this is what the Lord wants me to do, he will help me work it out."

"*If* it is what he wants," Ephraim said. "That is the critical word, Simeon." He was suddenly pleading. "Look, I'm not trying to throw cold water on your efforts. I know that you're trying to do what is right. But you can't ask God to help you if what you are doing goes against his law."

Simeon tried to ignore that. "That's it," he said, speaking to his parents. "It will take me a few days in Damascus and Jerusalem and Ptolemais to turn my holdings into cash. Then I'll go to Caesarea and make Pilate an offer. No intrigue, no elaborate schemes. I just offer Pilate the one thing he wants more than anything else." He shrugged. "If he chooses not to let his superiors know that the gold has been recovered, that's his decision, not mine."

"Are you at peace with this?" David asked.

"More than I've been in the last two weeks," Simeon answered without hesitation.

"Then let's sleep on it," David said. "We need time to think about it too. It does have a good chance of working, far better than the other scheme."

He stood, signaling that the discussion had ended. Ephraim stood too and went over to face his brother. "Simeon, I—" He took a quick breath. "Look. One thing that Jesus has said perhaps more than any other is, 'Come unto me.' 'Come follow me.' I'm not sure what that always means. I think we're all trying to work that out in our minds. But it surely means that we ought to use him as our example, that we try to live as he lives."

Simeon's eyes filled with pain. "Don't you think that is what I have been agonizing over for the past two or three weeks?"

"Yes, I do. I know that is what you want, but—"

"But the world is not quite that simple, Ephraim. The barbarians are at the gates. Our country is slowly being strangled by evil. Do we just stand by and watch it happen? Is that what you think Jesus expects of us?"

"Well, I—"

But Simeon bored right on. "Well, here's a question for you, Ephraim. There are violent and evil men in the world. There always have been, and I suppose there always will be until the great millennial age of peace is brought in. Do we just love everyone and pray for them and wring our hands while they rape the world?"

Taken aback by Simeon's passion, Ephraim faltered a little. Deborah and David just watched, for the moment letting the two of them play this out. "Well," Ephriam began, "Jesus did tell us to love our enemies, to turn the other cheek."

"Yes, he did. And as you remember, that infuriated me at first. But I've thought a lot about that. Does loving our enemies—remembering that they are God's children just as we are—does that mean that we ignore or excuse their evil acts? Is that love to be unconditional, no matter what they do?"

"I didn't hear Jesus put any conditions on it."

"Nor did I hear Jesus say, 'Ignore evil.'" He paused for a moment, then asked, "Do you think there is a new God in town now, Ephraim?"

"Simeon!" Deborah cried.

"No, Mother, I'm not being irreverent. This is the key question for me." He turned back to his brother. "Do you think Jesus is contradicting what God has done in the past?"

"Of course not. He is confirming it, perhaps even expanding it."

"Agreed. So, answer this for me. In Abraham's days, all the various kings in Canaan were at war. Abraham's nephew, Lot, was captured and taken prisoner. What did Abraham do—Abraham who is held up for all of us as a great example of faith? Did he sit back and wring his hands? Did he say simply say, 'I forgive them'?"

Ephraim had no answer.

"I'll tell you what he did, because I went to the synagogue yesterday and found that account in the Torah. The scripture says that he 'armed' three hundred and eighteen of his trained servants, and pursued those kings northward into Dan. And there he 'smote them.' Yes, Ephraim. That's the word that is used. He smote them and delivered Lot from certain death.

"Or let me ask you another question. Do you think Jesus is courageous?"

That caught all three of them by surprise.

"Or does all this talk of love and meekness and humility make him too submissive? Do you think he's a coward?"

"Of course not," Ephraim said, bothered that Simeon would even ask such a question.

"Neither do I. And here's something else for you to think about, Ephraim. Miriam and Livia told us about the day that Jesus drove the moneychangers out of the temple."

"Yes, and that alone proves he isn't a coward. He stood up to the soldiers without hesitation."

Simeon pounced on that. "Yes, he did. How did he do it?"

Ephraim hesitated for a moment. "If I remember right, Miriam said he braided a whip."

"That's right. And then he waded into them. He didn't walk around humbly pleading for them to mend their wicked ways. He didn't go to a far corner and pray that they would change. He took the whip to them. He broke down the pens. He overthrew the tables. Why? Because he was incensed at the evil he saw. These were evil men doing evil in his Father's house, and he would not tolerate that. The barbarians were not only at the gate, but inside the courtyard as well, and he drove them out."

Of David ben Joseph's two sons, Ephraim was most like his father in temperament and spirit. But there was a streak of stubbornness in him—if such had ever been part of David's life, it had long since been overcome. "He is the Son of God. He has the right to react in any way he feels is appropriate."

"No, Ephraim. You said that he has asked us to come unto him and to look to him for our example. So that's what I am doing. The same Jesus who said turn the other cheek also took a whip and drove the moneychangers from the temple. The same Jesus who says love your enemies and forgive those who despitefully use you also calls the Pharisees hypocrites and whited sepulchres. Don't I have to consider both sides of his example? Isn't there a time when I, too, can rise up and make a stand against evil, do my part to stop the barbarians from destroying something of great worth?"

"You had better be careful," Ephraim warned. "Is the only way to fight the barbarians to become a barbarian yourself? Is violence the only way to combat violence?"

"No," Simeon said. "And that is my struggle. I don't have all the answers, Brother. I wish I did. But it occurred to me that men of great faith in our past have taken the sword in defense of truth and right. Take Moses as another example. When it came time for Israel to enter the promised land, the Lord told Moses to extend an offer of peace to the Canaanites. If they had accepted it, they would have been spared. But they did not. They chose to fight against God and his people. I looked this up today as well, Ephraim. Want to know what God told Moses? 'If they will make no peace with thee, but will make war against thee, then shalt thou besiege them. Then shalt thou smite them with the edge of the sword.' Was Moses wrong? Was Abraham wrong?"

Ephraim sighed wearily. "Simeon, I know that you are trying to do what is right. I really do. But I cannot believe that Jesus would condone bribing a government official. There has to be a better way. I can't for the life of me picture Jesus doing that himself, no matter how just the cause."

Simeon didn't answer, but turned to his mother and father. "Here's what I have decided after much wrestling with this issue. I think Jesus is trying to teach us that our hearts cannot be filled with hate for any man, friend or enemy, as mine used to be. I think he's reminding us that even the Romans are our brothers and that we must feel love for them just as our Father in Heaven does. Isn't that what he said? 'Love your enemies'?"

"That's precisely the lesson he is trying to help us see," David answered.

"And is your heart filled with love for Pontius Pilate right now?" Ephraim broke in softly. "Are you telling me that *this* is why you're going to bribe him?"

"I wish I could say yes to that," Simeon answered. "But I can say this. My heart is no longer filled with hate. I don't glory in the love of battle anymore. That's a miracle to me, believe it or not. But Yehuda and two other men are in prison awaiting death because I asked them to help me do what I thought was the right thing. You're right, Ephraim. It is a bribe, and it's probably wrong to do it. But it is a far greater wrong to turn my back on these men. So I'll take that gold and I'll go to Pilate and sue for a peaceful solution. I'll try to add some faith somewhere in that process and trust more in the Lord. I'll keep trying to come to some resolution in my mind about what it means when Jesus says, 'Come unto me.'"

His head came up and his eyes were sad as they met Ephraim's one last time. "But if all that fails, then like Abraham and like Moses, I will take up arms against those who are evil. I will make my stand at the gates. And if it comes to that, I will fight violence with violence. May God forgive me if I am wrong, Ephraim, but that is what I have to do."

III

An hour later, Simeon still sat with his parents on the rooftop of their home. Ephraim had left without further comment after Simeon's final passionate declaration, and after a few minutes Leah and Joseph returned. Joseph immediately went off to bed. Leah joined the three adults to enjoy the cool of the evening.

By unspoken agreement, nothing further was said about Yehuda or Pilate or gold talents. They spoke of the harvest and all that had to be done in the coming weeks. They laughed together as Leah described Esther's cleverness in devising ways to delay being put to bed. Two or three times the conversation turned to Jesus—his latest miracle, or something he had said—but both Deborah and David deftly steered those conversations away from any attempt to suggest what those teachings might mean for them personally. Simeon participated, though he was quieter than usual. Two or three times, Leah gave him questioning looks, obviously wondering what had taken place while she had been over at Rachel's house.

About half an hour later, they were interrupted by the sound of someone knocking on the gate to the courtyard below them. Surprised, Simeon stood up and moved to the low wall at the edge of the roof. He looked down to see four hooded figures standing in the street below. "Yes?" he called.

They stepped back, looking up. "Simeon?" The one closest to the gate threw back his hood. "Simeon, it's me. Ezra the Sandalmaker."

There was no moon and it was too dark to make out specific features, but Simeon instantly recognized the voice. "Ezra?" He was astounded. "What are you doing here?"

His parents and Leah had come over beside him.

Below them, the figure standing beside Ezra reached up with both hands. As the hood fell away, Simeon could make out the shape of long, dark hair. "*Shalom*, Deborah," a woman's voice called out. "*Shalom*, David ben Joseph." There was a moment's pause. "*Shalom*, Simeon."

Simeon couldn't believe what he was hearing. "Miriam?"

There was a soft laugh. "We thought we might surprise you."

CHAPTER NOTES

It is difficult to calculate with exactness the worth of a talent in modern financial terms. Like most money of that time, a talent originally signified a measure of weight. Also there were talents of gold, of silver, and of brass, which obviously varied greatly in their worth. By the time of Jesus, a talent had probably become a fixed sum of money. However, various scholars cannot agree on exactly how much a talent in the time of Jesus weighed or what it was worth. Generally, a talent seems to have been around forty to fifty pounds (see Fallows, 2:1176; Hastings, 630; Alexander, 108.) Some put it as high as eighty pounds.

If we calculate the current value of gold at four hundred U.S. dollars per ounce, then a pound of gold would be worth $6,400. If we use fifty pounds as a rough benchmark for a talent, then a single talent would be worth $320,000.

What really matters in determining the value of money, however, is equivalent earning or purchasing power. As was indicated in this chapter, a day laborer in New Testament times earned a half-shekel per day. A talent consisted of about 3,000 shekels, so a talent could buy 6,000 days of work (or about nineteen years of work, at six days a week). If we assume a minimum wage of about $6 per hour for unskilled workers today, a "day laborer" would earn about $50 per day. Six thousand days of labor at that price would be worth $300,000. Thus, a talent of gold in today's market would have about the same purchasing power as did a talent back then.

The references Simeon uses about Abraham and Moses are found in Genesis 14:5–14 and Deuteronomy 20:10–13.

CHAPTER 8

WHY SPEAKEST THOU UNTO THEM IN PARABLES?

—*Matthew 13:10*

I

CAPERNAUM
30 JUNE, A.D. 30

Though they had talked late into the night, the entire household was up early the next morning. Their four visitors—Ezra, Lilly, Miriam, and Livia—had come to the Galilee to hear Jesus, and they were too excited to spend the time in bed. Deborah sent early for her household servants and had breakfast ready within an hour of sunrise. David reluctantly excused himself. There was much to do at work, and they had already closed their warehouses several times this month in order to hear Jesus. Knowing that he would soon be leaving for several days, Simeon decided that he had better help his father. They breakfasted on their own and were gone by the time the others came down.

They ate quickly, then stopped by Rachel's house. Ephraim volunteered to take Esther and Boaz to the warehouse—much to the children's joy and Rachel's relief. In the end, Ezra turned out to be the only man in the group that morning. He walked in the company of six women—Deborah, Leah, and Rachel, and the three he had brought with him from Joppa, Miriam, Livia, and his wife, Lilly.

Deborah led them to the house of Peter and Anna. It was the quickest way to find out where Jesus would be. To their surprise, Peter's wife was just coming out of the house with two other women. Deborah hailed her, glad they hadn't been a few minutes later and missed her. "Anna! Good morning."

"Oh, Deborah. *Boker tov.* Good morning."

Anna, a woman who was not much older than Miriam and Livia, motioned her two companions forward. "I have guests I would like you to meet." She turned to the older of the two, reaching out to take her hand. "It is my great pleasure to introduce you to Mary, widow of the carpenter, Joseph of Nazareth."

Deborah was reaching out to take her hand as well, but stopped in amazement. She should have noticed the resemblance. "You're Jesus' mother?"

Mary smiled warmly. "Yes."

Anna went on. "Mary, this is Deborah, wife of David ben Joseph, Peter's partner in the fishing business. This is her daughter, Leah, and her daughter-in-law, Rachel."

"And these are some friends who have just come to visit from Judea." Deborah quickly introduced Ezra, Lilly, Livia, and Miriam.

As Deborah finished, Anna turned back to Mary. "Simeon, who came to Nazareth to see you, is Deborah's son."

"Oh, yes," Mary said with genuine pleasure. She was about Deborah's age, in her middle to late forties. Her dark hair showed the first signs of gray, and a few wrinkles had started around the corners of her eyes, but she was still a woman of gentle loveliness. And her eyes. Deborah could hardly look away. They were so serene, so warm and attentive.

"I spent a wonderful afternoon with your son," Mary said.

Sudden joy welled up in Deborah's heart. "I know. Thank you. It was after that visit that he decided to become a disciple of *your* son."

Mary seemed genuinely surprised. "Really?"

"Yes, he will be so pleased to know that you are here."

Miriam stepped forward beside the two older women. "Simeon told us all about what you said to him, about when Jesus was born. Thank you."

Again the smile that seemed to spring from somewhere deep within lit Mary's face. "Even after thirty years with him, it's all still so—" She groped for the right word. "So incredible to me. As you know, the people in our little village of Nazareth have largely rejected him. That's why I wanted to come down and see all this for myself. Anna tells me the people come from everywhere to hear him."

"They do," Leah said, also coming forward to take her hands. "He touches all of us."

Anna turned to the second woman, who stood slightly behind her, smiling and waiting patiently while they talked. "And this is another Mary." She motioned her forward. "This is Mary of Magdala." Anna laughed lightly. "With two Marys in the house now, we call her Mary Magdalene."

Deborah had already noticed that this woman was much more finely dressed than Jesus' mother. Yet her robes were not lavish, but were tasteful and well-tailored. Her hair was deep brown, with a touch of auburn in the morning sunlight. It had a soft wave to it and was carefully brushed and tied back with an embroidered cloth of brilliant blue. Her eyes were a deep green, set off by high cheekbones and a delicate nose. Though younger than Deborah, probably near thirty, she, like Deborah and Miriam, was obviously a woman of some means. This was a little surprising to Deborah because Magdala was a small village. It was not a place where one would expect to find many of such comfortable circumstances.

"Where is Magdala?" Ezra asked. "Is it far?"

Mary Magdalene turned to him. "No, it is just a few miles down the western shore of the lake, about halfway between here and Tiberias."

Livia spoke up for the first time. "In Greek, *magdalanay* means a 'plaiter of hair.'"

Mary Magdalene nodded. "Yes, I know. I am sometimes asked if that is my profession, but I must confess it is not." Then she looked at Livia more closely. "You are Greek, yes?"

Livia blushed a little. "Yes. I am originally from Macedonia." Then, seeing the surprise not only in her eyes, but in Anna and the mother of Jesus too, she went on. "I was brought to Judea to be a servant to Miriam in her household."

"But now," Miriam broke in swiftly, "she is no longer my servant, but my dearest friend, and soon to be my sister."

Deborah and Leah were not surprised at that. The previous night Miriam had told them all about going to Rome and the bargain she had made with her father.

Peter's wife, Anna, spoke again. "Mary Magdalene has come to hear Jesus. We were just leaving to find him."

Miriam leaned forward eagerly. "That is why we have come as well. We arrived just last night. We—Livia and I—saw him twice in Jerusalem. Once when he cleansed the temple at Passover. But we—"

Anna was amazed. "You saw that? We heard all about it. Peter and Andrew were there, but not close by at the moment it happened. But you were actually there?"

"Yes," Miriam answered, "no more than ten paces from where he overturned the tables." She looked at Jesus' mother. "He was magnificent. I've never seen anything like it. It was at that moment that Livia and I decided we had to learn who he was."

"He told me what he had done," she said quietly. "He was still burning with indignation that night when he came back to the house where we were staying."

Miriam turned to her cousin. "Lilly and Ezra have never met Jesus, but they believe everything they've heard about him and are eager to meet him."

"Most eager," Lilly said.

"Well," Anna said, "you are just in time. Peter said they would be down by the seashore. Come, we'll all go together."

As they started away, the group walked slowly, staying in a tight group so they could all converse freely.

"Are you a follower of Jesus," Deborah asked Mary Magdalene, "or will this be the first time you will hear him?"

"Oh, no. I too am a disciple."

Anna, hearing that, turned her head. "Mary, tell them how you first came to know Jesus." She glanced at the others. "This is a wonderful story."

Mary seemed a little embarrassed, but nodded and, after a moment, began. "For a long time, I was afflicted with a terrible malady. It was partly physical. I would often be so weak and so tired that I could barely move about. But it was partly spiritual too. Sometimes I felt like my heart was coming apart at the seams. Some days I would be fine and feel quite happy, then suddenly I would plunge into the darkest of moods, going for days in the deepest depression. I would burst into tears when someone even said hello to me."

Miriam was staring. Here was a beautiful, educated, and intelligent woman. It was hard to picture her in such a state.

"The doctors could not determine what was wrong. They attributed it to an evil influence of one kind or another. I spent a great deal of money on every possible treatment, but nothing seemed to make any difference."

She looked from face to face, her expression quite solemn now. "One of my friends was also going through a difficult time." She spoke to Deborah. "In fact, you may know of her. She is the wife of Chuza, chief steward in the palace of Herod in Tiberias. Her name is Joanna."

"Oh, yes," Deborah answered. "I know Joanna. I had heard that she was sick and that the Lord laid his hands on her and she was immediately healed."

"She was. Joanna is some years older than I am and had so much pain in her joints that she could barely care for her family. She had heard about Jesus, but the stories seemed unbelievable, too wonderful to be true."

"So what happened?" Miriam asked, marvelling that she was speaking to a person who had actually been healed by Jesus.

The deep green eyes were filled with emotion. "One day, word came that Jesus was in Magdala. They said he was healing those who came to him. I had given up hope by then, but Joanna hired a carriage and came up from Tiberias. She came and convinced me to go with her to see him. We found him in the village square. I hung back, but Joanna was determined to see him."

Her voice grew very soft. Their pace had slowed as they listened intently.

"In one instant, Joanna was freed from the pain. She came running back to me. I was astonished at seeing her move about so freely. I was still afraid—afraid that I would impose, afraid that Jesus might think it was all a silly woman's nonsense. But Joanna wouldn't let me stay back." Her eyes were suddenly glistening. "Then Jesus turned around and saw me."

She looked directly at the other Mary now. "I shall never forget the look in his eyes. He has your eyes. Wonderful eyes." Then she continued, speaking again to all of them. "He came over to me. He didn't speak at first, just searched my face for what seemed like a very long time. Then he lifted one hand, pointed it at me, and commanded the evil that was in me to come out."

Livia was wide-eyed. "And?" she pressed.

"The only way I can describe it is that it's like when you enter a room that has been closed for a long time. Everything is musty and dark and oppressive. Then you pull back the curtains and light floods in. You throw open the windows and a fresh breeze sweeps everything away. In one instant everything within me was all light and freshness and—and joy!"

Miriam, realizing that her own eyes were burning, looked at Lilly. She was not surprised to see she too was near tears. So was Livia.

Now Anna spoke. "Peter was there that day. He told me that the Lord later told the apostles that he had cast out seven evil spirits from Mary."

"Seven?" Livia exclaimed.

Mary Magdalene's smile was tranquil. "Yes, that is what he said. No wonder I was so down, so depressed."

"But seven?"

Miriam turned to Livia. "In Hebrew, *sheva*, or seven, is a specific number, but it comes from a root which means 'whole,' 'complete,' or 'perfect.' We use it as a superlative as well as an actual number. For example, to say that we do something for seven hours every day means that we spend our whole lives in that activity."

"So . . . ?" Livia was obviously puzzled by what Miriam was implying. Even after living with Miriam for five years, she was still learning the richness of the imagery and metaphorical language of the Jews.

Mary Magdalene turned to her. "What Miriam is saying is that Jesus may not have meant there were literally seven spirits in me, but rather that I was completely cleansed, completely freed from the evil that was in me." Her eyes were still glistening, and her face was radiant. "He cast it all away. It was gone and I have been without the slightest trouble since."

Anna came in again. "Mary and Joanna and other women he healed that day have not only become followers of Jesus, but they are using their means to help support him and the Twelve in the work."

"It is not much," Mary Magdalene said quickly.

"It *is* much," Anna corrected her. "Peter has told me how it frees them and Jesus to do the work. It is of greatest importance."

Embarrassed by the glowing praise, Mary Magdalene looked at Deborah. "Anna tells me that your husband also gives freely to help the Master."

Deborah inclined her head slightly. She understood Mary's embarrassment and yet her joy at having an opportunity to serve Jesus. "It is the least we can do to help," she said.

"Exactly," Mary Magdalene said softly. "That is exactly how it is."

II

ON THE SHORES OF THE SEA OF GALILEE, NEAR CAPERNAUM

To Miriam's surprise, when they made their way through the throngs and finally saw Jesus, he was not standing on the seashore as she had expected. He was seated on a fishing boat, a few paces offshore. Miriam recognized him immediately and felt a thrill of satisfaction shoot through her. At last!

She turned to Lilly and Ezra. "That's him," she said. "On the boat. That's Jesus."

"Wonderful," Lilly exclaimed, peering at the solitary figure before them.

At the moment, Jesus was not speaking. He seemed to be waiting for the crowds to find their places.

Miriam turned at a touch from Deborah. "See those men at the water's edge? Those are the Twelve Apostles. The one holding the anchor rope is Peter, Anna's husband. He's the chief apostle."

Miriam and her group nodded. Anna had left them and was taking Jesus' mother and Mary Magdalene down to join Peter and the others. Peter smiled at his wife and slipped an arm around her waist, then greeted the two Marys. From the boat, Jesus gave his mother an affectionate smile.

"The one next to Peter is Andrew, his brother," Deborah went on. "Just behind them are James and John, who are partners in the fishing business with Peter and Andrew. The rest there with them are apostles too—Judas Iscariot, Bartholomew, Nathanael."

Leah stepped up beside her mother. "See the one in the blue robe? That's Matthew Levi. His call to be an apostle was a great surprise to us. He was one of the publicans here in town."

Ezra looked around quickly. "A publican?"

"Yes." Leah went on. "Father and I were there the day Jesus called Matthew. There was a lot of shock and some genuine outrage. Imagine! A publican, the vilest of sinners in the eyes of the Pharisees. And Jesus chooses him to be one of his leaders."

"Our own Uncle Aaron was one of those who was highly offended when that happened," Rachel added.

That caught Miriam by surprise. "You have an uncle who is a Pharisee?"

"He is my younger brother," Deborah answered.

"What does he think of you being a follower of Jesus?" Ezra asked.

A momentary look of pain passed across her face. "It would be fair to say that the day I was baptized considerable strain was introduced into the family."

"The Pharisees in Jerusalem are very disturbed by his teachings," Miriam said. "Deborah, you will remember Azariah, who was with us that day Simeon and Yehuda rescued us from Ya'abin and brought us to Beth Neelah."

"I remember him well," came the reply.

"He was especially upset by Jesus." She told them quickly about the woman taken in adultery and how Jesus had turned the tables on her accusers. Ezra and Deborah had already heard this story, but the others had not. Miriam's face clouded. "It was the very next day that my father told me I could never mention the name of Jesus again."

"I'm so grateful most of our family has been united in following Jesus," Deborah said. "It's hard to believe it's been only a month since we were baptized."

For the most part, Livia seemed content to listen to the others, but at that, she looked at Deborah quizzically. "When we were here before, Simeon had not yet been baptized. Is that still the case?"

Miriam's head came up at that question.

Deborah shook her head. "At the time the rest of us were baptized, Simeon was still searching for answers. When he finally began to find them, you three had come with the news of the trap at the pass. Things unraveled quickly after that, as you remember." Her eyes dropped, and her voice filled with pain. "Now I don't think he considers himself worthy. I fear he may think he is not a true disciple."

Leah suddenly had an idea. "Maybe since you have decided to be baptized, Simeon will be baptized too. He's feeling much better about things now."

Just then, out on the boat, Jesus stood up. A murmur swept through the crowd, and the Twelve began to motion people to settle into their places. Jesus was obviously about to begin. The family was at a spot where the beach was a combination of sand and small, smooth pebbles, so they sat down right where they were.

"I suppose he's on the boat to avoid being swamped by the crowd," Lilly suggested.

Deborah nodded. "That, and as you'll see in a moment, the water provides a natural amplification of his voice. It's almost like being in the bottom of an amphitheater, or cupping your hands when you shout at someone."

Almost all of the multitude were quickly seated, and a hush fell over the crowd. Jesus let his eyes move across the hundreds of faces, a look of pleasure in his eyes; then he began. "Behold, a sower went forth to sow."

Two things struck Miriam at once. First was that Deborah was right about the effect of speaking from the boat. Jesus' voice was neither elevated nor strained, yet they could hear every word with perfect clarity. Second, she had last heard that voice suggesting to a hostile crowd that whosoever was without sin should be the first ones to cast a stone at a hapless woman. The moment she again heard its rich, deep resonance, a sense of peace and satisfaction swept over her.

"And when he sowed, some seeds fell by the wayside, and the fowls came and devoured them up. Some of the seed fell upon stony places, where they had not much earth. They immediately sprang up, because the soil was not deep there, but when the sun was up, they were scorched. Because they had no root, they withered away.

"And some of the seed fell among thorns, and the thorns sprang up, and choked them. But other seeds fell into good ground, and brought forth fruit. Some brought forth an hundredfold, some sixtyfold, some thirtyfold."

Jesus stopped and sat back, searching the eyes that were fixed on him. Then with more gravity than before, he said, "He that hath ears to hear, let him hear."

III

An hour later, Jesus was done and the crowd broke up. Deborah got up and went over to see Anna and Peter, but the others with her stood and talked about what they had just heard as the people swirled around them. Each was clearly disappointed in what had happened.

That was the only comforting thing to Miriam about the morning. She was not the only one who had ended up puzzled by what Jesus had said.

After talking about the sower planting his seeds in various kinds of soils—an odd thing for a farmer to do, Miriam thought—Jesus had gone on in a similar vein. He gave one short allegory or analogy after another, in each case prefacing it with, "And the kingdom of heaven is like unto . . . "

"Help us, Leah," Miriam said. "You and Rachel have listened to Jesus much more than we have. What did we miss? He was teaching us about the kingdom, and some things were clear. The pearl of great price, for example. That made sense. The kingdom should be so precious to us that we would give whatever it takes to acquire it. But the story of the farmer and the seed really seemed strange to me. For one thing, why would anyone plant their seed in rocky ground? Or among the thorns?"

Leah shook her head. "I'm not sure. To be honest, we've not heard Jesus teach quite that way before. I thought he was going to go on and tell us what his stories meant, but he didn't."

Rachel who had been listening quietly to this point, broke in. "Think about it for a moment. How does a farmer plant his grain? He puts a bag of seed over his shoulder, then walks along casting handfuls of seed out in long sweeping movements. Sowing that way is called *broadcasting*."

Ezra's head bobbed in agreement. "That's right. So it would be natural that as he walks along, some of the seed would fall on the wayside, or the paths that border the field. There the ground is so hard, no seed could grow. And he doesn't deliberately throw seed among thorns. Remember, when he is sowing, the thorns haven't come up either. It's only later that they choke out the good seed."

"All right," Miriam said, "that makes more sense." She had grown up in Jerusalem, but she had a good understanding of how a farmer worked. "But why would he throw seed among a pile of rocks?"

"Not rocks," Rachel said thoughtfully. "*Stony* ground." She smiled at the look that won her from both Livia and Miriam.

"Rocks? Stones? What's the difference?" Livia asked.

For Rachel, this part of Jesus' teaching had been especially significant. "Let me tell you what I picture he meant. As you know, there are many, many places in Israel where the ground is strewn with rocks. In fact, we have a saying in our country that when God created the world, he gave one of the angels a huge bag of stones to distribute evenly across the earth. Naturally, he started his work in the Holy Land, but just as he circled overhead, the bag broke."

That was met with an appreciative chuckle from all. Throughout much of the country, miles and miles of rock walls marked the efforts to clear the land so it could be planted.

"But there are rocky places," Rachel went on, "and then there are stony places. You have all seen a threshing floor."

Miriam instantly saw what Rachel was suggesting and began to nod. Ezra and Lilly were nodding thoughtfully too. Livia, whose life had been even more limited to cities, shook her head. She knew what a threshing floor was, of course. One did not travel far from Jerusalem without seeing large areas where the soil had been swept away, leaving the smooth, flat limestone exposed—a "floor" made by nature, not by man. Here sheaves of grain were brought from surrounding farms and threshed on the hard, flat surface. But she didn't see how all of that related to the parable.

"Well," Rachel came back in, "when you think of stony places, don't think of a place with boulders scattered about, think of something like a threshing floor, only where the stone is covered with a thin layer of soil. Perhaps it is no deeper than the thickness of two fingers. From the surface, it looks perfectly fine. In fact, you can't really tell from looking at it that it is different from regular soil. But just below the surface is hardpan, solid rock that the seed cannot penetrate. It will grow up for a time, but once summer comes, it dies very quickly."

"Ah," Livia said slowly, understanding now. "The seed can't grow deep roots and it withers in the sun."

Rachel nodded, but then her face fell. "I understand the imagery Jesus used. That's clear. But *why* did he tell us that story?" She shook her head. "What was he trying to teach us? Was he trying to warn us of some spiritual danger? I'm sorry. I'm not sure."

Leah turned to look to where Deborah spoke with Peter, Anna, Jesus, his mother, and Mary Magdalene. "Maybe that is what Mother is asking Jesus," she suggested. "Maybe she can help us understand."

But a few minutes later, when Deborah rejoined them, it was not to talk about sowers and seeds. "Good news," she said.

"What?" Leah and Rachel asked.

"I have asked Jesus if he would have supper with us tonight."

Miriam drew in her breath, hardly daring to ask. "And?"

"And he agreed," Deborah said happily. "Anna, Peter, Jesus' mother—they all will be coming." She sighed happily. "I think we had better go to the market and get something ready." She looked at Leah. "Could you go to Phineas's home and see if he can hire some help for today?"

IV

CAPERNAUM

The spacious courtyard of David ben Joseph, merchant of Capernaum, was filled with people. They sat on benches, stools, and small wooden chairs. They sat on the stone steps that led to the rooftop, and some simply sat down on the paving stones wherever there was an open space. Here and there, others leaned against the stone wall, content to stand so they could see and hear better. Jesus sat near the center of the courtyard, his mother on one side of him, and Anna on the other. Livia, Lilly, and Leah were just behind them, talking with Mary Magdalene. At the moment, they were visiting quietly in pairs or small groups, waiting for the rest of the men to rejoin them.

When the meal was finished, David had told Deborah to take their guests out to the courtyard while he and Simeon and Ephraim helped their hired servants clear everything and put it away. Peter, Andrew, James, and John were up immediately, offering their assistance as well. Ezra did as well. More would have stayed too, but David insisted that there wasn't enough room and sent them outside.

Deborah looked around, counting idly. It shouldn't have surprised her how the numbers had swelled from the initial invitation. Even though only the closest of Jesus' associates and disciples had come, counting her own family and guests, it was still a large crowd. Rachel, Deborah's daughter-in-law, sat with the wives of Andrew and James, listening but not participating for the moment. She had brought Esther and Boaz with her, but as soon as supper was over, young Joseph had asked if he could take his niece and nephew out to play. So many adults in the house did not bode well for children, he was sure. Rachel had gratefully given her consent and was enjoying the chance to visit.

She turned to look the other way. To Deborah's surprise, Livia was on a bench near the fountain, speaking to Luke, the family physician, and a long-time friend of David's. Deborah overheard snatches of Greek. Of course, she thought. Livia was Greek, sold into slavery with her family and finally rescued by Miriam's father. Greek was her native tongue. Though he was Jewish, Luke also spoke fluent and very literate Greek. Much of what was known about medicine had been developed and codified in Greece during the golden age of Athens centuries before. Luke had taken up the language early so that he could study those texts for himself. Deborah's eyes softened. It must be a wonderful thing for Livia to have someone to converse with in her own tongue.

Luke served as the physician for Peter and Andrew's family as well and so had been introduced to Jesus early on. Like David, Luke almost instantly accepted Jesus as the Messiah and had been a loyal disciple ever since.

Through the window, Deborah saw shadows moving back and forth and heard a heavy thud. The men were putting the extra tables away. She let her eyes come back, still counting. With her own family and their visitors from Judea there were ten, not counting Joseph and the grandchildren. With the Twelve and their wives—John, the youngest of the apostles, was not married as yet—there were twenty-three more. James and John had also brought their aged parents, Zebedee and Naomi, and Bartholomew and his wife had their two oldest sons, handsome and respectful young men. Andrew's father-in-law rested on a bench with his eyes closed. That made five more.

There was also Luke and his wife. In addition, Matthew the Publican had invited a neighbor who was just beginning to accept Jesus as the Messiah. Mary Magdalene and Mary, the mother of Jesus, made two more. And, most important of all, Jesus himself.

Deborah shook her head. Forty-four in all, if she had counted correctly. That was a record, even for her. As the wife of one of Capernaum's successful merchants, she often hosted suppers for David's associates or clients. But two dozen had been the most she had ever served at one time. It gave her a sense of pleasure and satisfaction to know that things had gone as smoothly as they had.

There was an air of expectation and excitement in the group. Some, like Miriam, Livia, Ezra, and Lilly, were eager, new followers of Jesus. Others had been with him from the first. All had come hoping that in this more intimate setting perhaps he could and would say things he might not share with the multitudes.

Deborah let her eyes come back to Mary and her son. The

resemblance between them was notable, but not striking. Until they laughed. Then it was unmistakable. It warmed Deborah to watch the tenderness between them and the great deference and respect Jesus held for the woman who had given him birth. Anna said something to Mary, which brought another smile as she looked up at her son. He slipped an arm around her waist, and when she leaned in against his shoulder, he bent down and kissed her on the top of her head.

The sound of the door opening brought Deborah around. The men trooped out with David bringing up the rear. All conversation immediately died as they made their way to where wives and family waited for them. Deborah was especially pleased to see Ephraim and Simeon sit down together. The tension of the night before was now completely gone.

As the last person got settled, everyone turned to Jesus and waited. To their surprise, that only seemed to amuse him, and he said nothing. The silence stretched on for several moments, until Peter finally stirred. "Master?"

Jesus turned to his chief disciple. "Yes?"

"Today, when you were speaking to the people, why did you speak to them in parables?"

Miriam shot a quick glance at Deborah. On the way home, they had shared their perplexity with her. Had Deborah told Peter to ask for clarification?

Jesus eyed the stocky fisherman thoughtfully for several seconds, but before he could speak, Matthew answered his fellow apostle. "Did not the writer of the Psalms, speaking of the Messiah, tell us that 'He will open his mouth in parables; he will utter things which have been kept secret from the foundation of the world'?"

Every head turned to look at the man who until a few weeks before had been a tax collector, one of the detested *publicani* who collected revenue for Rome. David, who now sat beside his wife, was not one of those who was surprised by the comment. Matthew was somewhere near David's age. He wore a skull cap on his balding head. Eyes that were solemn and filled with wisdom looked out from beneath heavy black brows. The lower part of his face was covered with a dark but thin beard giving some hint as to what his hair must have looked like when he was a young man. David had been one of the few who knew Matthew well, and they were longtime friends. David had told Deborah that within the inner circle of the disciples, Matthew was greatly respected. He was wise, experienced, and balanced in his counsel. His knowledge of the scriptures was prodigious—in spite of the fact that the Pharisees accused him of being unlearned in spiritual things. He had an uncanny ability to link things that Jesus did or said to the prophecies of old. As Peter put it, Matthew did not speak up often, but when he did, all the rest of them listened.

John looked at his colleague with respect. "Does it really say that in the Psalms?"

Jesus chuckled softly. "It does, John."

"Oh."

Everyone turned back to see what Jesus would say next. He only smiled at Matthew, showing his approval.

"So," Peter persisted, "why do you teach us in parables?"

Jesus turned slowly as he looked first at Peter, then the others of the Twelve, and finally the rest of the people. "It is a good question. Here is the answer. To you, it is given to know the mysteries of the kingdom of heaven, but to the people it is not given. There is a principle of spiritual knowledge, which is this: Whosoever has, to him it shall be given, and he shall have more in abundance. But whosoever has not, from him it shall be taken away, even that which he has."

He stopped, watching the puzzled looks that appeared on many of the faces around him. "Therefore, it is for this reason that I speak to them in parables, because they seeing, see not. And hearing, they hear not, neither do they understand."

"Master, I—"

"Yes, Peter, speak on."

"Master, I'm not sure I understand. What do you mean when you say that those who have, receive more and those who have not, have it taken away?"

"Could it mean," James broke in, "that some people hear your teachings, but they don't really hear them? Many people read the scriptures, but they read with their own eyes, and see only what they want to see."

"Yes, James. And in people such as that is fulfilled the prophecy of Isaiah, which says, 'By hearing, ye shall hear, and shall not understand. And seeing, ye shall see but shall not perceive.'"

"Are you speaking of the Pharisees, Master?" That came from Nathanael.

"I speak of any who will not hear and accept spiritual truth. Well did Isaiah say of them, 'For this people's heart is waxed gross, and their ears are dull of hearing, and their eyes they have closed. They do this lest at any time they should see with their eyes and hear with their ears, and should understand with their heart, and should be converted, and I should heal them.'"

"But," Miriam whispered, speaking almost to herself, "don't we want people to be converted?"

Jesus turned. Miriam had forgotten that she was just a few feet away from the Master; she could see he had heard her clearly. He turned to face her, though his eyes took in others, too. "But blessed are your eyes, for they see. And blessed are your ears, for they hear. Verily, I say unto you, many of the prophets and righteous men of old have desired to see these things which you now see, and they did not; and to hear these things which you now hear, and they were not privileged to hear them."

He turned back to Peter. "So hear now therefore the parable of the sower." He paused, as if he knew that what he was about to do would have to be digested carefully.

"The seed is the word of the kingdom." He stopped again, and

Miriam realized that what he had just said was the key to the whole parable. The seed was the word of God.

"When anyone hears the word and understands it not, then comes the wicked one, like the fowls of the air, and snatches away the seed, or the word, that was sown in his heart. This is he which receives the seed by the wayside."

Miriam looked at Ezra, who sat beside Lilly. That was exactly what Ezra had said earlier. The wayside was too hard for any seed to take root.

Ironically, Simeon thought of his Uncle Aaron at that moment. Aaron was an honest man, filled with integrity, deeply determined to put his life in harmony with God. Yet, in this one aspect, his heart was like the roadways of their country—hard as flint, without even the tiniest crack in which the words of Jesus could take hold.

"But he that received the seed into stony places," Jesus went on, "the same is he that hears the word and immediately with joy receives it. Yet he has not root in himself. He endures for a time, and the seed begins to grow, but when tribulation or persecution arises because of the word, then is he offended."

Jesus stopped again to give them time to consider his imagery. Rachel caught Livia's eye and smiled. Not rocky places, *stony* places, she seemed to say. And Livia saw it now. Some people were like that thin layer of soil. They immediately accepted the word of God, but there was no depth to their commitment. It didn't take much heat to see them wither away.

As for Miriam, she was almost floating. A sense of revelation was on her. It was as though Jesus had lifted a hood from over her eyes, and now she was clearly seeing the picture he had painted for them earlier that day.

Jesus began again. "He that received seed among the thorns is he that hears the word but then allows the cares of this world and the deceitfulness of riches to choke the word, and he becomes unfruitful."

Like my father. Miriam was startled by that thought and yet instantly saw it was true. And not only of her father, but of so many others of the rich and powerful that came to their home in Jerusalem. Choked by the deceitfulness of riches. What a powerful way to put it.

"But he that received seed into the good ground," Jesus said, "is he that hears the word with gladness and understands it. These bear fruit because the soil is good. And some soil brings forth an hundredfold, some sixty, some thirty."

He stopped, looked at Peter again, and smiled gently. "This, Simon, is the parable of the sower."

Peter had a look in his eyes that suggested to Miriam that he had experienced something very much like she had just experienced. "I understand," he murmured. "Thank you, Master."

Then another insight came to Miriam's mind. The word *parable* came from *mawshawl* in Hebrew, meaning a proverb, or a similitude. But in Greek, it was a much more vivid word. *Para* was a prefix meaning "alongside" or "parallel to." *Bolay* was the verb meaning "to hurl," or "to throw," such as in the word *ballista*, the catapults used by armies. Thus, a parable was literally to throw or place things side by side. That was exactly what Jesus was doing. The seed was the word. The soils were different kinds of people. She shook her head quickly. No, not people. Different states of the heart. A difference in how people accepted the word.

Now the word *mawshawl* took on greater meaning for her. It was a similitude. Jesus was taking things from the natural world and making them similar or parallel to things of the spiritual realm. And then Miriam remembered the last words Jesus had spoken after completing the parable of the sower. "Who hath ears to hear, let him hear."

Miriam bat Mordechai, daughter of one of Jerusalem's leading and most powerful citizens, sat back, marveling at what was happening to her in a courtyard in Capernaum.

CHAPTER NOTES

The first scriptural mention of Mary Magdalene, who figures so prominently in the accounts of the crucifixion and resurrection, is found in Luke 8:1–3. There she is mentioned as one of those who were among the followers of Jesus. Luke records that out of Mary "went seven devils" and that she and other women had been "healed of evil spirits and infirmities." We are not told what these infirmities were, so the details given in this account are only the author's suggestions.

Hollywood and popular literature have typically portrayed Mary Magdalene as a reformed prostitute. This comes from the fact that in some Christian churches, Mary is thought to have been a harlot prior to being healed by Jesus. She is even today seen by many to be the patron saint of prostitutes, and in some places harlots are still called "Magdalenes." This tradition, which has no basis in scripture, seems to have been derived from the fact that just prior to his introduction of Mary, Luke gives an account of an unnamed woman who was likely a harlot (see Luke 7:36–50). However, though Luke introduces Mary Magdalene shortly after that account, he does not in any way imply that it is the same woman and, in fact, he speaks of them as two different people.

Another argument against this conclusion is that typically prostitutes in the time of Jesus were of the poorest classes of society, often forced into their terrible life in order to survive. Yet Luke tells us that these women, including Mary Magdalene, "ministered unto him of their substance," suggesting that Mary Magdalene was likely a woman of some wealth (see Clarke, 3:417; Dummelow, 2:1122; *Who's Who in the Bible*, 287–88).

One of the difficulties in writing a historical novel based on the four Gospels is that the scriptural record provides very little personal information about the details of Jesus' daily life and the people who were part of it. For example, there is no Gospel account of Jesus explaining the parable of the sower at a supper at someone's private home. However, while it is necessary to fill in additional details required for a novel, the author has nevertheless stayed in harmony with what is known.

In this case, we are told that it was after he had taught the parable that the disciples asked him why he taught that way (see Matthew 13:10; Mark 4:10). We also know that Jesus often dined with people, both those who believed in him and those who were critical of him. In fact, it was such a common occurrence that the Pharisees used it as a basis for criticizing him (see Matthew 11:19; Luke 7:33–34). For this reason it seemed plausible that Jesus would be found in such a setting and use it as an opportunity to teach his more intimate disciples.

The author has *not* taken similar liberties with the teachings of Jesus. What Jesus teaches in the novel is always based directly on what the scriptural record gives to us.

In a similar fashion, we have little detail about the personal lives of the principals in the New Testament accounts. Even in the case of Jesus, the dominant figure of the Gospels, we are given very few details about his physical features, clothing, or personality traits. We know that he was thirty when he started his ministry and that Mary had four other sons and at least two daughters with Joseph (see Matthew 13:55–56). Beyond that there is virtually nothing.

Likewise, with the Twelve we get only snippets of information. We know Peter was a fisherman and that he was married because we are told that Jesus healed his "wife's mother" of a fever (Matthew 8:14–15). However, his wife is never named nor are we told if they had children. In the case of some of the apostles, we have nothing but a name. However, we can extrapolate certain things from what we know about the culture of that time. For example, we know that the emphasis on marriage was so strong in the Jewish culture that it is almost a given that the adult men were married and had children. They would have come under strong criticism from the religious leaders if that had not been the case. Because John was likely the younger of the two sons of Zebedee, always being named after James when both are mentioned, I have shown him as still not married at this point.

Matthew, whose Gospel is unique in that he constantly shows us how Old Testament prophecies were fulfilled by Jesus (see, for example, Matthew 1:22–23; 2:15, 23; 4:13–16), is the one who notes that Christ's teaching in parables fulfilled a Messianic prophecy (compare Matthew 13:34–35 with Psalm 78:2).

The apostle Paul called Luke "the beloved physician" (Colossians 4:14). Many modern scholars think Luke was a Gentile converted to Christianity, probably after Christ's death. However, as one well-known scholar notes, there are many, "ancient and modern," who believe that Luke is the unnamed disciple who saw the resurrected Christ on the road to Emmaus (see Luke 24:13–35; see also Clarke, 3:500). Luke is the only one to record that account in detail. Not naming himself would be in keeping with the practice of other Gospel writers when placing themselves in the narrative (see John 13:23 and Matthew 9:9 as examples). To have Luke in Galilee at this time shows a personal preference of the author and should not be construed to mean I think the issue is conclusively settled.

CHAPTER 9

COME UNTO ME, ALL YE THAT LABOUR AND
ARE HEAVY LADEN, AND I WILL GIVE YOU REST.
—*Matthew 11:28*

I

CAPERNAUM
30 JUNE, A.D. 30

David gave one last wave, called out one last farewell to their supper guests, then shut the heavy wooden gate behind them. He turned to the others who stood watching. He went to his wife and kissed her on the cheek. "Well, that was a wonderful idea, Deborah."

"I should have done it before," Deborah murmured happily.

"Oh, no," Miriam exclaimed. "If you had given this supper any earlier, then we wouldn't have been here."

"True," she answered. "And I am so glad you were."

"It's been a wonderful day," Lilly said, touching Deborah's arm. "Thank you again for having us here. It is all that we hoped for and more."

"Much more," Ezra said.

"So," Leah asked eagerly, looking at their four guests from Joppa, "did you speak with Jesus about being baptized?"

Lilly, Ezra, Miriam, and Livia all nodded at once. "We did," Ezra answered. "Jesus said to meet them where we were today, at about the second hour tomorrow morning. He asked James and John to baptize us."

"That is wonderful," Deborah said. "I'm so happy for you."

"I've never been happier," Miriam replied. "When Jesus was teaching us tonight, it was like my spirit was soaring. That's when I knew I had to be baptized. I don't care what Father says, or will say, when he finds out. I've been looking for this my entire life."

"Are you sure this is the right thing to do?" Simeon asked, speaking directly to Miriam.

The disappointment was instantly evident. "Aren't you?"

A smile stole slowly across his face. "Actually, yes I am." Now he looked at his mother. "That's why I asked Peter tonight if he would mind being there tomorrow too."

For a moment, it didn't register, then she threw herself at him. "You asked Peter to baptize you?"

"Only after I asked the Master if that was acceptable to him." He laughed at her expression. "I told you I was going to try to show more faith. Well, isn't this the first step?"

He was instantly surrounded by everyone trying to congratulate him. Leah couldn't believe it. "Really, Simeon?" she cried over and over. "You're really going to be baptized?"

"Yes, little sister. If Jesus will have me in the kingdom, which he said he would, who am I to hold back?"

"I am so happy, Simeon," his mother whispered, clinging to him tightly. "It's the best thing you could do to make things go right."

David gripped his son's hand. "Son, there is nothing you could have said that would give us greater pleasure."

At last it was Ephraim's turn. He grabbed Simeon by the shoulder and shook him gently. "Good for you, Simeon. Good for you."

"Did you get a chance to talk to Jesus tonight about your plan?" Deborah asked as things finally subsided a little.

Simeon shook his head. "No, everyone was around, and he was with his mother." He shrugged. "But I still feel that this is what I need to do. I'm not torn like I was before."

"Simeon?"

He turned to Ephraim. "Yes?"

"Are you still committed to trying to bribe Pilate?"

He winced. "Couldn't we use the word *ransom?*" he said, keeping his voice light. But finally he nodded. "Yes, I am, Ephraim. I don't see any other way out of this."

"I still think it's wrong."

"I know that."

"But if you really are committed to that plan of action, then I have a suggestion."

Simeon couldn't hide his surprise. "You do?"

"Yes. Make it three talents."

That brought a swift reaction from Simeon and several of the others. If anything, Rachel was even more shocked by what Ephraim had said than Simeon was. "Three?" she cried.

"That's right. One for each prisoner." There was a sudden brusqueness. "If you really are committed to this, then do it right. One talent per man. That's language Pilate will understand."

"Wait a minute," Simeon exclaimed. "Who kidnapped my brother and left this man in his place?"

"And you can take the third talent from my part of the inheritance."

Simeon had started another quip, still shocked at what he was hearing, but that stopped him short. He stared for a long moment into Ephraim's eyes. "Thank you," was all he could finally say.

II

Ephraim and Rachel went home to see how Joseph had fared with Esther and Boaz. Deborah was exhausted, and she and David retired immediately after that. Ezra and Lilly stayed to talk for another half hour, then they too left the night for the young.

Leah, Simeon, Miriam, and Livia stayed down in the courtyard rather than going up on the roof. The night had cooled, and the air was pleasant. They pulled their chairs around the fountain and settled in. For well over a minute, they were quiet, each caught up in their own thoughts; then Miriam spoke. "Who would have thought it that day you and Yehuda showed up at our camp in Samaria? None of us even knew about Jesus then, and now the three of us are being baptized on the same day."

"That is something," Simeon agreed, thinking back to that morning that now seemed like years before, even though it had been just a few months.

Miriam's eyes suddenly were filled with teasing. "There's something I've been wanting to ask you for a long time, Simeon, son of David."

Surprised at her sudden formality, he nodded. "Go ahead."

"Do you remember when we stopped to have lunch at the spring of Harod that day you rescued us?"

"Of course."

"We were just getting ready to leave and you asked Livia a question. You said, 'You're not Jewish, are you?'"

"I remember that very clearly," Livia said with a tiny smile, knowing what Miriam was up to. She had talked with Livia about this before.

"I do as well," Simeon said. "Livia said no. She said she was Greek."

"No," Miriam cut in quickly, "*I* said she was Greek."

"Oh," Simeon grunted, seeing the trap. "Yes."

Her voice dropped to a low growl as Miriam mimicked his angry tone. "'Do you see your slave as an ox who cannot speak for herself?'"

Leah, who had pulled her chair alongside Simeon's and had her hand resting on his arm, drew back in shock. "You said that?"

He didn't answer.

"Oh, yes," Miriam said gleefully. "He nearly took my head off. Gave me this lecture about slavery and the Law of Moses. Said it didn't make any difference whether we had given Livia her freedom or not. Walked up and down my back with hobnail boots when I said she wasn't a slave, only a servant." Again she dropped into a parody of Simeon's voice. "'*Only a servant!* If you call a donkey a horse, it doesn't change the fact that he is still a donkey.'"

Livia laughed heartily at the look on Simeon's face.

Leah was staring at him. "You really said all that?"

He looked away. "Something like that, I suppose," he mumbled.

Miriam wasn't about to let that pass. "Not *something* like that. I remember very clearly every word."

"So," he growled, on the defensive now, "is there a question somewhere in there?"

"Yes. I just realized it tonight. Your family hires servants. Your father has a chief steward, just like mine does. Your mother had three women here tonight helping with the cooking. So how come you were so high-handed with me about having a servant?"

For a moment, he was caught without a word. He hadn't seen that question coming at all. "Well," he began, obviously groping, "it's not the same."

Her look was scathing. "Why isn't it?"

"Well, for one thing, our servants were more like employees who used to come in on a regular basis, but they had their own homes.

They were paid a wage. Now, of course, since Mother and Father were baptized, we use them much less."

"True, but that wasn't the case when you said what you did. You think the fact that they lived somewhere else makes all the difference?"

Simeon turned to Livia, recovering sufficiently to go on the offensive. "Are you paid a wage?"

Livia had been enjoying the interchange to that point. Now she visibly flinched. "Well, no, but I—I have everything I need."

Simeon shot Miriam a triumphant look, but she fielded it blandly. "And that makes all the difference?" she needled him again.

"No," Simeon said, suddenly very quiet. "Here's the difference, Miriam. None of our servants ever felt like we owned them, like they were our property. They were employees. That's all."

Her face colored and she started to answer, but Simeon turned to Livia again. "Answer me honestly, Livia. Do you ever have the feeling that Miriam's father owns you, that you are his property?"

Livia's head dropped and her cheeks flamed. Miriam just stared at her. It was answer enough.

"And while I know it is no longer the case," he said, more softly still, "did you ever have that feeling about Miriam?"

Livia bit her lip, looked up quickly at Miriam, then away again.

"Never mind," Simeon said, watching without triumph the reaction and the resulting dismay on Miriam's face. "Don't answer."

Miriam's head had dropped too, and she was staring at her hands. Leah wasn't sure what to say. The exchange had shocked her.

"Now," Simeon went on quickly, "I want to say something else, in answer to your very thoughtful and fair question."

Miriam's eyes lifted to see if he was being sarcastic, but there was no mockery in his eyes. "Back when I said all that, I thought Miriam, daughter of Mordechai, was a pampered, egotistical, self-centered, aristocratic snob who desperately needed to be taken down a notch or two for her own good."

She gave him a wan smile. "So I made a good impression on you?"

He ignored her question and continued. "I also learned that she had a tongue that could take off your hide as effectively as a Roman scourge."

"You should talk!" she cried.

Leah clapped her hands at that. "Amen!"

Simeon went right on, not meeting her eyes now. "I have since learned that I was far too hasty in my judgment." He grinned momentarily. "Well, not about the part about her being rich and having a tongue of fire. But in the rest I was wrong."

She had started to react to his first comment, but then sat back. "You were?"

"Yes. I learned that Miriam, daughter of Mordechai of Jerusalem, was a woman of courage. I learned that she cared so deeply for her servant that she was willing to risk her life for her. I also came to see that she and her servant girl, Livia of Alexandria, were so filled with integrity and honor that they left that comfortable and pampered existence to come north to try to save the life of the very man who had treated them with such shameful contempt."

Leah reached out and took Simeon's hand and squeezed it hard. Miriam was speechless.

Now Simeon looked at Miriam directly. "In the wild melee of that night at the Joknean Pass, I only thanked the two of you briefly for what you did for me. You both have put yourselves in grave danger. I am greatly relieved that you are going to Rome, much as you hate the idea. I am also grateful that you were allowed to come here first so that one very humbled and penitent Simeon ben David could offer both his thanks and his apology. It is long overdue."

III

ON THE SHORES OF THE SEA OF GALILEE, NEAR CAPERNAUM
1 JULY, A.D. 30

The group waiting near the boat of Peter and Andrew was small, and Simeon was grateful for that. Peter had brought his family, as did Andrew. James and John were there, but alone. Mary Magdalene had come with Jesus and his mother. Luke and his wife were there too. That surprised Simeon a little until his mother whispered to him that she had seen Luke and Livia conversing in Greek the night before while waiting for the men to clean up after supper.

At the sight of Jesus, both Esther and Boaz broke free from their parents and ran to see him. Jesus was delighted, tossing Boaz up until he shrieked with joy; then Jesus gravely introduced the two children to his mother.

"*Shalom*," Peter said as he came over to join the family. "Are we ready?"

Ezra spoke for all of them. "We are ready."

He nodded and led them over to Jesus. As they approached, Esther took Jesus by the hand and pulled him down. "Do you know Miriam?" she asked in a half-whisper.

"Yes, I do," Jesus answered, smiling at her seriousness.

"She's beautiful. I like her."

Miriam blushed, touched by the simple innocence of the statement. "And I like you too, Esther. Very much."

Again Esther tugged. Jesus bent down again. "And this is Livia, Miriam's friend. She's going to be baptized too."

"Yes, I know. Isn't that wonderful?"

Esther cupped a hand to her mouth and spoke into his ear, thinking that would prevent the others from hearing. "I wish my hair was like Livia's."

Jesus chuckled richly, seeing Livia color now as well. "It is very pretty, isn't it."

Rachel just shook her head, smiling at this little imp with the face of a sphinx. Lilly leaned over beside her. "How did you ever get one as absolutely priceless as she is?"

"She is a gift from heaven," Rachel said.

To Lilly's surprise, Jesus walked over to her and took her hand. "*Shalom*, Lilly of Joppa."

"*Shalom*, Master."

"You are here to become one of us." It was a simple statement, not a question.

"Yes, Master."

He was looking at her closely. "Deborah tells me that you are as Sarah and Hannah of old. Your marriage as yet has not been blessed with children."

Lilly's eyes widened. She wasn't sure what to say.

"Both were choice daughters of God," he said gently, "and women of faith. Eventually, both received the desire of their hearts."

"Yes, Lord." Her heart had leaped within her. Though promised that she would be the mother of countless children, Sarah had gone childless until she was ninety years old. Then she had borne Isaac and became the great matriarch of the House of Israel. Hannah likewise had been barren and prayed year after year for a son. When the Lord finally opened her womb, she mothered the prophet Samuel. Was he saying . . . ?

Before she could finish that thought, Jesus turned and took Ezra's hand, but he continued to look at Lilly. "Does this man treat you well?"

Lilly's smile went suddenly misty. "Far better than I deserve."

Jesus nodded, obviously pleased. "That is as it should be."

He turned to Livia. As he took her hand, he glanced at Esther, who was watching all of this with her characteristic gravity. "I fear that you have created a touch of covetousness in our little queen," he said, teasing Livia just a little.

Livia started to answer, but he went on before she could. "I perceive that your heart is pure, Livia of Alexandria, as pure as that of this child." He squeezed her hand momentarily. "It is not by mere chance that you are here this day."

Like Lilly, Livia was left speechless. His words had come as a total surprise.

Next he turned to Miriam. "Peter and Anna have told me that your father is a member of the Great Council in Jerusalem."

"Yes," Miriam murmured.

"And what would he say if he knew you were here with me this morning?"

Miriam was astounded. How much had David and Deborah told him? But the kindness in his eyes engulfed her, and she could not but answer him in complete honesty. "He would likely disown me and send me from his bosom. He says that you must be destroyed."

Jesus only nodded. "Remember this, which I have said to others before." His voice had become like a touch on her cheek. "In the Law, Moses commanded us to honor father and mother. And rightly so. That is an obligation of great importance. But there are times when a man's foes may be they of his own household."

Her head pulled back as she stared at him.

"This is a hard saying, Miriam, but know this. If a person loves his father or mother more than me, he is not worthy of me. He that takes not his cross to follow after me, is not worthy of me."

Simeon was staring. Those were exactly the same words that Jesus had taught him several days before when he had asked Jesus about discipleship.

Without even realizing it, tears had come to Miriam's eyes. She was only aware of it when she felt the wetness start down her cheeks. "I know, Master," she whispered.

"Be of good cheer," he said. "You have chosen the better part."

"Thank you." She stepped back, embarrassed that her emotions had spilled over so easily.

Simeon wondered if Jesus had deliberately waited to speak to him last. He tensed slightly as Jesus finally turned to him. "*Shalom*, Simeon."

"*Shalom*, Master."

"Last night, at supper, you seemed at peace."

"Yes, Lord. I am much more at peace since you spoke to me that day about being a disciple."

"You have not given up on your friends from Beth Neelah?"

"No. I have what I hope is a better way to try to help them."

Jesus gave an approving nod. "Greater love has no man than this, that he lay down his life for his friends."

Simeon's mouth opened slightly. *Lay down his life?* Was he suggesting—?

But Jesus went on. "And what did you learn from what I said?"

"I learned that no man, having once put his hand to the plow, can turn back and still hope to enter the kingdom of God. I learned that if we lack faith, we can sink into the waters of despair. I learned that, as the prophet Jeremiah says, man should never trust in the arm of flesh, even if that arm is his own."

"That is good, Simeon ben David."

Simeon turned to look at Miriam. "And I have learned that when you ask us to take up our cross and follow you, that may require very different sacrifices from each of us."

"Yes, very different," Jesus responded.

"It isn't always easy, is it?" Simeon asked quietly.

The brown eyes widened slightly. "Easy? Did you think it would be?"

Simeon couldn't meet that penetrating gaze. "No, I suppose not."

"I would that you should remember this, Simeon ben David. If you come to a time when you feel as though you can bear things no longer, when you feel as if you will be overcome with the weight you carry, remember this one thing."

His eyes peered deeply into Simeon's, and it was as though they were the only two people in the world at that moment. His voice was softer, more filled with gentleness and love than Simeon had ever heard before. It offered an invitation that could not be ignored. "Come unto me, all ye that labor and are heavy laden, and I will give you rest. Take my yoke upon you, and learn of me, for I am meek and lowly in heart, and ye shall find rest unto your souls, for my yoke is easy," he concluded softly, "and my burden is light."

"Yes, Lord," Simeon murmured, barely able to speak. Jesus had seen into his soul.

Jesus stepped back. "Peter, we have five people here who wish to enter the kingdom of God. Let us proceed."

IV

Simeon fully expected to be disappointed. He had watched Miriam and then Livia and then Lilly come out of the water radiant with joy. As they wiped the water from their eyes and pulled back the wet hair from their faces, it was as though something in their very countenances had changed. Peace and serenity and fulfillment shone from their eyes.

Ezra had been much more subdued in his reaction when James drew him out of the water, but Simeon had seen something in his eyes as well, something that Simeon couldn't define.

Now as he stood here, waist deep in the water, and listened to Peter's brief prayer, Simeon was suddenly afraid he wouldn't feel anything. And if he didn't, what did that mean? Was he not ready after all?

"Amen," Peter said.

"Amen," Simeon murmured, realizing he hadn't heard a word that Peter had said.

Peter laid one hand firmly on Simeon's back and another on his chest, then smiling broadly, he pushed him backwards.

Simeon almost gasped as the cold water enveloped him, but clamped his mouth shut in time. He felt the pressure of Peter's large hands for a moment, then was suddenly lifted up again. As his head broke the surface and he released his breath, Peter let go. Simeon tossed his head, flinging the dripping hair backwards, then wiped the water from his eyes.

"Welcome to the kingdom, Brother," Peter said, his voice filled with emotion. "Thank you for letting me be the one to bring you in."

"Thank you, Peter." He turned, aware of hands clapping and cries of approval from the shore.

Smiling, he moved forward even as he searched himself inwardly. There was nothing unusual. Nothing out of the ordinary. He felt gladness, satisfaction. He had wanted to do this for some time. But there was nothing like what he had seen on Miriam's face or in Ezra's eyes. Trying to hide his disappointment, he reached the shore and was swept up in his mother's embrace. "You did it, Simeon."

"I did, Mother. Thank you for not giving up on me."

He shook hands with his father, who said nothing. He didn't have to. His eyes shone with pride. Ephraim, Rachel, Leah, John, Anna, James—one by one he accepted their congratulations, murmuring the right responses, nodding at the right places. Esther let him touch her cheek but refused to hug him because he was all wet. Boaz seemed content to watch it all.

Finally Simeon turned to Jesus, who waited quietly a step or two behind the others. He dreaded this moment. What if Jesus could see into his heart and sense that nothing had really changed?

Then without a word, Jesus extended his hand and gripped Simeon's firmly.

"Master, I—Thank you."

And at that instant, as if they had been formed in letters of brilliant white, the following words came into his mind. *Come unto me, all ye that labor and are heavy laden, and I will give you rest. Take my yoke upon you, and ye shall find rest unto your souls.*

He let go of Jesus' hand, staring at him in wonder. Now he understood. It wasn't joy, though joy was there. It wasn't serenity, though he felt calmer than he could ever remember feeling. It was peace. A deep, abiding peace had flooded into his soul and he was . . . he searched for the word, then realized it was already there. He was at rest. At long last, his soul was at rest.

He lowered his head, acknowledging the presence of the one who stood before him. "Truly, Master," he whispered, "truly thou art the Son of God."

CHAPTER NOTES

There is no specific description in the four Gospels of a baptismal experience where newly converted followers of Christ were brought into the Church. However, we know that such baptisms did happen. Jesus taught Nicodemus that one could not enter into the kingdom of heaven without being born of the water and the Spirit (see John 3:5), and his final commandment to the Twelve was to go unto all the world and preach the gospel, promising that "he that believeth and is baptized shall be saved" (Mark 16:16; see also Matthew 28:19).

There is one specific reference in John that tells us that Jesus and the apostles baptized (see John 3:22). After Jesus' resurrection, we see numerous references to baptism as the mode of entry into the kingdom of heaven (see, for example, Acts 3:38; 8:36–39; 10:47–48; 16:33).

Christ's teachings about one's foes being from one's own household is found in Matthew 10:34–38. The statement about showing love by laying down one's own life for one's friends is based on John 15:13. The beautiful passage about taking the Savior's yoke upon us is found in Matthew 11:28–30.

CHAPTER 10

FOR THOU HAST POWER OVER LIFE AND DEATH; THOU DOST LEAD
MEN DOWN TO THE GATES OF HADES AND BACK AGAIN.

—*Wisdom of Solomon 16:13*

I

CAPERNAUM
2 JULY, A.D. 30

Deborah clung to Simeon, holding on to him fiercely. "Can't you stay just one more day?" Seeing the answer forming in his eyes, she shook him roughly. "You were just baptized yesterday, Simeon. A mother has a right to savor some happiness before she has to start worrying again, doesn't she?"

He put his arms around her, pressing his cheek against her hair. "If Pilate were to change his mind and move up the date of the execution, I would never forgive myself."

"It's going to take him several days," David said, "maybe a week, to convert our assets to gold. You don't just walk in and raise three talents of gold overnight."

"I know," she whispered. "I know."

They were in a small corral behind the warehouse where the incoming wheat crop was currently being stored. Simeon's horse was saddled and ready. At Simeon's insistence, only his mother and father had come to see him off. He had said his farewells to the family and their guests from Joppa the night before. He wanted to be off. He had never liked saying good-bye.

"Are you sure I shouldn't come with you, Son?" David asked Simeon. "Two of us can get more accomplished in less time."

He shook his head. "I feel bad enough leaving you at the height of the harvest season, Father. I'll be fine."

"Did you know that Miriam volunteered to help?" Deborah said.

"Help? How?"

"By raising one of those talents herself."

"Oh, Mordechai would love that," Simeon retorted.

"Miriam told me that several years ago, her father gave her part of her inheritance and taught her how to invest it. Where she is his only child and he has no male heir, I suppose he wants her to be ready to inherit everything when he dies. As bright as she is, she has done very well for herself. She says she can get to that money without her father's permission."

"Maybe so, but I'll wager she can't do it without his knowledge, and that would be the final blow for him. No, Miriam has more than done enough. I hope you told her no."

"We did," David answered. "But she meant it. She wants to help."

Simeon nodded. It was an impressive offer, and he would have to remember to thank her for that as well on his return. "Are they still planning to leave for Gaulanitis later today?"

"That's what Ezra said. They'll be gone two or three days. Leah tried to talk the women into staying here while Ezra goes so they can spend more time with Jesus, but Miriam promised her father that she would stay with Ezra. She won't break that promise."

"That's wise. Mordechai will question her about it when she sees him again."

"That will still give them about a week to listen to the Master before they have to travel to Caesarea."

"Speaking of Caesarea," Simeon said, "once I have the money, I'll probably go straight there. I don't like the idea of wandering around with three talents of gold in my bags."

"Oh, Simeon be careful."

"I will, Mother. I promise."

"So many things could go wrong. Are you sure you shouldn't go back to Beth Neelah? Issachar and the others want to free Yehuda almost as much as you do."

He was shaking his head before she finished.

"Even half a dozen men, Simeon. You are so vulnerable if you go in all by yourself."

"I've mulled this over and over in my mind. I have to have faith. Remember what Jesus said to Peter as he was sinking? 'Wherefore did you doubt?' I can't start doubting now."

"But—"

"This isn't blind faith, Mother. I'm not going to just blithely walk in and hope the Lord drops manna from the sky. I've tried to foresee every possibility, but I feel strongly that this is the right way. This is my answer. But it's only for me. The moment I start thinking about dragging others into it—Issachar, Father, Miriam—any sense of peace I have leaves me."

His father's eyes were calmer than his mother's, but they still showed anxiety. "Are you sure you've worked out a way to get out of there if Pilate decides he wants you *and* the gold?"

Simeon wished he hadn't asked that question. "Yes," he said, more firmly than he felt. He had worked it out in his mind. Over and over and over. It was a good plan. A tight plan. But who knew what that cunning old lion would do when the gazelle walked right into his lair?

He felt like a further answer was needed. "I can't depend on Pilate. In the first place, I don't know him. I don't know how to predict his reactions. I'm going to work through Marcus. He's part of all that we are fighting against, but I believe him to be a man of integrity." He took a quick breath. "And like it or not, I did save his life at the pass. Surely there will be some sense of obligation there."

He looked back and forth at these two people who were everything in the world to him, and a sudden pang of doubt swept over him. If he was wrong—and he had surely been that before—he might never see them again. Or tease a smile out of Esther. Or—

He shook his head, suddenly angry at himself. *O ye of little faith, wherefore do you doubt?* "It is going to be all right, Mother. I have to believe that. I have to."

Deborah sighed and stepped back. "Go, then," she said, her head high. "Go with God, my son."

II

CAESAREA

7 JULY, A.D. 30

Simeon was surprised at his patience, a trait for which he had never been renowned. In fact, his mother had once commented that he had been born impatient and greatly increased his birthright. But a great calm had settled over him. Ever since his baptism the week before, he had not lost the sense of peace, the sense of all being right.

It had been a long and tiring week. Simeon had gone first to Tiberias, then over to Ptolemais, the port on the Mediterranean coast about thirty miles north of Caesarea. His hope had been to raise the full amount between those two cities where his family did so much business, but he hadn't been able to do so. So, praying that he wouldn't be seen by anyone who would recognize him from his previous trip, he returned to Damascus, then finally back to Ptolemais. His sense of urgency was such that he had paused on the Sabbath only to attend the local synagogue, then continued on. He had risen before dawn this morning and started south. Now he sat with his back against the wall a few strides away from the entrance to the Praetorium, the palace of Pontius Pilate, governor of Judea. And he waited.

He had arrived to the north of the city just after dark, which was as he had planned. He buried the gold, then rode into the city. For the last two hours he had sat here in this narrow alley, which was not quite straight across from the main gate of the great Roman compound. There had been no changing of the guard since his arrival, but he knew that would eventually happen. He was neither frustrated nor tempted to alter his plans. Twice now, observing through the great gates, he had seen Tribune Marcus Didius pass through the great courtyard lit by torches mounted on the walls. That was the important thing. He had feared that Marcus might be out of the city on assignment somewhere and that the letter Simeon carried in his tunic would sit on a table somewhere for several days.

But Marcus was here. The first possible obstacle was behind him.

Simeon glanced up at the sky. The stars were out in their fulness. Later there would be a quarter moon, but now it was totally dark. The city was quieting and to the west of him, he could hear the faint wash of the sea on the massive pier built by Herod the Great.

It shouldn't be much longer now. In the Roman system, a typical "watch" was about four hours, and this, the first watch of the night, had to be near its close.

Simeon leaned back against the rough stones of the building that formed one wall of the alley. The air was stifling in the narrow passageway. The breezes from the Great Sea had not penetrated here as yet, and he could feel the stickiness everywhere on his body. That was all right too. He would be moving again soon enough.

Simeon straightened as he heard the crunch of sandals. It was an unmistakable sound. Soldiers in the legion had sandals with short iron spikes in the soles. No other sandals sounded quite like these. He straightened, brushing at his shoulder in case he had gotten dust on his tunic. Once again, as that first time in Damascus, Simeon was dressed as a young Roman gentleman.

Four new soldiers came through the gate with spears in hand and swords at their belts. They saluted the four waiting there. Simeon went immediately into action. He cut across the street, moving confidently, but not swiftly. The slap of his sandals on the paving stones brought all eight heads around. The oldest of the first watch took a step forward, one hand on the hilt of his sword. He was not wary, but he was definitely alert.

Simeon stopped ten paces away and the man visibly relaxed. "Sir," he said in Latin, speaking with obvious deference, "I have a letter to be delivered to Tribune Marcus Quadratus Didius. I see you are about to go off duty. Would it be possible to have you carry it to him?"

All eight men were watching him curiously. "A letter?" the senior man said.

"Yes." As he reached in his tunic for the folded piece of parchment, with his other hand he fished out three *denarii* and rattled them softly. That immediately changed everything.

The guard came forward and took the letter and the coins, ignoring the sudden hungry look of his companions. "Do you require an answer?" he asked.

"No. There are instructions in the letter on how the tribune is to contact me." He paused for a moment. "Do you know if the Tribune is in the Praetorium at this time?" The last time he had seen Marcus was almost an hour ago. There might be a second gate, which Simeon had no way of covering.

"Aye, he is," one of the new arrivals said. "I saw him just a few minutes ago."

"Good. Thank you."

The coins disappeared and the parchment followed. "Very well then," said the man, "if you require no answer, we shall be off."

Simeon moved away. Just before he turned the corner, he looked back and saw the four old guards disappear through the gate as the relief detachment took up their watch. He let out his breath slowly. Second possible obstacle down.

III

CAPERNAUM AND ON THE SHORES OF THE SEA OF GALILEE
8 JULY, A.D. 30

The courtyard was quiet except for the soft twittering of a bird that Miriam could not see in the branches of the pomegranate tree. She sat beneath the trellis covered with grape vines, enjoying the cool morning air. She had been awakened when she heard David slip out of the house about an hour before and had finally gotten out of bed and dressed. Careful not to wake Livia or anyone else in the house, she went outside.

It surprised her to see how dramatically her habits had changed since coming north. In Jerusalem, she always poked and puttered around until late at night, long after the rest of the household went to bed. Then she would sleep until the third or even fourth hour of the day, lazily taking another half an hour in bed even when she did finally wake up.

Here, in the household of David ben Joseph, she was up early every day, even when she stayed up late in the night. She found herself sleeping so deeply that she awoke early, completely refreshed. She loved having time to herself to savor what was happening to her.

The noise of the door opening brought her head around. Her mouth softened at the sight of Leah, dressed but barefoot. She straightened and waved a hand. Leah waved back and came directly over to join her. "*Boker tov*, Miriam."

"Good morning, Leah."

The girl dropped down on the opposite bench. "You're up early." She smiled. "Again."

"I love it," Miriam said enthusiastically. "I love this time of the day."

"As do I. I often go for walks down by the seashore."

"Really? Does your mother need help with breakfast? If not, I would love to go for a walk with you."

"No. Mother promised to help Father catch up on things at the warehouse. She's helping Father with the books. They've already eaten and gone. We're on our own for breakfast."

Miriam stood. "Then let's leave a note for the others. We can eat when we return."

Leah stood too. "No need. Phineas is just leaving too. I'll ask him to tell them." Phineas was her father's chief steward, and while they no longer had household staff, he often came to the house to confer with her father on matters. He had offered to clear away breakfast and insisted Deborah and David go on ahead.

She ran into the house and reappeared a moment later, now with sandals on her feet. Miriam moved to join her, and together they exited through the gate and into the street.

One of the things Miriam loved about Capernaum was how quickly you could be out of the city and at the water's edge. Even at its widest part, the city was not more than five or six streets from the sea.

They passed the main pier and started westward, where the beach was strewn with smooth, round rocks, but level and easily traversed.

Neither spoke. Leah was humming a tune that Miriam didn't know. It was lilting and joyous, and Miriam wondered if it was a song of the Galilee. She dropped back a step so she could watch Leah without her noticing. There was nearly three years difference between them—Leah would be sixteen in October; Miriam would be nineteen four months after that—but Leah seemed older than her age. Her features were those of a mature young woman. More to the point, she was mature in her outlook. She was wise and judicious, not at all giddy or frivolous as were so many of the girls her age that Miriam knew in Jerusalem. Her skin was quite fair even though her hair was dark, lustrous now in the rays of the sun coming from behind them. It occurred to Miriam then that Leah was a wonderful combination of both her parents. Already slightly taller than her mother, her countenance was also an inheritance from Deborah. By the time Leah was five or ten years older, Miriam guessed that she would look very much like Deborah. Yet in temperament and personality, she was mostly David. Gentle and patient, she would weigh her words carefully, speaking only after she had considered the feelings of others. She often acted as peacemaker when conversations got a little too heated.

And her faith. Miriam felt that most keenly. According to her father, Leah had accepted Jesus from the beginning and had been instrumental in bringing Ephraim, Rachel, and even her mother to that same point. Miriam had been impressed with Leah when she had met her briefly during her first visit here. Now, staying with the family for this time, she had come to feel the deepest affection and admiration for her.

Suddenly, Leah stopped humming and looked at her. "I'm so glad you're back."

"Me, too. But I loved the Golan Heights. I'm glad Ezra had to go up there."

"You should have seen it a couple of months ago. It is beautiful in the spring. The wildflowers make it look like a rainbow has fallen from the sky. The grass can reach up to the belly of a horse."

"Yes, we saw that, though it's all dry and brown now. Ezra was elated. The cattle are like fat old men and women, barely able to waddle around the hillsides. He says the leather is of excellent quality. Now he can honestly tell my father that this trip was very worthwhile for his sandal business."

"I'm glad."

"Last night your mother said that Anna thinks Jesus and the Twelve will be back today or tomorrow." It had been a disappointment to Miriam to return from Gaulanitis and find that Jesus was not in Capernaum.

"Yes. They only went up to Chorazin and some of the other small villages to the north of us. They'll be here today."

"Is his mother still with him?"

"No. Mary returned to Nazareth the same day you left."

"That is too bad. She is such a lovely woman."

They continued on. Miriam walked right along the water's edge, loving the soft rasping sound her sandals made on the wet rocks. "Oh, Leah. I love it here. I don't want to leave."

"So do I," Leah said happily. "This is my favorite place in the whole world."

The light in Leah's eyes was enchanting, and Miriam suddenly remembered a question that had come to her mind earlier. "Have you been promised to anyone, Leah?"

Leah's face was instantly pink. "Promised?"

"Yes, betrothed. You soon will be sixteen." She moved up beside her, poking her lightly in the shoulder. "You can't tell me there aren't a dozen suitors trying to arrange a match with your father, pretty as you are."

The pink turned to scarlet.

Miriam laughed lightly. "I'm sorry. It's none of my affair."

"Oh, no, it's just that—" She was completely flustered now. Her chin dropped and she was suddenly fiercely interested in her hands. "Yehuda once asked my father if he would consider Daniel as a suitable husband for me."

Miriam stopped abruptly. "Daniel!" she blurted. "Yehuda's brother?"

Leah nodded. "My parents declined, though. Papa thought I was too . . . " She hesitated. "Too tender for a man of Daniel's nature. I think Papa knew how hard it would have been for me to marry a Zealot warrior." Leah slowed her step, her countenance falling. "I wept when I learned of his death."

"I, too, wept," Miriam said, taking Leah's hand.

"Father would like me to marry an honest, hardworking man. But all he really cares about is that it is someone with whom I can be happy."

"Your father is a wise man, Leah."

"He has told me that who I marry must be my choice too. He is often criticized because I am not promised yet, but I am glad." She shrugged, her color deepening again. "So far I have found no one to my liking."

Miriam slipped an arm around her. "It would have been wonderful to keep it in the family."

Leah's head came around. "In the family? I do not understand."

"You and Daniel. Simeon and Shana."

Leah stopped dead, pulling away from Miriam's grasp. "But do you not know?"

"Know what?"

"The betrothal has been canceled."

Miriam's eyes registered her surprise.

"Yes," Leah went on sadly. "Because of Simeon, Daniel was killed and Yehuda was captured. That was too great a thing between them."

"I know, but that wasn't Simeon's fault. Simeon was trying to prevent a tragedy."

Leah looked at her strangely for a moment. "Of course, but Daniel is still dead. Can a woman be happy with the man responsible for her brother's death? Maybe even responsible for the death of two of her brothers, if Simeon is not successful in freeing Yehuda. Simeon took the bill of divorcement to Beth Neelah himself. He understands her feelings and wanted her to be free of any obligation."

Miriam didn't know what to say. She had been in Beth Neelah. She had seen the adoration in Shana's eyes whenever Simeon was near. "Perhaps if Simeon *is* successful on this trip, Shana will reconsider."

Leah shook her head slowly. "I suggested that to Simeon. All he would say is that he may bring Yehuda back from Caesarea, but he can never bring Daniel back from the grave."

Miriam started forward again. "I didn't know. I'm sorry. For both of them."

"It makes me want to weep each time I think of it. Shana and I were very close. She would have made a good wife for Simeon."

"Yes, I saw that."

They walked in silence. The surface of the sea was smooth like polished brass. The coolness of the morning was already diminishing as the sun rose higher above them.

"Miriam?"

"Yes?"

"What about you?"

"What about me?"

"You will soon be nineteen. Are you promised to anyone?"

Now it was Miriam who felt her face go hot. She should have expected to have the conversation turned on her, but she hadn't. "No, I—"

Leah gave her a dubious look. "No? That's all. Just no?"

Miriam couldn't help herself. She laughed softly at the persistence of this gentle peacemaker. "No, I'm not promised to anyone at this time."

Leah's nose wrinkled and her eyes were teasing as she quoted Miriam's previous words. "You can't tell me there aren't a dozen suitors trying to arrange a match with your father, pretty as you are."

"And as wealthy as my father is," Miriam added somberly.

"Yes, that too." Leah giggled again. "Especially that."

More serious now, Miriam decided to be honest. "Well, for one thing, in the circles in which my family lives, betrothal at the age of fifteen or sixteen is not as common as it would be up here in the Galilee or out in the countryside of Judea."

"Oh?"

"Yes, more typical would be about eighteen."

"You are eighteen."

"I know," she sighed, "but I am like you. If there was even one among the many who come calling who had even a pinch of promise, it wouldn't be so disheartening."

Leah sighed. "So we both have the same problem."

Miriam laughed at her morose countenance. "Let's make a pact, Leah. Let's both of us agree to marry only when we find the right man. And if the other men don't like it, then let them marry a camel."

Leah laughed aloud, the sound like a crystal bell in the morning air. She moved her hand, turning it into a firm handshake. "Done!" she cried.

Laughing together, they put their arms around each other's shoulders and continued slowly on. After a long silence, Leah looked at her. "I wish you weren't going to Rome."

"Oh, Leah, me too. I dread it. More than anything in the world."

"Then don't. You can stay with us. Moshe Ya'abin won't know you're here."

This time Miriam's sigh was filled with sorrow. "Father would never hear of it, and he's probably right. Ya'abin is a cunning and evil man.

He could track us down anywhere here. But it's more than that. If I go with him, then Father has agreed to consider the possibility of me adopting Livia as my sister."

"Yes, and that is wonderful. Livia is wonderful."

"She's the sister I never had," Miriam said. "And then, there's also her brother. There is a much better chance we can find him if we are actually in Rome."

Leah nodded gravely. "When you told us that her brother was still a slave somewhere, it made me sick. Mother and I were nearly taken as slaves once, and—"

"She told me," Miriam broke in. "That must have been horrible."

"More than you can imagine. If it were *my* brother that was lost, if Joseph was a slave in someone's household somewhere, I would do anything to find him again."

"That's why I'm willing to go to Rome."

To Miriam's surprise, Leah looked away. For a moment, Miriam thought she had broken out in tears and was touched by her emotion, but when she leaned forward, Miriam was taken aback to see not tears, but that Leah's face was flaming again. "What, Leah?"

She responded with a quick shake of her head.

"What is it? Tell me."

"I can't."

"Why? I thought we were friends."

"That's why I can't say it."

Miriam stopped and took her by the shoulders, turning Leah to face her. Even then, Leah wouldn't meet her eyes, her face almost glowing with her embarrassment.

"My goodness, Leah," Miriam said, thoroughly puzzled. "What is it?"

"I was hoping you could stay—" she bit her lip—"until Simeon gets back."

Miriam dropped her hands, stunned. "Simeon?"

"Yes." There was a shy, tentative smile. "I was hoping that you could be here at least for a few days together again before you leave and he leaves."

"I—" Then Miriam just blurted out. "What are you suggesting?"

Leah's head came up with a touch of defiance. "Well, he is no longer betrothed. And you're not promised to anyone."

Miriam had to turn away, feeling as if her own cheeks would burst into flame.

"Well?" Leah said, stepping up beside her.

"Well, what?" came the stammering reply.

"Are you too particular to even look at Simeon?"

Miriam turned to this young girl who seemed wiser than some grandmothers. She started to answer, took a quick breath, then still couldn't find the words. Finally, she just shook her head.

Leah nearly leaped into the air. "I knew it!"

"Don't you dare say a word to Simeon, Leah. I mean it. Don't you even think it."

"But you do find him interesting?"

She finally surrendered. "He is . . . " She smiled fully now. "Yes, he is interesting."

Leah was deeply pleased. "I knew it."

IV

A SHORT DISTANCE SOUTH OF CAESAREA

Simeon circled slowly, moving through the brush with the utmost care. In the darkness it was impossible to make any progress without making at least an occasional sound, but he was confident that the sound of the surf smothered any noise he was making. It struck him with a sorrowful irony that much of what he knew about being stealthy he had learned from Yehuda over the three and a half years they were comrades in arms. Simeon had once watched his friend—who was large enough to knock down a small tree—move to within thirty paces of a deer in the forest without its being aware of his presence. Well, perhaps now, he thought, the training Yehuda had given him would prove to be a blessing to them both.

Stopping every step or two, Simeon peered through the brush at the solitary figure standing beside his horse on the beach. Marcus Quadratus Didius was about a hundred paces away. The quarter moon was up now, and Simeon saw it glint dully from the brass breastplate and plumed helmet. The Roman tribune kept turning his head, searching the darkness, but he was not looking in Simeon's direction, and Simeon knew that so far he did not know where Simeon was. Simeon smiled grimly to himself. Yehuda would be proud.

Simeon had chosen this spot—about two miles south of the city—because not only was it totally deserted, but it also put Marcus out in the open where he could be seen from any direction. And was close enough to where the sand ended and the thickets of willow and myrtle began to provide Simeon with good shelter and a quick escape if needed. What Simeon was doing at the moment was making absolutely sure Marcus was not also making use of the undergrowth to hide anyone.

Simeon had debated long within himself whether to give Marcus a full twenty-four hours from the time he received the letter until they actually met. That much time allowed considerable preparation, more than enough to set a trap. On the other hand, if Simeon had asked Marcus to come immediately upon receiving his letter, he would have had to have chosen a place closer to the city. So he had purchased some bread and cheese and a flask of wine and had spent the day on a small hillock, making sure no one slipped in to back Marcus up. No one had appeared all day, and Simeon's confidence increased. Now he was making one final check to make sure no one was trying to slip in under cover of darkness.

Satisfied, he stepped out of the brush and moved swiftly across the sand to where the other man waited. At the sound of his footsteps, there was a soft whinny and the horse turned his head. The Roman turned too, clearly not alarmed.

"Convinced we're alone?" Marcus jeered.

Simeon merely nodded, stopping a few feet away from his adversary.

Marcus eyed him for several long moments, then shook his head sardonically. "That night in the Joknean Pass, I had about decided you were mad. Risking your life to save me and Sextus and the very powers you are sworn to destroy."

"Only a Roman would think it madness to honor one's oath."

He stiffened, then forced a contemptuous laugh. "Oh, I could name many more than that who feel that way." When Simeon didn't say anything to that, he leaned forward slightly. "There are some who would say this is your second act of madness. You know that, at this very moment, my men could be sealing off every road out of Caesarea."

"Yes, you could," Simeon shot right back, "and you know that at this very moment I could have a dozen men with bows drawn and arrows aimed at your heart. Maybe I'm not the only one who is mad here."

Marcus fought back a look of surprise. Without realizing it, Simeon had just given him the one piece of information Marcus was most concerned about. He was alone. He hadn't come with his band of Zealots. There was no one out there in the bush.

Marcus's mind was racing, considering the implications of what he had just learned. He had come here fully expecting that Simeon would have most, if not all, of his men with him. In fact, after reading Simeon's letter, Pilate had been convinced that this was Simeon's way of luring Marcus into a trap so that he would have an important hostage with which to negotiate. The governor strongly warned Marcus not to go, and when Marcus insisted on doing so, Pilate flatly declared that there would be no negotiating if his guess proved to be correct. Marcus had come because, based on what had happened that night of the aborted ambush, he trusted Simeon's integrity, foolish though it might be. And he came because his curiosity was piqued. Almost certainly Simeon was determined to free his friends from prison. But Simeon was no fool. The Jew had something he thought would be of such value to the Romans that they would consider a trade. So what was it? Was he willing to give them the name of their betrayer in exchange for the prisoners? That probably wouldn't be sufficient, but it would strongly tempt Pilate. Was he going to offer them money? Pilate had released more than one political prisoner for the right consideration. Marcus had gone over the possibilities many times throughout the day.

And yet, as he had ridden down the deserted path and onto the beach half an hour earlier, he had felt the hair on the back of his neck prickle. He could be wrong. Simeon was probably incensed that the Romans had taken his comrades prisoner after they had tried to save Marcus and his men. Maybe he really did want a hostage. As he had stood there in the faint moonlight, he had braced himself for the silent whir of an arrow, or the rush of men breaking out of hiding. Now he felt like throwing back his head and roaring with laughter. Simeon was alone. The man really was mad after all.

It was hard not to let the triumph show in his voice. "So what do you want?" Marcus demanded.

"I want Yehuda and my men."

"Surprise, surprise! I should have thought of that and brought them out to you."

"You know I wouldn't be here if there wasn't some benefit to you."

"To me personally, or to Rome?"

"I thought if you were truly Roman there was no difference."

Marcus grunted. For all his desire to smash this towering confidence—this insufferable arrogance!—he felt a grudging respect. This Jew not only was brave—perhaps to a fault—but he was shrewd, intelligent, a worthy foe.

"I have come to strike a bargain."

Marcus laughed shortly. "A bargain suggests a mutually agreeable arrangement between two parties. I know what you want—or better, *who* you want—but what could you possibly bring to the table that would interest us?" One hand came up quickly. "And please. Don't insult me by reminding me that you saved my life and by suggesting that now I am somehow in your debt. I harbor no such sense of duty."

Simeon wasn't fazed by that in any way. "I understand that there were two bars of gold that night that have never been recovered."

The Roman's eyes narrowed. Knowledge of that loss was a closely held secret. "So?" he finally managed.

"A talent of gold is a lot of money," Simeon mused.

Marcus couldn't help himself. "You found them?"

Simeon watched him steadily for a moment, then finally shook his head. "No."

"Then . . . ?"

"I shall be completely honest with you, Marcus Didius, so you know that I mean what I say. I have brought gold with me. They are not the same bars as those you lost, but they are of the same worth." He gave a quick shrug. "What does it matter where they come from?"

"You are putting up two talents of your own gold?" Marcus asked incredulously.

"Actually three. One per man."

This was staggering. An offer of money had been one of the possibilities Marcus had considered, but three talents! He removed his helmet and ran his fingertips through his hair. "So you're offering us a bribe?"

Simeon laughed softly, and Marcus was not sure why the Jew found his words amusing. "Surely a bribe would offend our noble governor's integrity," Simeon said with heavy irony. "I thought of it more as a ransom for hostages taken in battle."

Marcus's mind was racing. This would interest Pilate very much. One talent was a small fortune. A man who knew how to invest and use money wisely could live comfortably off one talent for many years. Three talents could turn the head even of a wealthy man, especially a man who was desperate for funds, as Pilate was. Technically, the gold belonged to the Syrian legate, but Marcus knew Pilate would feel little obligation to let his superior know about this.

Simeon waited, suspecting what was going on behind the shadowed eyes.

"Only three men?" Marcus finally asked. "We took many more captives than that."

"Only three were of my band," Simeon affirmed. "Yehuda, Barak, and Samuel. All from the village of Beth Neelah. The rest must be Ya'abin's men. If that thief wishes to strike his own bargain, let him come forward."

"I would like that," Marcus said tightly.

Simeon started to back away. "Take my offer to the governor. Let him mull it over for a day. Tomorrow night, exactly one hour after sunset, leave the Praetorium alone, as you did tonight. Go east this time. A messenger shall be waiting at the city gate to give you instructions on where we shall meet again."

He turned and started away, then turned back. "Pilate's reputation for treachery and extortion is well known among my people, Marcus Didius. I am offering more than a fair price. Encourage him not to underestimate us."

With that, he turned again and jogged away.

Marcus reached for the reins of his horse and swung up into the saddle. For a moment he was tempted to race after the receding figure, run him to ground. Simeon didn't have the gold with him—Marcus was sure of that—but an hour or two under the careful coaxing of a scourge—the multistrand whip with small pieces of bone or lead woven into the leather—would bring forth the information they wanted. But he didn't move. In the first place, Simeon was halfway back to the thicket and would be gone before Marcus could reach him. In the second place, Marcus wasn't absolutely sure Simeon would break under torture. It was likely, but not guaranteed. Three talents was a lot to lose. In the third place, there had to be something else. He surely had not come here totally alone with nothing but an offer of gold. If Marcus acted precipitously, he wasn't sure what that would trigger. In the fourth place . . .

He reached up and replaced his helmet. In the fourth place, though Marcus would never speak of it with this Jew, Simeon had pricked Marcus's sense of honor. This Jew understood the qualities of the Roman character—self-discipline, respect, honor, integrity. Those were what had made Rome what she was today, and they were deeply instilled in the heart of Marcus Quadratus Didius. It irritated him greatly to think that Simeon had made that sense of honor part of his calculations. It annoyed Marcus even more to know that he had done so correctly.

He watched the dark figure disappear, then clucked softly to his horse, turning back the way he had come. For now, at least, Marcus Didius would let this little drama play itself out. He would see where this would take them. He would see just what this Jew known as Simeon the Javelin was up to.

V

CAESAREA

"He dares to bargain with us like we were a harlot of the night?" Pilate slammed his fist down on the table, creating circular ripples in their wine cups. "That is my gold!"

Marcus said nothing. He knew this would be the initial reaction, and until Pilate vented his fury there would be no reasoning with him. He certainly wouldn't appreciate it if Marcus pointed out that it really wasn't the gold Pilate had lost.

"Why didn't you seize him while you had the chance?"

Marcus spoke evenly, calmly. "For one thing, he could have had a dozen men in the thicket in case I tried something." Marcus didn't feel he had to share his feelings about Simeon being alone. One didn't have to bare all of one's soul. "For another thing, we have no idea where the gold is. It seemed that we had nothing to lose by letting this play out for another night."

From his expression, one would have guessed that Pilate had heard none of that, but after almost a year of working with his governor, Marcus knew that Pilate was a master of masking what was going on behind those eyes. Finally, he straightened, took the cup, and drank deeply. He wiped his mouth with the back of his hand, then looked at his tribune. "Do you think he really has it?"

"Unquestionably," Marcus answered at once.

"Three talents!" There was naked covetousness in the man's eyes.

"That is his offer. Three talents, three men."

Pilate pulled at his lower lip, thoughtful now. The anger still smouldered, but it was no longer his driving emotion. "Did he say how the trade will be arranged?"

"No, but you can be sure that he will be very wary of a trap."

"He would be a fool if he weren't," Pilate snapped. "But let him be as careful as he pleases. The finest of snares are never visible to the prey until it is too late."

Marcus felt a ripple of uneasiness. "You're not going to deal with him, sire?"

"Oh, to the contrary," Pilate answered with obvious relish. "I am going to deal with the Javelin once and for all."

CHAPTER 11

I

EAST OF CAESAREA
9 JULY, A.D. 30

"Pilate accepts your bargain."

Simeon almost sagged with relief, but the reaction was short-lived.

Marcus looked away, afraid that Simeon might see the shame in his eyes. "But there is one additional condition."

"What condition?"

"That you give us the name of the person who betrayed our plan."

For a long moment there was no sound in the night silence. This second meeting was not on the beach, but on a small hillock east of the city. At the moment the air was still; there wasn't even the whisper of a breeze in the branches above their head.

In that stillness an image sprang into Simeon's mind. It was Miriam. She was being tied to a scourging post. Pilate stood behind her, raging at her for betraying him at the Joknean Pass. Simeon looked squarely at Marcus, anger deepening his voice. "I have come here at enormous risk. I have brought Pilate a huge fortune in order to save my friends, people that I value highly, from a horrible death. Does your governor really think I would give him someone else instead?" His laugh was sarcastic and cold. "I had heard that whatever else Pilate may be, he has a brilliant mind. So much for that piece of information."

"I told him that you wouldn't bargain on this," Marcus said calmly, "but he won't budge. He wants to know who sabotaged everything we had worked for."

Simeon said nothing. This was not a total surprise, but the bitterness was still like bile in his mouth.

Marcus went on, his voice uncompromising. "To be honest, I had to talk very persuasively to get Pilate to even accept this much. He wants you, Ha'keedohn. He wants you very badly. But I finally convinced him that you were not the one primarily responsible for our fiasco that night. It was the person who gave you the information."

"The answer is no. You will never learn who it was from me."

Marcus shrugged. "I am only the messenger. Those are Pilate's conditions."

"Oh, you are far more than a messenger, Marcus Didius," Simeon cried. "Do you think you can sidestep your honor by pretending to be a fawning servant? You are a trusted counselor with much influence. You know that and I know that."

Simeon shook his head, his eyes cold and hard. "When I told my father that I planned to negotiate with you instead of directly with Pilate, he said that was good. He said that you were a man of decency, a man on whose word one could depend." He made a sound of utter disgust. "So much for that piece of information."

Marcus flared instantly. "It is not my honor that is under question here tonight."

Simeon gave him an incredulous look. "If you believe that, then you have fallen farther than even you realize." He raised a hand, pointing a finger at the Roman. "You return to your noble governor," he said, his voice tight, "and you tell him this. What I am asking him to do is not unusual. Perhaps Pilate thinks that the arrangements he made in the past to free prisoners in exchange for money is a great secret, but it is not. It is common knowledge that Rome is a whore that can be bought by the highest bidder."

"Now listen—" Marcus said, fully angry now.

"No! You listen. One gold talent for each man—men who saved you from disaster!—is far more than Pilate deserves. If that is not good enough for him, then you give him this message: If he refuses to accept this offer, then I shall not simply return to the Galilee with my gold. I will go to Sepphoris. Gehazi, leader of the Zealots, is still bitter that he came away with so little that night. Three talents of gold will buy many arms and outfit many new warriors. Not only will Pilate's treasury be three talents poorer, but he will see a war of attrition launched against Rome that will cost him ten times that amount. Furthermore, a letter detailing Pilate's refusal to recover his lost gold will be sent to Vitellius so that the legate knows the real cause of the outbreak of further hostilities."

Marcus's chest rose and fell as he fought to control his breathing. "You dare to threaten the procurator?" But Simeon's words had sent a chill through Marcus. Three talents of gold would buy a lot of rebellion. And it was a rare Roman official who was comfortable with the idea of someone making full disclosure of his acts to his superiors.

Simeon just shook his head, the weariness almost more than he could bear. "I know that you and Pilate think you can get everything you want in this—the gold and the name of this person—but you are wrong. He has two options and two options only. He can walk away with three talents and have three fewer people to crucify at his precious Roman games, or he can face a rebellion that will bring down the wrath of the emperor upon his head. I swear that to you on my life, Marcus. So you go back and you counsel him, Counselor."

Marcus shrugged diffidently. "I will tell him what you have said. If you expect that it will send him running to his bedroom trembling with fear, you are a bigger fool than even I thought."

Simeon didn't answer that. "There is one more thing you need to tell him. I am told that in Roman culture, an honorable man will sometimes take his own life rather than face disgrace or dishonor."

Marcus was taken by surprise by that comment. "That is so," he admitted.

"Well, in our culture, taking one's own life is seen very differently. It is a terrible evil. We believe that life is a gift from God, and no man can throw it away without the gravest of eternal consequences."

"Yes." Marcus was aware of that, but he wasn't sure what had brought this turn in the conversation.

"I accept that as true," Simeon said softly, "but hear me well, Marcus Didius. I would take my own life before I revealed the name you seek and put that person or those persons into Pilate's bloody hands."

There was a long, low sigh from Marcus, who was feeling equally tired now. "I understand."

"No!" Simeon cried fiercely. "You *think* you understand, but you don't. It matters not what Pilate offers me or threatens to do to me, that information will never pass through my lips. Make him understand that. He thinks he can have it all, but he already has my best offer. There is nothing else on the bargaining table."

He reached inside his tunic and withdrew a small folded parchment. "He has until midnight to decide. Here are my instructions on where to meet again if he accepts."

Marcus was shocked. He had expected that Simeon would try to bring things to a conclusion tonight, but midnight was less than three hours away.

"You will bring Yehuda, Barak, and Samuel to the place indicated herein by midnight, or the offer is withdrawn."

"But it is midway through the first watch already. There is not enough time to return to the palace, persuade Pilate, and return with the prisoners to wherever it is you want us to be."

"You have time enough if you ride hard," Simeon said, his voice like a stone. "But there will be no time to waste, no time to put together a plan to ensnare me. If you are not there by midnight, or if my instructions are not followed precisely, you will not see me again. Not until we meet over crossed swords somewhere in the Galilee."

"Then your friends will die," Marcus shot back, angry at the stubbornness of the man. "Pilate is already raging. You threaten him and he may decide to have them executed this very night."

"If so, it will be only the beginning of a new day of conflict, Marcus Didius," came the quiet reply. "If you have any shred of honor left within you, go back and convince Pilate of that."

Before Marcus could answer, Simeon spun around and disappeared into the darkness.

II

ON THE MEDITERRANEAN COAST, NORTH OF CAESAREA
10 JULY, A.D. 30

When King Herod the Great decided to create a new port on the eastern shores of the Great Sea, he chose a spot where there was a reliable source of water. What he hadn't counted on was the growth that his man-made harbor would generate, or that the Romans would eventually make Caesarea the capital city of Judea. That spawned even more growth, and soon Caesarea needed additional sources of water, especially during some of the great festivals, when large numbers of people came to the city.

The most abundant source of water along the eastern coast of the Great Sea was Mount Carmel, about twenty miles north of Caesarea. Rising fifteen hundred feet above the level of the sea, the mountain, whose name means "a garden place," received considerable rain and drew down heavy dew from the moist sea air as well. The area had numerous springs of clear, unpolluted water. Over the years, many had talked about bringing water from Carmel to Caesarea, but Pontius Pilate had done more than talk. He set about creating an aqueduct to carry the water from the mountain. It moved south along the coast from Carmel in an almost straight line, the water channel itself gradually dropping in elevation to keep the water flowing by gravity. Where the ground rose, the aqueduct became a ditch. Where the ground fell away, the channel was lifted up and carried by a series of graceful stone arches after the Roman style.

Things had moved swiftly at first, but as the aqueduct approached Caesarea the engineering challenges increased dramatically. There was a long stretch along the coastal plains where the elevation was lower than Caesarea itself. For a stretch of several miles the stone arches had to be fifteen and twenty feet above the level of the ground so as to take the water into the city. It was not a difficult task—Roman engineers had surmounted far more challenging topography in other provinces— but it was costly and slow. After several years, the massive project was still a mile and a half from reaching the northern walls of the city. The south end of the aqueduct ended abruptly in bamboo scaffolding. In the sand surrounding the scaffolding, there were no fresh footprints. The project had come to a halt awaiting further funds.

Simeon had moved to the top of that aqueduct, and stretched out in the empty water channel directly above the fifteenth archway north of where the aqueduct ended. The channel was about a cubit deep, just enough to hide a man from view. He had carefully chosen this place for the final meeting with that important fact in mind. He could see anyone coming from any direction without being seen himself.

He lifted his head and peered over the edge of the aqueduct at the moonlit sand fifteen feet below him. To Simeon's left, on the east side of the aqueduct, the sand was smooth and unbroken for two or three hundred feet before the vegetation finally began to take hold. On the opposite side was the sea. The high-tide mark was no more than fifteen or twenty paces away from the stone structure that stretched away into the darkness. In the moonlight, the surf rolled toward him in long strips of rippling white. Satisfied that he was still alone, Simeon turned over on his back and closed his eyes.

O ye of little faith, wherefore do you doubt? He sighed. Those words had become like a litany to him these past few days, but now they did nothing but add to his pain. If anything, they only sharpened the doubt he so desperately kept trying to push aside. Ten days ago, as he had come out of the waters of the Sea of Galilee, a great peace had enveloped him. That peace had stayed with him through his travels to Tiberias, Damascus, and Ptolemais to get the gold. It had been with him as he waited outside the gates of the Praetorium to deliver that first letter to Marcus. It had even been with him tonight as he waited for Pilate's answer.

Now it was gone. Simeon had never felt such raging turmoil before. Question after question marched through his mind, each one stirring up more turbulence within. Was Marcus even now moving in troops to encircle him? Was Marcus right? Would Pilate only sniff in contempt at Simeon's threats? Had Simeon ransomed off a substantial part of his family's wealth only to see the money taken with no return?

But those were not the most troubling questions that tore at him. Why had he had such strong feelings of confirmation that he had finally found the answer to his dilemma? He had been *so* sure. Yes, it did seem to be sheer madness to come here totally on his own, with no backup, no one to pull him out if something went wrong—but it had felt right! Even after many hours on his knees. *It had felt right!* Now, all hope had gone out of him. Despair was like the point of a spear pressing in against his chest.

No! He was suddenly fierce in his self-rebuke. He couldn't lose hope now. *O ye of little faith, wherefore do you doubt?* He had to trust those feelings. He was trying to do the right thing. He had to believe that God would bless him in that. Wasn't that the essence of faith? That you trusted even when all seemed hopeless?

Wherefore do you doubt?

He raised up and looked toward the water. It took a moment before his eyes found the dark shape anchored just five or six paces out into the surf. When he had told his mother that he wasn't just trusting blindly in God, he meant it. He had planned carefully for any possible treachery on the part of the Romans. The boat he had anchored there an hour before was big enough for four men. It had a sail and two stout oars. Let Marcus close off every road, every path. Who could patrol the sea?

He sighed again and looked upward. He calculated the distance between the quarter moon and the dark shape of the foothills to his east. The moon was noticeably higher than the last time he had looked. Simeon had no way of knowing the time precisely, but his inner sense, which had always served him well, told him that it was very near the midnight hour, if not already past it. And still nothing. This was not good.

Unbidden, the memory of Peter's face rose in Simeon's mind. He was standing on the surface of an undulating sea. The fisherman's eyes were wide with terror as he suddenly began to sink beneath the waves. Now Simeon understood more clearly what Peter had felt that night.

He closed his eyes again. "Master," he whispered, "Master, I perish! Save me!"

III

As Tribune Marcus Quadratus Didius passed the last of the undergrowth lining the road, he slowed his horse to a walk. The other six horsemen behind him did the same. He stood up in the stirrups, searching the expanse of sand before him. There were no figures standing within view, and his eyes moved to the dark shape of the aqueduct. Once again he felt a little shiver. What if he had been wrong after all? What if Simeon did have a dozen or two dozen men waiting beneath those arches?

He reined his horse to the left, heading directly for the place where the aqueduct abruptly ended. This was where Simeon's instructions had said to meet him. As he approached the end of the great stone mass, he stopped again, holding up his hand to stop the others as well. Marcus could see the geometric web of bamboo scaffolding left by the workers. "Wait here," he said. "And stay alert." As he moved forward again, he didn't turn to see if his command was obeyed. He knew he had said it as much for his benefit as for theirs.

He was about thirty feet east of the aqueduct, moving north, parallel with the stonework. Over the soft sound of the surf, he could hear the heavy breathing of his horse. They had run hard to get here in time. His mount's neck was wet, and there were flecks of foam at its mouth. Marcus let the mare take her own pace in the soft sand, every nerve attuned to the night around him. He began to count beneath his breath as he passed each arch. The letter told him to go to the fifth arch from the south end of the aqueduct, then stop and wait.

As he moved past the fourth arch, a voice rang out in the night. "That's close enough."

Marcus reined up, his eyes lifting in the direction of the voice. It was from above him, which meant Simeon was in the water channel.

Wise. Not only did it hide him from any view from below, but it also diffused his voice so it was hard to pinpoint exactly where he was.

"I told you that you were to bring no one but the prisoners," the voice said accusingly.

"I brought one guard for each prisoner," Marcus answered calmly. "I am certainly not fool enough to bring three known rebels out here by myself."

There was a moment of silence, then, "Tell your men to dismount and move away from their horses. Get the prisoners down too."

Marcus turned in his saddle. "Help the prisoners down," he called. "Then stand clear of the horses." He swung down himself, gave his horse a reassuring pat, then moved forward toward the voice.

"I said that's close enough."

He stopped, watching as the three legionnaires who had accompanied him lifted the prisoners down. Chains clanked softly in the darkness.

"Yehuda! Is that you?"

There was a muffled sound from behind Marcus. "The prisoners are gagged and bound," Marcus said. "I brought torches. May I have your permission to strike a flint? Then you can see for yourself who they are."

Again several seconds went by before the answer came. "You may light one torch."

Marcus waved a hand. His men were close enough to hear whatever Simeon was saying, and he spoke in Latin so they would understand him. The soldier nearest to Marcus began fumbling in the pouch at his belt. In a moment there was the sound of stone striking steel, and a spark flashed. Twice more, then the torch, soaked in a mixture of pitch and camphor, caught. In an instant the flames engulfed it, and the flickering light lit up the beach and threw the aqueduct into sharp relief. Marcus quickly turned his head away, not wanting to lose his night vision. "Show him the prisoners," he barked.

The three men in chains were already standing close together. The legionnaire with the torch moved to them and lifted it high.

Yehuda lifted his chin and turned his face so it was pointing in the direction from which the voice had come. He didn't need to ask who it was. The Romans had told them nothing, just awakened them with a kick and dragged them from their cells. For a time, he had assumed that they were being taken out to be executed. Only as they continued onward did he dare to hope that something much more acceptable might be happening. Simeon had come at last.

"Remove their gags," Simeon commanded.

Marcus shook his head. "Not until I see the gold."

"You have my word that it is within fifty paces of where you stand."

Marcus hooted in derision. "And you have my word that your friends can still talk and have not been harmed. Now let's stop playing children's games."

"Remove at least Yehuda's gag," came the answer. "I need to know that they are all right."

Marcus fought the desire to jerk his head up. The voice was noticeably closer. Simeon was moving in on him. He tensed, picturing Simeon with a bow in hand and an arrow trained directly at Marcus's chest. He fought back the fear and called out. "Take the gag off the big one."

There was a quick movement; then a deep voice boomed out. "Simeon, you old dog. Is that you?"

"It is," came the happy cry. "Are you all right?"

"We've picked up a few fleas since we last saw you, but other than that, we're fine."

Marcus swung around. "All right, now where is the gold?"

"Light a second torch," Simeon commanded, almost directly above Marcus now. "Have one of your men hold it close to the prisoners so I can watch them while you work. You may take the first torch with you to where the gold is hidden."

A simple nod from Marcus, and a second torch was produced and lit. The man ran it quickly to his commander, then trotted back with the others. Marcus held it high, looking up, but there was still nothing to be seen.

"Marcus Didius." The voice had changed position yet again. It was to his left now, so he could watch Marcus's back as he moved forward. "Do I have your word of honor as a Roman officer that you will release my men when you see that I have delivered the gold as promised?"

Marcus flinched slightly.

There was the scrape of sandal on stone above him. "Well?"

For a moment, Marcus stared at the ground; then, finally, he nodded. "You have my word. When I actually see the gold, I shall release the prisoners."

"Your word of honor?"

"Come on, Simeon!" he snarled. "You heard me."

There was a long moment of silence, and Marcus found himself holding his breath. Then, "Did you bring a shovel as instructed?"

Marcus retrieved a short-handled wooden spade from the back of his belt and held it up, relief flooding over him. Simeon had bought it.

"You are standing beside arch number four. Move north three more arches. Start digging directly beneath the center of the arch. You will have to go down about a cubit and a half."

Marcus almost laughed out loud. The gold had been this close all that time. He had feared that Simeon would lead them into the mountains or some other isolated spot. Turning his head, he called out to his men once more. "Stay with the prisoners," he said.

Beneath the seventh arch Marcus stuck the torch in the sand and began to dig. The sand was firm but easily cut through. A minute later there was a solid clunk as wood struck something hard. He felt a burst of exultation. Grabbing the torch, he knelt down beside the hole. Scooping out the sand with one hand, in a moment he had uncovered a white cloth wrapped around something square and hard. In one quick movement he had his dagger out and slashed open the cloth.

He sat back on his heels. It was there, just as promised. Three bars of gold glowed like an amber lamp from within the hole. He heard a gasp, then realized it came from his own mouth. It was hard not to take in breath at the sight of this kind of wealth.

"Satisfied?" the voice said, directly above him now. Marcus jumped to his feet, grabbed the torch, and moved out from under the arch. He could still not see where Simeon was.

"Release my men," Simeon demanded.

Marcus turned. "You heard him," he shouted. "Release the prisoners, then step back to your horses." A crouching shadow flitted past the corner of his eye. He fought the temptation to look up, keeping his eye fixed on his men. The other two gags were removed, the chains unlocked and allowed to fall to the ground. As soon as that was done, the three soldiers moved back to stand beside their horses.

"Yehuda," Simeon called. "There are bows and swords just behind the first arch." As Yehuda, Barak, and Samuel started to move, Simeon stepped into view directly above Marcus. "Tribune, I'll ask you to wait by your horses until we are gone; then you can have your gold."

Marcus answered with a derisive bark. "I don't think so," he shot back. Then he cupped his hands. "To your bows!" He leaped backward, darting beneath the arch again to where Simeon could no longer see him.

Yehuda, Barak, and Samuel whirled. The three men at the horses had obviously anticipated this command, for they now had bows out and drawn. Metal tipped shafts gleamed in the torchlight. They were pointed directly at the three prisoners who had been in bonds just moments before. The three Zealots froze, shocked into immobility.

"Tell your men to hold, Simeon, or they die."

To his credit, Simeon did not drop back down to hide in the water channel. He stood in astonishment, staring at the bowmen. "So this is how you honor your word?" he cried.

"You need to be more careful what you ask for," Marcus sneered. "I told you I would release them, which I have done. Now come down before your men die."

"You think honor is a game of words?"

"Listen to me, Simeon!" Marcus hissed. "Pilate himself gave these men their instructions. It will not make any difference what I say to them. If you or your friends make a move, these soldiers are instructed to kill all of you."

"Better the swiftness of the shaft than the horror of the cross." It was a hoarse cry, the pain so twisted his voice.

"Your choice," Marcus said softly, "but make it before I count to five, or we'll make it for you."

Simeon glanced over his shoulder toward the water, knowing that he could jump down to the soft sand below, keeping the aqueduct between him and the Romans, race to where the boat was anchored, and live to fight another day. Just as quickly, he knew that it would end the lives of the three he had come to save.

He turned back, withdrew the sword from his scabbard, and tossed it down. He stepped to the edge of the stonework and dropped to the sand below. When Simeon straightened, Marcus had Simeon's own sword in his hand. In an instant it was at his throat. He saw that his men had the three prisoners again and gave Simeon a shove. "Move."

Simeon didn't stir. "You and I carry scars from that day you came to our home, Marcus Didius," he said, his voice low. "I on my chest, you on your arm. That was a day of shame for you. I could see it in your eyes. But what you have done this night will leave a scar on your heart that will live with you forever."

"I had no choice," Marcus answered, clearly stung. "You were a simpleton not to see that. Now move, or die."

IV
CAESAREA

"Yehuda?"

Simeon listened intently in the silence of the dungeon, hearing nothing but the occasional drip of water from the far corner—the corner nearest to the sea, if his sense of direction had not failed him.

"Yehuda!" He whispered louder this time, more insistent.

From the cell next to him, he heard something stir.

"Yehuda! Can you hear me?" He cocked his head in the direction of the stairs. When he had tried this about two hours before, it had immediately brought down one of the guards, who kicked at him savagely. His side still hurt every time he moved, and he wondered if the man's boot had cracked a rib. But all above them had been quiet now for over an hour. He hoped the guard was asleep.

More stirrings, and then he heard the soft clinking of the chains. Their cells—no more than narrow rectangles open on one end—each had thick iron rings embedded about waist high in the rear wall. The manacles attached to his wrists were heavy and thick. Whatever blacksmith had been hired to forge the bonds had done his work well. The metal edges had already rubbed skin away, and both of Simeon's wrists were on fire. The chains were long enough to allow only enough movement for him to reach the small bucket in the corner or to shift positions slightly when he was laying on the cold floor.

Holding his arms up so as to minimize any rattle of the chains, he edged as close to the front of his cell as possible. "Yehuda?"

"I hear you."

"Are you all right?"

"Actually, I seem to have two heads at the moment, both of them pounding rather fiendishly in perfect harmony."

As they had reached the main gate of the Praetorium, Marcus Didius had dismounted to help the two guards on duty open the gate. The moment he was off his horse, Yehuda had lunged for the soldier next to him. Though his hands were manacled he had managed to grab the man's throat, and they crashed to the ground. Unfortunately, Yehuda had been on the bottom, and his head hit hard against the paving stones. That abruptly ended whatever wild scheme he had in his mind. "That was a foolish thing you did out there."

"You're talking to *me* about being foolish?" Yehuda asked incredulously.

Simeon shifted his weight slightly, wincing as the iron bracelets cut into his wrists again. He moved back a little to give himself more slack. "I thought I had it worked out so carefully."

"You thought that the tribune would keep his word, didn't you."

Simeon didn't answer. There was nothing to say.

"What's happened to you, Simeon?"

"What's that supposed to mean?"

"The Ha'keedohn I once knew would have had that Roman trussed up on the ground like a chicken waiting for slaughter, not depending on his word—" there was a mimicking tone—"as a Roman officer."

"I didn't trust him," Simeon began. "I—" But then he stopped. What did it matter now?

"What has this Jesus done to you?"

Simeon closed his eyes and laid his head down on his arms. That was a question echoing in his own mind at the moment.

When he didn't answer, Yehuda's voice grew sharper. "And you're still convinced that he is the Messiah?"

"More than that, Yehuda. Much more than that."

"What is that supposed to mean?"

There was a sound from off to their left, and both men froze for a moment. Another chain clanked, and they realized it was one of the other prisoners farther down the line. Simeon relaxed again.

"How are Shana and Daniel?" Yehuda asked after a while.

Simeon's breath drew in sharply, and a cold more penetrating than the stones beneath the thin layer of straw seeped into his body. "Have you had no word at all since your arrest?"

"What?" he scoffed. "Do you think they bring us mail with our daily ration of moldy bread and filthy water?"

Simeon took in a deep breath. "Daniel's dead, Yehuda."

There was the scrape of metal on stone, and a soft grunt of pain, as if he had been struck.

Simeon began to talk, his voice strained with emotion. He described that night—how, as he charged down the hill, he suddenly realized that Daniel was no longer by his side, how he had found Daniel with the arrow in his stomach, how he had carried him on his back for what seemed like an eternity, and finally how he and his father had buried Daniel somewhere in the forest.

When he stopped it was silent for a long time; then, finally, Yehuda's voice rumbled in the darkness. "Ah, Daniel, Daniel." Then, after another long silence, "And Shana?"

Simeon paused for a moment. "I released her from our betrothal."

There was a deep sigh. "I'm sorry."

"No, *I'm* sorry," he cried. "I asked for your help in a cause that was not yours, to do something that you did not believe in. She is right to hold me responsible."

Yehuda didn't answer. Three or four minutes went by and Simeon pictured his silent grieving for his younger brother. Then finally, "I knew you would come." There was a bitter chuckle, tinged with irony. "I wasn't sure how you would do it. I couldn't imagine that you would be so stupid as to actually try something like this. But I knew you would try something."

Simeon pulled a face. How he loved this old friend with whom he had shared so much. "So you were sure it would be stupid?"

"I was."

"This was my *best* idea," Simeon said sardonically. "You should have heard my other plan."

Another sigh. "But thank you. At least that much hasn't changed."

"I had to try. I am so sorry, Yehuda. For everything. For Daniel especially."

"Well, we always said that if we were going to go, we'd like to go together."

"Have they told you they're holding you—holding us—for some Roman games in the fall?"

"Yes, they did tell us that much. You've got to love these Romans. String out the anticipation and horror for as long as possible."

There was another long pause; then, much more subdued, Yehuda spoke again. "You know what they want, don't you?"

Simeon's head lifted. "Yes." He hesitated. "Did they—?"

"Oh, they threatened me a couple of times. They took me to the room where they have all their little devices—a rack, a scourging post—but I guess I convinced the tribune I knew nothing before it got out of hand. It wasn't anything I couldn't handle." He didn't mention the stripes on his back.

The silence stretched on for another minute. "It's time to worry about yourself, Simeon. I convinced Marcus that I didn't know anything, but they know that *you* know. There will be no mercy for you."

Simeon shrugged in the darkness.

"It won't be pretty, Simeon."

"I *won't* tell. I can't. There's too much at stake."

"You may not have a choice."

"There is always a choice," Simeon answered softly.

Finally, after a long time, Yehuda spoke again. "I'm sorry about

Shana, Simeon. I really am. I wish we could get word to her somehow. Knowing what you did last night would make a difference to her."

"I think it's a little late for that," Simeon responded. He uttered a short, bitter laugh. He lifted his arms and rattled the chains a little. "Actually, I'm pretty sure it's a little late for much of anything now."

He pushed back into the cell and sat up against the cold stones. If his despair earlier in the night had been sharp as a spear point, now it completely engulfed him, like a desert sandstorm sweeping in upon him, choking him in smothering darkness.

Simeon knew that by nature he was brash, impetuous, and often overly bold. There had been times when that brashness had nearly brought disaster. But this time he had been so careful. He had not rushed off to action. His motives were profoundly different. He had prayed and pondered and searched. He had never felt so confident before that he had chosen the right path.

That confidence was utterly shaken now. Would he ever be able to trust his own judgment again? Three talents of gold and what had it bought? A cell and a cross for himself. Absolutely nothing for Yehuda, Barak, and Samuel. The gravest danger for Miriam and Livia.

For all his brave words to the contrary, Simeon knew that Yehuda was right. The Romans were capable of breaking any man, no matter how fierce the determination to resist. There would be no opportunity to take his life to protect his secret, as he had so foolishly boasted to Marcus. The tribune had given the strictest instructions to the guards that he be given nothing he could use to hurt himself. Not only had he failed in every way for himself and his comrades, but now Miriam was also at terrible risk.

He folded his arms on his knees and laid his head down on them. "O God, what did I do wrong? I wanted to do thy will. I was so sure that all of this was from thee. Is this what my faith has wrought?"

The only answer was the soft drip, drip, drip of water in the far corner of the dungeon.

CHAPTER 12

HOWBEIT THIS KIND GOETH NOT OUT BUT BY PRAYER AND FASTING.

—*Matthew 17:21*

I

OUTSIDE CAPERNAUM
10 JULY, A.D. 30

They were seated on the ground in a tight circle, eating the simple meal that Deborah and Rachel had prepared for them. At the moment, the family of David ben Joseph and their guests from Joppa and Jerusalem were eating. Jesus had stopped his teaching about half an hour before, when Peter and others of the Twelve brought some food for him. When it became obvious there would be a break for a time, those wise enough to bring food with them had also sat down to partake. Others had started quickly for Capernaum, no more than half a mile away, to eat at home or purchase what they could if they were from another village. Now the crowd was mostly back, and they expected Jesus to start again soon.

The family talked quietly about the events of the day. There had been nothing spectacular, not in terms of miracles or other remarkable events, but Miriam, Livia, Lilly, and Ezra were completely satisfied. Jesus had stayed close around Capernaum for several days, and they had been able to hear him every day. Miriam especially was grateful for that. This was their next to last day here. The day after tomorrow they had to leave for Caesarea if they were to meet her father in time to embark for Rome. No one talked about that now. It brought too much pain to all of them.

Suddenly young Joseph tugged on his mother's sleeve. "Mama, look. It's Uncle Aaron."

Startled, Deborah turned around and raised up to her knees. They were in a large meadow, used as winter pasture for a small herd of cattle and sheep. During the summer, as it was now, the animals went to the hills to feast on the high grasses there. Empty now, the pasture made a good assembly point for a large crowd. It was from the south end of the field, next to the main road between Capernaum and Tiberias, that a tight knot of men was approaching. They were led by Amram, the chief of the Pharisees in Capernaum. But alongside him was Deborah's younger brother.

For a moment Deborah thought they might be coming to hear Jesus, but they passed by, shooting glaring looks and uttering imprecations as they went.

"I don't think they liked Jesus calling them hypocrites the other day," Ezra said with a smile.

Two days before, while Jesus was teaching the multitudes, this same group of Pharisees had accosted Jesus about eating his food without going through the proper ritual purification. With his usual practicality, Jesus told them that it was not what went into the mouth of a man that defiled him, but what came out. Then Jesus had turned the tables on them. He called them hypocrites for worrying about such things while they neglected more important parts of the law, such as caring for one's aged parents or watching out for the widows and orphans that dwelt among them. Greatly offended, they had stomped off and not been back since.

Livia responded to Ezra's comment. "Did you know that *hypocrite* comes from a Greek word? It has a very interesting derivation. Do you know of it?"

David answered. "I know it means a person who pretends to be something he or she isn't."

"Yes," Livia said, "but originally, a *hypocrite* was an actor. In the ancient Greek dramas, actors would hold up masks before their faces so that their real identity was hidden. Isn't that the perfect description of people like Amram?" she asked. "They want people to think they are one kind of person, but it's really only a mask."

David was intrigued. "And when Jesus tears the mask away for all to see, they are furious with him."

Deborah barely heard the interchange. She was still watching Aaron. He turned one last time, obviously looking to see if his sister was among the crowd. She didn't think he had seen her. She sighed and looked at David. "So my brother is still here in Capernaum."

David nodded. "I wonder how Hava feels about that." He turned to the others. "Hava is Aaron's wife. They have three little children, and Aaron has been here for two weeks at least."

"Well," Leah said, tartly, which was very much unlike her, "I think it's terrible that he won't come and see us anymore just because we were baptized."

Deborah just sighed. She felt a touch on the shoulder and turned. It was Miriam. "Your brother. My father. No wonder Jesus said that sometimes our foes would be those of our own households."

"Yes. It becomes one of the hardest choices, doesn't it."

Miriam moved over closer to this woman whom she was coming to love and respect so deeply. "Papa says we may be in Rome as long as a year. I hope not. I hope they'll catch Ya'abin sooner than that. But however long it takes, when we return, I'm coming back here to listen to Jesus. And this time, it won't be in secret. If my father doesn't like that, well then . . . " She shrugged.

"If your father doesn't like that," Deborah said firmly, "then you will just come and live with us. You and Livia both."

"We would like that," Miriam said, touched by her offer. "I already feel like we are part of your family." Then she blushed slightly as she saw the look Leah was giving her and remembered their earlier conversation on the seashore.

"It has been a wonderful time for us," David said, "to have the four of you here. All of you are welcome in our home at any time."

Lilly started to answer, then broke off at the sound of a cry from behind them. They all turned to look. A small group of people were pressing their way through the seated crowd, calling out for everyone to make way. An older man was in the lead. He had a husky young man in tow, a boy that looked to be fifteen or sixteen years old.

Miriam looked more closely at the boy, struck by several oddities. She saw that he was very distraught. His hair was disheveled and his clothes were covered with dust. There were dark smudges on his face. She couldn't tell if they were dirt or bruises. The boy's eyes were wide and vacant, with deep, dark circles beneath them. He seemed unaware of those around him as his father—Miriam assumed it was his father—led him forward. He stared off to one side, keeping his eyes above the heads in the crowd.

"Master!" The man in the lead cried out. "Master, help me."

Every eye turned to Jesus. He set aside the bread he was eating and stood up. He started forward, coming directly toward where Miriam and the others were seated, which was the closest path to the approaching group. David stood and motioned for the others to follow his lead. They needed to make room so there would be a place for Jesus and the man to meet.

"Master, I beseech thee," the man cried, letting go of the boy's hand and running forward. "Look upon my son, for he is my only child."

Jesus glanced at the boy, who shuffled to a stop when his father let him go. "What is it?" Jesus asked.

The man dropped to his knees at Jesus feet, clutching the bottom of his robes. "Lord, have mercy on my son. He is lunatic and sore vexed."

Miriam turned quickly to look at the boy again. The man had used a word whose general meaning was "demented" but which literally meant "moonstruck." She felt a shudder run through her body. Though many physicians weren't willing to confirm the connection, it was common folklore that severe seizures were caused by the influence of the moon.

"Master," the father cried, almost wailing in his anguish now, "the boy has a dumb spirit. Usually he is speechless. But then suddenly the spirit will take him, and he will cry out. It throws him about, sometimes into the fire, other times into the water. He foams at the mouth and gnashes his teeth terribly. The spirit tears at him and hardly leaves him alone."

Peter, John, and others of the Twelve had stood and followed Jesus and now nearly surrounded the two figures. The man glanced at them; then his eyes dropped. "I brought him to thy disciples, Master, but they could not cure him."

For a long moment, Jesus didn't move; then finally he turned as well. No one man had been named. His eyes swept across all of them, and Miriam saw the disappointment there. Each of them stared uncomfortably at the ground.

"O faithless and perverse generation," Jesus said sorrowfully, "how long shall I be with you? How long shall I suffer you?"

He swung back to the father and lifted him up from his knees. "Bring the boy here to me," he said gently.

A look of joy sprang into the man's eyes. He turned and quickly went to his son. However, as he took the boy's hand and started with him back toward Jesus, the boy suddenly stiffened. His eyes rolled up into his head, and his body began to jerk convulsively.

"No!" the father cried, grasping his son by the shoulders. Miriam saw his fingers whiten as he tried to hold the boy steady, but the power unleashed in the young body was far too violent, too explosive. The boy yanked free. An agonizing scream was torn from his throat as he fell to the ground, his body seized by terrible, violent tremors. He clutched at his chest. Then the hands, like claws, tore at his stomach. As the head rolled back and forth, covering the cheeks with dust, Miriam gasped in horror. White bubbles were coming from his mouth as his jaw clenched and unclenched furiously. All around them people shrank back, as though a wild beast had suddenly been loosed in their midst.

Jesus moved forward to stand beside the father, who stood horrified and helpless, watching his son torn by the terrible force within him. Jesus seemed neither surprised nor dismayed at what was happening. He laid a hand on the father's shoulder. "How long has this trouble been upon him?"

The father half turned, and Miriam saw tears in his eyes. "Since he was a little child." He shook his head, fighting for composure. "The spirit seeks to destroy him. O Lord! have compassion on us. Help us!"

Jesus moved slightly, until he looked directly into the man's face. The father had started to turn back to his son, but he stopped as Jesus' eyes locked with his. "If you can believe," Jesus said softly, "all things are possible to him that believeth."

The man seemed not to comprehend; then suddenly his mouth twisted. The tears spilled over. "Lord, I believe!" Then his face crumpled. "Help thou my unbelief!"

Jesus nodded, gripping the man's shoulder briefly. Then he stepped past him so that he stood directly over the boy. All around, people craned their necks or leaned forward to see what he would do. On the ground, the boy still twitched and moaned, rolling back and forth in the dust.

"Thou dumb and deaf spirit!"

Miriam jumped as did those around her. Jesus had cried out with a commanding voice that cracked like thunder.

"I charge thee to come out of this boy and enter no more into him."

The boy's body stiffened as though he had been stabbed. He screamed out in terrible pain, his fingers tearing at the ground. Then as suddenly as the attack had come, it was gone. There was a great shudder, an explosion of breath, and the body collapsed. One last shudder rippled through the prostrate form; then he was still.

No one moved. Every eye gaped at the two motionless figures—one lying on the ground, the other standing above him, looking down calmly upon him. The father stared at his son, his face white with shock. Miriam realized she, too, was suddenly having trouble breathing.

"He's dead!" a man's voice cried out.

"O mercy!" a woman exclaimed, "the evil spirit has taken his life. Look! He's dead! He's dead!"

That broke the silence of the crowd. Others took up the cry, and it leaped from mouth to mouth.

The father stepped forward. Stricken, he looked at Jesus. "Master?" It was like the cry of a young child, pleading for help, pleading for comprehension.

Jesus turned his head. To Miriam's utter surprise, he smiled as he reached out and laid a hand on the father's shoulder. Then, totally ignoring the tempest of voices, he leaned over and took the boy's hand.

Miriam gasped. The eyelids fluttered; then, after a moment, they opened. The head lifted, turning as the boy looked around. The dark eyes were no longer vacant and tormented but clear and bright and alert. A sob tore from the father's throat as Jesus pulled the boy up to a sitting position. The Master leaned over and whispered something in the boy's ear. He responded with a nod and a soft laugh; then Jesus helped him to his feet and gave him a gentle nudge toward his father. With a cry of joy unlike anything Miriam had ever heard before, father and son fell into each other's arms.

Miriam's throat constricted, and something inside her breast twisted sharply. Then, realizing what it was, she gave way and began to weep with joy.

II

They were walking slowly, moving eastward toward Capernaum. There were only about thirty or forty of them left. The multitudes had dispersed, many to noise abroad the fantastic news of what they had just seen. As Deborah looked around, she realized that this was very much the same group that had been at their house for supper a week or so before. She was pleased. It was a group that felt comfortable with each other. There were no strangers here.

Jesus was at the head of the small group. The Twelve were around him in a half-circle. The rest followed behind. No one spoke. They were still overwhelmed by the healing of the young man.

Deborah glanced at Miriam. Miriam seemed particularly subdued, and Deborah wasn't sure if it was because of the healing or because they would be leaving Capernaum in the morning. She felt a pang of sorrow at the thought.

"Master?" The voice up ahead of her cut off her thoughts.

Deborah saw the Lord's head turn, but she was near the back of the group and could not tell who had spoken nor to whom Jesus now turned.

"I've been thinking about the young man back there." Maybe it was Nathanael, she thought, still trying to see.

"Yes?"

Deborah quickened her step so she could hear better. The others were moving in closer as well.

"You heard what his father said. He brought the boy to us, your disciples, and we could not help him."

"Yes." Jesus stopped, and the group circled in around him.

"Why could we not cure him?" the questioner asked in obvious sorrow.

"Because of your unbelief." Jesus spoke without condemnation, but simply and frankly.

To Deborah's surprise, Andrew picked up the questioning. "Yes, you said that before, Lord. But we're trying to understand. What is it we did wrong?" He pursed his lip, deeply thoughtful. "I guess in a way, we are like the boy's father, Master. We believe, Lord, but will you help our unbelief?"

Jesus nodded slowly, accepting the spirit in which the request was made. "It is a matter of faith. If you have even as much faith as the grain of a mustard seed"—his hand swept out toward the hills that rose sharply from the level of the Sea of Galilee to the west of them. Most prominent was Mount Arbel, which ended in a sharp precipice that plunged almost straight down to the lowlands around the Sea of Galilee. "If you have the faith of even a seed of the mustard, you could say to this mountain, 'Remove hence to yonder place!' and it would be removed."

That brought soft exclamations of surprise and shock. The eyes of Jesus only became more penetrating. "With the faith of which I speak, nothing shall be impossible to you."

Deborah saw the eyes of the apostles drop, and they began to shuffle uncomfortably in their places. They had asked to know what they lacked, and Jesus had told them forthrightly and without any attempt to soften it.

Jesus watched them, noting their discomfort; then he added one thing more. "Nevertheless—"

Their heads came up, and they were suddenly hopeful.

"Nevertheless, *this* kind cometh not out except by prayer *and* fasting."

With that he turned and began walking again. Deborah waited for a moment, then moved up to join her husband, who fell in with Peter and Andrew. David, seeing her, reached out and took her hand.

"Will we ever have that kind of faith?" Peter asked of no one in particular.

Andrew just shook his head, clearly troubled.

"What do you suppose he meant by that last statement?" Ephraim asked of Peter.

Peter looked up. "Faith is the key, but I think the Master was saying that some things require greater power than others, so you seek to increase your faith by adding fasting to your prayer."

Matthew was just behind them, listening intently. He moved forward to come up alongside them. "Isn't that what the scriptures teach us?"

They all turned, and Matthew looked a little embarrassed, but he pressed on. "Remember what the Psalmist said?" He began to quote, somewhat self-consciously, "'I humbled my soul with *fasting*; and my *prayer* returned into mine own bosom.'"

Deborah saw that Miriam, Leah, Ezra, Lilly, and Livia were listening too, curious about what was being discussed.

"And when the prophet Daniel, laden with sorrow for the captivity of Israel in Babylon, sought the Lord's help, he said, 'And I set my face unto the Lord God, to seek by *prayer* and supplications, with *fasting*, and sackcloth, and ashes.'"

"How do you do that, Matthew?" Peter asked sheepishly. "I

thought I knew the scriptures, but you come up with passages that don't even sound familiar to me."

Matthew colored slightly. "When you are a publican, your circle of friends is somewhat restricted." He smiled, almost like a shy boy. "That leaves a lot of time for reading."

"Well said, Matthew."

They all looked up in surprise. They had been so engrossed in their conversation that they hadn't noticed that Jesus had drifted back to join them.

"Master, I wasn't presuming to teach—"

Jesus cut in with a gentle wave of his hand. "It pleases me when you seek truth and understanding among yourselves."

"Master?" It was Peter.

Jesus turned to him.

"You have taught us about prayer before—about what our prayers should contain, and that we should pray in secret so that our Father can reward us openly. Since we lack sufficient faith, is there anything more you would have us understand? Why prayer and fasting?"

Jesus nodded immediately, stopping while once again everyone moved in closer. "I would speak a parable unto you, to teach you that men ought always to pray, and not lose heart and give up."

"Say on," Peter said meekly, clearly pleased that his question had brought a direct response.

"There was in a city a judge. This judge feared not God, neither regarded man. And there was a widow in that city, and she came to the judge, saying, 'Avenge me of mine adversary.'"

He let that sink in for a moment, then continued. "And the judge would not for a while. But afterward he said within himself, 'Though I fear not God, neither regard man, yet because this widow troubles me, I will avenge her, lest by her continual coming she weary me.'"

He stopped again, looking around the circle slowly. "Hear what the unjust judge saith. Shall not God avenge his own elect, which cry day and night unto him, though he bear long with them?"

There was evident surprise when it became obvious that he was finished. That was it? Miriam wondered.

Jesus watched their expressions, smiling at their bemusement. But he said nothing more. He started walking again, leading them back to Capernaum.

III

CAPERNAUM
12 JULY, A.D. 30

Miriam watched in the semidarkness as Ezra put her leather case in the back of the carriage. He shoved it forward, then put Livia's in beside it. He leaned over the backboard, pushing and tugging to make sure things were secure. Finally, he turned to the others. "I think that's it. We're ready to leave." He looked up at the sky, which was just lightening in the east.

Deborah turned toward where the gate that led into their courtyard stood open. "David! They're ready to go."

There was no answer. Ephraim looked at his mother. "I'll go get him."

"He said he had to get something," she answered, indicating for him to go back into the house.

As Ephraim left, Ezra stepped forward and began to check the harnessing on the team. The six women turned their attention to one another, realizing that this was the moment they had all been dreading. Tears were very near as they began to say their good-byes, vowing that they would see each other again.

"Will you kiss Boaz and Esther good-bye for us?" Livia asked Rachel.

"I will. They both wanted me to wake them up, but Boaz especially just can't do without his sleep."

Miriam touched her arm. "It's much too early for them, but do hug them tightly for each of us. We love them both."

Rachel's eyes were suddenly soft. "Last night as I was putting them to bed, they both talked about how much they'll miss you." She looked at Livia. "Then Boaz—my sweet little Boaz—sat straight up in bed and folded his arms and said, 'I go Rome with Livie.'"

"Oh," Livia cried, "did he really?"

Rachel was struggling to keep her voice level. "Yes. He adores all of you, but you, Livia—you are his Livie. You really made a friend there."

"Don't," Livia protested. "I can hardly bear the thought of not seeing him again for a year or more. And Esther too. They are such sweet children, Rachel."

"For a two year old, Boaz has such a tender heart," Deborah said.

"I told him that Rome was a long, long ways away," Rachel went on. "That it might be dangerous for a little boy." She had to stop and swallow quickly. "You know how he's always talking about bears. He always wants Ephraim to check outside and make sure there are no bears around before he goes to sleep. He's always going to fight the bears when he gets big."

"That's all he ever talks about," Leah said with an affectionate smile. "And he's so dramatic about it."

They all laughed, for that was the perfect description of Rachel's youngest. He could be so serious when he talked. His face would screw up. His eyes would become enormous, and he would use his hands as though he were a merchant in the marketplace. It was not unusual for him to entertain a whole room of adults with his conversations—especially when he was talking about bears.

"Well," Rachel continued, "when I told him that he couldn't go with you, that it might not be safe, his eyes got real big. He wanted to know if there are bears in Rome."

"Did he really?" Deborah exclaimed.

"But before I could answer," Rachel went on, "he shook his head with great solemnity. 'I no care,' he said, sticking his jaw out like he does. 'I go with Livie. I keep her safe from the bears.'"

That did it. Livia, who was usually the most controlled of them all, turned away and dropped her head. Miriam and Deborah fell into each other's arms, weeping. Leah and Lilly clasped hands.

"You have to promise to write," Deborah said, finally pulling back. "As soon as you know where you are staying in Rome. Then we can write too."

Just then, David and Ephraim came out of the courtyard. Both were carrying leather bags that were round and heavy. "Here are some oats for the horses," David said. "There should be enough to give them some each day. That will help them to keep going longer."

"Thank you. I plan to push them pretty hard." Ezra turned to his wife. "It's time, Lilly," he said. Then to Miriam and Livia. "We have to go."

As they climbed up into the carriage, Miriam turned to David. "May I ask you a quick question, David?"

"Of course."

"It was something Jesus said yesterday. I've thought about it all night."

"What?"

"The parable about the judge."

There was a soft smile from David. "Did you find it somewhat troubling?"

Her face registered her surprise. "You did too?"

"And I as well," Leah chimed in, as David nodded.

"What particularly did you find troublesome?" he asked Miriam.

She pursed her lips, trying to find how best to express it. "Well, it sounded as though Jesus was saying that we need to pester God in our prayers until he finally relents and answers us. At least that's what happened with the woman and the judge."

"Yes," Leah said, pleased that she was not alone in this question. "The judge didn't give the woman what she wanted because it was right, or because he cared about her; he gave in only because she wouldn't leave him alone. Is that really how God is?"

David nodded. "That's what it sounded like, didn't it?"

"But you don't think that's what Jesus meant, do you?" Miriam said. "I mean, surely God isn't like the unjust judge."

"No, he's not. We know that for sure."

"Then—"

Leah broke in, her mind working quickly. "Maybe Jesus was saying that if an unjust and hardhearted judge will respond to importuning, to persistent pleading, then how much more will a loving Father hear and answer our prayers."

Now Deborah came in. She hadn't said anything to David, but she too had been troubled by that brief little parable. "That's true, Leah, but here's what bothers me. Remember what Jesus said that day he gave the sermon up on the mount? He said that God knows what we need *before* we ever ask him."

"Right," David said. "So why should we even have to ask at all? We can never surprise God with a request, so why pray at all? Why not just sit back and wait for him to give us what we need?"

"Exactly," Deborah said. "That is what troubles me."

Miriam shook her head. "I hadn't thought about that part of it." She pulled a face. "You're supposed to help me understand it, not confuse me even more."

David laughed gently. "Sometimes, the more I think about some of the things Jesus teaches us, the more perplexing they become. And I've decided that he sometimes does it deliberately so that we have to think."

Ezra finished stowing the two bags of grain and climbed up onto the driver's bench. "So, David, have you come to any conclusions?"

"I have some thoughts, but—" He stopped as they heard the crunch of sandals on the graveled street.

To their surprise, a dark figure was approaching at a rapid walk, though with a distinct limp. The eastern sky was noticeably lighter now, but within the narrow streets it was still quite dark. Then David grunted, a look of concern passing over his face. He looked quickly at Deborah. "It's Sextus Rubrius," he said in a low voice.

"Who?" Miriam asked. Then she remembered the name. He was the Roman centurion who had escorted her and her father from Caesarea to Jerusalem after the attack by Ya'abin.

"The Roman centurion here in Capernaum," Deborah whispered. "He's a friend."

"Yes, I've met him before."

They watched as the figure came closer, able now to see the helmet, the leather breastplate, the sword swinging at his belt.

"David ben Joseph?"

"Ho, Sextus. Good morning. What brings you out at such an hour?" David's voice was amiable, but Miriam saw that his body was as stiff as the sword the other man wore. That puzzled her. If this man was a friend—

Then it hit her. A hand flew to her mouth, hoping against hope that she was wrong.

"I didn't expect to find you up and about," Sextus said as he reached them. He looked at the others curiously.

"We have had guests from the coast," David said smoothly, not offering to introduce them. "They're traveling to Caesarea this morning."

Sextus nodded, then motioned with his head at his friend, stepping back. "There is word from Caesarea," he said gravely. "I need to speak with you."

Deborah gasped. "Simeon?"

The grizzled old veteran obviously had hoped to speak with David alone, but seeing that Deborah had gone instantly white, he nodded. "Yes. A messenger came in last night to alert our garrison of possible trouble." He paused; then his eyes dropped. "Simeon has been arrested."

Deborah felt her knees go weak, and she groped blindly for the side of the carriage. Ephraim stepped to her side and steadied her.

"Arrested?" David said in a hollow voice. "But why? He brought the gold."

There was shame in Sextus's eyes. "Pilate got the gold as well. He refused to bargain—" He glanced quickly at Deborah, then away again. "He said there was to be no negotiating with the man who was responsible for the disaster at the Joknean Pass." He dropped his gaze as he continued. "Simeon will be held with Yehuda and the others for the games in September."

As Deborah gasped at that announcement, David spun around. "I'm going with you to Caesarea, Ezra. Let me get my things."

The centurion leaped forward and grabbed his friend's arm. "No, David! That would be madness."

"I'll speak with the governor. We can offer him more, if that's what it—"

Sextus shook him gently. "Listen to me, old friend. Marcus Didius sent a private note. He tried to convince Pilate to accept Simeon's offer. Marcus thought you might try to do something. He asked me to warn you—it's his way of repaying you and Simeon for saving us the night of the ambush. Since you were there that night, Marcus suspects you know as well as Simeon who it was that betrayed us. If you go,

Pilate will take you as well. The governor is adamant on this matter. He wants to know who was responsible for that disaster."

Miriam blanched and felt her body go weak. She and Livia exchanged horrified glances.

Fortunately, Sextus was not looking at them. What he had not told them was something else Marcus had said in his letter. Simeon would be tortured to get the information they wanted. If they could not break him, then Pilate was talking about sending a contingent of legionnaires to Capernaum to arrest David ben Joseph. Sextus knew that was pure insanity, and he didn't think it would actually come to that. But if David went to Caesarea, there was no question about what would happen to him.

Deborah went to her husband in three quick steps. "He's right, David. You can't go."

David's shoulders fell, and his whole body seemed to sag.

Rubrius watched him for a moment, then spoke softly. "I'm sorry, David. If there is anything I can think to do, I will let you know." There was no optimism in his face. He started to back away. "I'm sorry." Then, without looking at the others, he turned and walked swiftly away.

The moment he was out of earshot, Miriam leaped down from the carriage and ran to Deborah. "I can do something," she cried. "As soon as we get there, I'll talk to Marcus."

Now it was Lilly who went white. "Miriam! *You* are the one they are after! You heard what the man said. You are the one in danger here." She turned to her husband. "I don't think we should take her back to Caesarea. What if Simeon—"

She stopped, seeing the look on Deborah's face. "I'm sorry. You're right. Simeon will never tell them."

Miriam's jaw tightened. "It was Simeon and Yehuda who saved our lives once," she said. "My life and Livia's, and my father's. My father is a hard man, but he has not forgotten a debt such as that. I'll have him talk to Pilate. Perhaps we can offer him even more, convince him to take the gold and let Simeon go."

She looked at Deborah, suddenly forlorn. "I won't let them kill him, Deborah. I promise."

It was a tiny straw in a tempestuous sea, but it was all there was, and Deborah grasped for it desperately. "Yes, Miriam. Go! Take great care, but go! You are our only hope."

CHAPTER NOTES

The account of the "healing of the demoniac child," as many scholars call this event, is recorded in some detail by three of the Gospel writers (Matthew 17:14–21; Mark 9:14–29; and Luke 9:37–43). The description in this chapter draws on all three accounts but relies most heavily on Mark's account.

The people at the time of Jesus spoke Aramaic, a sister language to Hebrew, but the New Testament manuscripts were written in Greek. Therefore, we do not know what Aramaic word was used to describe the boy's condition. In Greek, the word which the King James Version translates as "lunatick," is *selaynayAHDzo*, which literally means "moon struck"—*seLAYnay* is the Greek word for the moon (see Vine, 2:36–37; and Vincent, 1:61–62). Based on the description of his symptoms, most scholars agree that it was likely epilepsy, and some modern versions of the Bible use "epileptic" in place of "lunatick" in their translations.

The parable of the unjust judge (or the importunate woman, as it is often called) is found in Luke 18:1–9 and likely did not happen at the same time as the healing of the boy. It is linked here with the other lesson on fasting and prayer to show more of what Jesus taught on this subject.

In the parable, the King James Version uses the phrase, "that men ought always to pray, and not *faint*." That term is misleading to modern readers, to whom "faint" generally means to lose consciousness. The Greek word used in that verse means to lose courage or to lose heart, and thus to give up (see Vincent, 1:204).

CHAPTER 13

I

CAPERNAUM
11 JULY, A.D. 30

Leah stopped at the door to her parents' bedroom. It was open part way and in the light from the lamp she was carrying, she saw that both her mother and father were on their knees at the side of the bed. She stepped back, pulling the lamp away so that its light did not shine directly through the doorway.

Finally, after more than a full minute, she heard the rustle of clothing, then the scrape of feet on the floor. She moved forward again. "*Eema? Abba?*" Even though Leah was now an adult, in the privacy of their home she, like her brother Joseph, always used the more intimate diminutives "Mama" and "Papa" that younger children used, rather than the more formal *Eem*, "Mother," or *Ahv*, "Father."

"Come in, Leah," David said. He came to the door and opened it wider.

"Uncle Aaron is here."

Her mother was immediately at David's side. "Aaron?"

"Yes, he arrived just a few minutes ago. I told him I thought you were in bed, but he said he must speak with you."

Deborah reached behind the door and got her outer robe, wrapping it around her as she stepped out into the hall. She looked at David, who followed close behind her. "Aaron? At this hour? Something must be wrong."

He was in the main sitting room, pacing back and forth, his head down, his *peyot*, or side curls, dancing and bobbing as he moved. At the sound of their footsteps, he stopped, then quickly came to Deborah. He reached out and took both of her hands. His face was drawn, his eyes dark with anguish.

"What is it, Aaron?" Deborah exclaimed. "What's happened?"

"I just heard about Simeon, Deborah."

"Oh." Deborah was partly relieved. She didn't need another tragedy in the family at the moment. She was also significantly surprised.

"Let's sit down," David suggested. "It was kind of you to come, Aaron."

He shot his brother-in-law a sharp look. "We may disagree about matters of faith, David, but I haven't forgotten who my family is."

Caught off guard by his vehemence, David nodded quickly. "I know, Aaron. I didn't mean to imply otherwise."

Deborah collapsed into a chair and began rubbing her temples. "The—" She caught herself, not sure how Aaron would react to the word that it was a Roman soldier who brought the news. "The person who told us said he expected additional information in the next few days."

"Sextus Rubrius," Aaron supplied, faintly amused by his sister's reticence. "I spoke with him just about an hour ago."

Both David and Deborah showed their surprise. "You did?" David asked. "You went to the house of a Gentile?"

"Yes." He waved the implication away with disdain. "The centurion told me that the sentence will not be carried out immediately. Something about some Roman festival in the fall."

Deborah was still reeling. "You went to see Sextus Rubrius?"

He again waved it away, clearly pleased to shock them a little. "I didn't go into his house, and I didn't touch him, so with a month or so of ritual purification, I'll be safe once again."

She just stared at him. For a moment she thought he was joking about having been in contact with a Gentile, and a Roman soldier at that, but then she saw he was completely serious.

His demeanor grew very serious. "I was very concerned when I heard, Deborah. It's no secret that Simeon and I disagree about his approach to solving our problems with Rome, but he is still my nephew. And, if I understand it correctly, this was not just some raid on the Romans. He was trying to secure the release of his associates, I believe."

Leah was still standing near the door. She answered for her parents, who were clearly still taken aback by all of this. "Yes. You've met Yehuda of Beth Neelah before, Uncle Aaron. He and two others were captured during a clash at the Joknean Pass. Simeon took a ransom payment to the governor for their release."

"That's what the centurion said as well. That is a noble endeavor and worthy of commendation. Only the deepest of love for one's fellowmen generates that kind of courage."

"Thank you," Deborah said, touched with emotion. "That means a great deal to me to hear you say that, Aaron."

He reached in his robes and withdrew a letter. "I have just come from Amram. We have drafted a letter to the governor. I will be leaving immediately for Caesarea to deliver it."

It was one astonishment after another. A small triumphant smile formed at the corners of his mouth. "I know what you think of us, and our—as you call it—obsession with the Law, but we have not forgotten the primary virtues—love, courage, integrity."

"Amram?" David said. "This is the Amram we know, chief of the Pharisees here?"

"Don't be haughty, David. Yes, that Amram. Though he does not carry the same influence with the Romans as someone who sits on the Great Sanhedrin in Jerusalem; nevertheless, Capernaum has one of the most influential councils in the province. Amram has agreed to formally intervene with Pilate in Simeon's behalf."

David could scarcely believe it. "What does this letter say?" He could see it was sealed and therefore could not be opened.

"Amram reminds the governor that the Pharisees represent the largest majority in all of Israel and that we have been instrumental in keeping the people at peace in times of unrest."

David nodded. That was not only true, but he knew that the Romans also knew that it was true. They didn't particularly like the Pharisees because of their arrogance, but they recognized their power with the people.

"Amram mentions the influence you and your family have in this community, David, and he asks the governor to consider granting Simeon a pardon, especially in light of the fact that it was Simeon who prevented a greater massacre of the Romans last month."

What Aaron didn't say was that Sextus Rubrius had also told him of the governor's desire to learn who had betrayed the secret of the ambush to Simeon. Torture of their newly acquired prisoner was a high likelihood. Amram had specifically and strongly condemned the possibility of any physical mistreatment of the prisoner, reminding Pilate that such barbarity was against the Mosaic Law and therefore highly offensive to the people. *Highly offensive.* In light of some of Pilate's past blunders in underestimating the religious fervor of his subjects, that contained a not so thinly veiled threat.

"You would do all of that?" Deborah whispered, her eyes filling with tears. She rushed to him and threw her arms around him. "Thank you, Aaron. Thank you."

"After all you have done for me, dear sister, did you think I would simply turn my back on you?" He touched her cheek. "We can argue about Jesus later. Right now, this is a family matter." He smiled softly. "And I am still family."

II

In the Galilean highlands and the Jezreel Valley
13 July, a.d. 30

The four travelers did not go to Caesarea by way of Ptolemais, as Ezra had originally planned. It was the safer way, but it would take almost a full day longer. Speed was now of the essence. Ironically, the shortest route from Capernaum was up and across the Nazareth Ridge, then down through the Joknean Pass to the coastal plains.

They stopped the first night a few miles west of Nazareth and south of Beth Neelah, taking lodging in a small wayside inn that overlooked the Jezreel Valley. They rose early the next morning and came together in the small main room downstairs. They were the only ones in the inn who were up, so they spoke in soft whispers.

"I have a proposal," Ezra said. "We can purchase a simple breakfast from the innkeeper, but not until about sunup. We can wait and eat here, or we can eat the bread, cheese, and dried figs we still have. There's a small spring about three hours from here. We could stop and have breakfast there."

"Let's go on," Miriam said without hesitation.

"I agree," Lilly chimed in.

They turned to Livia, fully expecting her to agree, but to their surprise, she didn't respond.

"Livia?" Ezra asked.

She seemed to come out of her thoughts. "I think I understand it now," she said.

Miriam, still sleepy from a short and miserable night on a straw pallet, looked blankly at her. "Understand what?"

"The parable."

For several seconds, that won her only blank looks; then Lilly spoke. "You mean the parable about the unjust judge?"

"Yes." Livia colored slightly at their puzzled looks. "It may help us decide about Ezra's proposal."

Miriam wasn't following this very well. "You mean about breakfast?"

"Yes, but it doesn't mean we stay here to decide. Let's start and I can tell you on the way."

Miriam gave her a strange look. Since yesterday morning, she had thought about little else besides Simeon and Yehuda in prison. It seemed like weeks ago that they had listened to Jesus speak about prayer.

They collected their things and went out to the corral behind the inn where the carriage was parked and the horse stabled. Fifteen minutes later they were on their way again, moving down a precipitous and serpentine road which dropped down into the Jezreel Valley. Lilly sat beside Ezra on the front seat of the carriage. Livia and Miriam were in the back.

"All right," Lilly said, once they were on level ground again and could relax. "Let's hear this explanation of yours."

Livia was a little reticent. She had blurted out her thoughts without thinking. Now she was a little chagrined. "I think I may know what Jesus meant. I'm not absolutely sure, but I'd like to know what you think."

Lilly swung her legs over and slid back to sit between the other two women. "Go on."

"Well," Livia began, "the key for me was the question David asked us yesterday morning."

"Which question?" Miriam demanded.

Livia was thoughtful. "You have to remember that the very concept of God being a loving heavenly Father, a being who knows us and cares for us and hears our prayers, is still quite strange to me. In Greece our gods were barely worthy of adoration, let alone real worship. So when David asked why pray at all if God already knows what we need, that was an intriguing concept to me."

Ezra turned his head. "That is the key question for me, too," he admitted. "Jesus suggested that we not only ask, but that we ask again and again."

"That got me thinking," Livia said, "about my own parents, or especially my mother. My mother loved my brother and me very deeply. So when I asked her for something, I didn't have to beg, if—" She stopped. "And this is a big if. If it was something she felt I should have."

"Go on," Miriam encouraged.

"I mean, sometimes she didn't want me to have something, so she simply said no."

"As I assume God does for us," Lilly responded.

"Yes. Then it occurred to me there were basically only three ways my mother would answer one of my requests. She could say no, which she often did. She could say yes, which she did if she thought it was best for me." She stopped, hoping one of them would see the third alternative, but they didn't, so she finished it for them. "Or she could say, not yet."

"Not yet?" Lilly asked, clearly puzzled.

"For example, one time I remember asking Mother if she would teach me how to sew. My mother made beautiful dresses for the mistress of the house in Alexandria. I wanted to be able to do that, so I asked her if I could learn how to do it. Her answer was yes, but not yet."

"Why?" Miriam asked, finally seeing that Livia really had thought this through.

"Because I wasn't ready. She said that first I had to learn about taking flax and turning it into linen, about how to card wool, or how to weave cloth. When I had done that, then I could begin to sew. She didn't object to my request; it is just that I wasn't ready for it. I had to do some other things first."

When the others began to slowly nod as that concept sunk in, the excitement in Livia rose. She was talking more quickly now. "I was thinking about Mother when I remembered what Jesus said as he started the parable. Remember? He said it was meant to teach us to pray *and not give up*. Why would he say that?"

She didn't wait for them to answer. "Think about it. If God is really a loving father, then he can say yes to our requests, or no sometimes. Or he can say . . . " She let her words hang expectantly.

Ezra swung around, his eyes showing surprise. "Or he can say yes, but *not yet*."

Livia could have shouted aloud. "Yes, Ezra! I wasn't happy with my mother's answer about sewing. I didn't want to do all those other things first. I wanted my answer now. For a time, I decided I would just give up on the idea."

Miriam was staring at her friend as comprehension dawned on her too. "So what we think may be a 'no' answer, might simply be *no answer—yet?*"

"I hadn't thought of it in quite that way," Livia said, "but yes. And then we give up and stop asking." Her eyes were alive with excitement as she looked back and forth between Lilly and Miriam. "Now think about what Jesus taught the disciples when they asked why they couldn't cure that poor boy the day before yesterday. He said some things require prayer *and* fasting. Why?"

"Because 'this kind,'" Ezra answered softly, "'this kind,' as Jesus said it, won't come out with just the normal effort. Something greater has to be done." Then he snapped his fingers. "That's it!" he exclaimed. "The disciples had tried to cure the boy, but when they couldn't, they gave up. They assumed the Lord's answer was, 'No, you can't do this.'"

"Exactly!" Livia exulted.

Miriam was concentrating fiercely, the understanding starting to unfold, like a rose slowly opening its petals. "So then . . . " She stopped, not sure yet how to express it.

But Lilly was ahead of her. "If God didn't hold back the answer sometimes, we would never go to that higher level of desire and effort. If he said yes to every request immediately, we would never experience any growth."

Livia was ecstatic. "Does that make sense to you? It isn't that prayer changes *God's* mind. It changes *our* minds."

Miriam sat back, filled with wonder. This was a side of Livia she had never seen before, and it left her humbled and feeling ashamed of her own denseness. Why hadn't she seen all that?

The carriage rolled on for almost a full minute with no one speaking. Then, finally, Livia brought the conversation around to what had started it all. "Ezra," she said, "what if when we get to that spring, we don't eat breakfast at all? What if while the horse is resting, we spend our time in prayer and begin a fast. I would say that having Simeon in prison is a problem large enough to merit a special effort to get an answer, wouldn't you?"

III
CAESAREA

"Hey, you! *Acus!*"

Simeon lifted his head, trying to pull himself up out of the depths of a fitful sleep. He jerked as a sharp blow slammed into the bottom of his bare foot.

"Wake up, O Great Needle. You've got a visitor."

Scrambling back deeper into the cell to escape another blow, Simeon saw two things at the same time. He saw that this was a new guard he hadn't seen before. He had a huge bulbous nose and crooked front teeth. Simeon also noticed that the stairway in the far corner of the dungeon was visible and the light, though dim, was not yellowish. So it was day again. Somewhere up above them the sun was actually shining. It was the only way he had of knowing.

Then a second figure stepped into his narrow field of vision. "I'll be fine. Leave us."

The guard saluted sharply and backed away. As he disappeared, Simeon heard a raucous cackle and a muttered comment about *acus* and *pilum*.

When the guards had brought Simeon in that first night, one of them had told the others they had finally caught the famous Zealot leader called the Javelin, or in Latin, *pilum*. Then in contempt, he said, "He is not a *pilum* now. He is only an *acus*, a common tailor's needle." His comrades had found that uproariously funny and now threw it in his face each time they saw him. It said much about their existence in this place of foul smells and fouler deeds that they found so much amusement in such a jibe.

The figure stepped to the opening of Simeon's cell, and Simeon realized instantly who it was. "Come to gloat a little, have you?"

Marcus Didius squatted down so his face was at the same level as Simeon's. "Your good fortune is holding, Simeon, son of David."

Simeon just shook his head. "Thank you for coming to tell me that, Tribune. Otherwise I might not have noticed."

"Pilate went to Jerusalem yesterday. He won't return until the day after tomorrow."

"And I had hoped for regular visits," Simeon said dryly.

Marcus just shook his head. "Listen to me, Simeon. Your flippancy, even if admirable, will only win you more pain down here."

Simeon didn't respond.

"Aren't you going to ask me why this is a fortunate turn of events?"

"All right. Why is it a fortunate turn of events?"

"Because your little outing at the Joknean Pass has put Pilate in a mood like I've never seen him before. He won't let us start questioning you until he returns."

Simeon fought hard to keep his eyes expressionless, but he was sure the Roman must have seen the relief that leaped into them for a moment.

Marcus was still a little awed by the hatred he had seen in the governor's eyes. "He says he wants to be here to watch you totally broken."

"I'm disappointed to hear that," Simeon said sarcastically. "When your primary entertainment is watching gladiators tear each other apart, I just assumed watching a man tortured might seem a little dull."

Marcus ignored that. "That means you've got two days, maybe three to think this over. I appreciate your courage, and I know you really do think you can hold out against us, but please believe me. You will not."

"Believe you? A man of your integrity? How could I ever doubt your word, Marcus?"

Marcus blew out his breath. "Look, you can sit there and be

insulting, or you can listen to what I'm offering you. I can't promise anything for sure, but if you would tell us who betrayed us, then I think I could persuade Pilate to let you go."

"And what about Yehuda and my other two men?"

"Pilate knows that your men were just foot soldiers in all this. Yes, he might even agree to let them go too."

"And do I have your word on that as a Roman officer and gentleman?" Simeon asked softly.

Marcus flushed and straightened abruptly. "You think about it. I know you don't want to betray a trust, but isn't it better to lose one and save four, including yourself?"

"One? And what if it is more than one person who betrayed you?"

"I don't care. Give us one name. Give us the person most responsible, and Pilate will be satisfied. He doesn't have to know about anyone else." Marcus stepped back. "Think about it, Simeon ben David. I am not fool enough to think I can frighten you with tales of what a man skilled with a hot iron can do, but make no mistake. You *will* give us the name. You may not even be aware of what you are doing by then, but you will break. And if that is the case, all of this is for nothing. Save yourself and your friends."

Simeon rolled onto one side, the chains clanking softly, turning his face to the wall of his cell.

For a long moment Marcus stared at the rigid back. Then, disgusted, he whirled and went back up the stairs without a word. Simeon didn't turn his head. He reached over to his left wrist and gently began to rub beneath the manacle where the skin was raw. So he had at most three more days before the contest of wills began. It almost saddened him to learn that. That meant three more days of living with his thoughts. Three more days of unanswerable questions.

He wasn't praying anymore. It wasn't that he had turned his back on God. It was that he feared that it was an insult to Deity to ask for deliverance when it was his stubborn determination to do things his own way that had brought him into captivity in the first place.

He changed hands, working on his right wrist. Then he sat up and began the same therapy around his ankles, forcing himself to concentrate on what he was doing to stop the thoughts from coming.

As he finished and lay down again, trying to find some position of comfort on the cold floor without pulling on the chains, he suddenly stopped. In his mind, as clearly as if someone had spoken them aloud, he heard these words. *Greater love hath no man than this, that he lay down his life for his friends.*

Simeon sat up again, very slowly. The words of Jesus hung there in his mind. To his surprise, his eyes were suddenly burning. He lifted his hands and stared at the manacles and the heavy chains that were attached to his leg irons. He felt the hot, wetness start down his cheeks. He didn't care. He dropped his head and closed his eyes. Stupid or not, he had not been forgotten. He was not alone.

"Thank you, Father," he whispered. "Thank you for loving such a fool as I."

And then, with equal clarity, came the next: *Come unto me, all ye that labor and are heavy laden, and I will give you rest. Take my yoke upon you, and ye shall find rest unto your souls.*

IV

Marcus moved across the main entry hall of the great Praetorium, his sandals slapping sharply on the marble floor. "Miriam! How good to see you again. Did you have a safe journey down from the Galilee?"

She managed a tired smile. "Good evening, Marcus. Yes, we did. Thank you."

"You're early. We didn't expect you until tomorrow night."

"We decided to push on and come all the way in today." She half turned, motioning for the others to come forward. "Marcus, this is my cousin Ezra, and his wife, Lilly. And I believe you have met Livia before."

"Yes, up on the Temple Mount some months ago." Marcus bowed slightly to her, then to Ezra and Lilly. "Welcome to the governor's palace. Unfortunately, the governor is not present to greet you, but I've sent word to have the guest rooms prepared immediately. In the meantime, though the dinner hour is passed, I will have some food prepared and—"

The four of them looked at each other quickly; then Miriam spoke. "Supper will not be necessary, Marcus. We have had our needs well satisfied on the road today." Before he could question her further, she went on. "Is my father here yet?"

"No. Actually, Pilate is in Jerusalem on official business. He will bring your father with him when he returns in a day or two." A shadow briefly darkened his eyes. "I don't wish to worry you, Miriam, but an attempt was made a few nights ago to enter your home and—"

"What! Is Father all right?"

"Yes, yes. He has been very cautious. He has several bodyguards. The intruders were caught before they made it past the outer courtyard."

"Ya'abin's doing?" she asked, still shaken.

"Most certainly," Marcus said grimly. "That's why the governor went to Jerusalem. He's taken a large contingent of soldiers from here. He wants to put some fire into the garrison commander and double the patrols out in the wilderness."

He glanced quickly at Ezra and the others. "This is why I am most pleased that you have returned. That is one less thing we have to be concerned about." Then to Ezra: "Thank you for caring for Miriam so well. Mordechai said that he had the utmost confidence in your ability to keep her safe. Did you have any trouble?"

Ezra could have answered in a dozen ways, but he didn't hesitate at all. "None. Our presence in the Galilee was not noticed by anyone that caused us concern."

"Good." Back to Miriam: "Pilate told me that if you didn't arrive by tonight, I was to go out looking for you. That's why he left me here instead of taking me with him. The ship taking you and the delegation to Rome—one of the large grain ships—is already in the harbor loading wheat. We are scheduled to sail four or five days hence, so we were getting a little concerned about you." He gave Miriam a warm smile. "Only when we've set sail can we truly let down our guard."

"Marcus?" Miriam looked at the others, not unconscious of the instant concern her one word had triggered. "I have a matter of great urgency. May I speak with you?"

Surprised, he nodded instantly. "Of course. But you have just arrived. Would you like to go to your room and rest for a short time first?"

"No, if it is convenient, I should like to speak with you now."

"Of course." He clapped his hands one time and immediately three servants came through the arched portico. Marcus gestured. "Show these guests to their rooms. See that baths are drawn. They have come a long way, and a hot bath will do much to revive them."

"Thank you, Tribune Didius," Lilly said. Then to Miriam: "We'll see you in the morning." She moved forward and went up to kiss her cousin on the cheek. "Be careful, Miriam," she whispered into her ear. "Be very careful."

"Thank you," Miriam said brightly as Lilly stepped back. She watched until they were led away, then turned to Marcus.

"You look tired too, Miriam. I'm sure the strain of travel this last while has taken its toll. Are you sure this matter can't wait until you are refreshed a little?"

"No, Marcus. I must—" She moved away from him, biting at her lip. "As we passed through Capernaum day before yesterday, we heard news of the capture of one of their citizens."

Marcus's eyes narrowed almost instantly. "Oh?" he said cautiously.

"Yes. Simeon ben David. I don't know if you know him. His father is David ben Joseph, a prominent merchant in Capernaum. Simeon is a leader of—"

"I know who he is," Marcus said shortly.

"Is it true?"

"Miriam, I—" Then his eyes became even more focused on her. "And why would that be of interest to you? Do you know this man?"

Feeling her heart begin to race, Miriam took a moment before she answered. The difficult thing was trying to keep straight in her mind what she could safely say. Of course, Marcus knew that Miriam had met Simeon and Yehuda—her father had given Marcus the record she made when Mordechai had met with them to arrange the so-called trap. But as far as Marcus knew, Miriam didn't know that he knew. She almost wanted to laugh. It was like trying to make your way through a labyrinth in the darkness. One wrong slip and she could put herself into deep jeopardy, along with Lilly, Livia, Ezra, and most importantly, Simeon and Yehuda.

"But," she said, feigning surprise, "don't you remember our experience earlier this spring in Samaria?"

"What experience?"

"We were on our way to try to arrange a conference with the Zealots for the Great Sanhedrin. Moshe Ya'abin attacked our camp. My father's chief steward had betrayed us. It was Simeon and Yehuda and their band that saved us that day." A tiny tremor of horror rippled through her body, and that was not feigned. Any time she thought of that morning, when Ya'abin had grabbed her by the hair, she went completely cold. "We came here to Caesarea shortly thereafter. Remember? That was the first time I met you."

"Oh, yes, I do remember that now."

"Well, it was this Simeon and Yehuda of Beth Neelah and some of their men that rescued us and spared us from a terrible situation."

"But perhaps this is not the same man," Marcus said, acting almost bored.

So he was playing the same game as she was. She could see it in his eyes, calculating how much to say and how much to pretend innocence. "I know only what we heard in Capernaum," she answered smoothly. "If it is the same man, I and my father would like to speak with you and the governor about possible clemency. We owe him and this Yehuda a great debt."

That clearly startled him. "I'm not sure that would be a wise thing to do, Miriam."

"Would you at least take me to see him tomorrow, so I can see if it is the same man?"

He laughed shortly. "The dungeons are no place for a woman, let alone a lady of your grace and position."

"It would greatly relieve my mind, Marcus. If it is not him, then the matter is settled."

"I would not dare give permission for such a visit without Pilate's consent. He would have my head if it displeased him."

"What are the charges against this Simeon?"

"Treason. Rebellion. He was part of an attack on a Roman column."

She tried to look shocked. "Oh? Did he kill anyone?"

Marcus watched her evenly. "We lost twenty-eight men that night."

Miriam wanted to shout at him. Simeon hadn't killed those men— Moshe Ya'abin had. But she let none of that show on her face.

"I understand your desire to repay a debt, Miriam, but I do not think it wise to bring this up with the governor. This particular prisoner has created serious problems for us, and the governor has strong feelings against him."

"Is it true that he brought in three talents of gold as a ransom for his men, which the governor seized, then took the man captive anyway?"

Marcus actually jerked around at that question. "Where did you hear that?"

She shrugged. "The same person who told us of the arrest. This David, Simeon's father, is a prominent citizen and highly respected. If what the man said is true, the arrest will stir up great agitation in the countryside. They say Simeon is the famous Ha'keedohn, the Javelin. I don't know if you knew that."

"Oh, we knew," he murmured.

Suddenly Miriam's eyes fell on Marcus's forearm. A six-inch streak of white was visible through the dark hair on his arm. Startled, she remembered Deborah's story of that day last fall when the Romans came to collect taxes from David ben Joseph. Simeon had grabbed the Roman tribune and cut his arm badly. Miriam stared. She had never made the connection until this moment. It was Marcus who was there that day.

"What?" Marcus said, noting her look.

"I—I had never noticed that scar before."

He looked down, then dropped his arm. "A minor skirmish, quickly forgotten."

"So is it true?"

"What?" He was still thinking about the day of his "minor skirmish."

"That Pilate took the gold and arrested the man too?"

"Miriam, as a Roman officer, I am not at liberty to discuss any circumstances related to our garrison." Then seeing the look of triumph flash across her eyes and knowing she had read it for exactly what it was—an admission that she was right—he went on blandly. "But I can tell you that most rumors have little basis in reality. They multiply like frogs in a swamp."

"Please let me see him, Marcus," she said, completely contrite now. "That morning in Samaria, Moshe Ya'abin had me by the hair. He was dragging me back into my tent to—" She shook her head and closed her eyes. "If Simeon had come even two minutes later my life would have been ruined. I have to know if these are the same men who saved me that day."

"I'm sorry, Miriam. Only the governor can authorize that." He smiled again, putting all of his considerable charm behind it. "When he returns, I will come with you when you talk with him. I will put your cause to Pilate with as much force as possible. Fair enough?"

Miriam knew when she had lost. "Fair enough. Thank you, Marcus." She sighed. "Now, you are right. I am very tired." She looked around briefly. "Suddenly a hot bath and an early trip to bed sounds most wonderful."

He was clearly disappointed. "I would like to hear what you did in the Galilee. Your father said you were going to Gaulanitis. That is a place I have not yet visited. Are you sure you won't have supper with me?"

"Quite sure. I'm sorry, Marcus. I am very tired. Perhaps tomorrow."

He bowed low. "As you wish. I shall see that you are not disturbed."

CHAPTER 14

EASY IS THE WAY DOWN TO THE UNDERWORLD:
BY NIGHT AND BY DAY DARK DIS'S DOOR STANDS OPEN;
BUT TO WITHDRAW ONE'S STEPS AND TO MAKE A WAY OUT
TO THE UPPER AIR, THAT'S THE TASK, THAT IS THE LABOUR.

—*Virgil*, Aeneid, *vi. 128–31*

I

CAESAREA

15 JULY, A.D. 30

There was a sharp knock on the door. Miriam looked up. She was combing out her hair with a sandalwood comb in front of a highly polished brass mirror. "Come in."

She moved sideways a little so she could see the reflection of the door in the mirror. Nothing happened. "Come in," she called more loudly.

There was a click; then the door opened. She saw only a dark shape standing in the doorway. She set the comb down and turned. Her mouth fell open and a cry exploded from her. "Papa!" She was up in an instant and flew across the room.

He opened his arms and drew her in. "Good afternoon, Miriam," he laughed, caught totally by surprise at her enthusiasm.

"But Marcus said you weren't going to be here until late tonight or tomorrow."

"Pilate finished his business in the city more quickly than he expected. And all of my affairs are in order now, so we came most of the way yesterday."

He stepped back, holding her at arm's length. "Are you all right?"

"Of course."

"Marcus said that you haven't been eating much these last two days. You're not sick?"

"I'm fine, Papa. Really."

"Good." His brow lowered. "I suppose Marcus told you about what's been happening?"

"About someone breaking into the house? Yes, he did."

"Yes, yes," he said. "But it's much more than that. Ya'abin grows more bold every day. He's raiding the King's Highway across the Jordan. He's kidnapped three prominent citizens of Jerusalem in just the last two weeks. He is hitting Roman patrols at will and making them look like fools. The night before we left, word came in that he had killed six more legionnaires. Men are flocking to his band. The whole of Judea is trembling with fear."

He exhaled slowly. "It is a very good thing we are out of Jerusalem, Miriam. I don't know how soon they will run him to ground."

"Are you sure you are all right?"

"I'm fine. We caught the intruders and put them in chains. In fact, Pilate brought them back with us. They'll be interrogated, but Ya'abin's too shrewd to send someone who could lead us back to him."

The word interrogated sent a chill through her. "Papa, I—"

"Where's Ezra? I want to thank him and Lilly. It was a wonderful idea to get you out of Jerusalem. It was such a relief to me to not have to worry about you."

"Ezra and Lilly left for Joppa yesterday morning. Ezra has been gone from his sandal shop for so long he wanted to get back as soon as possible."

"I shall see to it that his service is greatly rewarded."

"He won't take anything, Papa. You know Ezra."

"I know. So I've arranged for some of the shopkeepers in Jerusalem to buy all of their sandals from him in the future."

Touched by his genuine gratitude, she laid a hand on his arm. "That's wonderful, Papa. He and Lilly were very good to Livia and me."

"I know." He took her hand. "Come, dinner is almost ready. Pilate has invited us to eat with him and Marcus."

Miriam pulled free and stepped back. "Papa, we have to talk first."

"It can wait until—"

"No!"

He was startled by the sharpness in her voice and felt a flush of irritation. She took a quick breath and plunged ahead.

"Papa, they have arrested Simeon ben David of Capernaum. He's here in the prison."

One eyebrow lifted suspiciously. "Yes, I know all about that. But how do you know?"

"The word is out all over the Galilee. Everyone is talking about the ambush at the Joknean Pass."

He grunted something. That wasn't too surprising.

"Did Pilate tell you why he was so determined to catch Simeon?"

"Of course. Simeon is the one who engineered the whole disaster there that night."

"Oh?" she said quietly. "I thought that was *you*, Papa."

He was momentarily startled; then his eyes narrowed. Miriam knew she was flirting with danger now. She could see that her father was tired from the journey, and when he was tired, his temper quickly shortened. But she pressed on.

"They're saying that one of the reasons Pilate was so anxious to catch Simeon is that he's the only one who knows who betrayed the Romans. The governor wants to force that information out of Simeon."

"That's true. Pilate is still in a rage over what happened there. We—" He caught himself. "He had the whole of the Zealot movement within his grasp, then lost it all."

"What difference does it make?" she asked. "So what if Pilate finds out who told Simeon? What can he do?"

"Nail him to a cross," Mordechai snapped.

"And how will that change what happened that night?"

He was looking at her in disbelief. "You know as well as I do that the Romans don't take kindly to being made to look like fools. They will have their revenge. If they don't, every ragtag band of rebels in the empire will think they can take them on."

"So why aren't *you* afraid, Papa?" Miriam asked quietly.

"What?"

"Pilate is going to force Simeon to tell him who it was that betrayed the Roman column to the Zealots."

"Yes? So?"

"Why doesn't that worry you? *You* are the one who brought Simeon and Yehuda to our house and told them all about the arms and the gold. *You* are the one who brought Ya'abin in on this in the first place. You said it was an elaborate scheme to finally get your revenge on that old bandit, and that the Zealots would profit greatly from it. That's what you told me, and that's what you told Simeon and Yehuda. So why aren't you afraid that it will be *your* name Simeon gives to them?"

"I—" He clearly had not seen that one coming at all.

Miriam turned and walked back to her dressing table. She sat down heavily, staring at him in the mirror. "I've been thinking a lot about what we heard in the Galilee. They are saying that the whole thing was a cleverly engineered trap, not to catch Moshe Ya'abin, but to destroy the whole Zealot movement. They're saying that someone on the Great Council in Jerusalem was behind it. Then someone came and told Simeon what was really happening, and he and his father stepped in and changed the outcome. And they're saying it was Simeon who actually stopped Ya'abin from annihilating the Roman column."

"You've been listening to too much gossip."

"Oh, really?" she retorted. "Well, if it isn't true, then why is Pilate so determined to find out who helped Simeon?"

"Because the Romans lost twenty-eight men that night. It was an embarrassing defeat. Pilate is seething."

Miriam saw that her father's neck had turned red. She knew that sign. It was the first indicator of a towering rage. She had seen it only three or four times, and it had frightened her a great deal. But that was all right, because she was feeling a deep anger and outrage of her own. She gave a short, bitter laugh. "When Marcus told me that Pilate had gone to Jerusalem to get you, shouldn't I have been worried? Was he going there to arrest you and drag you back in chains? But no. Marcus told me Pilate was providing you safe escort back from Jerusalem. Pilate has arranged for us to go to Rome. Pilate has invited us to dine with him. We are honored guests in his palace. Why is that? Why aren't you a suspect in all this, Father? Why aren't you worried that Simeon will be tortured and give them *your* name?"

Mordechai's eyes were flashing dangerously. "You have said enough, Miriam."

"No, I haven't, Father. When you came back from Alexandria, why weren't you more concerned that the whole thing at the pass had fallen apart?"

"Not concerned? I was furious when I heard the news."

"Furious, yes. But worried sick about your own safety? No. Why, Father? Why did you come to Jerusalem with Marcus, the very man who should have been wanting to get his hands on you? And now, you're not in the least concerned about them putting Simeon on the rack. Why is that, Papa? Could it be because Pilate already knows all about your part in this whole affair and that it doesn't bother him at all?"

Jaw tight, eyes suddenly cold, he said, "You are interfering in things that do not concern you, Miriam. I'm warning you. This ends now."

"You used me, Papa! You used me to convince Simeon and Yehuda that you really were trying to help them, to give the whole thing some legitimacy. Don't tell me this doesn't concern me."

He took a step forward, his face as dark as smoke from a furnace. But at that moment, there was a sharp knock on the door. "Master Mordechai?" It was the voice of the servant assigned to care for Pilate's guests.

He turned. "Yes."

"Dinner is served, sire. His Excellency requests the company of you and your daughter in the main dining room."

"We'll be right there."

Miriam stood up and swept past him, then stopped at the door. "I won't say anything of this to Marcus or the governor, Father, but I want you to intervene in Simeon's behalf. Ask Pilate for a pardon."

"What? Are you mad?"

"Simeon saved us!" she cried. "Have you forgotten that? He saved us from Moshe Ya'abin. Does that mean nothing to you?"

"It is out of my hands, Miriam. Out of our hands. And I don't want you—"

But she flung open the door and stalked out before he could finish.

II

Miriam was surprisingly calm at the dinner table. Once again the governor or his wife had placed her beside Marcus, and she spoke easily with him about the upcoming visit to Rome. To her surprise, the confrontation with her father had not dampened her appetite. Since arriving at the governor's palace, she had eaten only one meal, and that was yesterday at midday. Then she had started fasting again. In fact, that was the only full meal she had eaten in the four days since leaving the inn outside Nazareth where she and her fellow travelers had stayed. Her body felt it. After the clash with her father, she felt listless and drained. It was hard for her not to heap her plate and plunge in eagerly.

The meal spread before them was dazzling. It was the height of the summer harvest in Israel now, and the governor of the province obviously had his pick of the best. The table before them almost groaned beneath the weight of the food. There were great platters of sliced melon, deep red and speckled with seeds. Piles of purple grapes were stationed about every five feet. There were trays of dates rolled in chopped almonds and honeyed flour, sliced cucumbers, quartered tomatoes, and mounds of olives. One bowl held nothing but halved pomegranates oozing their deep scarlet juice. There were several different varieties of squash. Dried figs, boiled quail eggs, loaves of bread, hand-buttered rolls, and wedges of cheese filled every available space. Pitchers of wine, kept cool in great jars in the cisterns beneath the palace, were strategically placed on the table.

Though Miriam ate slowly and demurely, never had anything tasted so wonderful to her.

"I'm glad to see you finally eating, Miriam," Marcus said approvingly.

"It's wonderful," she replied.

They were semireclining on padded benches around the low, U-shaped table. Pilate and his wife sat at the head of the table. Her father sat to their right, the place of honor—another interesting indicator of what was going on here—and Miriam and Marcus were to their left. If there were other guests in the Praetorium at the moment, they had not been invited. Livia, as a servant, was of course not even given a second thought.

"Marcus tells me that you have been somewhat ill," Fortunata said. "It is a good sign if you have your appetite back."

Miriam turned to face the governor's wife. "Oh no, not ill" she said lightly. "I am fine. It was just that traveling from the Galilee in this heat drained my appetite."

"I can understand that," she answered. "I hate this accursed heat. I can hardly wait for the rains to come again."

Fortunata's skin was pale, almost translucent, and showed no trace of sun. The few times she went out into the open, she kept herself carefully covered under a canopy lest her delicate skin be damaged. It was common knowledge among the people of Judea how bitterly the governor's wife detested the country her husband ruled.

Marcus looked at Miriam's father. "You seem to have lost your appetite as well, Mordechai. Are you feeling well?"

Startled, Mordechai jerked his head up. "Yes, I'm fine." He picked off a grape from a nearby cluster and put it into his mouth to prove his point.

"You do look a little pale," Pilate observed. "Perhaps we pushed too hard to get back."

"Perhaps." Mordechai glanced quickly at Miriam, then away. "But really, I am just a little tired."

"Did the governor tell you that your ship is in port?" Fortunata asked Mordechai.

He looked up, obviously still distracted. "No, but Marcus did. He says it is one of the large grain ships from Alexandria."

She looked at Miriam. "That is good. It will make for a smooth voyage. Not that you should see much bad weather in the summer sailing season. Perhaps a thunderstorm or two in the Ionian Sea, but these ships are so large that when they are fully loaded they roll much less. I refuse to travel on anything smaller."

"Good," Miriam said, forcing a smile. "I have heard much about seasickness and do not look forward to that part of our experience." Then she turned to Pilate. "Excellency?"

Her father visibly started and shot her a sharp glance. She ignored it as Pilate waved a hand for her to proceed.

"Has Marcus spoken with you about my request?"

Marcus straightened, warning her off with his eyes. "I haven't, Miriam. Since the governor's return this afternoon, there has been disturbing news out of the Galilee. Our time has been occupied with that."

"Really?" she said, surprised. "What is that?"

Marcus glanced at Pilate, who nodded his approval for Marcus to say more.

"There has been an uprising."

Mordechai was instantly alert. "In the Galilee?"

"Yes, near Sepphoris. A band of Zealots attacked our garrison there—a small one—and drove our men out. One man was killed."

"Zealots?" Miriam said slowly.

"Yes," Pilate snapped. "Seems that word of the arrest of the Javelin has reached their ears. They think they can influence his sentence by offering a demonstration of their power."

Marcus said nothing more. What Pilate was choosing not to say was that the letter that had come from Sextus Rubrius was very sobering. It wasn't just Sepphoris. The reaction was erupting everywhere. A small group of men had scaled the walls at Beth Shean, a major garrison on the River Jordan, and set fire to the granaries, shops, and barracks. "Free Ha'keedohn or die!" had been painted on the outer gate. Four guards at the small armory in Capernaum had been overpowered during that same night, and a large cache of weapons was taken.

According to Sextus, word was out everywhere in the north that Pilate had accepted Simeon's offer of three talents of gold as a ransom, then turned and taken him prisoner anyway. The whole of the Galilee was aflame with outrage. David ben Joseph was a highly respected man. His family had mortgaged a significant part of their fortune in order to free the prisoners from Beth Neelah. Ha'keedohn, the Javelin, had been widely admired among the various Zealot bands. He had infuriated his fellow rebels when he insisted on giving the Romans safe passage out of the Joknean Pass, but he had done it for the oath's sake. They didn't like it, but it was something everyone understood. Now, to have the very ones he had saved that night violate their own honor and lure him in with treachery was the flash point needed to unite the squabbling bands of Zealots into one united front. Sextus was urgently requesting that two cohorts—more than a thousand men—be sent immediately to Capernaum to see if their presence might calm things.

Pilate turned to his young guest. "Yes, my dear," he said to Miriam. "You were saying?"

"Miriam!" Her father's voice was quiet, but there was a sharp edge to it.

That immediately caught Pilate's attention and he sat back, eyeing the two of them thoughtfully. "What request is this you speak of, Miriam?"

"I am told," Miriam started, deliberately avoiding the glares of both her father and Marcus, "that you have a prisoner here by the name of Simeon ben David of Capernaum."

The coarse and weathered features didn't change, but the narrow gray eyes suddenly glittered coldly. "Yes?"

Feeling her heart jump, she went on, choosing her words with great care. "Earlier this spring, my father and I were saved from a very dangerous situation by a man of that same name, also from Capernaum."

Pilate's eyes probed hers for several seconds; then he turned to Mordechai. "What is this? You have not told me this before."

"I did speak of it some time ago, sire," Mordechai said. "It was when the delegation from the Great Council went to the Galilee to arrange a meeting with the Zealots. Ya'abin struck our camp while we were in Samaria. The Zealot council had sent an escort, and fortunately they arrived in time to intervene. I'm sure I mentioned this to you when we came here to Caesarea on our way back to Jerusalem."

"Oh, yes, I remember now. Your chief steward betrayed you to Ya'abin."

"Yes, sire," Mordechai came in. "Ya'abin was on the verge of taking Miriam into her tent to have his way with her when Simeon and Yehuda appeared."

Pilate erupted. "Ya'abin? That pig! Is nothing below the man?"

Fortunata's hand flew to her mouth. "How dreadful!" she cried.

But Pilate was raging. He swung on Marcus. "The man attacks our columns, robs my custom agents, defies me at every hand. By the gods! I would give a fortune to get my hands on him, but the commander in Jerusalem cannot tell me that they are even close to finding and stopping him. Maybe it's time we give the man a few lashes to increase his motivation."

Marcus said nothing. He had already heard all of this earlier.

Miriam waited for Pilate's outburst to subside, then went on. "Even if Ya'abin had not taken our lives, my life would have been ruined." She made no effort to hide the pain on her face. "But just as I was about to be taken, this Simeon arrived and drove Ya'abin and his men away. We owe him a great debt, Excellency, me most of all."

She hesitated for a moment. Pilate was fully attentive, but there was also something else behind those eyes.

"When I arrived here, I asked Tribune Marcus if I could have permission to see this prisoner and discover for myself if it is the same man who helped us in Samaria."

"Sire," Mordechai broke in swiftly, "my daughter's feelings about this incident have overcome her better judgment. I apologize for her. We have no right to make such a request."

Miriam's head came up. "It is a great debt that we owe, Excellency." She shot her father a withering look. "*Both* of us."

"Sire?" Marcus broke in, trying to see if he could salvage this before it got fully away from him. "Miriam did speak to me of this earlier. I explained that only you could give that permission. I told her I would speak to you of it on your return."

There was a barely perceptible nod, but the governor's eyes never left Miriam. "And if it is the same man?"

"Then we should—"

Mordechai overrode her. "Though there is a debt there, sire, we would not feel it wise to intervene in your internal affairs."

"Sire, though I honor my father's feelings, because of what we owe to this man, I would ask that you consider clemency in his behalf."

"Not you too?" he grumped.

That was not what either Miriam or her father had expected. "Me too?" Miriam asked.

"Yes. I had a delegation of Pharisees call on me this afternoon. Couldn't even wait until I got the dust off my feet from our journey. I sent them away just before coming in here."

"And they came about Simeon?" Mordechai asked. Pharisees? This was not good news. "Were they from Jerusalem?"

"No, no. Mostly local leaders. But they had a delegation of three from Capernaum, including a man who claimed to be this Simeon's uncle. They carried a letter from the chief Pharisee on the council there in Capernaum asking that I reconsider my—" his voice was suddenly mocking—"*arrangements* concerning this Simeon." He snorted angrily. "I hate those people. Can't they ever just come straight out and say what they mean without all the innuendo and veiled threats?"

"Threats?" Marcus said.

"Yes," Pilate said with a dismissive wave. "They reminded me that the Pharisees carry great influence with the people and that an execution of this man might not be looked upon too favorably."

Pilate looked at Marcus, a sudden thought striking him. "Write Sextus, Marcus. See if he can find out if these Pharisees might have anything to do with the outbreak in Galilee. If they do, I'll clap the lot of them behind bars."

He nibbled on a dried fig, then flipped it aside and glared at Miriam. "Why is it everyone suddenly has an interest in this man?"

Mordechai was all smoothness. "I apologize, Excellency. Miriam's emotions, understandable though they may be, caused her to forget herself. We do not wish to make any formal request concerning your prisoners."

The betrayal was complete. She couldn't even meet the eyes of her father.

"Miriam?"

She raised her head slowly. Pilate was smiling at her, but his smile sent a chill clear through her body. "I am sorry, my dear, but it doesn't much matter whether this Simeon is the same man as the one who helped you or not. He and I are going to spend the day together tomorrow and discuss a few items that concern me." His voice went suddenly very hard. "Request denied."

III

"Oh, Livia, what am I going to do?"

Livia shook her head slowly. "I don't know, Miriam. I don't know."

Miriam was pacing back and forth in front of her bed. "I have to do something. Pilate is going to start torturing Simeon tomorrow."

"He said that?"

"He may as well have."

"Simeon won't betray you, Miriam," Livia said slowly. "No matter what they do to him."

"I know that, Livia," she shot back. "But I can't let them do that. I can't."

She stopped and swung around. "I'll go tell Father that if he doesn't intervene, we're not going to Rome with him."

Livia went instantly pale. "You can't say that. He'll bind you to the mast if he has to. And then there is Ya'abin. If he ever gets his hands on you again, Miriam . . . " She gave a tiny shudder.

"We'll go back to Capernaum," Miriam said, her words tumbling out. "I'll change my name. We'll go into hiding for a time." Her shoulders slumped, and she sat down heavily on the bed. When she looked at Livia, she was near tears. "As we left dinner, my father said that if I say one more word about this, he will see to it that no further search is made for your brother when we get to Rome."

Livia paled. "He said that?"

"Yes. He was so angry he could hardly speak. All he could do was say over and over, 'You'll ruin everything.'" She hesitated, then decided that Livia needed to know it all. "He also said that there will be no more talk about me adopting you as my sister."

Livia immediately moved to her. "That doesn't matter. What we have between us doesn't depend on a piece of paper."

"I know but—" She flung herself backwards on the bed, throwing an arm up across her face. "Oh, Livia, what can we do?"

Livia laid down on the bed beside her. "Keep praying. That's all we can do."

Miriam looked up in disbelief, almost as if she hadn't heard correctly.

"We can't give up, Miriam. That's what Jesus said. We have to pray and not lose heart."

Miriam sat up again. Her shoulders lifted and fell, then straightened again. "Yes. You are right, Livia. We can't give up." She got to her feet shakily. "Let's pray right now."

"Of course," Livia said.

Then Miriam's emotions rose again. "If only Ya'abin wasn't still free," Miriam wailed. "I could stay here. I could raise more money. Maybe three talents just wasn't enough for Pilate."

Livia knelt down at the bedside. She waited, then reached up and tugged at Miriam's hand. "Come, Miriam. We need to pray."

But Miriam had gone rigid. Her eyes had widened into enormous circles as she stared straight ahead at the wall.

Livia got up quickly, alarmed by the sudden change in Miriam. "What? What is it?"

"If only Ya'abin wasn't still here!" she whispered in awe.

"What are you saying? What do you mean by that?"

Miriam spun around. "I have to see my father."

"Now?"

"Yes!" She started toward the door, then stopped. "Keep praying, Livia. Don't give up. I'll be back as soon as I can."

IV

"Father, we have to talk."

His tired eyes instantly hardened. "It's over, Miriam. I told you, there will be no more discussion on this. I won't hear any more of this nonsense."

"I know how to free Simeon."

He started to shut the door again. "I don't care. Go to bed."

She stepped forward, blocking the door with her shoulder. "If Simeon breaks under torture tomorrow, I know the name he will give Pilate."

He stopped, surprise replacing anger. She pushed the door open. Looking quickly up and down the corridor, she stepped inside his bedroom and pushed the door shut. She noted that he was still dressed.

His bed was turned down but was unrumpled. Papers were scattered across one table.

"I'm in no mood for games, Miriam," her father said. "What are you saying? How could you possibly know that?"

"Because it was *me*, Papa."

He stared at her blankly.

"Yes, Father. Me! I'm the one who told Simeon all your plans."

Mordechai ben Uzziel, one of Jerusalem's most powerful citizens, went as pale as a sheet of linen. He stood there, feet apart, just staring at her. "I don't believe you."

She moved over and sat down slowly on his bed. "I was still awake that night that Marcus came to the house to make the final arrangements with you. I heard his voice and came down to the garden to say hello." Her face colored a little. "I didn't mean to eavesdrop. I just wanted to surprise Marcus. But I heard it all, Father. I heard everything you said to him." She paused, and then finished. "The morning after you left for Alexandria, I went to Capernaum and told Simeon everything."

One part of Mordechai was recoiling at such a preposterous notion, but the analytical part of his mind was dropping pieces of the puzzle into place. It answered all of the questions. It explained everything.

Miriam finally looked up. "Why do you think Simeon and his father were willing to put up three talents of their own money? Partly it was to try to save Yehuda, but partly it was to protect me, to stop Pilate from ever finding out the name that he so desperately wants."

Mordechai passed his hand across his eyes. He sat in the highest councils of the country. He worked with some of the nation's most powerful and influential men. He had brokered financial contracts worth major fortunes. It took a lot to leave him speechless, but that he was. He just continued to stare at her in disbelief as his mind completed the circle, and he knew with cold fury that she spoke the truth.

"I won't try to justify what I did to you. Nor will I try to convince you that what you did was wrong, terribly wrong, but—"

"Wrong!" he shouted, finally coming out of the daze. "You dare to talk to me about right and wrong?"

He whirled and stalked to the table. She saw that his hands were trembling as he stared down at his papers. Then with one mighty swipe of his arm, he sent them flying. He spun back around. "We had peace within our grasp," he exclaimed. "Not just for our time, but for generations to come. We were on the verge of the greatest victory for peace our nation has ever known."

"By sending a thousand men to their deaths?" she cried.

His mouth opened, then shut again. His eyes were like tiny points of black light. "Not a thousand men. A thousand fanatics! A thousand lunatics who think that God has given them some divine mission to overthrow Rome, the first government to offer us a chance for real peace and prosperity in six hundred years. By all that is holy, Miriam, what have you done?"

He kicked savagely at the padded, backless chair he had been using at the table. It skittered across the polished marble floor and slammed against the wall with a crash. Miriam shrank back, her eyes wide and round. He spun around, raging like a wounded bear.

Outside the door, there was the sound of running footsteps. They stopped; then there was a sharp knock. "Master Mordechai? Are you all right?"

"Get out of here!" Mordechai roared. "Leave us alone!"

But the interruption stopped the blind, mindless fury. Miriam sat huddled on the bed, head down, hands clenched tightly in her lap. For several minutes he vented his barely contained wrath. He swore, he cursed, he threatened, he fumed. She was no longer his daughter. He never wanted to see her face again. He would confine her to the house for the next ten years if that's what it took to teach her obedience. They would go to Rome, and she would never be allowed to return.

Her inheritance was cut off as of this very moment. She was no longer worthy to be his daughter. Maybe he would just tell Pilate himself so the governor would know that Mordechai had no part in her treachery. Twice, as the enormity of her betrayal sunk into his mind, she thought he was going to strike her.

When he was finally spent, he sat down heavily on one of the benches and dropped his head into his hands. Miriam didn't move for several minutes, watching his chest gradually stop its violent heaving.

Finally she stood. "If you wish to tell Pilate what I did, then let's do it now, Father."

He jerked up. "Stop it, Miriam! You know I can't do that. Won't do that. Justice would be well served if I did, that is true enough. But Pilate will strip you naked and feed your flesh to the vultures. The fact that you are my daughter will only make him all the more determined to use you as an example."

"If you say the word, I will leave tonight and you will never see me again."

"We are going to Rome, Miriam," he muttered. "Get that into your head. I will brook no more objections to that and no more disobedience from you. Do you hear me?"

"Yes, Father." She gave him another few moments, then asked the crucial question. "And what if Simeon doesn't hold out, Father? What if he gives Pilate my name? Then what?"

His fingers came up, and he began to rub at his eyes. "I don't know." There was an infuriated cry again. "What were you thinking, Miriam? What in heaven's name possessed you? Did the possibility of what the Romans would do to you if they ever found this out never even cross your mind?" He looked up at her, his eyes haggard and bloodshot.

"I did what I felt I had to do. I'm sorry that it has caused you so much grief."

He swore, softly enough that she wasn't sure what he said.

She took a quick breath. "There is a way out of this, Father."

He sat up fully, lips pinched into a tight line. "Free Simeon?" he scoffed.

"Yes. If he goes free, Pilate will never know who betrayed him."

"And what would you have me do to bring that miracle about? Barge into the governor's bedroom and read some scripture to him? Perhaps play some soothing music on a lyre? Offer him a handful of ripe grapes to soothe his mood?"

Miriam's head came up slowly. "If you get me in to see him, I can convince him to let Simeon go."

V

Clothing a Roman gentleman properly in his white toga was an art. It had to be draped just right over the shoulder and arm. The folds had to be precise and even. The skirt had to be perfectly level at the ankle. It could take even a trained slave close to quarter of an hour to get it right. Pilate had removed his toga after dinner and did not take the time to put it on again. He wore a simple brown tunic that came to mid-thigh, secured at the waist with a simple leather belt. He was shod in the sandals he normally wore only in his chambers. His feet slapped softly on the marble floor as he paced back and forth.

At the sound of the door opening, he turned. The expression on his face was moody and dark.

Marcus came in first, followed by Miriam and then Mordechai. Pilate gave his commanding officer a sharp look. "You are party to this too?"

Marcus bowed his head slightly. "Miriam and her father have come to me with a proposal, sire. They felt if I could not approve, there was no sense troubling you. I think it has enough merit to warrant your attention."

"And it had to be tonight?" he snapped.

Miriam came forward to stand beside Marcus. "Yes, Excellency. I'm sorry, but it is a matter of some urgency." He started to say something, but she went on quickly. "And my father is not responsible for my impertinence, Excellency. He tried diligently to talk me out of this course of action, but alas, his daughter brings him much frustration."

Pilate had a bemused expression as he looked at Mordechai. "So it was you who was trying to break my furniture?" he asked.

Mordechai flushed, then held out his hands. "Miriam's mother died when she was six years old. I fear that being raised by an old man such as myself has left her very headstrong and spirited, sire. It can be very exasperating."

Pilate nodded, pleased that the Jew had not tried to temporize or pretend not to know what he was referring to. "What is it then?" he said, looking at Marcus.

There was a moment's hesitation; then the tribune turned to Miriam. "It was Miriam who thought of this possible solution, sire. With your permission, I would suggest that she be the one to present it to you."

Pilate frowned, not particularly pleased with that protocol, but nodded. He moved to a large marble armchair that was almost like a throne and sat down. He didn't suggest they sit, and so none of them moved. "Go on, then," he said with a wave of his hand.

Miriam took one step forward. "Sire, the obligation I feel toward this Simeon may not seem as important to you as it is to me, but in our culture, when a person saves another's life there is an attendant debt of gratitude that cannot lightly be ignored."

"It is the same in our society."

"It is for this reason that I feel compelled to speak in his behalf."

His mouth pulled down. "I told you that this issue was settled, " he warned. "I thought I had made that quite clear this evening."

"I understand, Excellency. And I would not interfere in these affairs further if it had not occurred to me that there is a way to honor my obligation and at the same time offer solutions to some problems confronting you and your government."

His heavy brows wrinkled slightly. "You're going to tell me that helping this Simeon will be to my benefit?"

"Yes, sire."

He looked at her father, an amused expression on his face. "You are right, Mordechai. Her impertinence is almost breathtaking."

Mordechai only inclined his head and said nothing.

Miriam was churning inside. His comment had been half in jest, but there was a clear warning beneath the light tone. *This had better be worth disturbing me at this hour of the night.*

Speaking slowly, she continued. "Tonight, sire, you spoke of two frustrations you currently face, costly and dangerous frustrations. The first is Moshe Ya'abin. As you noted, he grows more bold with each passing day. After more than a month, your troops are no closer to caging him. This is not a surprise. The wilderness of Judea has served as a hiding place for those who wish to avoid capture since the time of our King David a thousand years ago."

Pilate's eyes had darkened. He was keenly aware of the failings of his garrison in Jerusalem, but he did not appreciate her taking note of that fact. "And my other *supposed* frustration?"

She didn't miss his emphasis on *supposed*. "It is the uprising in the north. Marcus tells us that it is spreading rapidly. I do not need to tell you, sire, that the Galilee has always been a tinderbox of rebellion. More than once they have been the cause of great problems for Rome."

He nodded curtly. "Go on."

She took a deep breath, held it for a moment, then plunged ahead.

"What if Simeon of Capernaum could eliminate both of those frustrations for you, sire? Then would you consider releasing him?"

VI

As Miriam and her father moved down the corridor toward their rooms, Mordechai spoke in a low voice. "If the answer from Pilate is no, Miriam, that ends it. Do you understand me?"

"Yes, Father."

"You have put us both at tremendous risk. Your actions could destroy everything I've spent a lifetime working to achieve. If Pilate rejects this proposal, you will not say another word."

Miriam had already decided that for herself. She knew she had skirted the edge of the volcano this night. "The fact that he asked Marcus to stay is a good sign," she suggested.

"Perhaps. Perhaps not."

"Do you think Marcus will speak in favor of the proposal?"

He shrugged. "It makes sense both strategically and tactically, and Marcus is a wise and experienced commander." He lowered his voice, looking around. "On the other hand, Pilate wants that name from Simeon very badly. His ego has been severely bruised, and that is no small matter with this governor."

They had reached Mordechai's door. Both stopped for a moment. Miriam watched him out of the corner of her eye. He was staring at nothing, deep in his thoughts. "Father, I—" But she stopped. She was not going to apologize to him for what she had done. Let his fury roll. She had done the right thing.

He turned, his face grim. "Let us hope that your idea solves our immediate problem, Miriam. But don't think for a moment that the other is forgotten. Your foolishness has wrought great harm. You have done tremendous damage to our cause. That simply cannot be ignored."

"If you are looking for a way to punish me, Father," Miriam said evenly, "you have already found it. Going to Rome is the answer. It is something I dread beyond anything you can imagine."

"Good night, Miriam." He opened the door and went inside, closing it sharply behind him.

Miriam stood there for a moment, then turned and walked on, knowing that Livia would be anxious for her return.

VII

16 July, A.D. 30

Simeon was calculating in his head.

His cell opened directly onto the corridor of the prison, with no door. It was approximately seven feet long, four feet wide, and perhaps six feet high. The low ceiling was covered with plaster, probably over laths and beams. Each of the side walls, as well as the main wall that formed the back of the prison, was made of bricks. There were seven hundred ninety-three bricks in each cell, if you counted all three sides. Yesterday, he had risked a hard kick when he inched as far forward as his chains would allow to see around the edge of the wall. He couldn't see all the way to the end in either direction, but he saw enough to estimate there were fourteen cells in this particular part of the prison.

That information had required him to start over again. He finally resorted to straws carefully laid out on the stone floor to help him keep track of the multiplication. Too bad Ephraim wasn't here. He had always been the quick one with figures.

He stopped. *Too bad Ephraim isn't here?* He almost broke into laughter. Ephraim surely would not agree with that wish.

So, seven hundred ninety-three bricks in each cell, and there were fourteen cells. He began to push the straws with his finger, careful not to let the chains dangling from his wrist brush across the floor and ruin his count again. The long straws each counted for a hundred—

His head came up as the heavy metal door at the top of the stairs screeched sharply. A moment later he heard the sound of footsteps starting down. He felt himself tense. The bread and water had been brought no more than an hour before. Was it time? Were they finally coming for him?

He carefully sat up and placed one leg over his "mathematics board" so no one could see what he was doing. He didn't recognize the step, and he knew every guard by now, especially the ones you had to be especially careful around.

Only when the footsteps stopped directly in front of the cell did Simeon look up. He fought back a look of surprise, and instead forced a bored expression as he looked into the face of Marcus Quadratus Didius.

"Good afternoon."

"Is it?" he asked. "Is it good? And is it afternoon?"

Marcus moved a step closer. "I need to ask you some questions."

"Save your breath. That issue is already settled."

For a moment, Marcus didn't understand; then he brushed Simeon's comment aside. "I'm not here to ask who betrayed us."

In spite of himself, Simeon raised his head slightly.

"How well do you know Moshe Ya'abin?"

"Ya'abin?" He couldn't keep the surprise out of his voice. Then he smiled. "Still haven't caught the old fox yet, eh?"

"He's doubled or tripled the number of his men since the Joknean Pass. And he's become much more bold."

"After what happened that night, I'm sure he feels he's got some scores to settle," Simeon said. "Are your soldiers still getting footsore looking for him out there in the desert?"

"Do you think you could do any better?"

"Are you looking for advice from me? Sorry, my fees would be a little steep for you."

"I'm not looking for advice. Yes or no? Do you think you could do better?"

Again Simeon took the measure of the man, especially watching his eyes. This was not a casual question and he wasn't sure why. Finally he shrugged. "Any man is catchable. The problem with you Romans is you act like you are hunting elephants when what you are chasing is a rabbit."

"And you think you could catch a rabbit?"

Simeon closed his eyes. "Actually, my schedule is pretty full at the moment."

For a long time, Marcus was silent, eyeing Simeon up and down. Then he dropped into a crouch. He talked swiftly and concisely, describing in short, hard sentences what was happening in the Galilee. Finished, he sat back on his heels.

Simeon tipped back his head and laughed. "So it's begun without me? I should have known that." Yet even as he taunted Marcus, his mind was racing. Why had he come to share this news with him? He shot the Roman a derisive look. "You should have foreseen it too. The Galilee is like a small village. Everyone knows everything. It looks like your decision to set aside your honor backfired. Did you come here expecting sympathy?"

Marcus's jaw tightened, but he said nothing. He knew what Simeon was doing, and he was determined not to be provoked.

"Suppose you were given a free hand. Could you convince your countrymen to stop this uprising?"

For a long moment their eyes locked and held; then Simeon raised his hands, rattling the chains that hung from the manacles around his wrists. "And just how literal did you mean 'a free hand'?"

"I meant it literally," Marcus answered quietly.

Simeon stared back at him, his mouth opened slightly in shock.

Amused that he had finally pierced that insufferable arrogance, Marcus smiled. "I come with an offer from Pilate."

"Go on."

"Your freedom in return for two things. Peace in the Galilee and Moshe Ya'abin."

Simeon couldn't help it. He jerked forward so quickly that the chains yanked on the wrist manacles, digging them into his flesh. He was tempted to laugh in Marcus's face, but something in the tribune's eyes let him know this was not some joke, some terribly cruel way to taunt him. "What about the name of the person who betrayed your great secret?"

"That was the hardest for Pilate to give up, but he has agreed. He'll trade that for Ya'abin and for your promise that the uprising will stop."

Simeon was silent, but his mind was working furiously. "Starting when?" he finally asked.

"This afternoon. You think about it very carefully. If you can give me your word that you will deliver on both of those conditions, then you'll be a free man before sundown."

"And Pilate has approved this?" he asked again, still reeling.

"Yes. I wouldn't be here if he hadn't."

Simeon lay back against the rear wall. Marcus waited, guessing at some of the questions going through this man's mind.

"How long would I have?"

"How long do you need?"

He licked his lips. "Peace will be tricky, but if I am released—" He stopped. "I'll need Yehuda, Barak, and Samuel too." He held his breath.

"I told Pilate that's what you'd say."

"Yehuda is my second-in-command. I can't go after Ya'abin alone. And from what you say, part of the fury in the Galilee is that you took those three men after they helped save your Roman necks. If they are not released too, then I can't—"

"Pilate has agreed to that condition."

Simeon rocked back. "He has? He will release all four of us?"

"Yes. You can take them with you today. So how long do you need?"

Simeon was clearly having trouble coping with the sudden changes of events. "The Galilee will take a month, maybe more. We'll have to go around and meet with each group."

"And what about Ya'abin?"

"You say he's tripled his numbers?"

"Yes. And more are flocking to him every day. He's been hitting caravans up and down the King's Highway, robbing the custom houses, making off with gold and huge caches of incense. He's got plenty of money and spoils to draw every criminal within a hundred furlongs."

"I assume you want more than just Ya'abin himself."

Marcus didn't hesitate. He and Pilate had discussed this late into the night and again this morning. "Ya'abin is to be delivered alive if at all possible. But the band has to be destroyed once and for all. Totally annihilated. Anything less will not be acceptable."

Simeon wasn't greatly surprised. "I will have to gather a force of my own."

"You can have as many of our troops as you need."

A scathing look was the only answer to that. "It will take some time to outfit my band again." Simeon was still thinking to himself. Then he turned. "I assume asking for your help in rearming my men would be unwise."

"It was your men from Beth Neelah who hit the armory in Capernaum. Do you really want me to go back and suggest that to Pilate?"

Simeon gave a quick shake of his head. Finally, he nodded. "I can start showing results in six to eight months," he said, trying to sound as positive as he could. "Enough to stop Ya'abin from bothering you and start him after us. I can have it over in a year. Fourteen months at the most, counting the time it takes us in the Galilee."

Marcus nodded and stood. "Pilate has agreed to six months. If you're certain you can show some results by then, I can convince him to give you one year. But no more. You'll have twelve months from today."

"We will need some money to operate." Simeon frowned. "For some reason, I'm short three gold talents right now. My guess is our noble governor has not made returning those part of his offer."

Marcus didn't have to answer that. "Mordechai ben Uzziel has volunteered to fund this. There will be a thousand shekels put into an account in Jerusalem. I'll have a letter this afternoon giving you instructions on how to get access to those funds. A thousand should be enough to get you started."

That really took Simeon aback. "Mordechai is putting up the money? Why?"

"Because Ya'abin has sworn to kill him. There's already been one attempt on his life. He also fears for Miriam's safety."

Simeon nodded slowly. "Yes, that would be Ya'abin's way. Of all of us, Ya'abin would see Mordechai as his greatest betrayer."

"They're sailing for Rome in a few days—father and daughter. They'll not return until they are sure the fox has been caged." He smiled grimly. "Or the rabbit has been run to ground." Then his voice went hard. "But know this, Simeon. If once you are free you decide to run—"

"I won't run. You have my word on it."

"If you decide to run," Marcus went on stiffly, "or try to take that thousand shekels as your own, we will march on Capernaum. Every man, woman, and child who survives—including your own family—will be sold as slaves. Do you understand that? Pilate wanted me to make that absolutely clear."

Any temptation to be flippant was long gone from Simeon now. "I understand," he answered soberly. "You have my word."

"Your word might be good enough for me," Marcus grunted, "but not for Pilate. Fail, and he'll level the town and sow the site with salt. Nothing will ever grow there again. There won't be so much as a mongrel dog left when he's finished."

Simeon nodded. Marcus gave him one last searching look, then turned and walked toward the stairs. "Guard!" He looked back over his shoulder. "I'll be back this afternoon. Have your answer for me then."

"I have your answer now."

Above them the door screeched as it was opened. "I'll be back."

In a moment he was gone. Simeon crawled forward. "Yehuda? Did you hear all of that?"

"I did," came the answering voice.

"Do you believe him? Or is this the cruelest kind of joke?"

There was a long moment of silence. Then, "No, it makes sense in an odd sort of way. Pilate must have real problems."

"Can we do it in a year?"

This time there was no hesitation. "Get me out of here, my friend, and I'll do it in whatever time you say."

Simeon moved back, placing his back against the side wall of his cell. He stared up at the low ceiling covered with moldy residue. He could scarcely believe it. Freedom. For all four of them. And Miriam's secret would stay safe.

He dropped his head and closed his eyes. "O Father," he breathed, "I thank thee."

And then the words of Jesus came rushing back, like the blast of a trumpet piercing the night. *O ye of little faith, wherefore did you doubt?*

CHAPTER 15

KEEP THY HEART WITH ALL DILIGENCE;
FOR OUT OF IT ARE THE ISSUES OF LIFE.

—*Proverbs 4:23*

I

ROME
10 MARCH, A.D. 31

It was a glorious spring morning. The week of rain had scrubbed the air clean. The haze from the tens of thousands of cooking and household fires was gone for now. Everything stood out in sharp clarity in the clear air. Beyond the buildings, the seven hills of Rome were newly green. Trees were coming into leaf, new grass was bursting forth in every open space, and here and there tiny splashes of color marked the first of the wildflowers.

Miriam breathed deeply, savoring the fresh air. She was walking slowly down the *Via Sacra*, the Sacred Way, the street which cut completely through the *Forum Romanum*. She stopped, turning slowly, ignoring the glares as people pushed around her. She didn't care. Her eyes took it all in—the dozens of monuments to famous persons from more than seven hundred years of history; massive government buildings; more temples than she could name; delicately carved columns everywhere the eye looked; towering arches celebrating the victory of this emperor or that; the *Curia*, or Senate building, from which Rome governed the world; the *Rostra*, a huge outdoor platform where orators exhorted—or, some would say, harangued—the crowds.

She loved it all. As much as that still surprised her, she truly loved it. Eight months ago, she had come here reluctantly, to please her father. She had dreaded it. But now, though she still longed for the day when she could return to her native land, Rome enchanted her.

She loved Italia too. The great villa of Antonius Marcus Didius, father of Marcus Quadratus Didius, lay in rolling vine country just a half hour's walk east of the city. She and Livia and her father had stayed there for the first month after their arrival, until Marcus had secured a luxurious apartment for them in the city. Even now that Marcus had returned to Judea, she and Livia would go out and spend a day visiting with Cornelia, Marcus's mother, while Miriam's father and Marcus's father went off into the study and worked through various financial matters. On those days, though her father always took a carriage, Miriam and Livia would walk, passing through the city gates into the quiet twisting lanes and narrow roads. She loved the countryside.

But there was something about the city.

It had been true of Jerusalem as well. From the time she was a young girl, Miriam would leave the Upper City and plunge into the streets of old Jerusalem, taking the pulse of the city and its people. The *Forum Romanum*, or the Roman Forum, held that same fascination for her, only ten times more, because it was ten times larger, ten times more complex, and ten times more varied. The Forum was the heart of the city, and the *Via Sacra* was its soul. Where she stood now was the center of culture, religion, politics, government, and social life for the mightiest empire the world had ever known. How could one not be impressed with that? When people said that "all roads lead to Rome," they really meant that all roads came right here to the Forum, right here to the *Via Sacra*.

How much history had this one single street seen? On their first visit here, the day after arriving on the ship from her homeland, Marcus had walked her along the Sacred Way, describing the great triumphal processions that often moved down its length. Kings, consuls, emperors, and generals who would go on to become emperors, had marched down this street, receiving the thunderous accolades of the masses. He regaled her with descriptions of the trumpeters who led the processions and called the city to attention. Then came the marching legions, helmets burnished and glowing in the sun, spears in perfect alignment as they marched by. They would be followed by the hundreds of carts filled with the spoils of conquest—chests of treasure dripping with pearls, rubies, diamonds; cages with pacing, snarling lions, tigers, or leopards; exotic linens, gold vessels taken from the temples and palaces of the vanquished. The greatest tumult was reserved for the captives. Generally, only the young and the beautiful or the most fearsome of the enemy were reserved for the triumphal march. He hadn't mentioned it, but Miriam knew that they would then be taken to the arenas and executed or sold to the slave markets.

Marcus had told her that right here in this part of the Forum, scarcely more than seventy years before, Julius Caesar had thrown a massive banquet to celebrate four major victories in one year. The feast lasted for several days, and Marcus swore that twenty-two thousand people had been served. It was ironic that within months Caesar would lie on the floor of the Senate, struck down by assassins, his blood ebbing onto the tile floor. She turned, her eyes picking out the mass of the *Rostra*. At the moment no one was on it, but it was there that Marc Antony had given his passionate eulogy extolling Caesar's greatness.

She started walking again. It was like being in a dozen worlds all at once. With the weather turned warm and dry again, judges were setting up tables around the *Rostra* to begin hearing the various cases that would be brought before them. The participants were already gathering—the litigants, the advocates, the witnesses, the perjurers. In a nearby square was a very different group. Here were the bankers, the investors, the usurers, the brokers, and the sophisticated, elegantly clad women. You also might see an occasional Senator, toga impeccably arranged, haughty and imperious. Down near the canal, which ran through part of the Forum and drained into the Tiber River, were the opposite end of society's spectrum—vagabonds and good-for-nothings, scandal-mongers, parasites begging for some crumb from the rich, charlatans and drunkards, ex-soldiers playing knucklebones and dice, pimps and strumpets and thieves.

"Miriam!"

She turned in surprise, trying to see who had called her name. It was mid-morning now, and the Forum was thronged with people.

"Miriam!"

Turning slightly, her eyes searched the crowd. Then she saw a hand wave. She gasped as Marcus Didius burst through a group of men and pushed around a flower vendor's cart. He was smiling broadly and waving as he came.

"Marcus?" She could hardly believe her eyes.

He trotted up, grinning like a young boy. He was in his uniform— leather breastplate, white tunic, scabbard with its short sword, and the dark brown military-issue sandals. As he reached her, he clasped both of her hands and swung her around. "Hello," he laughed.

She stared at him as she twirled, her eyes taking in the handsomeness of his face, the cleft in his chin, the deep green eyes that were alive with delight. "What are you doing *here?*" she cried, pulling him to a stop.

"My ship docked this morning. I came straight here from Ostia." Ostia was the port for Rome, about seven or eight miles southwest of the city. "I saw your father and he said I could find you here."

"But—" She was still reeling. "I can't believe it. You, here? Did Father know you were coming?"

"No." He motioned for her to follow, then led the way over to the steps that led into the Temple of Castor and Pollux. That took them out of the main flow of the crowds. "I didn't know I was coming until the day before we sailed. Things are quiet in Judea at the moment, and Pilate had some matters he wanted me to bring to the attention of the emperor."

"Can you stay long?"

"A week. Maybe two."

Her face registered her disappointment. "I don't know what to say," she said. "You've taken my breath away. You were surely the last person I expected to meet here this morning."

"I like that idea."

"What idea?"

His smile was suddenly teasing. "Of taking your breath away." Then he changed the subject. "What are you doing?"

"I was just walking. I walk every day now that the weather is so beautiful. I thought spring in Judea was wonderful."

He looked around, letting his eyes sweep across the surrounding hills, savoring what he saw. "I've missed it. This is wonderful."

"Actually," she said, "I came down here this morning hoping to see the procession of the Vestal Virgins. You told me about them on that day you first gave me the guided tour of the city, but I've never actually seen them. I usually get here later in the day and they told me the procession happens each morning."

He took her hand again. "It does. In fact, it shouldn't be long now. But you're not in the best place. Come on."

She pointed to a small, round building just to the east of them. "But isn't that the temple of Vesta?"

"Yes," he agreed, "but that's where the procession ends. It's best to see it from the beginning." He took her hand as naturally as if he had done it every day for the six months since she had last seen him. They moved back out into the stream of humanity going in both directions up and down the Sacred Way. He turned east, barking at the people to make way. When they saw his officer's uniform, they immediately complied.

The two of them stopped across from a U-shaped, two-story building. Its design was simple, but the trappings were luxurious. In the center court were a long reflecting pool, elaborate gardens, and columned cloisters. Once again Marcus pulled away from the center of the street and took Miriam up two or three stairs so they could look over the heads of the crowds. He gestured toward the building. "You know what this is?"

"Yes, it's the House of the Vestal Virgins."

"Right. This is where they live, of course, though it's more like a palace than a house, and so they always come out that door over there. We can follow them to the temple if you like."

"I would."

"Do you remember the history lesson I gave you that first day we came here?"

"About the Vestals, you mean?"

He nodded.

"A little. And of course I hear people talk about them all the time, but I still don't fully understand it all."

"Well, they are actually priestesses to the goddess Vesta, whom we venerate as the protectress of the family and therefore the guardian of the primary source of Rome's power."

"Yes, I remember that. And they tend the eternal flame."

"That's right. The Temple of Vesta is one of the least imposing and impressive of all the temples in Rome and yet at the same time it is considered to be the most important."

"You said it was built to resemble one of the huts of the original inhabitants of Rome."

"Yes, and in the temple an eternal flame is kept forever burning. There is an opening in the roof to let the smoke out. The flame is carefully tended by the Vestal Virgins. As long as it burns, so the legend goes, Rome will continue to stand."

"And how are the candidates for these priestesses chosen?"

"Well, what they call 'novices' are selected between the age of six and ten—usually, but not always, from patrician families. They are taken from their homes to the House of the Vestal Virgins and there begin their training. Do you remember the vow they are required to take?"

Miriam nodded. That was one of the things that had surprised her the most. "Thirty years of strict chastity."

Marcus chuckled at her expression. What he didn't know was that what had brought the perplexed look was not the length of time of those vows, but the strange incongruity of such a vow in a land where "Thou shalt not commit adultery" would be viewed by many as a quaint and foolish standard of living.

"Occasionally one of the Vestals violates her vow." He was clearly enjoying his role as tutor. "This is so serious that the woman is buried alive. But for those who are faithful, statues are often created, and they are given a great endowment from the state. They are held in the greatest veneration. Even the emperor is obligated to step aside when they approach, and if by chance their path happens to cross that of a condemned criminal, he is immediately pardoned."

That was new information to her, and she looked at him sharply to see if he was perhaps teasing her. But he was completely serious.

She turned back as the blast of a horn split the air and a cry went up from across the street. "Make way! Make way! Make way for the priestesses of Vesta."

The doors to the palace were thrown open. Instantly, the crowd hushed and fell back, making a wide path. Now a rhythmic sound could be heard. After a moment, an older woman appeared, dressed completely in white linen, moving slowly, almost flowing in her gracefulness. Miriam leaned forward eagerly. The woman, evidently the high priestess, was beautiful and regal. Her dark brown hair was in a single braid that came to her waist. She wore a simple gold half-crown and a gold bracelet on each wrist. Her feet were bare.

In a moment, two other figures appeared. These were girls, barely past puberty, each carrying a musical instrument. The first carried a sistrum, an instrument first invented in ancient Egypt. It was a looped metal strap about the size of a goblet, shaped like a pear and fastened to a handle. Small metal disks were attached to thin crossbars inserted through the framework of the loop; these rattled with each shake of her hand.

The other girl held a timbrel. This too was a percussion instrument. Animal skin was stretched tightly over a circular wooden frame about two hand spans across. This formed a small drum no more than two fingers thick. Again, small metal disks hung from all around the wooden frame. Thus, when the girl rapped the surface of the timbrel with her fingertips, it made a soft drumming sound. She also would tap it against her leg, causing the disks to rattle. The effect of the two instruments played together was that of great solemnity. It was almost mesmerizing.

Next came the rest of the priestesses, three abreast. All were dressed in white, but none wore any adornment except for a silver band in their hair. All together, Miriam counted fifteen ranks of three each. They were grouped by age, the oldest—Miriam guessed these were in their thirties and nearing the end of their service—were in front; the novices brought up the rear. Some were strikingly lovely. To Miriam's surprise, some were quite plain. But each moved with such majesty and queenly composure that one quickly forgot their individual facial features. The overall impact of the procession was quite moving.

No one made a sound as the procession went slowly past them. The distance between the palace and the Temple of Vesta was not that great, perhaps two or three hundred paces, but it took almost a full quarter hour before the procession disappeared. Only then did the people come alive again and go on about their business.

"Very impressive," Miriam said to Marcus, noting that he was waiting for a reaction from her.

"Yes. My father first brought me here when I was seven or eight. I've never forgotten it. It still gives me little shivers." Then he smiled. "But enough of this. Where would you like to go? I am your guide for the day."

"I just want to talk," Miriam cried. "I still can't believe you're here."

II

They found a spot partway up the Palatine Hill, the hill where the emperor had his palaces. From there they overlooked the Forum and yet were far enough off the main walkway up the hill that it was relatively private.

Miriam had fought back her eagerness, not wanting to ply Marcus with questions while they made their way through the throngs. The minute they were settled she turned to him and burst out with the most important question. "Has Moshe Ya'abin been captured yet?"

His dark brows furrowed and a frown pulled the corners of his mouth down. "No, not yet."

Her face fell. "I was hoping you had returned to take Father and me back to Jerusalem. If we left immediately we could be back in time for Passover."

"No. I'm sorry, Miriam. Ya'abin is more powerful and dangerous than ever."

She was crestfallen. "Is anything happening? I mean, it's been eight months now."

"Yes, but frankly Pilate is losing patience. He doesn't think things are happening quickly enough."

She caught his emphasis on the governor's name. "But you don't agree?"

He shrugged. "Simeon took over a month in the Galilee, working with the various rebel groups to quell the uprising, and I keep reminding Pilate of that. That problem is solved." His frown deepened. "At least for now. I'm not sure the Zealot problem will ever be solved until the whole movement is destroyed."

His coldness frightened her a little, but even more disturbing was the thought that Simeon might not meet the deadline imposed on him by the governor and be arrested again. "But has Simeon done nothing about Ya'abin?"

Now there was a grudging admiration in his eyes. "At first I thought his strategy was just plain wrong. Ya'abin is terrorizing all of Judea and Perea. He raids caravans, customs houses, and inns at will. He's got a hundred men, all on horseback and heavily armed. I expected Simeon to take his band—he has about two dozen men—and perhaps recruit some of the other Zealot bands, and go after Ya'abin directly. But he has not, and that is what is making the governor chafe a little."

"So what is he doing? I thought you said you would be willing to give them as many men as they needed to get Ya'abin."

"I did, but Simeon practically spat in my face at that suggestion. No, his strategy is very different, and now I have to admit it makes a perverse kind of sense. Just before I left, I got a report from Sextus Rubrius. I brought him down to Jerusalem to serve as a liaison with Simeon. They know each other and Simeon trusts him."

Miriam only nodded. Marcus had no idea that she had met Sextus the morning he had come to tell the family about Simeon's arrest.

"Anyway, after calming things down in the Galilee, Simeon and Yehuda went south."

"Just the two of them?"

"That's right. From what Sextus says, even Yehuda had a problem with this strategy of Simeon's. He is impatient and wants to strike at Ya'abin immediately. Even though they are greatly outnumbered, Yehuda thinks they should use hit-and-run tactics, strike from ambush, whittle Ya'abin's forces down a little at a time. His idea is that a cup of surprise is worth a bucket of power. But Simeon won't. He refuses to risk losing men in a fruitless confrontation."

Miriam chose her next words carefully. "While Livia and I were in the Galilee, we heard that Simeon and his family had become followers of a man named Jesus, who advocates peace and love."

"That is true. Sextus has reported the same thing, and evidently this is partly what is driving Simeon to do what he is doing. It is also what is frustrating his partner." He absently began to rub his arm and Miriam looked down. His fingers were moving across the long, white scar there. "I find it hard to believe, actually," he said. "The Javelin filled with love and peace? But that's what they are saying."

"So what is Simeon doing?" she asked.

"According to Sextus, thus far all he's done is lay a foundation for action."

"A foundation?"

"As you probably know, there are nomads who live in the deserts of Judea, Arabian shepherds who run their sheep and goats there."

"Yes, I've seen them in their black tents many times."

"Well, to survive in the wilderness, Ya'abin has been preying on those nomads. He demands a tribute of food and animals from them and sometimes takes their women. They greatly fear and hate him."

"That would be just like him," Miriam said, filled with loathing.

"A few months ago, Simeon and Yehuda went south. They quietly began circulating among these desert people, camping out in the wilderness, letting them gradually know of their presence. Then they started using the fund your father set up to restore what these nomads have lost to Ya'abin. I guess in one case, five or six of Ya'abin's men came into the camp where Simeon and Yehuda happened to be staying. They tried to take the daughter of the old chieftain. Simeon and Yehuda intervened and sent the men back to Ya'abin bloodied and broken."

Miriam's eyes were glowing. That sounded more like the Simeon she knew. "So he is trying to win their trust."

"Exactly. And according to Sextus, he has completely succeeded. The old chieftain sent word to all the tribes that they were to help Simeon and Yehuda in any way possible. Simeon's plan is to use the shepherds as his eyes and ears when he is finally ready to go after Ya'abin. As you probably know, our biggest problem was that we could never find exactly where Ya'abin was.

"Anyway, just before I left, Sextus sent word that Yehuda and Simeon were ready to move to the next step. They went back up to the Galilee to gather their band."

"But you said he has only about two dozen men."

"Simeon's got his own way of doing things, and nothing is going to change his mind. Six months ago, I would have agreed with Pilate. Now I've told the governor that we need to see what develops."

"But you think it will work?"

He considered her question. "Simeon has made some mistakes, but he is no fool. I'll be anxious to get a report when I get back." Then he gave her a searching look. "You seem very interested in this Simeon."

She flushed a little. "Because I want to go home. We can't do that until Ya'abin is captured."

That made sense and seemed to satisfy him. "Your father told me you like Rome. He seemed very pleased with your change of attitude."

"I do, Marcus. I love Rome." She motioned toward the Forum below them. "I love this place. I've made many friends here, and your family has been wonderful, especially your mother. We have become very close. But it's not my home."

He smiled with pleasure. "Mother wrote me and said the same. She likes you very much, Miriam."

"And I like her. Livia and I often go out to see her."

"Have you been able to keep busy?" he asked, wondering if she might be getting bored.

"Oh, yes. Your father found me a tutor, and I have been studying Latin."

"You spoke it flawlessly before," he said. "But now you sound like a native."

"Thank you. And I love the libraries here. I thought my father had a wonderful collection of books, but almost every family here has a library. I have always loved to read."

"Many of those families have no idea what they have," he said dryly. "I'm glad someone is looking at their collections."

"And we are constantly being invited to dinners and social gatherings," she went on. "In fact, about a month ago, we even went to a banquet given by Tiberias himself, as guests of your father."

"Really?"

She laughed. "It sounds much more impressive than it was. There were over four hundred people there, and if the emperor was aware of our presence, he gave no indication of it."

Then as he chuckled at that, she grew more serious. "But if you haven't been home yet, you must go and see your family. We can talk later."

"Yes, I am eager to see them too. My brother happens to be in Rome right now as well."

"For your father's birthday?"

"Yes, you know about that?"

"Your mother sent us an invitation."

"Good. I haven't seen Quintus in almost three years. He's a tribune with the Sixth Legion in Iberia."

"Then go. Perhaps you could have dinner with Father and me tomorrow."

He stood. "I would like that. Very much. Can I walk you back to your apartment?"

She shook her head. "The day is still young, and it's so pleasant. I think I'll just sit here for awhile."

"Then I shall see you tomorrow." As he turned, he suddenly remembered something. "And what of the slave hunter and his search for Livia's brother? I have received no report for several months. Has anything happened?"

Miriam shook her head slowly. "He came one time shortly after you left. He said he had some business in Macedonia and would be gone a couple of months but then would contact us again and give the matter his first priority. He's never been back."

"Then I shall make that *my* first priority while I am here."

"Thank you, Marcus. Livia has been really discouraged."

He lifted a hand in salute. "Tomorrow, then."

III

"Miriam!"

For the second time that morning, Miriam turned to see who was calling her name. She still sat in the place where she and Marcus had talked, so she stood and moved toward the walkway that led up the Palatine Hill. And then she saw Livia. Livia had already seen her and was coming swiftly toward her.

"I thought I would never find you," she said as she came up. "I've been all over the Forum."

Miriam grabbed her hand. "You'll never believe who came this morning."

"Marcus? Yes, your father told me that when I went over to your house to find you."

When Marcus had found an apartment for Mordechai and his daughter in one of the expensive *insulae*, or multistoried apartment complexes in Rome, he had arranged for a much smaller apartment just a block away for Livia. Since they had fully expected that Livia's brother would be found and freed within a matter of weeks, it was decided it would be better for them to have their own place.

Though Livia's brother had not been found, the apartment nevertheless proved to be a blessing. Even after eight months, things were still strained between Miriam and her father. In public, he treated her with studied amiability or cool affection, but alone, he still harbored a smouldering anger over her betrayal. Because of that, Miriam had never brought up the question of adopting Livia, knowing it would only give him an opening to lash out at both of them again. So while Miriam missed having Livia actually living with her, it lessened the complications with her father. And in fact, Miriam spent almost as much time at Livia's place as she did at home, which provided a welcome escape from the cold indifference she felt there.

"I was hoping that Marcus had come with news of Ya'abin's capture so that we could go home, but it hasn't happened yet."

Livia tried not to look relieved. For the past several months she had been dreading the possibility that word would come that they could return to Judea before they had found Drusus. She thought about her younger brother every day, her anxiety growing that he might never be found.

She reached into the folds of her robes. "A letter came this morning," she said. She waved a folded piece of paper. "It was delivered just about an hour ago."

Miriam saw that this was not the usual form of correspondence used by the Romans. Paper was very expensive, and parchment was even more so. So, even among the upper classes who could afford such luxury, unless it was of unusual length or of special importance, the typical "letter" in Rome was written on thin wooden tablets with indented centers that were filled with wax. One wrote the message in the wax with a stylus; once the letter was read, the recipient could smooth the wax and use the boards over again. Often two or three tablets would be held together with wire loops to form a small "book." The invitation they had received two days before to attend the birthday celebration of Marcus's father had been such a letter.

Livia held out the paper to her, and Miriam saw three things at once. The name on the front was "Livia of Alexandria, servant of Miriam bat Mordechai ben Uzziel." Second, the top line of writing was in Aramaic, not Latin. Third, someone had scratched that out and written the translation in Latin directly beneath it. The paper was quite coarse, a form of papyrus borrowed from the Egyptians. The ink was black, made from lampblack and various resinous gums. There were smudges on the paper and it was creased in several places, showing it had been handled a great deal. Miriam snatched it eagerly. "From Simeon?"

Livia smiled. "No, but from his mother."

"That's what I meant," she said quickly. "From Simeon's family."

"Yes. I think Deborah wrote it."

"You *think?*"

Livia nodded. "It is written in Aramaic. But I did recognize Deborah's name." Though Livia spoke Aramaic well, there were not many occasions for a servant to become proficient in reading.

Then Miriam remembered something. When Miriam had written Simeon's family several months before, she warned Deborah not to send a letter directly back to her. If Miriam's father knew she was corresponding with Simeon's family, it would be disastrous. So she had given specific instructions on how to get a letter to Livia. Obviously, it had worked.

"Let's read it together," she said. She moved back to the spot overlooking the Forum, and they both sat down. Miriam carefully unfolded the paper and smoothed it out. Feeling her heart racing a little with anticipation, she lifted it and began to read.

Greetings from Deborah and David ben Joseph of Capernaum and all the family.

The Aramaic letters were small and carefully written. Miriam thought she knew why. Aramaic was a much more compact and efficient language than Latin or Greek. By writing small, Deborah had gotten easily twice as much on the sheet as she would have otherwise.

It is our deepest hope that the bearer of this letter proves to be a man of integrity. He is a trader in wheat that David has worked with in Ptolemais for several years. He claims to know Rome well and promises to carefully follow the directions Miriam sent in her letter. We are sending a duplicate letter by another means, in case this one does not come through. We gave this man specific instructions to put it only into Livia's hands.

"Yes," Livia said, "the man who brought it asked me several questions before he would turn it over."

Miriam looked at the bottom of the page. It was common for a letter writer to date a letter after concluding it. And there it was: "It is dated the twentieth of January, so it took almost eight weeks to get here."

"Actually, the man apologized for that," Livia explained. "He arrived in Rome a fortnight ago, but was so involved in business that he could not take time to find us."

Miriam nodded. That made more sense. Typically a letter between Israel and Rome took about three weeks in transit, but that could be increased dramatically depending on who carried it and when they were traveling.

It has now been six months since you sailed for Rome, and will be close to seven or eight when this finally reaches you. Much has happened in that time that will interest you. First, news of the family. This for Livia. Boaz

made me promise to give his best wishes to his "Livie" and wants you to tell
him if you have seen any bears yet.

Both women laughed at that, their eyes softening at the memory
of the family.

Ephraim and Rachel send their love. Rachel gave us some wonderful
news during Hanukkah celebration a little over a month ago. They will pre-
sent us with our third grandchild late this summer.

Livia clapped her hands. "Wonderful! Deborah must be thrilled."
Miriam smiled and read on.

Rachel hopes it is a sister for Esther, but Ephraim feels like it will be
another boy. Esther will have none of that, however, and the other day told
her father that she has told Heavenly Father that if he must send a boy to the
family, to save it for next time. She wants a sister.

"Can't you just see her," Miriam said, "hands on her hips, those
beautiful dark eyes flashing, and telling Heavenly Father how to run
things in heaven?"

"Knowing Esther, I wouldn't be surprised if she doesn't get her
wish. I listened to her pray several nights. She has complete faith and
does not find it at all unnatural to speak with God as though he was
her actual father and right there in the room with her."

Miriam was nodding. She too had listened to Esther's prayers and
been touched by her simple faith.

Simeon was here last month for Hanukkah. Things are proceeding with
his quest in the wilderness of Judea but not as rapidly as he hoped. Your
father, Miriam, will probably have word of his progress from the Romans
and so I will say no more of that, since space is limited. With Simeon gone,
Leah takes a more and more important role in helping me keep the books for
her father and is proving to be gifted in this area. David found a possible
match for her a few months ago, but she seems little interested. Miriam, she
said you would understand why.

Joseph, who will be twelve in a few months, has started to grow like a
thorn bush. He still practices with his bow and has now taken up the javelin

as well. With Simeon in the south, that is all Joseph talks about anymore.
He hopes against hope that they won't catch Ya'abin until he is old enough to
join the band. Hopefully, once this is over, Simeon can help Joseph see that
there are better ways to prepare for life.

"I miss them, Livia," Miriam said wistfully. "I miss the family."

"As do I."

Simeon said that if I write to you, I was to tell you that he fears you will
find Rome too much to your liking. He specifically asked that I warn you to
be wary around Marcus. Simeon believes that you are naive in believing him
to be a man of integrity and honor. Those are his words, not mine. I think he
still chafes a little over Marcus's role in his betrayal—and the fact that on
more than one occasion, this man has nearly cost Simeon his life. When he
said that, however, David told him of your role in securing his release. He
did not know that and was greatly surprised. He was much subdued after
that.

Miriam lowered the letter to her lap, obviously stung. "Well," she
sniffed, "that's a nice thing to say."

Livia gave her an odd look, then looked away.

"What?" Miriam demanded. "What's that look supposed to mean?"

"Nothing."

"Livia!"

"Well, if the truth were known, I worry a little about that too."

"What?"

Livia finally met her eyes. "Would you like me to speak as your servant or as your sister?"

Miriam was taken aback. "As a sister, of course."

"You would find it easier if I spoke as your servant, because then I
would not be free to share my real feelings."

"Livia, just tell me!"

"All right." She took a quick breath. "When we first arrived, all
you could do was talk about Jerusalem and Capernaum, about how
soon we could return. I haven't heard you say that for some time."

Miriam's face flushed angrily. "The first thing I asked Marcus today was if Ya'abin had been caught. I'm going to ask Father tonight if we can't return with Marcus anyway."

"You're going to *ask?*" she echoed faintly. "The Miriam I knew back in Caesarea would have demanded."

"That's not fair, Livia. You know how things are now between Father and me."

"I do, and by the way, I think your father is right. I think it is a mistake to return home before Ya'abin is captured. All I'm saying is that Simeon is right. You do love Rome. You're not nearly as anxious to leave as you were when we first came."

Her mouth opened to protest further, then shut again. "Yes," she admitted. "Yes, I do love Rome. But I think about home all the time, almost every day." The moment she said it, she realized that her use of "almost" greatly diluted the power of her statement.

"So what else?"

Now it was Livia who colored. "I think I have said enough."

"No, what else? You have something you want to say about Marcus, don't you."

Her eyes dropped and her fingers began to play with the edge of her robe.

"Go on," Miriam said evenly, bracing herself even as she asked. "I want to hear it."

"Well," Livia began, obviously hesitant. "It was Simeon's comment about Marcus that really made you angry, wasn't it? Not just what he said about Rome."

Miriam started to shake her head, then nodded. "Yes, a little."

"And what *are* your feelings about Marcus Didius, Miriam?" Livia asked quietly. "And don't feel that you have to tell me. Just ask yourself."

And so she did. She asked herself what it was in the relationship with this son of one of Rome's most important families that would cause Livia to say that. "Well," she started, choosing her words with care, "I do enjoy his company. I admit, I was very happy to see him this morning. He has been a wonderful host. He's intelligent, educated, clever, witty."

"Handsome?"

She shot her a look, but then nodded sheepishly. "Very."

"And is he a man of integrity and honor?"

"Yes!" It flashed out. "I know that he's not what we expect, but he comes from a different culture, Livia. His values are different than ours. He views the world very differently from us. Isn't integrity being true to your values? Doesn't honor mean to stand fast in what you believe? If that's so, then Marcus has both."

Livia was thoughtful. "Yes, I suppose if you look at it that way, that is so."

Miriam was still trying to answer the question honestly. "I like to be with him. I enjoy talking with him. He's stimulating. He challenges me to think. But that doesn't mean I think his values are better than ours." Her voice rose slightly as she grew more defensive. "Nor does it mean that I have any romantic interest in him at all."

One eyebrow raised.

Miriam was incredulous. "You think that?" Appalled, she got to her feet. "Livia, this man talks about slaves as though they were a purse full of coins. When he talks about God—even his gods—it is with faint contempt. Religion in his mind is something for the weak. Can you imagine how he would respond to Jesus? How could I ever love a man like that?"

It was clear that Livia was greatly relieved at her response. "Does *he* know that?"

That caught Miriam up short. "What?"

"Does Marcus know you have no romantic interest in him? I ask that only because I have watched his eyes when he looks at you, Miriam."

"I—" She remembered his comment about taking her breath away. "I'll admit that he seems to find me attractive and enjoys my company, but he knows that we could never marry. We're too different. I love Rome, but I could never live here permanently." She pulled a face. "And somehow I can't picture Marcus moving to Jerusalem, can you?"

She lifted the letter again, but was still looking at Livia. "You do believe that, don't you, Livia?"

Livia laid a hand over Miriam's. "I do, and I'm very pleased to hear you say it. But I'm not as sure as you are that Marcus finds the differences impossible to deal with."

Miriam waved that away, ready to say more, then changed her mind. She started reading again, glad for the opportunity to move on to a different subject.

One other piece of news about the family. There has been a reconciliation between me and my brother Aaron. Your letter mentioned that you knew of his efforts to intervene with Pilate, which may have been a factor in Pilate's decision to release Simeon and Yehuda. I told Aaron that—though I did not tell him how we learned it. He was deeply pleased. His coming forth in our time of need has gone a long way in healing the breach between us. Aaron now stays with us when he comes to Capernaum. We still differ deeply about Jesus but have agreed not to talk about that.

Now for the news I know both of you are anxious to hear. We see Jesus regularly and continue to be blessed by his teachings and presence. He went to Jerusalem for the Feast of Dedication and will, of course, go up with his mother and brothers and sisters for Passover in the spring. We shall go with Peter and Andrew and their families and hope to see much of Jesus while there.

Miriam paused again. "Do you know that this will be the first time in my life I haven't been in Jerusalem for Passover?" She sighed, then continued.

Peter tells us that the opposition to Jesus intensifies, especially in the capital. The Great Council in Jerusalem talks about the "growing threat"

Jesus presents. The multitudes grow larger each time he goes out to teach, and this concerns them greatly.

Livia, I told Jesus about how you interpreted the parable of the unjust judge and how it led to all of you fasting in Simeon's behalf. He seemed very pleased and commended you for pondering on his teachings.

Jesus continues to astound us with his powers. Virtually every day we hear of additional healings—the blind see, the lame walk, the sick are cured. There was another miraculous case of multiplication of food. This time there were four thousand people and Jesus fed them with just seven loaves of bread. David and I were not there the day when Jesus fed the five thousand and touched Simeon's heart. This time we witnessed it with our own eyes. It still leaves me tingling when I think about it.

One last thing. We were both saddened and yet pleasantly surprised last month when Ezra and Lilly showed up in Capernaum. Lilly said that she has not written you directly because she fears your father will see her letter. Your father was furious with Ezra for taking you to Capernaum to warn Simeon about the ambush. Before you both sailed for Rome, Mordechai set things in motion that have totally destroyed Ezra's business in Joppa.

Miriam stopped, staring at Livia in shock.

Your father purchased the building where Ezra and Lilly live and have their shop, and then he had them evicted. No one dares extend them credit or help them because they fear Mordechai's wrath will be turned on them. Only a few of their closest friends have dared to stand by them. Surprisingly, they are not bitter about his vindictiveness but have determined to move to Capernaum permanently. David has already helped Ezra secure a place to begin a new shop. Capernaum could use an excellent sandalmaker. And this of course will bring them in close contact with Jesus again. Lilly says to tell you that they now see it all as a blessing and not to harbor bad feelings against your father over it. I have told her how to get a letter to you through Livia, and she promises to write soon.

Miriam looked away, wanting to cry. "Lilly loved Joppa," she whispered. "What have I done to them?"

Livia shook her head. "Your father is a man of enormous power, Miriam. It is not often anyone dares to cross him. The fact that it was his own daughter was an especially bitter blow."

"But to financially destroy your own kin?"

Livia was suddenly concerned. "You can't let him know, Miriam. You can't say anything to him about this. If he knows how you learned about Ezra, it will only set him off again."

Miriam lowered her head, her eyes burning. "Oh, Livia." Then her mouth tightened with sudden resolve. "I'm going back, Livia."

"No! Miriam, you can't!"

"I don't care about Ya'abin. I won't live in Jerusalem. I don't want to anymore."

"I know you're upset," Livia said, really alarmed now. "But you can't. If your father is angry now, he will be—"

"I'm going back," Miriam said curtly. "I cannot live with this man any longer."

CHAPTER NOTES

The details about the Roman Forum, the Vestal Virgins, the institution of slavery at this time, and the Roman means of correspondence are all accurately portrayed (see Johnston, 64–65, 288–89; *A Guide*, 5–32; Cornell and Matthews, 90–91, 114). The description of the various peoples in the Forum is actually taken from a play written by a Roman dramatist named Plautus, who lived in the second century B.C. (see *A Guide*, 21–22).

CHAPTER 16

APPEARANCES ARE DECEIVING.

—*Aesop's Fables; from the story about the wolf in sheep's clothing*

I

IN THE WILDERNESS OF JUDEA

14 MARCH, A.D. 31

Simeon raised his head slightly, peering through the thin cover of the bush across the ravine. The opposite ridge was a hundred feet higher than the spot where Simeon and Yehuda hid; directly level with them was the dark shape of a massive cave. To the right about fifty paces and somewhat below the entrance to the cave, a mixed flock of sheep and goats was scattered along the steep slope. A young shepherd boy, no more than twelve years old, was just ahead of the animals. He seemed oblivious to the gaping opening as he picked up a rock and threw it at a goat that was getting a little too far away from him. The bleating of the animals carried easily to Simeon and Yehuda across the space of the narrow canyon.

"Steady," Yehuda whispered, speaking not to Simeon but to the boy.

It took the flock another three or four minutes to make their way right up to the cave's entrance. The boy looked around quickly, then tentatively took a step forward. They heard him call out softly in the melodic tongue of the Arabians. Then he disappeared. If anyone was inside, something Simeon was sure was not the case, the boy was to say he had lost one of his goats and was checking to see if it had strayed inside the great cave.

A moment later the boy reappeared. He beckoned them to come.

Simeon waved back, then sprang up into a crouch. "Let's go." Yehuda was instantly up as well. He stood, looking down the canyon, then waved an arm. About half a mile away, a figure stood and waved back. That was Issachar, the second of Simeon's lieutenants. All was clear in that direction. They both turned, and Yehuda waved again. Above them, another figure waved. That was Barak. All clear up there as well.

Yehuda walked back several paces to where a lumpy bundle laid on the ground. Something was wrapped in a heavy wool blanket and tied securely with hemp ropes.

"Here," Simeon said, moving back to join him. "I'll take that."

"No, you get the bellows and the branches. I've got this." He hefted it up onto his shoulders, then jerked his head away. "Whew!" he exclaimed, wrinkling his nose in disgust. "I thought you said the blanket would keep the smell in."

Simeon grinned. "That was my hope."

"This is awful. Maybe you had better take it."

"Oh, no." Simeon backed away, one hand over his mouth. "You volunteered." He picked up the skin bellows they had purchased from a blacksmith in Jerusalem and the long branches they had cut from a Jerusalem pine two days before. "Let's go."

But as he started away, Yehuda didn't move. Simeon stopped again. "What?"

"Are you sure this is what we ought to be doing?" There was no mistaking the distaste in Yehuda's eyes. "Why not just wait for them to come back and jump them? We could hit them hard and be gone again before they even knew we were here."

Simeon sighed. They had had this discussion more than once in the last three months.

"First, because there's not enough cover. Ya'abin will have scouts out and see us a mile away. We're not dealing with someone who is stupid here. Second, because he's got a hundred men and we have twenty-one. Third, because a man whose opinion I have come to value once told me this: 'Just because you are fighting the barbarians at the gate doesn't mean that you have to become a barbarian yourself.'"

"Is that another one of your favorite sayings from Jesus?" Yehuda scoffed.

Simeon ignored the dig. "No, actually, it was my brother Ephraim who told me that. Now let's go."

II

"What about the rest of the cave? Do you want us to erase the footprints out here as well?"

Simeon, who was on his hands and knees, turned his head. Yehuda was in the main part of the cave, folding the blanket up and coiling the rope around one arm. His voice was nasal and odd sounding, and Simeon realized he was trying to hold his breath as he spoke. That was no surprise. Simeon was himself breathing in short gasps, blinking rapidly to keep his eyes from watering.

"No," he answered. "Back here will be enough." He reached for the pine branch. "Go. I'll finish up. Make sure that boy is clear out of here."

"He was gone the minute you gave him his money."

"Good." As Yehuda reached the entrance, Simeon turned back to survey the place they had chosen to leave their "offering." In the last ten or fifteen feet of the back corner of the cave, the ceiling was too low for a man to stand. Though there were a few chicken bones and other scraps of debris tossed there, that was all. It wasn't a place that lent itself to occupancy, and judging from the thick dust, no one ever went back there.

Simeon took the pine branches and dragged them back and forth across the crawling marks they'd made, and over the long gouge where they had dragged in the bundle before unwrapping it. Once the dust was smooth, he reached for the bellows. Working carefully, he pumped the skins carefully, blowing the air directly at the dirt. In two minutes, even the lines made by the branches were gone. The dust looked as though it hadn't been disturbed for centuries.

Pleased, he stood and took a deep breath. That was a mistake. He winced, nearly gagging, then turned and plunged out of the cave. Outside, he took in great gulps of air. "That is really bad," he said with obvious pleasure.

"What do we do with the blanket?" Yehuda asked, holding it at arm's length.

"We'll burn it once we're away from here." He sniffed the air in Yehuda's direction. "And by the way, I'd appreciate it if you'd sleep downwind from the rest of us tonight."

III

Eliab saw it first. The sun was down, and the light in the ravine was fading rapidly as they moved up the narrow canyon from where they corralled their horses. The scouts had already given the all-clear signal, so he was climbing steadily up the steep slope. Just ahead, the opening of the cave loomed above him. It was almost completely black inside. He stopped, holding up his hand.

Moshe Ya'abin immediately moved up beside his chief captain. "What?"

"Fresh sheep and goat droppings," he said, pointing.

Ya'abin stared for a moment, then swung around to the others, pointing at both sides of the ravine. "Scatter out. Make sure we're alone."

As they raced away, Ya'abin dropped to one knee. He picked up a sheep dropping and crushed it between two fingers, then let it fall away. "It's cold, but definitely fresh."

Eliab was walking forward slowly, peering at the ground. "Not a large flock. Ten, maybe fifteen animals. No more."

"Are the scouts still out?" Ya'abin demanded of the man just behind him.

"Of course. If somebody was nearby, we'd know it by now."

He looked around, scanning the ridge tops above them. He didn't like it. Animal droppings were not unusual. The wandering tribes of this wilderness part of Judea went wherever there was grass, and the spring rains had turned much of the land green for a brief time. Here in the canyon, the forage was not lush, but it was enough to bring a shepherd and his sheep. But the grass had been here when they left two days before and there had been no sign of animals then. Anything unusual raised his suspicions. That was how he had survived as long as he had.

He motioned to Eliab. "Check the cave."

Eliab jabbed his finger at three others and they ran forward with him. Drawing bows and swords, they disappeared inside. A moment later, the four of them came stumbling out again, arms across their faces. "There's something dead in there," Eliab called.

"What?"

"It's really bad," one of the others said.

Ya'abin couldn't believe that. He moved forward, cursing under his breath. Fools! Probably someone had left a bowl of stew sitting out, or perhaps some of the goat they had eaten three nights before. "Get one of the torches."

Covering his mouth, Eliab went inside again, returning a moment later with one of the long-handled torches they used to light the cave. "It is terrible, Moshe!" he said.

Ya'abin flicked his fingers impatiently. Two of the men sprang forward, pulling out flints. In a moment they had the torch blazing.

"Stay alert," Ya'abin commanded, taking the torch from them and moving forward. The stench hit him before he even passed beneath the overhanging rock. He too threw his arm across his face. "I'll have the head of whoever left that behind," he growled. Then he stiffened a little as another thought struck him. "Any animal tracks?" he asked, holding the torch high.

The answer to that was immediately clear. There were many signs of men here—not a surprise when you had a hundred with you—but nothing from either sheep or goats. So the shepherd had not come inside, at least not with his animals.

Now the men were groaning. The stench was overpowering.

"Shut up!" he snarled. He whirled on Eliab. "Look around. See if anything has been touched."

Eliab grabbed a second torch, lit it, then moved deeper into the cave. Less than a minute later he was back shaking his head. "Everything is just as we left it."

"Then find whatever it is, and find it quick." He shoved the torch at another man and stepped back, breathing through his mouth in quick, shallow breaths.

"Here it is!"

Ya'abin moved swiftly forward, then stopped when he saw Eliab bent over and peering into a deep cleft in the rock.

"It's a dead goat."

"A dead goat!" He swore again. He grabbed the other torch and started forward, bending over as the ceiling dropped. Then he stopped. The imprint of one set of footprints was clearly visible in the dust. They led to where Eliab stood. "Wait!" Eliab was partially blocking his view, but he could see part of a carcass. Something was wrong. "Eliab? Are there any footprints around you? Any marks showing how that got in there?"

Eliab peered around, then stiffened. "No, Moshe! There's not a mark." He started backing out, holding the torch out in front of him.

Ya'abin felt the hairs on the back of his neck prickle. "You're sure? No goat footprints?"

Eliab looked again. There was fear in his eyes. "Nothing, Moshe."

When Eliab reached him, Ya'abin thrust him roughly aside. Holding his own torch ahead of him, he dropped to his knees and crawled forward. He recoiled in disgust at what he saw. In the flickering light of the torch, he could see the matted black hair, the gaping stomach, the raw flesh where something had gnawed at the carcass. The goat had been dead at least a week. Maybe more. And yet he and his men had stayed in this cave just two nights before. It hadn't been here then.

Chills were marching up and down his back. There was not a mark in the thick dust other than where Eliab had been. Ya'abin's mind was working furiously. How could that be? Even if someone had stood back and heaved the carcass into this crevasse—which was probably not possible—there would be signs where the body had hit the ground and slid forward. There was nothing.

He backed out and stood up. His men stood staring at him. He saw a nervous tic pulling at the corner of Eliab's mouth.

"Get that goat out of here!" he commanded, cuffing the nearest man.

"How did it get here?" Eliab asked in a low voice. "There's not a mark in the dust."

"Demons!"

Ya'abin jerked around. One of the men behind him had whispered the word to his comrade. "What did you say?" he roared.

The man fell back, mumbling something, then stared at his feet.

Swearing under his breath, Ya'abin turned again. The man he had cuffed hadn't moved. "*Get that out of here!*" he screamed.

"We can't sleep here tonight," Eliab said. "It will take a day or more to air the cave out."

"We'll sleep up on top."

Ya'abin looked around. He didn't like what he saw in the faces of his men. He swore again. "It isn't demons. It isn't some evil spirit. It's a dead goat. That's all. Now get out of here and find us a place to make camp."

IV

ROME

15 MARCH, A.D. 31

In spite of all that she had said to Livia five days before, Miriam found herself looking forward to Marcus's arrival. He had gone with her father to Ostia to make arrangements for Mordechai's return to Judea. When they returned, Marcus had asked if she would like to accompany him to the theater that evening. So now she stood before the brass mirror on her wall and brushed her dark hair until it gleamed like oiled ebony in the lamplight.

"Handsome?" That had been Livia's question. There was no question about that. He was boldly handsome with his dark hair that curled slightly around the nape of his neck. His features were angular, with a distinct cleft in his chin. His cheek bones were high and the jawline strong. His deep green eyes often laughed at her from behind a sober expression. He was intelligent, quick of wit, and a thorough gentleman. He could be enormously charming when he set his mind to it but also exhibited depth and sensitivity as well. There was no mistaking the fact that he found her attractive, which was always a compliment to a woman. More importantly, he genuinely respected her as an individual and treated her as though she was his match in ability and intelligence. So many of the men who had been attracted to her had faintly demeaned her womanhood. To them, her role would be that of a dutiful, meek wife and mother to their children, but never as one who had any significant identity of her own.

And yet. She stopped, watching herself in the mirror. Was she romantically attracted to him? She had said no, almost too quickly, but it was true. She enjoyed being with him. Her life in Rome had been filled with interesting activities, but here was companionship that truly stimulated and stretched her. But that didn't change the fact that she was a Jew, and he was Roman. That went much deeper than her religion. In spite of his sensitivity, he had a Roman's natural arrogance and cultural sense of superiority. His callousness toward slavery still left her cold.

She had been tempted more than once during their many long talks to speak to Marcus about Jesus of Nazareth. She never did, of course, because of her father, but she had run through the imaginary conversation more than once. Where her father would react with fury if he knew of her baptism, she guessed that Marcus would show only tolerant boredom. "Well, Miriam," she could hear him say, "if that is what is important to you, well then . . . " He would give a diffident shrug and the whole matter would be dismissed, like a parent dealing with a child's request for some petty indulgence.

A knock on the door brought her around. She expected it to be one of the slaves assigned by Marcus's father to see to the needs of their visitors from Jerusalem, but it was her father. "Marcus is here."

"Thank you, Father. I'll be right down."

He watched her and something in his eyes softened. "You look lovely, Miriam."

She turned in surprise. "Why thank you, Father." She realized as she said it that she never called him "Papa" anymore. But she was touched by this sudden, if only brief, return to normalcy.

She looked at herself once more in the mirror, then started toward the door. He didn't move, just continued to watch her. Suddenly a little embarrassed, she forced a smile. "We're going to the Theater of Marcellus. There is a new satire that everyone is talking about."

He nodded absently and stepped back to make way for her. As she passed him, he finally spoke. "I'm glad Marcus is back," he said. "It has been good for you."

She gave him a startled look, then nodded. "Good-bye, Father. Marcus says that we shall be back long before midnight."

V

"Would you be terribly disappointed if we didn't go to the theater?" Miriam asked.

Marcus slowed his step, looking at her in surprise. Then a slow smile stole across his face. "I thought you liked the theater."

"I do, but it's such a beautiful evening. I'd rather walk."

"Well, actually I was misinformed. I was told it would be one of the new comedies. We've got several excellent satirists in the city at the moment, but it's actually a Greek tragedy tonight. Euripides, I think. They can be pretty depressing."

She looked up at him. "Then that settles it. Let's walk until it gets dark."

He laughed softly. "Wonderful." Then: "I shouldn't admit this, and my mother would be horrified if she heard me say it, but I far prefer a good chariot race in the Circus Maximus."

Miriam laughed with genuine pleasure. "Actually, I shouldn't admit this, and my father would be horrified to hear me say it, but I think I do too."

His expression made her laugh right out loud. "Does that shock you?"

"Oh, no, it's just that when we went to the races when I was here before, you seemed as though you were merely enduring the experience."

She was suddenly demure. "I was afraid if I leaped to my feet and started screaming for my favorite driver to go faster, you might think I was less than feminine."

"I know some very cultured women who are passionate followers of the charioteers," he said with a chuckle. "Including my mother."

"Really? But you just said she would be horrified."

"Oh, she doesn't object to my interest in the charioteers, only my lack of enthusiasm for drama."

"I knew there was more than one reason that I liked her." And Miriam meant it. She found Marcus's father somewhat distant and aloof, but she and his mother had become very good friends.

They were approaching the entrance to the Roman Forum, but he motioned them to the right. "Would you like to go up on the Capitoline Hill? That's always a pleasant walk and not nearly as crowded. Perhaps we can see the sunset as well."

"Yes." As they turned and started up the path, Miriam looked at him. "Actually, that is one of the things that has surprised me about Rome."

"That women like chariot racing?" he teased.

"No, the place of women in general. The women of Rome are

probably the most emancipated and independent of any in the world that I have heard of. I've noticed that women are held in the highest respect by all levels of society."

"That's true, not only because as mothers they bring forth the sons and daughters Rome needs to thrive, but also because they are the primary means of instilling the Roman virtues into their children. We view that as a most critical role. Why wouldn't we venerate them?"

"But it's more than just motherhood," Miriam said. "The women I've come to know here are truly helpmeets in their husbands' affairs. They often serve as trusted confidants and counselors. We believe that too—though many men may not practice it well—but in many cultures that is not the case. I read that in ancient Greece even wealthy women were confined to so-called 'women's apartments' within the home. Not so here. Take your mother, for example. She is the matron of your villa in the fullest sense of the word. She directs the servants and manages the affairs of a complex household."

Marcus was pleased at that comment. "As you know, in the Roman home, total authority rests with the *pater familias*, the father of the family. His authority is absolute. If he chooses, he can even have one of his children put to death if the offense is serious enough. But beneath that larger umbrella of the father's authority, the woman of a family does have tremendous power. And you've probably observed that even away from the home, women are treated with deference and respect."

"Exactly my point. Men make way for them in the streets. They are given special seating at religious ceremonies, public games, and affairs of state. Your mother even told me that a woman's testimony is acceptable in court—something that would be unheard of in some countries."

"That is correct." Then his face darkened a little. "Unfortunately, in the last few decades since the fall of the Republic and the rise of the Empire, some of that traditional esteem for women has eroded.

Divorce is on the rise, and more and more wealthy women find the burden of childbearing and child-rearing boring and tedious. That is one of the things I find admirable about your people, Miriam. Family is important to you too, and your women view motherhood as their highest duty."

She thought of some of her friends back in Jerusalem—wealthy, beautiful, aristocratic. Some of them found the idea of carrying a child inconvenient and destructive to their beautiful figures. This attitude was not widespread, but among the upper classes it was becoming more and more common.

They walked slowly on. There were many people out, enjoying the lingering daylight. Spring was here in its fulness, and it seemed like everyone was out to enjoy it. From time to time, someone would recognize Marcus and smile and say hello. As they passed on, they would give Miriam a careful scrutiny.

"I'm afraid we are starting considerable gossip tonight," she said after it happened for the fifth or sixth time.

"What's that?"

"Never mind. What were you thinking?"

He looked down at her. "At that moment I was thinking about Ostia."

"Father says you have a sailing date."

He frowned briefly. "Yes, a week hence, right after the birthday celebration for my father. That's assuming the weather does not change again. Spring sailings can be a problem, but Pilate wants me back in time for Passover. He wants me and Sextus to meet with Simeon and Yehuda personally and evaluate how they are doing with Ya'abin."

In her conversation with him earlier, Miriam had learned that if she exhibited too much interest in Simeon, Marcus grew suspicious, so she changed the subject. "Tell me something, Marcus."

"As you wish."

"When you speak of leaving Rome it is with obvious sadness."

"Ah," he said gallantly, "but that is partly because of you."

She brushed that aside with an embarrassed laugh. "Perhaps a little, but it is much more than that. You miss Rome, don't you."

"Oh, yes. Always. It's been wonderful to be back for a time. I'm glad Pilate had a need for some business with the emperor and would let me take care of that at the same time as my father's celebration."

"So, tell me, what it is about Rome that means the most to you? I've noticed that you often speak of Rome as if it were a person, a woman. So tell me about her. Tell me about her personality, her character. Introduce me to this woman you love."

He laughed easily. "Yes, perhaps that is the proper way to think about her."

They were approaching the top of the Capitoline Hill where stood the Temple of Juno, queen of heaven and patroness of women, and nearby, the Temple to Jupiter, her brother and husband. Both were elegant temples with high, fluted columns all around. Marcus motioned to a stone bench near the path that led to Juno's temple. "Ready to sit for a time?"

"Yes. I love it up here."

Once settled in, he leaned back, pulling up one knee with his hands. He was musing. "The character of Rome? That's an intriguing question, and yet really not difficult to answer, if you are talking about the ideal. You will recognize, of course, that the ideal is never achieved in totality. As I said, it has been eroding in some ways in recent years."

"It is no different for us," she answered. "But tell me about the ideal."

"This ideal—or better, these ideals—are the foundation of our character. We also believe they are the primary reasons why Rome has become what she is today. How does an obscure village on a rather unimportant peninsula become a great city, and eventually an empire more vast and powerful than any the world has ever known?"

"Good question," Miriam said, not really minding that she was playing to his vanity, this national pride that was so much a part of the Roman personality.

"We attribute all that we have, all we have done, all that we are to the *daemon* which inhabits the soul of every true Roman."

"Demon?" Miriam asked. While demon in her culture generally had a negative connotation, she knew that to the Romans the *daemon* referred to the inner spirit, the inner fire that possessed a person and motivated all he did. She wasn't sure how he meant the word in this particular context, however.

"Yes, we call it *pietas*, or duty. *Pietas* pervades every aspect of our lives. It shapes and molds all we do. It is drummed into us from the time we are born and reviewed and reemphasized until we die." He had grown very solemn now and spoke gravely. "*Pietas, virtus, gravitas, fides*. Duty, virtue, soberness, fidelity—these are the great imperatives of character, the sacred duties that constitute what it means to be Roman. They are the absolutes that infuse all other motives. There are other qualities as well, such as self-discipline, diligence, and austerity, but those four are the foundation of all that we hold sacred."

He smiled at her. "Do you know where the word *luxury* comes from?"

Miriam shook her head.

"It was first an agricultural term. *Luxus* describes a profusion of undesirable and spontaneous growth in vegetation—a garden gone to weed, a vine that proves to be all leaves and little fruit. Thus *luxuries* originally were anything that burst their bounds and got out of control. When a person becomes addicted to wealth and comfort and ease, he or she is lacking in self-discipline, and this gives birth to the baser instincts—greed, voraciousness, laziness."

This surprised Miriam. The family of Antonius Marcus Didius was one of the wealthiest in Rome. Their villa was huge, two or three times as large as her father's palace in Jerusalem. If anyone lived in

luxury, it was this family. And yet . . . Now she marveled. It wasn't really luxurious in the traditional sense of the word. Everything was of the highest quality throughout, but it was neither ostentatious nor pretentious. It was elegant and expensive, but simple and tasteful. Marcus had been in her home in Jerusalem. Did he view her family as living in luxury? It struck her as odd that it hadn't occurred to him that his comment might have applied to her and thus offended her.

He was watching her curiously. She realized she had gotten lost in her thoughts and smiled for him to go on.

"Anyway, these qualities, these character traits have a little different meaning for you than for us. Virtue for us means not compliance to some moral code given by the gods, but self-discipline, surrender of the *vir*—the inner strength of a man, what makes him 'virile'—to the greater good. The individual's will is always subject to the greater good of the *familia* and the *civitas*—the family and one's citizenship."

"Whereas," Miriam broke in, "for us, individual will and identity take priority. We believe it is a gift from God."

He grinned. "Yes. That's one of the reasons we Romans have such a hard time understanding you Jews. Some would say you are quarrelsome and intractable—" the grin broadened—"which I must admit I felt for a time when I first arrived. But I have come to see that this way of thinking is the product of a different way of viewing life. And that view leads you to value a fierce individuality."

"Yes," Miriam said, surprised at his insight.

"Let me tell you two stories that illustrate how we view this idea of surrendering one's own self for the greater good of the community. We have a legend that many years ago the earth opened up, creating a deep chasm in the Roman Forum. All efforts to fill the gap were unsuccessful. When a soothsayer, an oracle, was consulted about the problem, she said that the chasm would remain until *what most gave Rome her strength* was cast into the pit as an offering to the gods.

"While the citizens pondered and debated exactly what that meant and what would be required to close the abyss, a young man stepped forward. He alone understood that the real strength of Rome lay in her young men. He flung himself into the pit without hesitation, and the chasm immediately closed."

He stopped, watching her face. "That is a perfect example of what I'm saying. He sacrificed himself for the greater good."

She was nodding. "And that's why you leave your home to serve in the army in a far-off land. You are one of the young men, throwing yourself into the pit as well."

He gave her a sharp look. Now it was he who was impressed with her insight.

Miriam smiled. "Our people would have stood around the edge of the crevasse debating who should be the one to jump. They would probably be there still." She gave a wry smile. "I can think of one or two who might have pushed someone else in."

He laughed, thinking of some of the members of the Great Sanhedrin he had met. Then he sobered somewhat. "The second story you may find to be somewhat disturbing, but it too illustrates this national character of ours, this woman we love and call Rome. Before I tell it to you, you need to understand something about our concept of the family. We believe that while love and companionship and physical attraction are important elements of marriage, the primary object of the union between a man and woman is the birth and proper upbringing of children. In this way the permanence of Rome is assured."

"In our scriptures, we are told that the first man and woman were commanded to 'be fruitful'—" she blushed slightly—"and to 'multiply and replenish the earth.'"

"Yes, that would be a commandment for us as well. Because of that, if a woman is unable to bear children, it is viewed as a serious condition, not for her so much, but for the very foundations of the state. Therefore, *pietas*, or duty, the obligation to have children, even supersedes the bonds of marriage."

"How can you have a duty to have children outside of marriage?"

"Let me tell you the second story. And this one is not a legend. This actually happened. Some time ago, there was a man named Cato. He was happily married to a woman named Marcia, and they had three children. A longtime friend of Cato's, whose wife had been unable to bear children, confided to Cato one day that since he was in his advancing years, he was afraid he would die without offspring. Cato immediately offered to lend Marcia to him because she had already proven her fertility."

He saw the shocked look on Miriam's face and went on quickly. "Now here is what is interesting. When Cato consulted with Marcia about this, *she agreed!* She loved her husband, but it was her duty to see that Cato's friend did not die childless."

"So she went to his bed?" Miriam cried.

"No, no, not in the sense you mean. That would be highly improper. No, Cato suggested that they get divorced. Marcia agreed and they did, as did the other couple. Only then did she marry the other man. Marcia lived with Cato's friend until he died, bearing him children as he had hoped. After he died, Marcia and Cato remarried—" He held up his hand as Miriam began shaking her head in astonishment. "She and Cato remarried, but this did not result in them sharing a physical relationship again. They remained apart from each other until their death because that was the proper thing to do."

Now there was no lightness in him anymore. "Don't you see? Both Cato and Marcia followed the path of *pietas*, or duty. They did not let their personal desires, especially any carnal gratification of their senses, override their obligation to the greater good."

She was shaking her head, staring at the ground. "I'm sorry, Marcus, I can't believe it."

"I know what you're thinking. You're shocked by what you see as a terrible sacrifice for some abstract concept. In fact, you would probably label that as an immoral act, certainly on Cato's part, but possibly on Marcia's as well."

"Yes," she said softly, "I'm afraid I would. Or at least a tragic act. How awful for her."

"No," he shot back. "Not awful. Wonderful. Inspirational." His hand came up and took hers, cutting off her reaction. "I don't expect you to understand, Miriam. But you asked me to explain the character of Rome. Well, that is it. What you find as a repulsive, incomprehensible decision, I view with admiration and the greatest veneration. Marcia's decision was not an act of immorality. To the contrary, it was a most remarkable act of *moral courage!* And this is what has made Rome what she is today."

Her head came up very slowly. "Yes, I think I understand," she murmured.

VI

Marcus stopped at the front door to the large building that contained their apartment. They had already seen lights in the windows on the top floor, indicating that her father was still up.

"Thank you, Marcus. Thank you for a most pleasant evening."

"Better than a Greek tragedy?" he said, half-mockingly.

"Definitely."

He searched her eyes for several seconds, then stepped back a little. "Do you think it is possible for intelligent people to understand another person's values and principles without feeling like they have to accept them?"

She was caught off guard by the question but immediately nodded. "Of course."

"That is more than just an idle question, Miriam. Your people and mine have profoundly different values, completely different outlooks on life. We think ours is best; you think yours is. But isn't it possible that we could come to understand the other's way of thinking and feeling without being threatened by the differences?"

That was a much harder question, and she hesitated.

"I mean, think of what you said a few minutes ago. You said you believe your god gave you the gift of free will."

"Yes. Not just us. All men."

"So, isn't it possible that we Romans have used our free will to choose a different value system, a different view of the world than you? Does that make us evil in some way?" He held up his hand. "I know, I know. We are guilty of thinking ours is the best way, the only way."

She saw where he was going now, and it was a thought-provoking question. "So do we, Marcus. We are as guilty of that mode of thinking as your people. I guess that's just part of human nature. Our way is the *right* way. Our country is the best country. Our religion is the only true religion."

He pounced on that. "Yes! I got so frustrated when I first went to Judea. I couldn't understand how anyone could be so stubborn, so blind, so completely intolerant of other religions. But you and others have helped me understand that it's something deeper than stubbornness, something far more than pigheaded stupidity—which is, I'm afraid, how Pilate sees things there."

She was nodding slowly.

"I don't agree with what you believe, Miriam, but I can *understand* it. I can respect it and honor your right to hold to those beliefs. That's what I'm talking about."

"I see." And she did. It was an intriguing concept. How many problems in the world would that solve? But in the back of her mind, something was bothering her. He saw it in her eyes.

"What?"

She shook her head, not even sure yet what it was.

"If you don't agree with me, tell me, Miriam. That's one of the things I find so stimulating about our relationship. We can be completely honest with each other."

"No, I agree with you. We ought to build bridges of respect and understanding instead of hatred and prejudice and bigotry." She stopped, her mind still working rapidly.

"But?"

"But isn't it possible that one way really is better than another?"

He was clearly disappointed. "Like your way is better than ours?"

"I know it sounds like that, but . . . All right, let me give you an actual example." She gave him a quick, challenging look. "You won't like this."

He grinned. "I'm ready."

"Take slavery, for example. We believe that a human being is of infinite worth. No, it's stronger than that. We believe that *each* human being is of infinite worth. This stems directly from our concept of God. We believe that God is far more than some vague, imperfect deity. He is our Father. He created us. We are his children. Would you enslave your own brother? Well, ultimately, we think that is what we are—brothers and sisters, all come from the same divine source."

He was frowning deeply, his brows almost touching. "Do your people see us *goyim*, us Gentiles, as being your equals, as your brothers and sisters? I don't think so."

"No," she said. "You're exactly right, most of us do not. And we're wrong too. In our own way, we're making the same mistake you are. But that doesn't alter the other question. You—no, your society, your culture—sees nothing wrong with taking a human being and enslaving them. Whether that comes through conquest in battle or through a legitimate sale, your culture says that fundamentally slavery is acceptable. Our culture, our religion, says that it is wrong, terribly wrong."

She looked up at him, her eyes searching his, trying to make him understand. "Both views cannot be right, Marcus. They can't."

"But—"

"No, let me finish. You have dozens of temples here. I don't know how many gods and goddesses you have. We believe there is only one God. We believe he is real, not some myth or legend devised to satisfy men's desire to explain the mysteries of the world. We believe that he actually exists, that he knows us and cares for us and intervenes in our behalf."

"And isn't that just an expression of your own desire, your own free will, to find some comfort, some meaning outside yourself? I'll admit, strange as it was to me at first, I find a certain satisfying logic to your concept. It would be nice if there really were such a being. And if you want to believe that, Miriam, then I respect your right to do so. I don't feel like I have to convert you to my way of thinking."

"I know, and you're right about that. We need to respect each other's right to believe as we choose. But what I am saying is something different. We both can't be right, Marcus."

"Why not?" He was earnestly trying to follow her, but he hadn't seen it yet.

"Some things don't matter. Some things are strictly a matter of culture, or taste, or individuality."

"Such as?"

"The chariot races, for example. I find them enjoyable. I wish it was something that was part of our culture, but it isn't. But does that cultural difference make you wrong or me wrong? No, it's simply a matter of preference, of personal taste."

He was finally seeing it. "Go on," he said slowly.

"Some things are a question of truth, of right and wrong. Either there is one God or there is not. It doesn't matter what you believe or what I believe, or what we prefer. If there is such a god, then your concept is wrong. If there is not, then I am wrong and we can worship whomever or whatever we wish."

She lifted her eyes to challenge his. "Slavery is not just a matter of taste, Marcus. If human beings are of value, then it is terribly wrong. If we are only one of the many creatures that walk the earth, just another animal or insect, then let the strong prevail, let the powerful use the weak in whatever way they can."

He said nothing. He was still looking at her, but his eyes were far away now.

She laid a hand on his arm, deciding she had let her passion carry her away. "I can understand why you believe as you do, and I can respect your views and your way of life, but some things are fundamentally right or wrong, irrespective of what we feel or believe about them."

He blew out his breath ruefully. "I'll say this, Miriam of Jerusalem. You certainly know how to make a man uncomfortable."

It so surprised her that she laughed aloud. "I'm sorry. My father says I have to learn to control my tongue, not just blurt out whatever is in my head. He truly fears that my strong-mindedness shall keep me from marrying."

He shook his head reprovingly. "Don't be sorry. That's what I find so amazing about you. I'm going to miss these kind of nights."

She looked up at him, her eyes softening. "I will too, Marcus Didius."

Then catching her totally by surprise, he stepped forward, took her in his arms, and kissed her softly on the lips. He stepped back, smiling sardonically at the shock on her face. "Good-night, Miriam of Jerusalem. If it is all right, I shall call on you again tomorrow."

CHAPTER NOTES

The insights and details about the character of Rome come from Shelton, 2, and Grimal, 97–105. The story of Cato and Marcia is found in Grimal, 125.

Mention is made in this chapter of the theaters in Rome. During the early years of the republic, all dramas were held outside, and while quite popular, they were viewed by many as a threat to the general morals of the nation. There were comedies (both of Greek style and Roman satires) and tragedies, as well as pantomimes and what we might today call operettas. Construction of the first permanent stone theater was started by Julius Caesar and completed in 11 B.C. by the Emperor Augustus. He named it after his nephew Marcellus. It could seat twelve thousand people (see *A Guide*, 44).

To show how some things never seem to change, a playwright named Publius Terentius Afer (often called Terence), who lived two hundred years before Christ, wrote a comedy called *The Mother-in-Law*. A surviving document shows that as the play opened, the producer begged the audience to remain attentive and stay through the whole production lest "by your neglect, music and drama fade away" (Shelton, 347).

CHAPTER 17

I

IN THE WILDERNESS OF JUDEA
16 MARCH, A.D. 31

Moshe Ya'abin held up one hand and reined in his horse. In the bright moonlight, two riders—the scouts he had sent forward—were coming fast down the trail toward them. Behind him almost a hundred men pulled up too, reaching nervously for bows and spears. Was there trouble ahead?

Ya'abin nudged his horse forward to meet them.

"Someone's at the campsite, Moshe," the scout called as he reined up.

Ya'abin went rigid. "*What!* How many?"

"Not sure. We didn't dare get in too close. But they've got a big fire going and it was throwing shadows of men against the hillsides. There are several, that's for sure. We thought we'd better come and get you before going any farther."

Ya'abin leaped off his horse and dropped to a crouch. The whole column dismounted as well. Using hand signals only, signifying the numbers by holding up fingers, he waved Eliab, his second-in-command, and fifteen men straight forward, on foot. He assigned five to stay with the horses, then sent fifteen more men off to the right and fifteen to the left. As they disappeared into the darkness, he ran back to the remaining men. "You two," he pointed, whispering urgently, "backtrack the way we came. Make sure no one is following us."

"But Caleb and Orrak are back there—"

"Do it!" he hissed. Then he motioned for the rest of his band to fall in behind him, and he moved forward a hundred paces to where he had a better defensive position.

A quarter of an hour later, Eliab came back down the canyon. He walked wearily and without tension. "Well?" Ya'abin demanded, getting to his feet.

Eliab rubbed at his eyes. "There's no one there."

"You're sure?"

"We've got men out almost a mile in every direction. There is nothing. Not even a shepherd's camp."

"Then who?" he started.

In the moonlight, Eliab's face twisted. "You'd better come and take a look."

It was a place they had used on more than one occasion as an overnight camp. There was a small spring with a few trees nearby at the bottom of a narrow draw. Low hills rose on both sides so Ya'abin could put men up on the ridge tops and see quite a ways in every direction. That's why he liked it. There was no sneaking up on this place without being detected.

As they drew near, Ya'abin sniffed the air. "Lamb?" he said in surprise.

"Yes. There's a spit. Half a lamb is roasting nicely over the fire."

Now they were close enough that Ya'abin could see it for himself. The fire had died down somewhat, but he could see the spit and smoke coming from the meat. It smelled wonderful. "So who did we frighten away? Any clue?"

Eliab gave him a strange look, and Ya'abin again saw fear in his eyes. His captain moved forward until he was only ten paces from the fire. In the circle of light, Ya'abin saw his men standing back, looking around nervously.

"I saw the shadows too," Eliab said. "There were at least two men moving around the fire, but by the time we could sneak up here, there was nothing."

"So you let them get away?" Ya'abin said in disgust.

Eliab shook his head, and now the fear was palpable.

"What?" Ya'abin demanded.

"Notice anything strange?" Eliab said, pointing at the fire. "Look at the ground."

Suddenly the hairs on the back of Ya'abin's neck shot up. Everything looked perfectly ordinary except for one thing. In the soft dirt around the fire there was not a single footprint. Not a goat's track. Not even the mark of a lizard. They had been here not that many days ago; and yet there was not a mark. And there had been no rain in the interim.

Eliab had spoken in a low voice, but not low enough. A murmur of shock rippled through the men that had come up with Ya'abin.

"It's haunted," someone whispered. The man next to him swore softly, more an exclamation of fear than anger. The men edged back as the whispering leaped from lip to lip.

"Silence!" Ya'abin roared. He stalked forward, whipping out his dagger. "Well, the meat isn't haunted," he snarled, knowing there was no way he was going to stop what was happening. "Come on, Eliab. Let the rest of these cowering dogs go hungry if they will."

But Eliab's hand shot out and grabbed Ya'abin's hand. "What if it's poisoned?"

For a long few seconds, Ya'abin stared at his lieutenant; then, with a hoarse cry, he kicked at the spit, sending it collapsing into the fire. He kicked again, swearing and cursing wildly. Sparks shot skyward as a burning stick skittered away into the darkness.

II

ROME
19 MARCH, A.D. 31

It was the first time since Marcus's return to Rome that Miriam had gone more than one day without seeing him. The last they had been together was at the chariot races at the Circus Maximus two days before. Since his return from Judea, he had come to dinner once with her and her father. They had been out to the Didius family villa twice, once for a midday meal and once for the birthday celebration of Marcus's father. They had gone on several long walks, talking philosophy, religion, politics, and a wide range of other topics. More than once these had ended up in amiable though vigorous verbal jousts. Both agreed that neither of them could be declared a clear winner. But yesterday Marcus had not appeared, and there had been no word. When she casually asked her father if he knew where Marcus was, he had simply shrugged.

She had waited for an hour this morning before deciding that he wasn't coming this day either. So she and Livia went to the market to do Livia's shopping. Miriam and her father had been furnished three household slaves to care for their needs, but Miriam refused to make any direct requests of them. And Livia, of course, had none to help her. Mordechai also gave Miriam a generous living allowance, which she shared liberally with Livia. If Mordechai knew about it, which he probably did, he never spoke of it.

The two of them had come back and washed each other's hair in a large porcelain pot. Now they sat around as it dried, brushing it out as they idly chatted.

"So," Livia asked. "Have you said anything more about us going back with Marcus?"

Miriam shook her head. "When I brought it up that first night after Marcus returned, Father just exploded. I—" She blew out her breath. "I've never seen him quite like this, Livia. It almost frightens me."

"Then don't mention it again. It's better that we don't go back until something else happens with Ya'abin, so just let it go for now."

"That is what I have decided too. But I want to go back, Livia. I want to go to Capernaum and see Jesus again, and listen to him teach. I want to sit around with Anna and Mary Magdalene and Deborah and Rachel. I want to go for walks along the seashore with Leah and talk about nothing."

Livia laughed lightly. "About nothing? I thought you said that you and Leah talked about Simeon the last time you did that."

Miriam ducked her head. "Livia!"

"Well, isn't that what you told me?"

"We talked about many things." She looked away, clearly flustered.

Livia laughed as she reached up and began brushing her long hair again. Miriam turned to watch. The afternoon sun was coming through the window; it made Livia's hair look like spun gold.

"Your hair is beautiful after it's been washed."

"Thank you."

"Remember how Esther loved it? Jesus even said you were making her covetous."

The light blue eyes softened as Livia nodded. "I remember. I wish we could see Esther and Boaz again."

Miriam murmured her assent and began brushing her own hair once more. It was quiet for several minutes; then Livia spoke. "Are you thinking about Simeon?" she teased.

"Livia of Alexandria! What has gotten into you today?"

"Well," Livia said. "You had that faraway look in your eyes. I was just wondering."

To her surprise, Miriam didn't fight back. Instead a touch of color rose in her cheeks. "Actually, I was thinking about Shana."

"Shana?"

"Yes, Yehuda's sister. Surely you haven't forgotten who Shana is?"

"Of course not. But why were you thinking about her?" Then, as Miriam looked away, Livia put her brush down and reached out to touch Miriam's arm. "That's over."

"How can you say that? Yes, Daniel's dead, but Simeon saved Yehuda from prison. Yehuda has obviously forgiven him, so Shana probably has too. Wouldn't you?"

"If Simeon and Shana were betrothed again, Deborah would have said something in her letter. She gave us all the other news about the family."

Miriam just shook her head.

"She would. You know she would."

"It wouldn't happen fast. Maybe it's not been formalized yet, but— I'll make a wager with you," Miriam said. "I'll give you ten *denarii* if the next letter doesn't tell us they're betrothed."

Livia laughed aloud.

"What? You know I'm right."

"No, *Simeon's* right. You like Rome far too much. Now you are even wagering as though you were a spectator in the Circus Maximus."

Miriam laughed, coming out of her mood. "What can I say to that?" She set the brush aside and began piling her hair atop her head in a style that was popular with many of the young women in the city.

"Well, let's talk about you now," she said after a moment. "I saw you daydreaming the other day. Were you thinking of Yehuda?"

One of the things that Miriam loved about Livia was that she blushed at the tiniest embarrassment. There was absolutely no way that she could ever hide her true feelings. Now she went a deep scarlet.

"Remember that night you danced with him and the other villagers? When we go back to Capernaum, I'll bet you could slip up to Beth Neelah and do that again."

"Stop it," Livia said, shaking her brush at her.

Miriam laughed in delight. "So the tables are turned. But I don't hear a denial. Let's hear a denial, young woman. Tell me that you are—"

A knock on the door interrupted her. Both turned in surprise. The only company Livia ever received was Miriam. She stood. "Maybe your father is looking for you," she whispered.

But it wasn't Mordechai. It was Marcus. "Oh!" Livia stared for a moment before recovering. "Good afternoon, Tribune Didius."

He smiled. "Hello, Livia, and how long will it be before you call me Marcus as Miriam does?" He didn't wait for an answer. "Mordechai told me that Miriam might—" He stopped as Miriam stepped forward where he could see her.

"Hello, Marcus."

"Good afternoon, Miriam," he answered, giving a slight bow, something he had not done before, Livia noted.

"We were just finishing," Livia said, stepping back.

"No," Marcus said quickly. "Actually I was hoping I could catch you both. I have some news." He was frowning.

Livia felt her heart sink. "About Drusus?"

He nodded. "May I come in?"

"What is it, Marcus?" Miriam asked with great concern. Then, remembering her manners, she invited him to sit down on the padded bench where she and Livia had been sitting moments before. Marcus took his seat and they both sat on stools facing him.

"I've spent the last two days with a man by the name of Valerius," he began without further preamble. He looked at Miriam. "This is the man about whom I spoke with you before."

"The slave hunter?"

"Yes."

"Has he found my brother?" Livia exclaimed.

Marcus took a deep breath, his face grave. "You have to understand some things about the situation, Livia."

She sat back, her eyes lowering, not able to bear watching him as he spoke the words.

"First of all, there are an estimated one million people who now live in Rome. About seventy percent of those are slaves."

Both women nodded. Neither piece of information was new to them. Typically you could tell a slave by how they dressed—simple white tunic, cloth sash to fasten it at the waist, inexpensive sandals. Some slave owners, fearing runaways, branded their slaves with their own mark. This was done either on their foreheads or on the palm of the right hand, so that the scar could never be hidden. Every time Miriam went out into the city, she saw hundreds of men, women, and children who were instantly identifiable as slaves, no matter what manner of dress they wore.

"One of the great problems we are experiencing in Rome," Marcus continued, "in these modern times, is a growing laxity about record keeping. With the empire expanding as it is, tens of thousands of people are being taken in war as slaves every year. Many are shipped to Rome and sold without proper documentation. There is no control." He was clearly irritated by such shocking laxity. "After Julius Caesar conquered Gaul," Marcus groused, "so many slaves flooded the markets that for a time you could buy a slave cheaper than you could purchase a donkey."

Here in a single moment, Miriam thought, was her dilemma about this handsome Roman tribune. He could be charming, entertaining, and exciting, and then in one instant, he would toss off a comment that left her cold. Imagine! Not caring enough about one's property. Shoddy records. Flooding the market with the refuse of war. Shocking. Unconscionable.

The night of Marcus's father's birthday gala, the conversation had turned to slavery. The men began discussing this "sorry state of affairs" in the slave trade. If the ratio of slave to freemen got too high, it could spell disaster. Even though it had occurred more than a hundred years ago, the slave rebellion led by Spartacus still sent tremors of fear through every slave owner in the empire. Miriam had finally excused herself from dinner that night on some pretext or another, fearing she would be physically ill.

"Valerius thought he had identified where your brother was."

Miriam pulled herself back to the conversation. "He said before that Drusus had been sold to a patrician family either in the city or nearby."

"Yes. That's what we've been doing these past two days, trying to locate the owners. With me leaving Rome soon, I was getting worried about time running out."

Just then they heard the sound of footsteps on the stairs outside the door. Marcus looked up, then stood. "Oh, good. That will be Valerius now. I thought you might wish to hear his report personally."

Miriam and Livia stood quickly, both taken aback by this development. The slave hunter was actually here?

Marcus strode to the door. He paused for a moment, then threw it open with a flourish. Without a word, he stepped back, revealing the person who stood there.

Livia gasped. This was not a grizzled older man, as both she and Miriam had expected, but a young boy of about seventeen or eighteen. He was slender of build, almost frail. His skin was pale, with only a touch of color from the sun. He was clad in a simple white tunic, fastened at the waist with a cloth sash. His feet were shod in plain, leather sandals.

But that was not what caught and held Miriam's eyes. His hair was a golden blonde, only a shade darker than Livia's. The eyes were the same pale blue.

"Drusus?" Livia cried in a hoarse whisper.

"Livia?" The boy fell back a step, obviously dazed.

Livia's step faltered. "Drusus, is it you?"

He gave a strangled cry, and then the boy rushed forward and fell into Livia's arms.

Miriam turned to Marcus, her eyes as wide as catapult stones. "You found him?"

He nodded gravely. "Just about an hour ago." He reached out and took Miriam's hand. "Come. I think these two need some time alone."

III
21 MARCH, A.D. 31

Mordechai opened the door and motioned Marcus inside the spacious apartment. "Thank you for coming. I know you are leaving for Ostia in the morning, so I appreciate you taking time to come by."

"Actually, I had a matter I wanted to discuss with you as well."

"Oh?"

They moved into the main sitting room, and Mordechai motioned Marcus to a chair. Instead, Marcus moved to the doors and closed them. "Do you mind?"

Mordechai gave him a brief, quizzical look, but then he shook his head. "Miriam is still over with Livia and her brother. I've told the slaves to leave us alone. But if you wish."

He only nodded and sat down. Mordechai took a chair facing him. "That was a good thing you did, finding the boy," Mordechai said. "Livia is still half in a daze. It's been about six years since they were separated."

Marcus shrugged. "I should have done something about it sooner. That lout Valerius promised me he'd keep working on it after I returned to Caesarea, but he didn't."

"I would like to know what it cost you to free the boy," Mordechai said. "We don't expect you to cover that."

There was a dismissive wave of the hand, and Mordechai nodded. He would have done exactly the same had the situation been reversed. "Thank you. Miriam was almost as touched as Livia."

"Yes," Marcus answered with a smile. "These past few days with her have made me even more reluctant to leave."

Mordechai reached for a leather pouch on a table beside him. He opened it and retrieved two sheets of papyrus. Marcus saw that they were covered with writing. Mordechai folded each one carefully, took a stick of wax and held it over the candle flame. Once the wax softened, he pressed it against the fold of the first letter, then quickly stamped it with his signet ring. He repeated it with the second sheet.

Only then did he look up. "I have written a long letter to Pilate. Also one to the Sanhedrin. Could I impose upon you to include these in the pouch you are taking back with you?"

"Of course."

"The one for the Great Sanhedrin is actually for Caiaphas, the high priest. Once you are in Caesarea, I would appreciate it if you could find a trusted messenger and see that it is delivered directly into his hand for me."

"As I told you the other day, Pilate has asked that I go to Jerusalem upon my return so that I can get a direct report on the campaign against Ya'abin. I'll probably go there within a day or two of my arrival. I shall see to the delivery myself."

Mordechai tried not to show surprise. Mail between the various provinces of the empire was frequently carried by soldiers and other government officials, but Mordechai was a Jew. Despite the positive relationship he and Marcus had, the Roman could easily have seen the request as impertinent on Mordechai's part. To offer to hand deliver the letter to Jerusalem was especially surprising.

"That would be more than I could rightly expect," Mordechai said smoothly. He leaned forward and handed the letters to Marcus.

"Is anything wrong?"

"Oh, more troublesome than wrong."

"Anything I can help with when I get there?"

"It's this Jesus of Nazareth."

"The preacher?"

"Yes. I received a letter two days ago from Caiaphas. The popularity of Jesus grows every day. He challenges the traditional ways of thinking and has the Pharisees in a dither."

"That's not all bad, is it?" Marcus smiled.

There was an answering laugh. "No. Caiaphas said that Azariah— he's the chief of the Pharisees in Jerusalem—is so upset he has even approached Caiaphas about perhaps uniting with the Sadducees in an effort to deal with the problem."

"And that bothers you? It seems like a united front would be desirable."

"In one way, but . . . " His stroked his beard thoughtfully. "The differences between the Pharisees and us Sadducees run very deep. If Azariah is asking for our help, and if Caiaphas is seriously considering a collaboration, that says more about Jesus than anything else could."

Marcus wanted to smile. He had spent almost a year and a half in Judea now, so he knew of the squabbles and the bickering between the various sects. He found it all quite boring, but he was required to maintain an interest because Rome always kept a close eye on the local governments.

"So you have some religious charismatic challenging your traditions," he said, ready to dismiss this and get on to his item. "It will go away. They always do."

Mordechai shot him a quick look, clearly irritated. "Two months ago, Jesus had a crowd of over five thousand people come to hear him." He shook his head quickly. "No, not five thousand people, Marcus. Five thousand *Galileans*. Five thousand fanatics who will pick up a sword at the very mention of the name of Rome. Doesn't that give you some pause for thought?"

Marcus whistled softly. "Five thousand!"

"Yes, that's nearly a full legion. And it's the same everywhere he goes." There was a quick, shrewd look in Marcus's direction. "If he were ever to call on his followers to rise up, Rome could have a serious problem. A very serious problem."

Knowing that he had been mildly chastened, Marcus nodded nevertheless. "I shall look into it when I arrive."

"This information about Jesus is one of the things I have taken the liberty to point out to Pilate." He blew out his breath in frustration. "Curses on that Ya'abin. Of all the times to have to go into exile. It is not a good time to be away from the Council."

Something in the way that he said it caught Marcus's attention. "Are you changing your plans, Mordechai?"

"I'm aware that Ya'abin is still not contained, and that it is a real concern. But I am thinking of perhaps slipping back without letting anyone know. In fact, I've asked both the governor and Caiaphas to give the matter careful thought and to respond as quickly as possible."

This was a significant piece of news. "Would you take Miriam too? I'm not sure that's wise."

Mordechai shook his head emphatically. "No, not until the

danger is completely past. But I'm not sure *I* can wait that long. Things are developing too rapidly."

Marcus waved the two letters at him. "I shall deliver these for you and send you my assessment of both Ya'abin and this Jesus within a month of my arrival."

"That would be deeply appreciated. I need an objective view and not just what those old fools on the Council are telling me."

Marcus waited a moment; then when it was clear that Mordechai had finished his business, he took a quick breath. "That brings me to the matter I would like to discuss with you."

Mordechai gave him his full attention. "Yes?"

He looked down, hesitating.

Mordechai was surprised to see that he was suddenly uncomfortable. "Is it correct to say that Miriam is not promised to anyone in Jerusalem?"

Whatever it was that Mordechai had expected, that was not it. "You mean betrothed?" he blurted in surprise.

"Yes."

Mordechai spoke slowly, even as his mind began to race. "No. I have tried to arrange things with two or three of our prominent families there, but Miriam would have none of it." He sighed. "As you have surmised by now, I'm sure, Miriam is not a daughter who easily submits her will to anyone, even to me."

Marcus chuckled at that, thinking of some of their conversations.

Mordechai gave him a long appraising look. "Why do you ask?"

It was not Marcus's way to skirt around things, so he plunged right in. "I know how your people feel about marrying outside your faith, especially to a Gentile, but—"

To his surprise, Mordechai waved that away. "I am not bothered by foolish notions of what is appropriate and what is not." There was genuine interest now. "Far more important to me is finding the right family and the right circumstances for Miriam."

"And is the family of Antonius Marcus Didius that kind of family?" Marcus asked.

Mordechai sat back, his face a study in amazement. "I had wondered as I watched the two of you, but I did not dare to hope." Then he remembered the actual question. "The family of Mordechai ben Uzziel would consider it an honor of the highest order to join itself with the noble family of Antonius Marcus Didius."

"Thank you," Marcus said, a rush of pleasure warming his face.

"Does Miriam know you are having this conversation with me?"

"No, nor do I think the time is right to discuss it with her. First, I needed to talk with you. With your consent, I thought we could keep the arrangements informal for now. I am greatly encouraged by Miriam's attitude of late." He looked at his palms. "I believe that she has come to like Rome and that perhaps it is possible to work things out between us."

"She does," Mordechai said, trying to hold back the enthusiasm in his voice. "She loves Rome. I have been very pleased with this. She has made many friends. And, as you know, she and your wonderful mother have become close friends. And this latest, with you securing the freedom of Livia's brother, has done much to lift you even higher in her sight."

"Thank you. I was hoping it would."

Mordechai sat back, pressing his fingertips together as he thought. "You would have to keep a home in Jerusalem. She would never agree to it if she thought it meant leaving Judea forever."

"That would not be a problem. I have come to love your land too."

The Sadducee barely heard him. "Knowing this makes it easier for me should I decide to return without her. She would have your family here."

"Agreed," Marcus said, but then went on in a bit of a warning tone. "But it may take some time for Miriam to get accustomed to the idea. I would not want to say anything to my mother at this point. She would be so pleased that I don't think she could keep it from Miriam."

"No, no. I agree. I'm not talking about moving things along too quickly. But this would be good. If I have to leave, she could stay with your family. That would be appropriate under the circumstances, would it not?"

"Not only appropriate, but expected." Marcus was elated. "I would have spoken to you earlier, but I was not sure if there was any hope for me with Miriam. After the last two evenings together—" He smiled quickly. "Well, let us just say that I am much encouraged."

Mordechai sobered. "I understand the power of the *pater familias* in your culture, Marcus. Perhaps it is not as extensive in ours, but in our law, the father still has the final say about whom his daughter marries. To this point, I have not been overly concerned that she is not married. There have been no suitable candidates. But while Miriam is of a strong mind, she also honors my position as the head of the family."

Then seeing the look of concern that had come into his eyes, Mordechai went on quickly. "But there will not be a problem. Miriam likes you, Marcus. Even a blind man can see that."

"I would like to think so." He stood. "Then with your permission, along with my reports on Jesus and the situation with Simeon and Ya'abin, I shall send you a proposal on the betrothal terms. Once you look them over, you can adjust them to your liking."

Mordechai stood and came over to the younger man. He extended his hand and gripped it firmly. "Thank you, Marcus. I have worried much about Miriam, and not just about her coming back to Jerusalem. But also about the direction her life is taking. About her happiness. This removes a great burden from my shoulders."

"I am most pleased to hear you say that," Marcus said happily. "I shall sail tomorrow greatly relieved."

CHAPTER NOTES

Mention is made in this chapter of the Circus Maximus. *Circuses* in Rome were not variety shows as they are today, but great stadiums. These were designed primarily for chariot and horse racing, though "hunts" with wild animals were sometimes staged in the circuses as well. The races were highly popular among the Romans of all classes. The *circus* took its name from the circular track that was its primary feature. This ran around a *spina*, or center island. The Circus Maximus, literally, "Greatest Circus," was on a flat area of ground south of the Palatine Hill, below the palaces of the emperors. By the time of the empire, its marble benches could seat sixty thousand spectators. Under later emperors, it eventually was expanded to seat two hundred thousand (see Johnston, 232–42). Many people today have a vivid image in their mind of the Circus Maximus from the surprisingly authentic reproduction of the stadium and the staging of a chariot race in the movie *Ben Hur*.

CHAPTER 18

WOE UNTO THEM THAT RISE UP EARLY IN THE MORNING,
THAT THEY MAY FOLLOW STRONG DRINK; THAT CONTINUE
UNTIL NIGHT, TILL WINE INFLAME THEM!

—*Isaiah 5:11*

I

IN THE WILDERNESS OF JUDEA
6 APRIL, A.D. 31

Simeon turned as he heard the shuffle of feet in the sand. The dark bulk of Yehuda approached, then sat down beside him. He looked at his old friend. "Can't sleep?"

"I did for a few minutes."

"No sign of Issachar?"

He shook his head. Issachar, Simeon's second officer behind Yehuda, had left more than five hours before. This was not too alarming. He had a long way to go and much to do.

Above them, the sky was a brilliant canopy of stars. The spring rains had moved east and evaporated over the great Arabian Desert. The night air was cool, and both men had woolen shawls around their shoulders.

"What about the rest of the men?" Simeon asked.

"Mostly asleep. Some are talking quietly about going up to Jerusalem for Passover. They're excited to see their families again."

"I look forward to it too."

"What if this doesn't work tonight?"

"We're still going. Ya'abin will be here when Passover is through."

"Yes," came the droll reply, "but what I meant is, if this doesn't work tonight, *we* might not be going to Passover."

"If it doesn't work, we'll know right up front," Simeon said, ignoring the jibe, "and then we won't go in."

"Why not?"

He sighed wearily. "Yehuda, we've gone over it and over it. You know the answer."

Yehuda grumbled something unintelligible, but said nothing else. Simeon watched him out of the corner of his eye for a moment, then lay back on the sandy soil of the Judean desert. He was far more than just "looking forward" to being with his family. He needed that change right now. He was tired down to the core of his soul, tired of being on the run, tired of living mostly by night, of slinking from place to place, of rarely having the luxury of a fire, of cold food, when he had any at all. To be with his family again, in a warm, dry house, without standing watch all night, sounded like the purest luxury. He turned his head to look at his old friend. "If we fail to take him tonight, we'll take it up to the next step, after Passover."

Simeon couldn't see Yehuda's face, but sensed it was gloomy. "No answer to that?"

"And what is the next step? Stand on the hillsides and spit, hoping the wind will carry it into their faces?"

"You still think this is all foolishness, don't you."

"Not *all* foolishness," Yehuda grunted.

"But mostly."

He answered with a silent shrug.

Simeon smiled in the darkness. He understood his friend's

frustration. After their release from prison, the two of them had spent six weeks moving around the Galilee, meeting with Zealot leaders, reasoning and cajoling and pleading, trying to make them see that if they didn't pull back, it would launch an all-out war, and Rome would win. The time was coming, or at least that's what they kept saying, when that would no longer be the case, but for now it was reality. When those negotiations were successfully completed, Simeon had spent a week by himself, trying to work out in his mind how to trap the wily Fox of the Desert. Simeon and his band were Galileans. They had been in the Judean wilderness, but it was not their territory. It was Ya'abin's. How do you trap a fox in his own backyard?

When Simeon had finally worked out a plan, Yehuda had nearly left him. Yehuda was itching to go into action and had the men at fever pitch. There was some justification for his sense of urgency. Pilate had given them six months to show significant results. If they did, they would have another six months. If not, they would be on the wanted list again. Two of those months had already passed. So when Simeon announced that he didn't need the full band yet, that only he and Yehuda were headed south, his captain and old friend rebelled. Only when Simeon quietly began to pack and prepare to go it alone did Yehuda relent and go with him.

For three miserable months, the two of them were in the Judean wilderness by themselves. They melted by day and froze by night. They slept in the open—rain, cold, and one brief sleet storm. Sometimes they went days with only a few morsels of food. Gradually they let the wandering tribesmen grow accustomed to their presence. In the fourth month, they received their first invitation. The patriarch of the largest clan asked them to dip meat from his common cooking pot. When he asked why they had come and what they were doing, they told him they were there to destroy the hated Moshe Ya'abin. The reaction had been pleased surprise and open skepticism. So for two more months they lived with the Arabians. They slept in the black tents made of woven goat's hair; they spent their days out with the shepherds until they knew every hill, every ravine. That was no small accomplishment because the wilderness of Judea covered an area almost the size of the Galilee. They picked up enough language to converse comfortably with the Arabs in their own tongue instead of Aramaic. Simeon judiciously doled out money from Mordechai's fund to restore damage wreaked by Ya'abin on these simple people. Simeon and Yehuda gave demonstrations of their skill with the bow and arrow, much to the delight of the children.

A major turning point came when six of Ya'abin's band came into camp on the prowl for food and women. They were mean and looking for trouble. They found it. Led by Yehuda and Simeon, the men of the clan drove them off, taking two captive. There was a wild celebration that night; thereafter, the shrewd old patriarch sent word to all the clans. These men were their friends. Give them whatever help they needed.

Yehuda had really struggled through all of that. He understood Simeon's strategy and grudgingly admitted it was a workable one, but he had no patience for it. When they finally felt it was time to bring the whole band down to join them, Yehuda was craving action, any kind of action. But Simeon was not. He had twenty-one men, Ya'abin had nearly a hundred. So he waged a war of the mind. The cave, the campfire—those were only the opening salvos. Horses had disappeared, their tracks stopping mysteriously in the center of a road. Five times Simeon's band had picked off men from Ya'abin's force—two night sentries whose eyes were heavy, a straggler whose horse went lame, the two raiders on the shepherds' camp, two more men who slipped into one of the villages to get a woman, and a rider carrying a message between Ya'abin's lieutenants. Eight men was not a major loss, not when you had a hundred, but psychologically it had been devastating. When word came that all eight were in prison in Jerusalem, it shocked Ya'abin and his band deeply. More importantly, it was something tangible to give to Pilate to show that they were making progress.

"We haven't lost a single man," Simeon said quietly.

"Nor have we fought a single battle," Yehuda shot right back.

"Not of the traditional sort. But you have to admit, we're winning in another way. Our friends report that in the villages the word is the same. Ya'abin is spooked. His men are frightened. They haven't gone back to the cave since they found the goat. He's using half his force to stand guard at night, and that's wearing them down. If what we heard from Jericho the other day is true, he's even had some desertions. More importantly, the rush to join his band has trickled down to nothing." Simeon felt deep satisfaction in his summary.

"And at what point do we stand and fight like men, Simeon? So Ya'abin is spooked. He's still raiding the King's Highway. He hit a squad of soldiers on the Jericho Road two nights ago." His voice was a little sharp. "It's almost April, Simeon. That leaves us less than four months. When our year is up, Pilate isn't going to be satisfied with us telling him that we've given Ya'abin a bad case of the jitters."

"We'll make it."

"Will we?" Yehuda burst out. "Do you think you're going to convince Ya'abin to give up? Do you think he'll come forward and surrender, trembling like a child, begging us to save him from the terrible demons?"

"You know the answer to that."

"Then when, Simeon? When do we stop playing games? When do we stand and fight like men, as you know sooner or later we are going to have to do?"

"When we can turn the advantage in our favor." Now he was a little irritated. Yehuda knew all this. Simeon sat up again. "Haven't there been enough funerals in Beth Neelah?"

Yehuda's shoulders slumped a little. "Daniel is dead, Simeon. Shana has forgiven you. I have forgiven you."

Simeon's breath exploded in frustration. "Do you think that's what this is all about? Me trying to find expiation? Ya'abin still has ninety men. We have twenty-one!"

"Then we hit and run, use Ya'abin's own strategy against him. Hit him at night. Hit him at dawn while they're still getting the sleep out of their eyes. Take them out two or three at a time. Cut the odds more down to size."

"And lose a man or two every time we do? How long can we afford to trade man for man, Yehuda?"

"Every man here came out knowing the risks, Simeon. They want to go home. We've been here a month already. They're tired. I'm tired. If we can put this behind us once and for all, they're ready to die if necessary."

"Well, I'm not ready to have them die. There's a way to do this and keep our losses at a minimum. Maybe even return with no one tied across their horse."

Yehuda uttered a sound of disgust. "It always comes back to that, doesn't it."

"Back to what?"

"To Jesus. You are so afraid that you're going to get blood on your hands. Come on, Simeon! You can't have it both ways. Not out here. This is war, and you're not going to keep your skirts clean while you wage it."

"For someone who refused to come down to Capernaum and hear him, you sure are quick to decide what Jesus is saying, aren't you."

"I saw him in Nazareth. I don't need to hear any more to see what he's doing to you."

Simeon took a deep breath. "Are you ready to take command, Yehuda?" he asked softly.

He whirled at that. "No, Simeon. You know that's not what I'm saying."

"Isn't it? If you really believe that I am leading all of us in the wrong direction, then you take charge. I'll step down this very night. I will. I want to go home too."

The big man sighed heavily. "Simeon, I—look, I know that if it weren't for you coming to Caesarea, I wouldn't be here. Barak and Samuel and I would be dead by now. I can never forget that. But this whole thing with Jesus has got your mind so befuddled, you're not yourself anymore. Where's the old Simeon who struck from nowhere like a bolt of lightning or the thrust of a javelin? Where's the man who plunged into battle without hesitation and feared nothing? All I see now is someone who's tortured by the wrong decisions he's made and keeps asking himself over and over if what he is doing is the right thing, the best way."

"If you had seen what I have seen," Simeon said earnestly, "you would be a follower too, Yehuda. A twisted and withered hand healed in a single instant. A man walking on water like it was solid rock. A huge crowd eating from one small basket of food. Five thousand people fed and twelve baskets of food left over! How can you not believe he is the Messiah?"

Yehuda didn't answer, and Simeon knew why. Yehuda had no answer. He knew that Simeon wouldn't lie to him, and yet he could not—would not!—believe what he told him.

Then Simeon had an idea. "Will you come with me while we're in Jerusalem? I'm sure Jesus will be there. Hear him for yourself, Yehuda. See him for yourself." He stopped as Yehuda shook his head with emphatic finality. "Why not?"

"One befuddled mind in this group is enough. I don't want to see him. I don't need confusion. I don't want questions. I want answers!"

Simeon sighed. When Yehuda made up his mind, it was like trying to push Mount Hermon a mile to one side or the other. "That's a great way to find truth."

Pricked, Yehuda lashed right back. "You want to know what I

think? All right. I don't know how to explain the things you say you've seen—"

"*Say* I've seen?" Simeon cut in hotly. "So you don't believe me."

"I didn't say that."

"You think I'm delusional? That these are just hallucinations I've been experiencing?"

"I told you. I don't know what to think. I don't have any easy explanations. Maybe he is a miracle worker. Maybe he's a great magician. I don't know. Maybe we're all mad."

He stopped, breathing hard now. "But what I would like to know is this. Why it is that all you talk about when you tell me about Jesus are his so-called miracles? Why don't you talk about his teachings?"

Simeon had been preparing his next retort, but that caught him up short.

"You're the one who told me his teachings used to infuriate you." Yehuda waved his hand in grand eloquence. "Love your enemies. Turn the other cheek. Go the second mile. You once said it straight out. 'How could a man like that be the Messiah?'"

"Yes, but—"

"So why don't you ever talk about his message now? It's like you've pushed that out of your mind. It's miracle this and miracle that. If he is really the great leader you think he is, why aren't you trying to convert me to what he *says?*"

Simeon didn't know what to say. Was that really what he had been doing? The answer came swiftly. Yes. So why?

"You want to know what's bothering me, Simeon?" Yehuda said bluntly. "I am scared out of my head that you are going to go up for Passover and be with Jesus again and when you come back, it's going to be some new twist, some new burden of guilt you're carrying. You'll decide you've made another mistake, just like the Roman uniforms and the bars of gold. Then what do we do? Get harps and sing to Ya'abin from the hilltops?"

Simeon felt his cheeks burning. "If you really feel that way, maybe you *had* better take command."

"I don't want command," Yehuda said stonily. "Oh, yes, the men will follow me. But you're the one they admire. You're the one they respect." His voice softened. "You're the one with the natural ability to get men to follow you anywhere, any time. All I'm saying is, *do it*, Simeon. Come back to us. Lead us again. Let's get this over with so we can go home."

Simeon didn't look up. "I thought that's what we were trying to do tonight."

"If it works."

"If it doesn't, when we come back after Passover, we'll go after Ya'abin directly."

His head came up sharply. "I have your word? Bow and arrow? Sword in hand?"

"Yes." Simeon's voice was dull.

Yehuda leaned back, a little overwhelmed by the passion they had triggered in each other. They sat together in silence for a time; then Simeon got to his feet, looking back towards the camp. "I was hoping Issachar would be back by now," he said, ready to put this whole conversation behind them.

As if on cue, a voice called out. "There's a cart coming up the road."

"Good," Yehuda said, lumbering to his feet as well. "Let's get this over with."

As they started back, Yehuda spoke again. "Shana will be here for Passover."

Simeon stopped. After a moment, he shook his head.

"I was just wondering," Yehuda murmured. "I know she'll ask."

"Let me ask you, Yehuda, and you think about it before answering. If my feelings about Jesus bother you so much, do you really want Shana to be my wife?"

There was only a moment's hesitation. "No."

"Then it's better to leave things as they are. Tell her I'm sorry."

"That's what she said too."

II

Simeon walked around the cart, examining it closely in the starlight. There were five large clay pots in all, each filled with a bath of wine, or about six Roman gallons each. Each was sealed with a wooden stopper with a rope handle. He grabbed the nearest one and pulled it off with a dull plop. He dipped his finger in the wine and put it to his mouth. "Not bad," he said.

"I had to pay enough," Issachar replied. "It had better be good. And by the way, the banker said we are down to less than thirty shekels in the fund now."

Nodding, Simeon motioned for his men, who were also gathered around the cart, to remove the other stoppers. "I'll talk to Sextus while we're in Jerusalem. Mordechai is going to have to come up with some more money." He turned to Yehuda. "Ready?"

His second-in-command stepped forward, several narrow glass vials in his hand.

"How much?" Simeon asked.

"One full vial per pot." He handed one to Simeon, kept one for himself, then passed the other three to waiting hands. Simeon held it up to the firelight. It was filled with a white powder. Yehuda and Barak had purchased the vials from a Greek alchemist in the back alleys of Jerusalem, whose shop was called *Pharmakeion*. They had no way of knowing if the powder would really do what he promised it would do. No, Simeon corrected himself, there was one way to test it—in action. He uncorked the vial and dumped the powder into the wine.

"Mooli!"

Samuel, or Mooli as everyone called him, jumped forward.

"Get a stick and stir that in really well."

Simeon waited until Samuel was done, then dipped his finger in again. He put the wine on his tongue and half-closed his eyes. Yehuda, done with the last pot, watched him closely. Finally, he nodded. "I can't tell any difference. He's right. There is no taste to it."

Yehuda let out his breath slowly. "He'd better be right about the other too, or we are in for a very nasty night."

III

"Ho! Pull up there!"

Issachar pulled sharply on the reins. The donkey stopped and the cart creaked to a halt. Two dark shapes materialized out of the darkness. They carried spears. A twig cracked behind him, and Issachar felt the back of his neck start to prickle.

"What's your name and what's your business?"

"I am Reuben of Beth Shemesh." Beth Shemesh was in the heart of grape country. He hoped these men knew that.

He stiffened as he felt the point of a spear suddenly pressed against his back.

"Begging your pardon, sire," he stammered, "but I seem to have lost my way. Is this the road to Hebron?" It wasn't hard to put a touch of fear in his voice.

There was a raucous hoot. "Hebron? That's five miles back, fool!"

"What's in the cart?" the man behind him said, prodding him with the butt of his spear.

"Wine, sire. Destined for the tables of Hebron."

"Wine?" It was a voice from his left, and suddenly three more men came forward. The sharpness in his back disappeared, but Issachar didn't turn. He heard a soft plop as one of the plugs was pulled, then a soft exclamation.

He partly turned. "Perhaps I was mistaken," he said in a shaky voice. "Perhaps this wine was meant for someone closer to where we are now."

"How much?" the first man sneered.

Issachar licked his lips. "I was promised two shekels per jar, but would consider—"

A hand grabbed his tunic and jerked him roughly off the cart. He fell to his knees. He lowered his head, fawning, beseeching them now. "Please, sire. What I meant to say was that I would consider it an honor if you would accept this as my gift to you." He jumped back, barely escaping the man's kick.

"Get out of here!" the man snarled.

Issachar got to his feet and stumbled away, calling out his thanks for their boundless kindness. As he heard the cart begin to roll again, the guards hooting and hollering with joy, he looked one last time over his shoulder; then, grinning, he took off at a run back the way he had come.

IV

Yehuda was disgusted. He had fully expected the sentries to be awake. None were. One of the jars was standing next to their post, two-thirds empty. Eight men lay snoring heavily in the sand and brush. He turned to Simeon. "This is going to be like spanking a baby."

"Let's hope so." Simeon motioned the others forward. "Stay alert. I don't want anyone harmed, unless we have to."

What they found a half mile farther on was both exciting and a disappointment. The camp was like a field of dead men. Men were sprawled everywhere, heads back, mouths open. The fires were down to burning coals, and horses stood untended on the far edge of the tents. This was the payoff for those months Yehuda and Simeon had spent building trust with the local shepherds. Now they knew almost every day exactly where Ya'abin and his band were. Simeon's band lit their lamps using sticks from the fires, and then it quickly became obvious that this was only half of Ya'abin's force. The shepherd boy who had brought them word of where the enemy was camped had sworn there were only about forty men, but Simeon had hoped that he had counted wrong. More devastating than the lack of numbers, however, was that Moshe Ya'abin was not among them. In the captain's tent, they found only Eliab and one of Ya'abin's other lieutenants.

Yehuda cursed in a low voice when he saw that. "If we could have taken Ya'abin tonight, we could have ended this in another month," he muttered.

Simeon didn't answer. The disappointment was bitter in his mouth as well. But they didn't have time to stand around and wring their hands. Twenty-one men might keep forty prisoners in check long enough to get them to Jerusalem, but not with forty or fifty others in pursuit. They were going to have to leave them.

He looked up to where Issachar and Yehuda awaited his command. "Leave me the bowl we brought; then search the camp. I want anything and everything you can find that they've taken as spoils. Clean them out. I want to be gone in five minutes. Ya'abin might still be coming here tonight. And remember, leave no trace. Nothing!"

Yehuda carried a clay bowl of fresh goat's blood, covered with a thick cloth to keep it from spilling over. He handed it to Simeon, then darted out after Issachar.

Simeon pulled the covering back. The blood was dark and starting to thicken. He took the cloth, dipped it in the blood, then smeared it on his hand. With a thin smile, he reached out with his other hand and carefully smoothed the edge of Eliab's robe against Eliab's leg, then pressed his bloody hand against the cloth. It left a perfect imprint.

He repeated the motion, leaving a second hand print on the pillow. He stood, wiped his hand on the blanket that served as Eliab's mattress, then knelt down beside the sleeping form.

Simeon grasped Eliab's tunic with both hands and yanked him up, shaking him hard. The bandit groaned softly. Simeon slapped his face twice, not hard enough to leave a mark, but sharply. The eyes fluttered opened, stared up at him for a moment, then started to close again. He shook him roughly again. "Eliab!"

The eyes were half-frightened, half-confused.

"Look at me! Do you know who I am?"

The lips moved, but only a mumbling incoherence came out.

"It's me. Ha'keedohn, the Javelin. I'm back. Tell Ya'abin I'm back."

He let go and Eliab fell heavily back on his blankets. Would he even remember? Simeon wasn't sure. He reached inside his tunic and took out the signet ring a goldsmith had made for him in Jericho. He dropped it beside the motionless form. Then he began a swift but careful search of the tent. What he was looking for was under Eliab's head in a large leather pouch. Simeon hefted it, hearing the soft clink. Two hundred shekels, he guessed, maybe more. Roman gold? The purse of some merchant on the Incense Road? Ransom from an unwary traveler headed for the Holy City for Passover? There was no way of knowing. Not that it mattered.

V

7 April, A.D. 31

Moshe Ya'abin was raging. He stalked back and forth, muttering and cursing, arms flailing. Eliab kept his head down, waiting for the storm to abate a little.

"What were you thinking, Eliab? Letting the men have access to that much wine. No wonder they were unconscious."

Eliab felt a little flash of defiance. "I would like to have seen you stop them from helping themselves. These are not disciplined troops you lead. They're rabble. They live by taking whatever spoils they can find."

"Maybe so," Ya'abin shouted. "But the sentries? Even an ox would know better than to give wine to the sentries."

"I didn't know they had any, not until this morning." The man who admitted that he had left one jar with the outpost was now being flogged. If his chief had his way, the man would be dead now. But Eliab hadn't completely lost his senses. Eight men had disappeared over the past few weeks. Ten more had deserted. Now the eight sentries were gone. That was more than two dozen men they had lost. Worse, with rumors of their camp being inhabited with evil spirits, the flow of new men had been cut off sharply. They couldn't afford to lose even one more man.

Ya'abin's voice dropped, though it was still thick with rage. "Same old story. The sentry's outpost looks as though there had never been anyone there. Not a footprint. No tracks from the cart. Everything here in camp looks perfectly normal."

Eliab felt his skin start to crawl again. He reached down and touched the dark handprint on his robe. Then he looked at the second print on his pillow. "There's something else."

Ya'abin picked up a cup and flung it across the tent. Eliab ducked, even though it wasn't aimed at him. "Something else? What else could there be? The chest is gone. The purse is gone. Five bags of incense are gone. What else could there possibly be, Eliab? *What?*"

The man who had been with Ya'abin longer than anyone else let out his breath slowly, knowing this would bring yet another eruption. "I think I know who it was."

Ya'abin stopped his pacing. "Who?"

"I'm not sure. I thought at first I was dreaming. But someone shook me in the night." He swallowed quickly. "He said he was Ha'keedohn."

"What! Ha'keedohn is dead." Ya'abin slammed his hand against one of the tent poles, causing the tent to shudder. "You weren't dreaming. You were drunk. Sloppy, stupid drunk. Pilate crucified the Javelin last September, along with all the men we lost at the Joknean Pass."

Eliab looked sick. Fear had contracted the pupils in his eyes to pinpoints. And it wasn't Ya'abin that was causing this reaction. He was thinking about the blurred face that swam before his mind. "That's what I thought too, but then I found this." He opened his hand and held out the ring.

Ya'abin snatched it up and looked at it in the light coming through the tent flap. It was a signet ring. There was a sharp intake of breath. He didn't recognize the family crest, but the Hebrew letters were perfectly clear. "Simeon ben David," he read in an awestruck whisper.

Eliab felt a small rush of triumph at the sudden fear that sprang into his captain's eyes. "I don't like this, Moshe," he ventured. "What is going on? Dead goats? Bloody handprints? Miraculous camp fires? Yes, we drank too much last night, but it wasn't *that* much. They must have come and gone like ghosts. Not a soul in the whole camp was awakened. I'm telling you, the men are getting terrified."

Moshe Ya'abin was quiet for a time, his beard twitching, his head bobbing up and down as he continued to stare first at the ring, and then at Eliab. Finally he lifted his head. "I'll tell you what is going on. Someone is trying to drive us mad. And they are very clever, Eliab. Very clever. But it isn't ghosts that did this. And the only *evil* spirits in this camp are the ones that follow me." He laughed at his own joke.

He began to pace again, jiggling the signet ring in his cupped hand as he did so. "I should have listened when we heard that rumor out of the Galilee. The Javelin wasn't killed after all."

Eliab's eyes widened. "You think he's alive?"

Ya'abin barely heard him. He was staring up, speaking to no one.

"Yes," he murmured. "Now it all makes sense." He clenched the ring tightly in his fist and shook it at the ceiling of the tent. "You made a mistake this time, Simeon ben David. We shall find our ghosts and demons, and then it will be our turn to see who has terrible dreams in the night."

Chapter 19

WISDOM IS THE PRINCIPAL THING; THEREFORE GET WISDOM:
AND WITH ALL THY GETTING GET UNDERSTANDING.

—*Proverbs 4:7*

I

BETHLEHEM
8 APRIL, A.D. 31

"Look at you," Deborah said, reaching up and rubbing at the short, stiff beard. "Is this *my* son?"

Simeon laughed. "I hate it, actually. I have been so long without a beard, it's driving me mad. But I can't be wandering around the wilderness looking like a Roman, not if I want to survive. Even our Arabian friends would be suspicious of that."

Deborah stepped back, eyeing him up and down. "You've not been eating right, have you?"

He laughed again. "If I told you what we've been eating, you would be downright covetous."

Leah came forward, holding out her arms. "Don't tell us." She threw her arms around him. "*Shalom*, Simeon."

He pulled her tightly against him, burying his face in her hair and smelling deeply. "*Shalom*, little sister. I've missed you."

"And we've missed you." She held him even more tightly. "Oh, Simeon, it is wonderful to see you again."

He stepped back and looked at Ephraim and Rachel. "Where are the children?"

"They were so tired after three days of traveling," Rachel said, "they went right to bed."

Disappointment crossed his face. "I was hoping they would still be awake." Then he looked more closely at Rachel, then made a motion with his hands that emulated the noticeable swelling of her stomach. "Congratulations."

She blushed, smiling happily. "Yes, just three more months now."

"Boy or girl?" he asked.

"Esther and I are hoping for a girl. Ephraim and Boaz are sure it's a boy; and the way he was kicking me all the way down from Capernaum, I'm afraid they may be right."

Ephraim came over and gripped his hand. "It's a boy," he whispered, "but don't say that to Esther." Then he too looked at Simeon's beard. "And don't have too many expectations. You know how Esther is about being kissed when we are 'scratchy,' as she calls it. She may not have anything to do with you now that you're bearded again." His grip tightened. "How are things going out there in the wilderness?"

"Well," Simeon said, looking around at all of them, still a little awed at how wonderful it felt to be back with them. He turned to his father. "We haven't lost a man yet, and so far we have not had to take a life."

David nodded, the pleasure showing in his eyes. "We stopped briefly at the Antonia Fortress and talked to Sextus Rubrius as we came through Jerusalem this afternoon."

"You did?"

"Of course," his mother answered. "We were very anxious to hear any news of you."

Simeon was appropriately chastened. "Mother, we don't dare risk sending a letter out. If Ya'abin were ever to intercept it—"

"I know," she said, "but we knew that you report regularly to Sextus, so we stopped to see what he knew."

Simeon nodded, not really surprised. "Yehuda and I are going to see him tomorrow and give him the latest news. He's a good man. A good friend. If it weren't for his reports to Marcus, I'm afraid Marcus would not have persuaded Pilate to give us the extended time he promised us."

"He is a good man," David agreed. "And he said he's quite impressed with what you are doing. You've taken eight of Ya'abin's men prisoner?"

"Actually more than that now, but Sextus doesn't know it yet."

"Good," David said quietly. "Sextus says Marcus is going to need something concrete before he'll be convinced you're making progress."

That stopped Simeon. "Marcus? Here in Jerusalem?"

"Sextus said he arrived just yesterday. Came back from Rome in time for Passover."

That was a second surprise. "He was in Rome? What about Miriam and her father?"

Deborah shook her head. "With Ya'abin still out there, they'll stay in Rome for awhile longer."

"Good. We've been nipping at Ya'abin's heels, and I don't think he's had much time to think about getting revenge; but until he's in the cage, it's better that Miriam isn't here."

Then, realizing there were two people he hadn't yet greeted, Simeon went over to them. "*Shalom*, Uncle Benjamin. *Shalom*, Aunt Esther."

They greeted him warmly, with Esther giving him a kiss on the cheek. "Welcome, Simeon. It is so good to have you with us again."

In actuality, Benjamin was his father's cousin and therefore was Simeon's cousin also, but he had always called them uncle and aunt.

Benjamin was a shepherd of the priestly order assigned to watch over the flocks of sheep destined for sacrifice in the temple. For a time he had moved to Jerusalem, but now he was back in the family home in Bethlehem. David's family had been staying with them for so many years when they came up for the festivals, they were like immediate family. In fact, Aunt Esther had mothered Deborah's children so much that Ephraim had named his first daughter after her.

Simeon turned back to his parents. "So what about Jesus? Did he come up from the Galilee too?"

"Of course," Deborah answered. "And Peter and Anna and all the rest. They're all here."

"Where are they staying?"

"Jesus is in Bethany, on the east side of the Mount of Olives. There's a family there he always stays with. Anna and Peter are there as well. As you remember, John has a relative who is a servant to the family of Caiaphas. So John and James and their parents are staying in the Upper City."

"Will Jesus be teaching tomorrow?" Simeon wondered.

"I'm sure he will. Peter said we'd likely see them on the Temple Mount."

"Good, I've missed that." He had a sudden thought and turned to his cousin. Benjamin had been with Simeon's father that night on the shepherd's fields, thirty-one years ago this very season. "Have you two had a chance to hear Jesus yet?"

"No," Benjamin answered, "but we're going with you tomorrow. We're very excited to hear Jesus after everything your parents have told us about him."

"Does it seem a little strange to think this might be the same baby you saw that night so long ago?"

He nodded emphatically. "I don't think there's any question about 'might be.' And now at last we see the promise fulfilled." He looked at David. "Do you remember what the angel said that night?"

"Perfectly," David said without hesitation.

"'For unto you is born this day,'" he quoted softly, "'in the city of David, a Savior, which is Christ the Lord.'"

Esther reached out and took her husband's hand. "And tomorrow we shall finally get to meet him." Her eyes shone with excitement.

They were quiet as they thought about that; then finally Leah spoke up. "What about Yehuda and the others? Did they come up to Jerusalem with you?"

"We all came in together, but they've got friends or relatives here too, mostly in Jerusalem," Simeon said. "Yehuda sends greetings to all of you."

"Is Shana with them?" Leah asked.

Simeon gave her a sharp look and then nodded.

"Are you going to see her?"

There was a quick shake of his head.

To his surprise, his mother nodded at that. "That's probably for the best, Simeon." Then she turned to Esther. "Well, we are all here now."

"Wonderful. Supper is waiting."

II

JERUSALEM

9 APRIL, A.D. 31

"We are here to speak with the centurion, Sextus Rubrius." Simeon spoke in near-perfect Latin.

The guard eyed Simeon and Yehuda up and down warily. "Names?"

"Just tell him that we are two wanderers from the wilderness of Judea."

"I need more than a clever reply to trouble one of our officers," the man said with an insolent sneer.

Simeon pulled his hood back and looked the man straight in the face. "You'll need new skin on your back if Sextus learns that you delayed the report for which he is waiting."

The use of the first name did it. There was a flash of anger, but at the same time, the guard weighed the consequences if this was not just a bluff. "Stay here," he grumbled, then turned and went through the huge gate of the Antonia Fortress.

Simeon and Yehuda moved over against the wall of the fortress where the morning sun had not penetrated yet and the air was cool. They didn't have long to wait, nor were they surprised when two figures appeared instead of one. They straightened as Sextus Rubrius and Marcus Quadratus Didius joined them.

"Well, look at who is back," Simeon said, feigning surprise. He had decided it wouldn't be wise to indicate that Sextus had met with Simeon's family yesterday.

Marcus nodded curtly. "Yes." His voice was cool as he took the measure of the two of them.

"Did Miriam and her father return with you?"

"No. And what concern would that be to you?"

Simeon caught the testiness in the tribune's voice. He shrugged. "Since part of the reason for our release to track down Ya'abin was the danger to Mordechai and his daughter, I was hoping they had not returned too early."

"We'll be the judge of that, not you," he snapped.

Simeon was surprised. The relationship between him and Marcus had seen some tense moments, but he sensed something more today. It was like the tribune was trying to goad him somehow. Simeon looked at Sextus Rubrius. His eyes were hooded, his face impassive.

There would be no clues from that direction. He looked back to Marcus. "And welcome home to you too."

"Let's go inside," Marcus grunted. "Sextus has briefed me, but I want to hear everything from you."

"We have something to deliver to you."

"What?"

"It's too large to carry. We'll meet you outside the walls, down in the Kidron Valley in front of the Tomb of Zachariah." He looked at Sextus. "You'll want to bring some men with you, maybe two quaternions." Ignoring the look of surprise on both their faces, Simeon turned and walked away, Yehuda beside him.

III

IN THE KIDRON VALLEY, EAST OF JERUSALEM

During the season of heavy rains, the Brook Kidron, which ran between Mount Moriah, or the Temple Mount, and the Mount of Olives, could become a torrent. Now it was barely a trickle. Another week or so and it would be only a dusty creek bed once again. Simeon and Yehuda waited in a stand of cypress trees about fifty paces from the brook. They were just outside the entrance to the Tomb of Zachariah.

The tomb was one of several massive funerary shrines hewn out of the rock face that formed the base of the Mount of Olives. Supposedly built to honor the king of Israel by that name, it was probably of more recent origin than that. The monuments were not the only tombs, however. Many people believed that if one was buried here on the Mount of Olives, he or she would be the first to come forth from the grave when the trumpet for the resurrection sounded. The lower slopes near the monuments were already filled with graves. In fact, this was the very reason why Simeon and Yehuda had chosen the spot.

Under the statutes of the Mosaic Law, any contact with the dead made a person unclean. When a person died in a house or tent, everyone and everything in the house became unclean for seven days. To come in contact with a dead body, to walk on a grave, or even to touch a single bone of a skeleton rendered a person unclean for one full week. An elaborate purification ritual was required to purge oneself of such uncleanness, including bathing and washing one's clothing. Priests were under even more stringent requirements in this regard.

Simeon's father had explained this to him once, saying it was a symbolic reminder of a spiritual reality. Death was the ultimate proof of the corruptible nature of this mortal existence. Being perfectly holy, nothing God did was corruptible, nor could any corruption be allowed into his presence. So this prohibition was God's way of teaching the people that they should make every effort to avoid spiritual corruption.

Whatever the reason, burial sites all over Israel were carefully marked so people could avoid stepping on a grave and polluting themselves. Sepulchres were often whitewashed to clearly mark them as places of the dead. Because of all that, people went to cemeteries only when a burial was required; otherwise, they might inadvertently step on a grave and be forced to undergo the rituals of purification. Knowing all of that, Simeon had specifically set the Kidron Valley as the place of meeting. There was plenty of space without graves, and that was where they were right now, but no one would risk being contaminated during Passover week, for then they would not be allowed to participate in the feast. Thus, even with tens of thousands of people overflowing the city, there was little chance that he and Yehuda and the Romans would be disturbed here.

"There they are," Yehuda said, pointing through the trees.

Simeon had already seen the movement of a column of men

through the trees. He moved forward a little to see better. Marcus stopped the column, said something to his men, then moved forward with Sextus Rubrius behind him.

"All right," Marcus said curtly, "let's see what you have to show for almost nine months of freedom."

There it was again. It wasn't open hostility, but it was belligerent and provocative. Simeon just smiled. "Did you not sleep well on the ship, Tribune?"

Marcus bristled. "What's that supposed to mean?"

"You seem to be looking for a fight. I'm not sure why. Would you like to settle something first so we can get on with this?"

Simeon thought he saw just a hint of amusement in Sextus's eyes, but he couldn't be sure. Marcus glared at him for a long moment, then finally muttered something. "Show me what you have," he said.

Simeon led the way back into the trees where a donkey was harnessed to a small two-wheeled cart. Marcus moved in immediately, sniffing the air. "Incense?" he asked.

Simeon laid a hand on one of the five large sacks that took most of the room in the cart. "These were taken six days ago by Ya'abin. He attacked a small caravan near the ford below Jericho. Two merchants were killed and three Roman escorts." Simeon pulled the top of one sack open, lifted a handful of the small chunks of hardened resin, and let them trickle through his fingers. "Incense is going for three hundred shekels a bag last we heard."

Marcus said nothing, but he too picked up a handful of the aromatic and put it up to his nose. Incense was neither as beautiful nor as valuable as gold or silver, but it came in a close third. Ground as a powder and burned, it produced a powerful fragrance, which in the Jewish religion was called "a sweet savor to the Lord." Many other religions also used it as part of their ceremonies. It was also used to make perfumes and scented body oils. Taken from trees far to the south on the Arabian Sea, the sap or gum was dried, then shipped north up the

King's Highway. It was a highly lucrative trade and therefore a strong temptation to men like Moshe Ya'abin.

Marcus let the crystals fall back into the bag and brushed his hands off on his tunic. Five full bags was no small thing. Pilate would be pleased. But he let none of that show on his face. "What else?" he demanded.

Simeon stepped around to the back of the cart and lowered the gate. There was a large, ornately carved wooden chest. He heard Sextus draw in a sharp breath. "From the customs house?" the centurion asked.

Simeon nodded. "That's our assumption. We didn't stop long enough to ask for details."

Sextus moved forward and lifted the lid. Gold coins gleamed brightly in the dappled sunlight beneath the trees. He looked at Marcus. "This fits the description of the box stolen from the customs station near Jerash about two weeks ago. We had a garrison just ten minutes away, so we thought it was safe. Ya'abin came in broad daylight and was gone again before an alarm could be sounded."

"Six of your men dead is what we heard," Yehuda said without expression, which Sextus confirmed with a nod.

Marcus moved forward and fingered some of the coins.

"It's just under a talent," Simeon said.

Marcus was impressed in spite of himself. This recouped two major losses and would represent a significant setback for their foe. It wasn't Ya'abin himself, but these were results you could measure.

Simeon moved around to the other side of the cart, reached over the side, and brought up a large leather pouch. There was a soft metallic rattle as he held it up. "We found this under the head of Ya'abin's chief captain. It is about two hundred shekels, probably taken as ransom." He shook it softly. "We've used almost all of the fund Mordechai set up for us. We can either keep this, or you can take it and have Mordechai put some more on account for us."

"Sextus tells me you've used the fund mostly to bribe the local shepherds."

"Bribe?" He felt his hackles rise a little. "They would be offended to hear you use that word. We've used it to restore things Ya'abin stole from them, to repair things his men destroyed. We call it 'a friendship offering.' But those were not the only expenditures. My men also have to eat."

Marcus ignored the tone. He was thinking. If Pilate knew about this bag, he would likely demand the money, but Pilate didn't know, and Mordechai was in Rome. Getting the fund replenished would take time. It said much that Simeon had produced the bag and given Marcus the choice of what to do. They could have kept it and said nothing. "Keep it," he said with a dismissive wave. "If you need more, let me know."

"We will."

Marcus looked inside the cart. "Anything more?"

"Back in the trees." Simeon looked at Sextus. "You may want to bring your men up now."

The centurion turned and walked swiftly away. In a moment they heard him barking commands. As the group approached the entrance to the monument, Marcus stopped. In the deep shadows, stood a man with a bow. His eyes darted to the right. And there was another.

"Issachar!" Simeon called. "Barak! Bring them out."

The two men stepped forward, and Marcus saw they had ropes in their other hands. In a moment, they led a chain of men out from behind the trees. As they did so, Sextus came trotting up with the eight soldiers. He stopped in surprise. "More captives?"

Yehuda gave an impudent laugh. "Strangest thing. These eight were supposed to be on guard duty, but we found them sleeping. Actually, we're doing them a favor. Ya'abin is renowned for his short temper."

Sextus gave a command, and his men moved forward to take the ropes from the two bowman.

"Take the cart and the donkey," Simeon said. "We'll get them from you later." Sextus gave another command, and one of the soldiers turned toward the cart. In a moment the legionnaires were moving through the trees with the prisoners and the cart in tow. Issachar and Barak melted away again, leaving the four men alone.

Sextus turned to Simeon with open admiration. "That's sixteen prisoners you've taken now."

"So far," he acknowledged. "Word is that more have deserted."

"Ten more," Sextus confirmed. "And our source expects that to go up. He says that Ya'abin's men are truly frightened."

That was good. The Romans had paid informants in many of the towns and villages. Their information would be very reliable. "If that's true, then he's lost almost a quarter of his force now. I assume you'll make it known that these eight are in your hands too?"

"Of course," Sextus said. "That word will be on the streets before sundown." He looked at his commander. "It's common gossip that Ya'abin's group has been cursed, that they are haunted by evil demons. He's having trouble getting new men to join him."

"The gossip is true." Yehuda's face was deadpan. "I think we may have actually seen one or two of those demons ourselves, haven't we, Simeon."

Simeon smiled briefly, but he was watching Marcus. "Satisfied?"

Marcus was watching his men and the prisoners move out into the sunlight where they stopped to wait for the two officers. "And how many men do you have?"

"Twenty-one," Simeon answered.

In one part of Marcus's mind, he was impressed. He had arrived in Jerusalem ready to give these two an ultimatum. He was tired of the months of set up with nothing to show for it, and so was Pilate. Mingling with the wandering tribesmen to build their trust might be clever, but it proved nothing—though Marcus was fair-minded enough to admit that the Roman approach the previous summer had gotten them nowhere either. Sixteen prisoners. Ten desertions. And now valuable goods recovered. It wasn't Ya'abin, but it was something tangible he could share with the governor.

And yet he was still irritated. Something in him was not willing to be satisfied. Part of that was their smug confidence, their flippancy. Part of it was . . . He wasn't sure, but he realized in the back of his mind that Simeon was right. He was half looking for a fight. "You'll never take him with twenty-one men," he said abruptly.

Simeon only laughed. "Well, you couldn't take him with six hundred, so who are you to say anything?"

Marcus fought back a flash of anger. "How soon? That's what Pilate is going to want to know. It's been nine months now. How soon can you end this?"

"It's a little more complicated than that," Yehuda said, miffed by the curt tone. "After our raid on his camp the other night, Ya'abin went across the Jordan into Perea and Moab again."

"So?"

"We don't have the support there that we need," Simeon explained. "No way to track him. No one we trust. We'd be going in blind. We'll have to wait. He'll be back."

Marcus's smile was wintry. "Your time is running out. Don't think a few prisoners or one cart filled with captured goods is going to buy you an extension."

Yehuda's face contorted. "Look, you," he started, rising to his full height, "just—"

But Simeon cut him off. "Pilate said we had a year. Or are you telling us that once again the vaunted Roman honor means nothing?"

The Roman's eyes narrowed dangerously. "Watch your tongue, Javelin. That's gotten you in trouble before."

"Do we have the year or not?" Simeon snapped.

"Yes, but no more."

Simeon looked at Yehuda and Sextus in exaggerated surprise. "Did I miss something? Did either of you hear me ask for more time?"

Marcus answered immediately. "You will."

Simeon's eyes went as cold as the tribune's. "Then wait until we do before you start whining about it." He jerked his head at Yehuda and they started away.

Marcus was furious. He was tempted to run after them and slap them in irons. But he held back and watched them disappear into the trees. "Ya'abin's still got some seventy-five men," he said to Sextus. "There is no way they can take him in the next three months. They'll be back, crawling on their knees asking for more time."

Sextus said nothing.

"And they won't get it. Not one day!"

IV

Simeon, Yehuda, Barak, and Issachar crossed the Brook Kidron and started up the steep path that led to the Golden Gate, the eastern entrance to the Temple Mount. Now they were back with crowds of people again, most of them going to the temple as well. At the place where the path split and led to Mount Ophel, south of the temple, Issachar and Barak left them to go find their families. The morning sun was halfway up in the sky, and the temperature was climbing rapidly. Both Simeon and Yehuda were sweating and breathing heavily as they made their way up the inclined pathway.

They had not spoken, other than to say farewell to their two companions, since leaving Marcus and Sextus. "So," Yehuda grunted. "Would you like to tell me what that was all about?"

"What?"

"You know what. That little exchange between you and Marcus."

Simeon just shook his head. "He's got a sliver under his fingernail, that's for sure. Don't ask me why. Maybe he's angry because we're succeeding." He didn't want to talk about it anymore. "Where are you supposed to meet Shana?"

"Near the east entrance to the Court of the Women, but I thought we'd be a lot longer than this. She won't be there until midday."

"Oh."

They walked on for several paces more; then Yehuda took him totally by surprise. "Samuel talked to me about Shana last night."

That brought Simeon's head around. Samuel had been in prison with Yehuda in Caesarea. He was single and about the same age as Simeon.

"Yes. He hasn't said anything before because he was afraid that you might . . . " He shrugged. "When I told him and some others that you and Shana are not going to reestablish things, he asked if I might consider him as a possible suitor."

"Well, well," Simeon said, truly pleased. "Samuel is a good man."

"Yes. And Shana has always liked him."

Simeon blew out his breath. "Then when things get hot out there, I want him kept back. Let him stay with the horses or something."

Yehuda gave him a hard look. "You want to tell *him* that?"

"Shana has had enough men in her life taken away. I won't be party to another Daniel."

"Aside from Samuel, do you know how Shana would react to that comment? Remember, I'm not the only Zealot in this family."

There was nothing to say to that, and Simeon walked on. They began to slow now, for as they approached the massive gates that loomed above them, the crowds were eight and nine people deep. Simeon half turned and glanced up at the sun. "If Shana won't be here for another hour or more, come with me and say hello to the family.

I'm meeting them under the apse of the Royal Portico. They were asking about you last night."

Yehuda hesitated, suspecting there might be more to the invitation than Simeon was saying, but then he nodded. "That would be nice."

Together they joined the throngs and moved slowly through the gates onto the great Temple Mount.

V

THE TEMPLE MOUNT IN JERUSALEM

The massive Court of the Gentiles that surrounded the temple proper covered more area than many villages. It was packed with people. Jerusalem normally had a large population, well over a hundred thousand people, but during Passover, the greatest of all the festivals, that swelled by five or ten times.

The family of David ben Joseph, including his cousin Benjamin and Benjamin's wife, Esther, moved slowly along, trying to stay together in the press of the crowds. David, who with Benjamin was in the lead, turned and pointed. "As warm as it is," he called, "I would guess that Jesus will stay in the shade beneath the porticoes." He was pointing to the south end of the temple complex, where the great, massive bulk of the three-level Royal Portico towered above them.

That made sense, and they started pushing their way in that direction. Ten minutes later David's assessment proved correct when they heard someone call out to them. "David! Deborah!"

It was Peter.

"*Shalom*, Peter," David said, moving over to him and gripping his hand.

"*Shalom*, David." He looked around. "No Simeon?"

"He was to meet with the Romans this morning. He'll be joining us as soon as he can."

"Good. How are things progressing?"

"I think quite well, all in all." David turned. "You remember my cousin Benjamin and his wife, Esther?"

"I do," Peter said warmly. "*Boker tov.*"

"And good day to you."

Just then Leah gave a little cry. "There's Simeon now. And Yehuda!" She darted away to meet them.

When they came back over, Simeon introduced Yehuda to Benjamin and Esther as well. Then, as the family gathered around Yehuda and inquired after his family, Simeon stepped to Peter. "Is Jesus teaching today?"

"Yes. In fact, several members of the Sanhedrin have him cornered now. We were just going over there." He gave Simeon a probing look. "How are things, Simeon?"

"Good," he said, meaning it. "Things are going well."

"Just this morning, Jesus was asking if we had any word of you."

That pleased Simeon. "Tell him that while God has not chosen to light our path more than a step or two ahead of us, he does allow us to see far enough out that, so far, we have not stumbled."

"'Trust in the Lord with all thy heart,'" Peter quoted softly, "'and lean not unto thine own understanding, and he shall direct thy path.'"

It was from the Proverbs written by King Solomon. "That's it exactly," Simeon said.

"I shall tell him that." Peter swung around to the family. "Come. Andrew and James have saved us a place by one of the columns."

Yehuda started to say his good-byes, but Simeon quickly went to him. "Come with us. Shana won't be there yet."

"No," he said, a little too quickly, "I'll wait there in case she comes earlier."

"You're afraid, aren't you?" Simeon said with sudden insight.

"Afraid of what?"

"Afraid that if you listen, Jesus might convert you too."

"Don't be ridiculous. I just want to make sure I don't miss Shana."

"Come on, you stubborn mule," Simeon said, grabbing his arm. "As hardheaded as you are, there's no great danger anything will penetrate that thick skull."

Leah had been listening to their interchange and took Yehuda's other arm. "Just for a little while. It's cool under the portico."

Reluctantly, Yehuda allowed himself to be led along. As they moved into the shade and made their way between the towering columns, they saw the others—Anna, Andrew and his wife, James and John, Matthew, Bartholomew. They were all there.

Just beyond where the others waited, directly under the great dome that formed the apse of the Royal Portico, Jesus stood amidst several men in long, flowing robes. It was clearly a confrontation. The men surrounding the Master were shouting angrily, gesticulating wildly.

"Looks interesting," Yehuda drawled.

Curious, they moved in closer so they could hear.

CHAPTER NOTES

The prohibition against coming in contact with the dead is given in Numbers 19. The purification for this pollution involved being washed with water mixed with the ashes of a red heifer specially sacrificed and burned on the altar as a sin offering. Hyssop, an herb that is frequently used as a symbol of purification, was also used (see Fallows, 1:509).

The Tomb of Zachariah and the Pillar of Absalom are two massive monuments, several stories high, that can still be visited in the Kidron Valley today. Though folklore attributes them to a much earlier time in Israel's history, archaeologists agree that they were probably carved from the solid rock in the first century before Christ. A major portion of the western slope of the Mount of

Olives is still an extensive Jewish cemetery. It is considered by many Jews to be a special blessing to have that as one's final resting place because those buried there will be the first to be resurrected when the Messiah comes.

On the opposite slope of the Kidron Valley, or the eastern slope of Mount Moriah, the Temple Mount, there is a Moslem cemetery. During the time of the Ottoman Empire, according to modern guides in Israel, the Moslems decided to bury their dead there because they knew of the Jewish belief that when the Messiah comes, he will enter Jerusalem through the eastern or Golden Gate. Since the Messiah is a *cohen*, or priest, he cannot come close to anything that is dead. Therefore, he will not be able to go through the cemetery there and his coming will be thwarted.

It is also part of both Jewish and Islamic tradition that the judgment will take place in the Kidron Valley between the Mount of Olives and the Temple Mount. An Islamic tradition states that Mohammed will sit on a pillow by the Dome of the Rock, the beautiful mosque that is now the dominant feature of the Temple Mount. A wire will be stretched from there to the Mount of Olives, where Jesus will be. (Moslems accept Jesus as one of the prophets.) All mankind will be required to walk across the wire. Those who are righteous will make it. The wicked will lose their balance and fall into the valley and perish (see Berrett, 275).

CHAPTER 20

AND WHO IS MY NEIGHBOUR?

—*Luke 10:29*

I

JERUSALEM

9 APRIL, A.D. 31

"By what authority do you presume to criticize us?" The man who spoke had a thin face and pinched lips. The anger in him was so hot his cheeks had turned a mottled red. "You and your disciples violate the Law on every hand. One of our number invited you to dine with him last evening. He said that you and your followers didn't even bother to wash before eating. You have no regard for the Sabbath. You blaspheme by suggesting that you are equal with God, whom you call your Father. How dare you point your finger at us—we who honor the Law in both word and deed? We who have placed a fence around the Law so that it is not desecrated."

Suddenly Jesus' calm patience was gone. He got to his feet, his eyes blazing with indignation. "Woe unto you, scribes and Pharisees. You hypocrites! Why do you make clean the outside of the cup and platter, but inwardly you are full of ravenous greed and wickedness?"

The reaction that triggered was not surprising. There were gasps of outrage, spluttering denials, a fist raised and shaken in Jesus' face. "Away with him!" someone shouted.

Jesus overrode them. "You love the uppermost seats in the synagogues, and for men to call greetings to you in the streets, but I say unto you that you are like graves which are not marked and men walk over them because they are not aware."

Simeon winced. The imagery was like the crack of a whip. These were dead men, polluting everything they touched, but with no warning signs to alert the unwary.

A man who had been near the back of the accusers pushed forward. From his dress, Simeon guessed he was a lawyer, one of the experts in the Law. "Master," he said petulantly, "by speaking thus of the Pharisees, you reproach us as well."

Though he was now surrounded by more than half a dozen very angry men, Jesus did not fall back even a step. He lifted a hand, pointing a finger directly at the man who had spoken. "Woe unto you also, you lawyers! You place burdens on men which are grievous to be borne, and yet you yourselves will not so much as touch those burdens with one of your fingers.

"Woe unto you, lawyers! for you have taken away the key of knowledge. Not only do you refuse to enter therein, but you hinder those who would."

For a moment, Simeon thought the man was going to lunge at Jesus. His hands were balled into fists; his mouth worked spasmodically. Jesus never moved. His eyes held the man like some magnetic force, and finally the man dropped his hands.

He swung around. "Come on!" the lawyer shouted. "This man curses against our Law. Take him. Take him to the Council."

"Yes!" cried the man with the pinched lips. "He blasphemes. Seize him."

But one look at the crowd and the men visibly recoiled. There was anger on the faces of the crowd, but it wasn't directed at Jesus.

"He speaks the truth," a man just behind the Pharisees shouted. "You are pompous hypocrites."

"Leave him alone," a woman cried out. "He speaks for God."

The muttering of the crowd rose to a ominous rumble. "Go back to your gilded thrones," someone called. "Go back and let us listen to this man."

The lawyer was staring, his head jerking back and forth. He moved closer to the thin-faced man and whispered something. He nodded and they whispered to the others. Closing in tightly together, they started backing away. "The Council will hear about this," the lawyer shouted, shaking his fist one last time. "We'll be back."

The crowd quieted as the agitators moved away. Yehuda nudged Simeon, even as he watched them plunge into the crowd. "No wonder they want to kill him," he said softly.

Simeon jerked around and gave Yehuda a sharp look.

"You haven't heard that?" Yehuda asked.

"What?"

"I've heard it from three different people since arriving here last night. Word is that the leaders of the city are so enraged with Jesus, they're trying to find a way to have him killed."

"They wouldn't dare."

"That's also what some are saying. The people would riot if they tried it." He shook his head. There was obvious admiration in his eyes. "I have to admit, Simeon. Your Jesus is no coward."

Before Simeon could respond, Jesus spoke. Now he was looking at the faces of the people. "Beware of the leaven of the Pharisees, which is hypocrisy."

Simeon and Yehuda exchanged looks again. "Couldn't say it better myself," Yehuda said softly, grinning. "I've always thought that some of the Pharisees are puffed up like loaves of bread with too much yeast in them. Someone needs to poke them with a stick and deflate them a little."

He realized that Deborah had turned and was watching him with saddened eyes. Then Yehuda remembered Simeon's Uncle Aaron. He kicked himself. "I'm sorry, Deborah. I didn't mean . . . " He let it die, because in actuality Yehuda found Aaron to be one of the very kind Jesus was talking about.

Simeon felt a touch of shame too, for Aaron had come to his mind as well. And yet, he thought, Aaron had come to Caesarea to try to influence Pilate to let Simeon go. That was more than many of Simeon's other friends and associates had done.

"I say this unto you, my friends," Jesus went on, completely calm again. "Be not afraid of them that kill the body, and which, after that, have no more that they can do to you. But I shall forewarn you about whom you should fear. Fear him who has the power to cast both body and soul into hell."

To his surprise, out of the corner of his eye, Simeon saw Yehuda nod. *Good. You wanted to hear what Jesus teaches? Well, here it is.*

As was characteristic of him, Jesus let his eyes sweep across the faces of his listeners as he let his words sink in.

"Let your loins be girded about, and your lights burning. You should be like unto men that wait for their lord when he returns from the wedding. When he comes and knocks, the men are ready to open to him immediately. Blessed are those servants whom the lord shall find watching."

Leah half turned and looked up at Yehuda. "He's speaking about the coming of the Messiah."

Yehuda gave her a surprised look, then turned back to look at Jesus.

"And if their lord shall come in the second watch or in the third watch and find them watching and waiting, blessed are those servants. And this know, that if the goodman of the house had known what hour the thief would come, he would have watched and not have suffered his house to be broken into. You should be therefore ready also, for the Son of man comes at an hour when ye think not."

Simeon wished fervently he could climb inside Yehuda's mind at that moment and see what was happening. Neither his expression nor his eyes gave any indication.

Suddenly, Peter spoke up. "Lord, do you speak this parable unto us, or even to all?"

"Who is that faithful and wise steward whom his lord shall make ruler over his household? Blessed is the servant whom his lord, when he comes, shall find so doing. Of a truth I say unto you that he will make him ruler over all that he has."

Peter and some of the other apostles exchanged looks. Jesus once again had not answered the question directly.

"But if that servant says in his heart, 'My lord delays his coming,' and begins to beat the menservants and maidens, or to eat and drink and be drunken, then the lord of that servant will come in a day when the servant looks not for him, and at an hour when he is not aware. And that servant, which knew his lord's will but prepared not himself, neither did according to his lord's will, shall be beaten with many stripes."

There was another pause. "For unto whomsoever much is given, of him shall be much required: and to whom men have committed much, of him they will ask the more."

Simeon started. He had been thinking strictly in terms of how Yehuda was taking all of this. Now the words pressed into his own mind. He and his family had been given much. They had not only been richly blessed with the temporal things of life—a successful merchant business, good health, a loving family—but they had been among the first to hear and accept Jesus. What was expected of them? He stopped. No, not expected. *Required!*

"Uh, I'd probably better go see if Shana's here."

Simeon gave his friend a hard look. "You said it would be closer to midday. That's another hour yet." But he knew there was no sense protesting. He could see it in Yehuda's eyes. He was bored. Now that the confrontation with the Pharisees was over, what Jesus was saying wasn't making any kind of impression on Yehuda.

"Just a little longer. Then—"

Jesus was continuing, and his words drew both of their heads around. "I am come to send fire on the earth; and how I wish that it were already kindled."

Yehuda leaned forward slightly, his eyes intent on Jesus now.

"Do you suppose that I am come to give peace on earth? I tell you, Nay. Rather I am come to bring division, for henceforth there shall be five in one house, and they shall be divided, three against two, and two against three. The father shall be divided against the son, and the son against the father; the mother against the daughter, and the daughter against the mother."

"Is he saying what I think he's saying?" Yehuda said, interest finally showing in his face.

Simeon shook his head sadly. "No, Yehuda. He is not."

"But he said—"

He took his arm and moved away as Jesus continued. Once they were to one side, Simeon went on. "I know what it sounds like, but he's not calling for war."

"Oh, really? 'I come to send fire on the earth?' That doesn't sound like peace to me."

"I want you to think about something, Yehuda, then you'll understand what Jesus is saying. Up until a few months ago, you and I were one—in heart, in mind, in purpose, in action. Would you say that's true?"

"Yes."

"And now?"

Suddenly Yehuda saw it. His mouth pulled down. "Where there

was once unity, now there is division. Where there was singleness of purpose, now we are of two minds."

"And the cause of that division?"

Yehuda turned his head and stared at Jesus, saying nothing. He didn't have to.

"That's right," Simeon said despondently. "That's the fire he came to kindle, Yehuda, a fire in men's hearts. Can't you see it? Can't you feel it?"

His jaw set. "Shana might come early. I'd better go."

He pulled free of Simeon's grip and walked away without looking back.

As Simeon watched him until he was out from beneath the portico and into the sunlight again, he shook his head. "'I am come to bring division,'" he murmured, "'and henceforth, shall brother be divided against brother.'"

II

THE TOP OF THE MOUNT OF OLIVES

As they reached the top of the Mount of Olives, they stopped to rest for a few moments, winded from the long climb. They automatically turned to look across the Kidron Valley to the city of Jerusalem. The crest of the Mount of Olives was about three hundred feet higher than the top of Mount Moriah, where the Temple Mount sat, so they looked down upon the whole complex.

No one spoke. It was just four of them now—Simeon and Leah and their parents. Ephraim and Rachel had returned with their children to Bethlehem, accompanied by David's cousin and his wife. It had been a long and exciting day for young Esther and Boaz, and they needed their sleep. Even Joseph, though he was eleven now, was ready to go home and declined the invitation to attend the supper in Bethany.

The sun was low in the west and shining directly into their eyes. The buildings on the Temple Mount, including the temple itself, were in silhouette, but the sun painted the rest of the city in a shimmering, amber glow.

"Jerusalem the golden," Deborah murmured, thoroughly enchanted.

"It's beautiful," Leah whispered.

"This would be a fantastic view in the morning," Simeon said thoughtfully. "The sun would be at our backs and light up the whole city. Then you could see everything."

Leah slugged him playfully. "Can't you just enjoy what is? Do you always have to be looking for a better alternative?"

Surprised, he rubbed at his arm. "It is beautiful," he agreed, "but I was just—"

She laughed merrily, cutting him off. "No buts, Simeon. Just say, 'It is beautiful.'"

"I just did."

"Come," Deborah said. "We told Martha we would be there by sundown. We'd better keep moving."

As they started off, moving eastward up and over the crest of the hill, Leah slipped her arm through Simeon's and leaned her head against his shoulder. "It is so good to have you with us again, Simeon. I've missed you."

He put an arm around her and pulled her in tightly against him. "As have I," he said. "In fact, it's getting so that home sounds better to me all the time."

III

ON THE ROAD TO BETHANY

Bethany was a small village on the back side, or the eastern slope, of the Mount of Olives, about three-quarters of an hour's walk from Jerusalem. The whole area was given to orchards of fig and olive trees and grapes. Stone walls ran everywhere, defining the various plots of ground. From this close to the top of the Mount of Olives, no trees blocked their view, and they could see a vast stretch of the wilderness of Judea, mostly brown with just a brush of green from the spring rains. But from here to the Dead Sea some fifteen miles away, the picture was of utter desolation. The sight of it sobered Simeon. In a few days, he and Yehuda would be returning to the desert to once again start the hunt for Moshe Ya'abin. The thought left him a little depressed.

Deborah spoke, bringing his thoughts back. "Martha says that her house is right on this road, near the eastern edge of the village."

Peter and Anna had told David and Deborah about the family in Bethany and explained that they would be staying there with Jesus during Passover, but Deborah and David had not met Martha until that afternoon. At midday, as Jesus took a break from teaching, Anna and Peter brought Martha, and her sister and brother, Mary and Lazarus, over and introduced them to David's family. They had spent the rest of the day together, following Jesus as he moved among the people.

Martha's invitation to dinner had come as a pleasant surprise. Jesus would be there, and that meant an opportunity to be with him without the huge throngs pressing in on him at every moment. They had immediately accepted. Hungry to spend as much time as possible with Jesus before returning to the wilderness of Judea, Simeon had been greatly pleased when Martha made it clear that the invitation included him and Leah as well.

They crested the hill and started down again, the road bending back and forth to soften the incline. "Look," Leah said, as they came around one of those bends.

Up ahead a crowd of about two dozen people filled the middle of the road. They were moving slowly down the hill. As they drew closer, it was not surprising to see Jesus was in the middle of the group. The people were gathered in around him, for he was speaking even as they walked.

"They must have been delayed on the Temple Mount," Deborah said. "Peter and Anna and Andrew are there too."

Simeon was pleased when he caught a glimpse of Jesus' mother, walking alongside of him. "Look," he said to Deborah, "Mary is with Jesus. Wonderful. I would like to speak with her again."

As they approached the slow moving group, Luke the Physician turned and saw them coming. He immediately moved back and greeted them warmly. "*Shalom, shalom,*" he said with a broad smile. "Anna told me you were coming tonight."

"*Shalom,* Luke," Deborah said, taking his hand. "This is a surprise. Do you know the family of Martha as well?"

"I do. I was here with Jesus at the Feast of Dedication last winter and got to meet them. Did you know them before?"

"No," Deborah said, "just today."

"Well, Martha's probably wondering where everyone is. We left the temple more than an hour ago, but you know how it is. Jesus can barely go anywhere because of the people." He chuckled. "In fact, I think we still have several with us who were not invited to supper."

Luke looked at Simeon. "*Shalom,* my friend. How are things going out in the wilderness?"

The question didn't catch him off guard. The facts of what he was doing were well known to the tight circle of disciples in Capernaum.

"Very well, thank you. I'm hoping we can bring it to a close in the next few months."

"That is good. Well, know that we are all praying for you."

"Thank you. We can use every prayer in our behalf."

The crowd slowed and then stopped. Jesus was talking with a young man, perhaps a little older than Simeon, who was wearing a richly cut outer robe and an embroidered turban on his head. He was talking earnestly. Jesus was listening, nodding from time to time.

Just then David gave a soft exclamation. An older man with white hair had stepped out of the crowd and was coming towards them, smiling broadly.

"Joseph?" David exclaimed.

"David! What a pleasant surprise." They clasped hands, holding them tightly for a moment.

The older man turned to Deborah and took both of her hands. "Deborah, you grow more lovely every time I see you. Being a grandmother must agree with you."

"It does," she laughed. "How good to see you again, Joseph."

Simeon watched curiously. Here was a man of obvious wealth. He was portly, but his robe was so cleverly tailored that it softened the effect of his weight. His outer robe was of a light, silky fabric and trimmed generously with gold braid. His inner tunic was of a deep blue, a fabric that Simeon knew came from Egypt and was very costly. A gold chain served as a sash around his waist. His sandals were encrusted with silver buckles.

David motioned for Simeon and Leah to come closer. "Joseph, let me introduce you to two of my children. "This is Leah, our youngest daughter. She is sixteen now. Leah, this is an old friend and associate, Joseph of Arimathea."

"I'm very pleased to meet you," Leah said, inclining her head respectfully.

The older man looked at her closely, then at Deborah. "You would have a hard time denying this one belongs to you, Deborah. She is as lovely as you are."

"Thank you," Leah said, coloring at the compliment.

"And this is my second son, Simeon," David said with evident pride. "Simeon, this is a friend from many years back."

Simeon shook his hand, immediately liking the firmness of the grip even though the hand itself was fleshy and soft. This was obviously a man who did not have to earn his living by the sweat of his brow. But he liked his eyes—generous, friendly, and intelligent. "It is a pleasure to meet you," Simeon said.

"Oh, we've met before," Joseph said.

"We have?"

There was a deep chuckle. "Yes, but you were only about this high." He marked a spot on his leg just above the knee. "As I remember, you were wrestling with your older brother at the time."

"That had to have been Simeon," Deborah said, laughing.

David stepped back a step, sizing up his old friend. "I must admit this is a great surprise, Joseph. Are you a follower of Jesus?"

When he nodded, Simeon registered even greater surprise. The older man saw it and smiled. "Yes. Believe it or not there are a few of us on the Council who feel something other than hostility for Jesus. We haven't made that fact known very widely yet, for there is great opposition among our brethren, but Nicodemus and I—" He turned to David. "You remember Nicodemus?"

"I do."

"He and I are both impressed with what Jesus is and what he does. But I doubt Nicodemus will come. He tried to convince me that it was a mistake for me to come, but it is not a public gathering. Martha was kind enough to extend an invitation, and so here I am. Actually, I brought a young acquaintance of mine with me. He is one of the scribes and wanted a chance to ask some questions of Jesus."

He pointed. "That's him with Jesus now. His name is Reuben ben Eleazar, of Jerusalem."

They turned to look. Jesus had come to a complete stop now, and the rest of the people had gathered in around him and the young man.

"Perhaps I had better go over and make sure he doesn't offend anyone. He is a good young man, but filled with the enthusiasm and self-confidence of youth."

That was fine with Simeon. Judging from the earnestness of the conversation, Simeon wanted to hear what Jesus was saying. The scribes were the experts in the Mosaic Law and closely allied with the Pharisees and the lawyers, the very ones who had confronted Jesus earlier in the day. It would be interesting to hear what questions he was asking. Simeon and Leah fell in behind their parents as they followed Joseph back over to where he had been before.

As they moved in close enough to hear, the young man was asking a question. "Master," he said. Simeon was pleased to hear that his voice was respectful. "You often speak of eternal life. That means a great deal to me. My question for you is, what must I do to inherit eternal life?"

Jesus nodded. "What is written in the law? How do you read it?"

There was a satisfied look, almost a smugness as the man pulled his shoulders back. "'Thou shalt love the Lord thy God with all thy heart, and with all thy soul, and with all thy strength, and with all thy mind.'"

Simeon found himself nodding. The passage he was quoting was perhaps the most famous passage in all of the Torah. It came from the book of Deuteronomy and formed part of the *Sh'ma*, the most sacred of all prayers to a Jew.

"And also," the man said, pleased to see his answer had won him a nod from Jesus, "'Love thy neighbor as thyself.'"

"You have answered right. This do and you shall live."

The man was suddenly flustered. He obviously had expected more than that. Jesus waited, watching him steadily.

"So," Reuben said, groping a little, "so who is my neighbor?"

Jesus was thoughtful for a moment. The crowd was watching the exchange with interest, so when Jesus began to speak, it was no longer just to the scribe in front of him. "A certain man went down from Jerusalem to Jericho and fell among thieves, who stripped him of his raiment, and wounded him, and departed, leaving him half-dead."

There were nods all around at that. The road from Jerusalem to Jericho was notorious for its violence. Dropping some four thousand feet in just fifteen miles, from the highlands of Jerusalem to the shores of the Dead Sea, it was steep, narrow, and passed through many places that provided excellent opportunities for ambush. Moshe Ya'abin was one of those who made his living preying on people along the Jericho Road.

"And by chance," Jesus continued, "there came down a certain priest that way. And when he saw him, he passed by on the other side." He stopped to let that sink in.

"Perhaps he thought he was dead," Joseph murmured in David's ear.

For a moment, Simeon wasn't sure why he had made that comment, then suddenly realized exactly what he was suggesting. If it was a dead body, contact would bring automatic uncleanness, especially for a priest, who would be under special obligation to avoid such spiritual contamination. On the other hand, if the man wasn't dead, there was no problem. By crossing the road, there was no way he could ascertain if the man was really dead or not.

Then another thought struck him. The man had been ambushed by thieves. Anyone who stopped also put himself at risk.

"And likewise a Levite," Jesus went on, "when he was at the place, came and looked on him, and passed by on the other side." Again Jesus paused to let the people consider the circumstance.

It was essentially the same thing. The Levites were an order of the priesthood as well and would be under the same obligations to avoid contamination as the priests. Then a second thought struck Simeon. The priesthood was given of God to serve others, to perform religious rites and ceremonies so others could be blessed. Of all Israel, shouldn't a priest be most inclined to care about another human being?

The people around Jesus were totally rapt as they waited. This was a compelling story he was giving them. "But a certain Samaritan, as he journeyed, came where he was."

It was as though the whole group suddenly drew in a breath. A Samaritan? The priest and Levite were the revered among society. A Samaritan was one of the detested ones, an unclean and hated enemy. Even walking on the soil of Samaria could contaminate one spiritually, according to the Pharisees.

Jesus seemed to sense their reaction and went on, speaking more slowly. "And when the Samaritan saw the man, he had compassion on him, and went to him."

No one breathed. Every eye was fastened on the Master as he spoke.

"And the Samaritan bound up his wounds, pouring in oil and wine. Then he set him on his own animal and brought him to an inn and took care of him."

Jesus looked around, letting his eyes stop briefly on each person's face. "And on the morrow, when the Samaritan departed, he took out two *denarii*, and gave them to the host of the inn, and said unto him, 'Take care of this man, and whatsoever you spend more than this, when I come again, I will repay thee.'"

Simeon was almost reeling. This was astonishing. A Samaritan! He too was at risk by stopping to help. The thieves along the road didn't harbor any such worries about contact with the unclean. If the Samaritan had merely carried the man to the inn and dumped him there, hoping someone might help him, he would have done far more than either the priest or the Levite. But to pay, and then to leave a pledge of credit. Unheard of! Simeon shot a look at his father. Was this a true story?

Jesus now looked directly at Reuben the scribe. "Which now of these three do you think was neighbor unto him that fell among the thieves?"

Reuben was bewildered. "I—" But there was only one possible answer. He dropped his eyes. "He that showed mercy on him."

"If you would have eternal life, go then, and do likewise."

IV

BETHANY

The home of Martha, Mary, and Lazarus was a spacious two-story house set behind a high stone wall. The house was larger than Simeon had expected, based on the fact that just three people lived here, though it was not palatial by any means. The courtyard, however, was even larger than their own in Capernaum. He noted that one end of the courtyard had a series of recessed arches. In one of those, Simeon could discern the dark shape of an olive press. In another, there was a large millstone for grinding wheat.

The courtyard was filled with people standing about or sitting on the benches. Only a few of the crowd that had come with Jesus had continued on when they reached Martha's house. Most had come in. It was clear that Martha was surprised and a little dismayed to see the numbers that had come. So Deborah and Leah immediately left David and Simeon talking with Joseph of Arimathea, and went into the house.

"We're here to help," Deborah said, pushing back the sleeves of her dress. "What can we do?"

Martha turned in surprise. Anna, Peter's wife, was there, as was Ruth, Andrew's wife. They sat at a long wooden table with Mary, the mother of Jesus, peeling and cutting onions, potatoes, carrots, and beans into a large pot. Lazarus, Martha's brother, was at a wash basin sorting clusters of grapes onto platters. Martha shook her head. "No, no. You go out and listen to Jesus. We're doing fine."

Deborah just smiled. "There'll be time for that after supper." She saw a knife on a small chest and picked it up, then took the last remaining chair at the table alongside the other three women and started to work. "We had Jesus to our house for supper too," Deborah explained. "We know how much work there is to do."

Martha gave them both a grateful look. "Thank you. I am running a little behind. I thought we were going to have only about fifteen people. Now it's closer to thirty."

Leah nodded. "The night Jesus came to eat with us, Peter told us to expect about a dozen. We ended up serving over forty."

Martha smiled briefly, then wiped at her forehead with the back of her hand. "I haven't counted lately. Maybe there are even more than I thought."

Leah saw that she was perspiring slightly. She also saw the lines of weariness around her mouth. Martha was in her mid-twenties, Leah guessed. She thought about what Peter and Anna had told them about this family. Widowed within a year of her marriage, Martha had not as yet remarried. She was the oldest of the three children and thus the matron of the house. Lazarus was a couple of years younger, about Peter's age, and was not married either, though Peter had not indicated whether this was because Lazarus had never married or was widowed as well. Mary, the youngest of the three, who seemed to be about

Leah's age, was not promised to anyone as yet. The three of them lived in the home of their parents, who had both passed away unexpectedly several years before. As the oldest child, Martha inherited the house, but as was the custom in Israel, she had the responsibility to share that inheritance with the other children.

Leah liked Martha very much. She was quiet by nature and yet had a warmth in her that made you feel comfortable almost immediately. She was lovely in her features, though not as striking as either Mary or Lazarus. She exhibited a deep maturity in spiritual things. It was obvious even from what little interaction Leah had seen between this family and Jesus that the Master was very close to them and enjoyed staying with them while he was in the Jerusalem area.

Realizing that she was just standing there, Leah looked around. There were three melons sitting on the table, but no other knives with which to cut them. "What can I do?" she asked.

A frown passed briefly across Martha's face. "Did you see my sister, Mary, out there?"

"Yes," Deborah answered. "She was with Mary Magdalene a few moments ago. They were both listening to Jesus when we came inside."

"Then Leah, could you go tell her that I need her. The chickens are almost done, but there's still a lot to do before we can start serving. Then once you get her, if the two of you could check the bread before you come back in, that would be the best thing. Mary can show you where the ovens are."

"All right." Leah turned and went out the door and ran lightly down the stone stairs to the courtyard. Simeon and her father, who were visiting now with Luke and Matthew and John, started to move toward her, thinking she might want something, but she waved them back. She moved around the edge of the crowd, her eyes searching for Mary. She could hear Jesus speaking and caught the words, "kingdom of heaven," but not much more. Then she saw her. Mary was on the far side of the group, still standing beside Mary of Magdala, her eyes fastened on Jesus as he spoke. Not wanting to interrupt what Jesus was saying, Leah moved quietly around to the two women.

Mary Magdalene saw her and smiled, but Martha's sister did not turn. Feeling a little embarrassed, Leah touched her shoulder. Surprised, Mary looked around. "Martha needs you in the kitchen," Leah whispered.

"Oh. All right. Tell her I'll be right there."

Leah nodded and stepped back. Mary Magdalene had heard what she said and moved with her. "Can I help?" she whispered.

"Probably. Martha is worried about having everything ready on time."

They waited a moment, but Mary had already forgotten them. She was totally engrossed in what Jesus was saying. The two women looked at each other, and Mary Magdalene shrugged.

"Do you know where the ovens are?" Leah asked. "Martha wants us to see how the bread is doing."

"Yes. They're behind the olive press."

Giving Mary one last look, the two of them moved away.

When they went back upstairs into the kitchen, Deborah and Anna were still cutting up vegetables, talking about the story of the good Samaritan. Jesus' mother and Martha were pitting olives. Lazarus had finished the grapes and was now washing some figs. At the sight of Leah with Mary Magdalene, Martha frowned.

"The bread should be done in about five more minutes," Leah said. "It looks good."

"And smells wonderful," Mary Magdalene said, wrinkling her nose in pleasure.

Martha looked toward the door. "Where's my Mary?"

"She said she'd be here in a minute," Leah answered.

There was a soft sound of exasperation; then Martha turned. "Lazarus. Will you get some of the men and set up the tables and benches in the courtyard? We will be ready in about ten minutes." She moved to the window and looked down on her guests. "Let's put them on this end. There's shade there and then you won't have to disturb Jesus until we're ready to eat."

"Good idea." He wiped his hands on a towel.

"And tell Mary I need her," she said, quite earnestly this time.

He nodded and went out.

"What can we do?" Leah asked. "Put us to work."

Martha went to a small box and retrieved two more knives. "You can slice the melons. Leah, there's a large platter in the chest there."

V

Ten minutes later, everything was in readiness. The round loaves of bread sat steaming on flat serving boards, the crust softened with melted butter. Bowls and platters were filled with melon slices, olives, figs, dates, pomegranates, almonds, grapes, and half a dozen other bounties from the fields and orchards. Eight roasted chickens were taken from the spit in the large fireplace and placed neatly on a bed of grape leaves.

Martha looked up and down the table, her eyes checking everything. "All right, I think we're ready to start carrying it down to the courtyard." Her brow creased and she walked swiftly to the window. She leaned partway out. "Mary!"

Leah moved forward enough to see. Below them, Mary was still where she had been when Leah spoke to her, still concentrating completely on Jesus. Several heads turned, but not her sister's.

"That girl!" Martha said, half-smiling, half-irritated.

"I'll get her," Leah said. She picked up the platter filled with the melons she and Mary Magdalene had cut, and went out. To her surprise, as she reached the tables and set the platter down, Martha was at her side. She set a bowl of almonds and a bowl of olives down with a sharp thud.

"I'll get her," Martha said shortly, and started across the courtyard. Without really thinking about it, Leah followed, curious to see what Martha would say to her sister. When they reached the spot where Mary was, Jesus was answering a question from two women on the other side of the group. Mary was rapt with attention.

Martha laid a hand on Mary's shoulder, causing her to jump slightly. "Mary," she said in a low but urgent voice. "I need you."

Mary looked up, surprised at the edge to her sister's voice. Jesus also turned. Flushing a little when she saw the Master was watching them, Martha spoke to him. "Lord, do you not care that my sister has left me to serve alone? Bid her to come and help. It is time to serve the supper we have prepared."

For a long moment, Jesus just looked at her. His eyes were large, searching her face with studied care. And then he spoke. Leah could not remember ever hearing more kindness and love in his voice than there was now. "Martha, Martha," he said, "you are cumbered about with much serving. You are careful and troubled about many things."

He smiled then and it was filled with infinite gentleness. "But only one thing is needful. And Mary has chosen that good part. And that shall not be taken away from her."

CHAPTER NOTES

The interchange between Jesus and the Pharisees, as well as the parable that followed concerning being a watchful servant, is found in Luke 11 and 12. The bitter anger depicted here was based on Luke's comment that "the scribes and the Pharisees began to urge him vehemently, and to provoke him to speak of many things" (Luke 11:53). In this chapter, the setting for those teachings was Jerusalem. Though Luke doesn't specify a place, it is more likely that it happened in the Galilee.

The Parable of the Good Samaritan, as it is commonly known, is found in

Luke 10:25–37. Since Luke is the only Gospel writer to record this parable, the author has placed him in the story at the time the parable was given. There is no setting specified by Luke for the giving of the parable. Immediately following the account of the Good Samaritan, Luke says that the Savior went on his way and entered into the house of Martha (Luke 10:38). Then follows the account of Martha's frustration with Mary not helping when she was "cumbered about with much serving" (see Luke 10:38–42).

It should be noted that while it is called a parable, Jesus may have been recounting an actual incident, as the story of the Good Samaritan does not fit the traditional form of a parable.

We know from the New Testament record that Jesus was very close to the family of Martha, Mary, and Lazarus. No details are known about them personally other than what is briefly given in the Gospels, mostly by Luke and John. The fact that it was Martha's house and that she was in charge has caused some commentators to assume she was the oldest in the family and not married at the time, and thus may have been a widow (see Fallows, 2:1119). The author's suggestion of age and marital status for the three siblings is added here merely to give detail to the novel and is not based on information found in the New Testament. Other details of this incident are also fictional.

In daily conversation, we glean enormous clues about what a person intends to communicate not only from *what* is said, but also *how* it is said, meaning the tone of voice, facial expression, and so on. Unfortunately, we are rarely told how Jesus said something. Knowing of his love for Martha, it felt right to assume that Jesus' correction of her on this day was not a sharp chastisement, but was given with great love and tenderness.

CHAPTER 21

BUT ONE THING IS NEEDFUL: AND [SHE]
HATH CHOSEN THAT GOOD PART.

—Luke 10:42

I

THE ROAD FROM BETHANY TO JERUSALEM
9 APRIL, A.D. 31

The full moon that ushered in the Passover season was up when they left Bethany. There was a breeze coming off the Mediterranean Sea some twenty-five miles to the west of them, and the air was cool and pleasant. When they reached the spot at the top of the Mount of Olives where they had stopped earlier that day and looked out across the city, they paused again. Bethlehem was still about five miles away, and it wouldn't do to push too hard or they would grow weary before they reached Benjamin and Esther's house.

Where before the city had been bathed in gold, now it glowed a faint silver. The temple itself almost seemed to float on a sea of soft light. The lines were muted, almost surrealistic. If anything, it was even more beautiful than it had been before.

They stood in silence, drinking in the scene, breathing in deeply the air that smelled faintly of the sea. Then as David led out again, starting down the path that led into the Kidron Valley, Leah spoke for the first time since leaving the house of Martha.

"I'd like to say something," she said with some solemnity.

Simeon was thinking about his interchange with Marcus Didius earlier that day and barely heard. David turned to look at his daughter, but it was Deborah who actually spoke. "What is it, Leah?"

"I—" She took a quick breath and started again. "I know I shouldn't say this, but . . . "

Her father half turned. "But what?"

"But I didn't like what Jesus did tonight."

Simeon's head came around, Marcus Didius banished from his thoughts. He looked at his sister closely to see if he had heard right. It was hard not to show outright shock. Of all of the family, Leah had been the one to give herself to Jesus without reservation. She never had anything but praise for Jesus, and if anyone started asking questions about something Jesus had said, she would jump to his defense, even if he wasn't under attack.

Deborah was also staring at her daughter in surprise.

Leah rushed on. "I don't mean to be critical, but I felt really terrible for Martha."

"What happened to Martha?" Simeon asked.

So Leah told them quickly. She told it all, from her first trip down to get Mary to the final exchange between Martha and Jesus. She was the only one who had seen the whole thing unfold. Deborah had been in the kitchen and had seen Martha's exasperation with her sister, but she had not seen what happened. David had been there when Martha asked Jesus for help, but he did not know anything of what had brought it on. Simeon had not seen any of it.

"I expected Jesus to correct Mary," she concluded. "After all, it's Mary's house too. I'm sure Lazarus and Martha would have loved to sit and listen to Jesus, but someone had to get supper on." She looked down, the guilt starting to rise as she realized the depth of her passion about this. "Instead, Jesus chided Martha and said that Mary had chosen the better part."

David was watching her closely. "So that was it. I wondered when it happened what was going on. Martha was dismayed by what Jesus said."

"I'm sure she was really hurt, Papa. Why? Why would Jesus do that? I was so positive that he would chastise Mary a little, not Martha. I fully expected him to say something like, 'Look, Mary, Martha's right. We can talk later. She needs your help.'" Her shoulders fell a little. "I know I shouldn't be critical, but it just really shocked me."

Deborah put her arm around Leah. "I'm sure there was a reason. We may not know everything that was going on," she murmured.

Simeon turned to their father to see what he would say. On the surface, at least, Simeon's sympathies were with Martha, based on what he had heard. It was very unlike what Jesus would do. But his father was deep in thought and said nothing. Embarrassed by her outburst, Leah fell silent as they made their way downward.

It was almost ten minutes before David slowed his step and looked at Leah. It was as though there had been no break in the conversation and he was answering the question she had asked just moments before. "What is really interesting is what happened just before that."

"What are you talking about, Papa?"

"Before we got to Martha's house, Jesus told the story of the good Samaritan. Think about that for a moment. What happened with that young man, the one named Reuben?"

"He asked, 'Who is our neighbor?'" Simeon said, not sure what his father was thinking.

"Ah," David said slowly. "That was what Reuben asked, but that is not what Jesus taught him. And us." David smiled, pleased that they all were looking at him quizzically. He had their attention. "Think about it. Reuben asked what he had to do to inherit eternal life. The two great commandments were then cited—'Love God and love your neighbor'—and Jesus confirmed that was the right answer. Then Reuben asked, 'Who is my neighbor?' In other words, Reuben wanted to know who he has to love in order to get eternal life."

A slow smile stole across David's face. "And if you ask that, you are also asking who you *don't* have to love, aren't you?"

Again there was a long silence; then suddenly Deborah understood. "Jesus didn't answer Reuben's question," she said.

Simeon and Leah turned around. "What?" Simeon said. "Of course he did. The whole story of the good Samaritan was the answer."

"No," she said, her face thoughtful. "No, think about it. Who was the neighbor? The priest? The Levite?"

"The Samaritan," Leah said. "He's the one who helped the man." But even as she said it, she shook her head. "No." It was said in wonder. "The neighbor was the wounded man. He was the one in need."

"Exactly right," David breathed, pleased that she saw it too. "The question that young man Reuben should have asked was not *whom* do I have to love to gain eternal life, but *how* do I have to love. That's the lesson of the story."

In that instant, Simeon understood as well. He had puzzled over the story all during supper and had finally given up, not quite sure what was bothering him about it. It was a wonderful story about caring for others, but something in the back of his mind had been nagging at him. He had the feeling there was a specific message in the story for him at this particular moment in his life. Now he saw it clearly. His task was to learn how to love God and his fellowman. Then he remembered what Jesus had said earlier that day. "Unto whom much is given, much is required." That was it. This was what Jesus required of them. *To change how they loved*.

Leah still wasn't satisfied. "All right, I see what you're saying, Father, and it makes sense to me. But it wasn't the story that bothered me. It was what Jesus said to Martha. I know there has to be a reason why he said what he did, but I can't see it. It seems unfair."

"Remember that he spoke to her with great love and tenderness," David said. "But don't you see any relationship between the parable and what happened at the house a little while later? Doesn't it strike you as odd?"

"Odd?" Leah exclaimed. "Jesus chastising Martha was odd. That was so unlike him."

"Maybe he wasn't chastising her," Deborah interjected quietly. "Maybe he was teaching her."

That set Leah back a little. "Teaching her? Teaching her what?"

"This is what comes to my mind. What are the two great commandments of the Law, according to the lawyer?"

"To love God with all our heart and to love our neighbor as ourselves."

"You listed those two commandments in the same order as Reuben did tonight. Is there a reason for that?"

"Of course," Leah answered. "To love God is the most important. Loving your neighbor would be second."

They had reached the bottom of the Kidron Valley and were in shadow. The moon was not high enough to penetrate its depths yet. From here, they would take a path that led south in a more direct route to Bethlehem. Deborah stopped, not to rest after coming down the hill, but to face Leah in the near darkness. "Now think for a moment, Leah. Which commandment was Mary keeping tonight, and which was Martha?"

For a moment, it seemed like a question that didn't make sense, and then once again the flash of insight came. Simeon suddenly felt like a child. Under his mother's gentle probing, suddenly it all became so clear, so evident, yet he hadn't even caught a glimpse of it before. "That's it," he breathed. "Now I see what you are saying."

Leah saw it too. "Mary was putting her love for the Son of God first," she said slowly.

"And Martha?"

"She put dinner first."

"No," Simeon said, "it was more than that. She was showing love too, for us, for her guests, for her 'neighbors.'"

"That's right," Deborah said, "and that is wonderful. What a fine woman she is to care for our needs, to want to make sure we are fed and made welcome. But of the two—feeding your friends, or loving Christ so much you can't bear not to listen to him, which is more important? Or as Jesus put it, which is the one thing that is 'needful—that good part'?"

Leah was completely contrite. "I see now," she said meekly.

Deborah had one last thought. She asked the question as much of herself as of the others. "Jesus has said that he is the Bread of Life, and that if we partake of what he has for us—his life, his teachings, his gospel—we shall have everlasting life. So who had more to offer tonight? Martha to Jesus? Or Jesus to Martha?"

II

BETHLEHEM

10 APRIL, A.D. 31

Simeon yawned mightily as he shuffled over to the table and sat down beside his niece and nephew. "*Boker tov*, Uncle Simeon," young Esther said, eyeing him gravely.

"Good morning, Esther. Good morning, Boaz."

Boaz looked up. He was forming a snake on his plate with the olive pits that remained from his breakfast. He gave Simeon a happy grin, then went back to his work, biting on his tongue as he concentrated fiercely on his task.

Rachel, who sat across the table from them, looked at her brother-in-law. "What time did you finally get home last night?"

Simeon yawned again before he could answer, winning a smile from her. "It was after midnight," he said. He reached across and picked up a dried fig. "Are Mother and Father still asleep?"

"No. Father has already gone with Benjamin to see to the sheep. Mother and Aunt Esther went for a walk. They'll be back in a little while."

He groaned. "A walk? After yesterday? I'll bet we walked ten miles all in all."

Esther answered that one. "Granmama likes to walk. Her and me go for walks too."

"I know." Simeon smiled and reached for her hand. "How would *you* like to go for a walk with me today?"

The serpent was forgotten as Boaz's head shot up. "Me too, Uncle Sheemon?"

"Yes, you too, Boaz."

Rachel gave him a strange look. "But we're going into Jerusalem again today."

"I know." He looked at the two children. "But Esther and Boaz and I are going to go together, aren't we."

A tiny smile lit up Esther's eyes. "Just us?"

"Just us. Mama and Papa are going to go with Pampa and Granmama."

"Go where?"

They all turned as Ephraim came through the door.

"To Jerusalem, Papa," Esther exclaimed. "Uncle Simeon's going to take us to Jerusalem."

Ephraim frowned slightly as he turned to Simeon. "What are you talking about?"

"I'm going to take the children to listen to Jesus today. All day. You go with Mother and Father." He was looking at Rachel. "Go listen to Jesus without worrying about them."

"But—"

"You deserve some time without the children." He laughed. "Except for the one you're carrying with you. I can't do much about that one." His face softened. "I know how much you and Ephraim wanted to go last night. So today, it's your turn."

"I can't do that," Rachel started. "You—"

But Simeon cut her off. "Let's take a vote. How many of the children here would like to spend the day with Uncle Simeon?"

Both hands shot up, waving wildly.

"And how many want to go with Mama and Papa?"

Boaz jammed both of his hands under his legs, so that there would not be the slightest chance of anyone misunderstanding his wishes. Esther folded her arms and looked at her mother triumphantly.

"See there!" Simeon laughed. "You lose. I'll find a cart going into the city so they don't have to walk the whole way."

"Are you sure?" Rachel asked softly.

Simeon nodded. "We're going to hear Jesus too, but let me worry about the children."

Boaz jumped out of his seat and started a little dance, fists clenched and punching the air, chanting triumphantly.

Rachel got up and came around the table. She bent down and kissed Simeon on the cheek. "Thank you," she murmured.

He reached up and touched her hand. "It's not just for you, Rachel. I've missed these two and I won't get to see them again for a while."

III

The rest of the family prepared to leave about half an hour later. Esther and Boaz were still getting their sandals on, so Simeon went to the small courtyard to say good-bye.

Ephraim came over and gripped his hand. "Thank you, Simeon. Rachel is almost as excited as the children."

"We'll see you up there, I'm sure, but don't worry about us. We'll be fine."

"More than fine," Ephraim said with a smile. "I've not seen those two this excited in some time."

Rachel came over. "If they get tired, just come and find us."

"Don't even think it," he said. "They are mine all day."

"Remember," Deborah called as he opened the gate into the street, "tonight is Passover Eve. We have to get back here at least an hour before sundown."

"We will," Simeon promised. "Who is going to stop by the temple and get the paschal lamb?" The key element in the Passover dinner was the lamb that would be roasted and completely consumed this night. But it could not be just any lamb. Though there would be thousands of sheep prepared for the families in Jerusalem this night, every one had to be carefully inspected by the priests to ensure there were no blemishes or defects, and then each animal had to be sacrificed and prepared in a precise ritual. In Hebrew, the word meaning "to pass over" was *pesach*, thus the name paschal lamb.

Ephraim lifted a hand. "If you have the children, we can do it."

"Good."

As the rest of the family moved through the gate out into the street, his mother suddenly turned and came back to Simeon. She went up on tiptoe and hugged him tightly. "Thank you, Martha."

For a moment he was startled; then he laughed, pleased that she understood. "Rachel deserves at least one time when she can be Mary."

"Yes, she does."

They stood there awkwardly for a moment. "Do you know what I want?" he asked gruffly.

"What?"

"When I grow up and get married, I want to be just like you and Father."

IV

JERUSALEM

"Tell us about this," Simeon said to the vendor, pointing to a thin narrow roll of something dark brown but with tiny points of light glistening in the sunlight.

The man behind the little two-wheeled cart picked one up. "It's a date stick. We grind up the flesh of the date, press it into a flat sheet, sprinkle it with chopped almonds and soak it in honey. Then we roll it up onto a stick and let it harden." He looked down into Boaz's wide brown eyes. "It's very good," he said.

Boaz was sold long before the explanation. "I want one," he said to Simeon.

Simeon looked at Esther. She wasn't sure yet. "Could you give us a little sample? Our little queen here needs to pass judgment before we make such a significant purchase."

The man smiled. "Of course." Breaking off two small pieces from the end of one, he handed them to each child.

The reaction was almost instantaneous. "Umm," Esther murmured. "That's good, Uncle Simeon." Boaz was nodding enthusiastically.

"Give us six of them," Simeon said, pulling out his purse.

They walked on slowly, savoring their purchase, Simeon holding on to their hands as they made their way through the heavy crowds. As they approached the temple, Simeon tried to explain to them in simple terms what they were seeing. They were walking along the *soreg*, or wall of partition. This was the low fence that marked the point beyond which no Gentile could go without risking death. He was explaining how the partition separated the Court of the Gentiles from the inner courts of the temple proper when they nearly bumped right into Yehuda and Shana.

"Oh!" Shana exclaimed. Then she quickly recovered. "*Shalom*, Simeon." Her color deepened and she looked down.

"*Shalom*, Shana. *Shalom*, Yehuda."

Yehuda was a little taken aback by this unexpected meeting too, but reached out and shook Simeon's hand. Then he looked down. "And what have we here?"

"You remember Yehuda and Shana," Simeon said to the children. "We went to their home in Beth Neelah up in the Galilee last year, remember?" Then to them he said. "These are Ephraim and Rachel's children, Esther and Boaz. Esther is five now, and Boaz will be three next week."

Esther had her head cocked, looking up at Shana curiously. Then she tugged at Simeon's hand, pulling him down. "I remember. She's your wife, Uncle Simeon."

Simeon flushed. Shana went a deep scarlet. "Well, we were betrothed, Esther," Simeon said, recovering quickly, "but not any longer."

"Oh."

"What's 'trothed,'" Boaz wanted to know. He took a bite of his date stick and munched on it as he waited for the answer.

"It means you promise to get married," Esther told him.

Simeon was just standing there, feeling very awkward. Shana was likewise uncomfortable. Then suddenly Shana stepped forward and kissed Simeon softly on the cheek. "I'm sorry, Simeon. I'm sorry it didn't work out."

"No," he whispered. "*I'm* the one who's sorry, Shana. I'm sorry for the pain I caused you."

She stepped back beside her brother. Her eyes were shining. "I know. But you brought Yehuda back to me. That helps to make things right again. Thank you." And with that she walked away, not looking back.

Yehuda watched her go, then finally looked at Simeon. "I talked with her about the situation, why it may be best not to try to go back to how things were before. She agreed. I think she's accepted it now."

"I hope so. I wouldn't want to hurt her anymore, Yehuda."

"I know." Yehuda turned. "We saw your family a little while ago in the same place as yesterday."

"Was Jesus there?"

"Yes."

"I guess you aren't interested in—"

"No," he cut in. "Do you still plan to leave the morning after Passover week is done?"

Simeon nodded. "I'll come get you."

With a brief wave, Yehuda moved away. Simeon took Boaz's hand again, but he looked down at Esther. "Would you like to go see Jesus?"

"Oh, yes."

"Then stay close. There are lots of people today."

As they started walking again, Boaz looked up at Simeon. "She's pretty."

"Shana? Yes, she's very pretty."

"She must really like you," Esther observed, sounding very old.

What had this five-year-old seen that brought that comment? Simeon wondered. The near tears in Shana's eyes? The look on her face? Or had she caught the tremor in her voice? "Why do you say that?" Simeon asked.

"Because she kissed you even though your face is all scratchy," Esther said, greatly impressed.

Simeon laughed loudly enough to draw curious looks from several people. Still chuckling, he put a hand on her shoulder. "Do you know what? I am really glad you two voted to come with me today. This is going to be a wonderful day."

V

By the time Simeon located Jesus, more hampered by the slowness of the children than any difficulty in finding him, Boaz had asked to be lifted up and then immediately fell asleep against Simeon's shoulder. As they approached the east end of the Royal Portico, Simeon saw that most of the crowd gathered around Jesus were seated on the great marble slabs that formed the floor. The only ones standing were those around the edges of the group. As he moved into the deep shade, a couple about the age of his parents saw him and waved him over. They were seated on a stone bench and offered it to him.

He gratefully sat down, letting the weight of Boaz's young body transfer from his arms to his body. "*Todah raba*," he murmured. "Thank you very much."

They smiled and moved away. He made sure Esther was comfortable beside him, then looked around. Straight across from him he saw his family. Rachel gave him a questioning look and made signs that she would come and take the children. He shook his head firmly, then looked away before she could argue with him further.

To his surprise, when he looked to the front, Jesus was watching him. Simeon nodded and received a smile and nod in return. Then Jesus' smile broadened, and he lifted a hand and waved. Looking down, Simeon saw that Esther was waving to him, smiling as happily as she had when Simeon had bought them the date sticks. Simeon put his arm around her and she snuggled up against him.

He jumped a little as someone sat down next to him and turned to see Rachel beside him. "Are you sure you don't want me take Boaz, at least?"

Simeon shook his head. "That is a firm no," he whispered. He laid his head against his nephew's. "Why should you be the only one to get these kinds of opportunities?"

Rachel's mouth softened as she looked at her son, his face in perfect repose. Then she peered around Simeon. "Esther, would you like to come over with me and Papa and Pampa and Granmama?"

Esther shook her head without hesitation.

Simeon felt the pleasure infuse his entire body. "Sorry," he murmured. "I'm the man of the hour today. You'll just have to get used to that."

She touched his arm, then stood and made her way back to the rest of the family. Simeon returned his mother's warm smile with one of his own. Then he turned back to listen to Jesus. He was teaching the people about the cost of discipleship again, sharing the same parable of building a tower as he had done before. Simeon let his eyes run over the crowd. They were of every kind and social class. The greatest number were commoners. They were the laborers and farmers and shopkeepers and artisans that made up the backbone of Israel. Plainly dressed in tunics and robes of their own making, none of them had the trappings of the leaders of the two main parties of Judaism. They had come to hear for themselves this preacher from the Galilee.

In sharp contrast to that, three or four elegantly dressed Sadducees stood near the back of the crowd, their heads together as they muttered darkly to each other. Nor was Simeon surprised to see Azariah, chief of the Pharisees in Jerusalem and a member of the Great Council, on the other side of the group. He was in the midst of about a dozen other scribes and Pharisees, including several that Simeon recognized from the day before. Then Simeon's eyes widened a little as he recognized one of the faces. It was his Uncle Aaron. He had seen Simeon too and inclined his head slightly to acknowledge that fact. Simeon smiled back. He had not seen Aaron since he, Yehuda, Barak, and Samuel had been released from prison, but he had written a short letter expressing his thanks for the part Aaron and Amram had taken in trying to convince Pilate to free him.

But seeing Aaron was not his greatest shock. Not far from where Jesus was sitting, Simeon saw a plumed helmet. Peering more closely, he recognized Sextus Rubrius. He was alone and stood back from the rest of the crowd, as though assigned to make sure nothing got out of hand. But Simeon saw that the centurion was listening as intently as the others.

There was a stir among the crowd, and Simeon turned to see what had caused it. There was a third surprise. Matthew, the publican who had been converted to Jesus in Capernaum, then called to be one of the Twelve, was leading a group of three other men forward. One look at their dress and Simeon knew who they were.

He felt a nudge and looked down at Esther. "Who is that?" she asked.

"The man in the front is Matthew Levi," he explained. "He's from Capernaum. He's a close friend of Jesus. The others are all publicans, friends of his, I would imagine."

Simeon wasn't the only one who had recognized this group for what they were. An angry murmur rippled through the crowd. The man seated on the floor directly in front of him stared for a moment, then spat in disgust. "Publicans!" he muttered.

If Matthew was aware of the stir he was creating, he gave it no heed. He went up to the Master and began introducing his friends to

Jesus. Jesus spoke amiably with them and shook their hands. When the introductions were done, Jesus invited them to sit down nearby.

Before they were even seated, Azariah called out, sputtering like a setting hen knocked off her nest. The chief Pharisee didn't speak to Jesus, but to the assembled people. "This man—" Azariah flung one arm in the direction of Jesus—"receives sinners, as you can see for yourselves."

Dozens of heads began to nod, and the angry mutter swelled. The tax collectors were almost universally hated, especially by the common people who could least afford their assessments. Matthew watched the accuser with a calm expression, but the other three had dropped their heads, their faces flaming.

Azariah, pleased with the response from the people, cried all the louder. "These men are despicable. They serve Caesar by sucking the blood of their own people. Yet Jesus treats them as though they were equals. I have learned that he even sups with them in their houses." That last was added almost in horror.

The mood of the crowd had turned darker. Simeon watched closely, prepared to take the children away quickly if things began to unravel.

Jesus was seated on one of the stone benches as he taught. He watched Azariah for a moment, then stood, letting his eyes move across the crowd. That silenced the murmuring immediately. Azariah stepped back to join his colleagues, smugly convinced that he had done the necessary damage.

"What man of you," Jesus finally said, looking directly at the group of Pharisees, "having an hundred sheep, if he lose one of them, would not leave the ninety and nine and go into the wilderness after that which is lost, until he find it?"

Simeon's eyes moved automatically to his Uncle Benjamin. Being a shepherd was his profession, and Simeon saw that he was listening raptly.

"And when he has found the lost sheep, he lays it on his shoulders, rejoicing. When he returns home, he calls together his friends and neighbors, saying unto them, 'Rejoice with me, for I have found my sheep which was lost.'"

Now his eyes burned with indignation, and he looked directly at Azariah. "I say unto you, that likewise there shall be more joy in heaven over one *sinner* that repents—" his voice was suddenly biting—"than over ninety and nine *just persons*, who need no repentance."

Simeon winced. That was not just a barb. That was a shaft sent right to the heart. The Pharisees knew it too. They were so proud of their righteousness, so quick to condemn those who weren't as holy and pious as they. Azariah looked as if he might have apoplexy. His companions were looking at each other in shocked outrage.

"Or consider this," Jesus went on, speaking to the multitude again. "What woman having ten pieces of silver, if she were to lose one piece, would not light a candle and sweep the house, and seek diligently till she find it? And when she finally finds it, what will she do? She calls her friends and her neighbors together, saying, 'Rejoice with me; for I have found the piece which I had lost.'"

Again his head swung around to look at the muttering group before him, but when he spoke, he spoke to the crowd. "Likewise, I say unto you, there is joy in the presence of the angels of God over one sinner who repents."

The Pharisees were forgotten now as Simeon gazed at the Master. He was not speaking of lost sheep or lost money at all. He was talking about lost souls. Simeon looked down and to his surprise saw that Esther was listening closely too. The stories had caught her attention.

Now Simeon saw people gesturing angrily for the muttering Pharisees to be quiet. When they did, Jesus continued, this time his tone more mild and thoughtful. "A certain man had two sons," he began, "and the younger of them said to his father, 'Father, give me the portion of goods that falls to me.' And the father agreed and divided unto his two sons his property.

"And not many days after that, the younger son gathered all that he had received, and took his journey into a far country. There he wasted his substance with riotous living."

Jesus stopped, giving them a moment to put that picture into their minds.

"And when the son had spent all that he had, there arose a mighty famine in that land. And the man began to be in want, and he went and joined himself to a citizen of that country to be his servant. And the man sent him into his fields to feed swine."

There was almost an audible groan from the crowd. In a matter of two or three sentences, the Master had painted a picture of the grimmest of circumstances. Under the Mosaic Law, swine were unclean animals. Though certain other animals and birds were also unclean, pigs had come to symbolize all that was polluted and impure. Not only would Jews refuse to partake of swine's flesh, but they would not raise pigs or even let them into their villages and towns. The very word was considered to be an abomination. For this young man to end up as a swine herder dramatically conveyed the depths of his fall.

Jesus watched their eyes, seeing the shock and revulsion. Then he went on, emphasizing each word carefully. "So desperate was the condition of this young man that he began to fill his belly with the husks that the swine ate, because no man gave unto him."

Simeon felt his stomach twist a little. It was one thing to have to care for pigs—but to eat with them?

Jesus moved over and sat down again. There was not a sound beneath the portico now. Even Azariah was watching Jesus intently.

"Finally," Jesus went on, "the young man came to himself, and said, 'The hired servants of my father have bread enough and to spare, yet I perish with hunger! I will arise and go to my father and will say unto him, "Father, I have sinned against heaven and before thee. I am no more worthy to be called thy son. Make me as one of your hired servants."'

"Then the son arose and returned to his father. But when he was yet *a great way off*, his father saw him, and had compassion, and *ran* and fell on his neck and kissed him. And the son said unto him, 'Father, I have sinned against heaven, and in your sight. I am no more worthy to be called your son.' But the father said to his servants, 'Bring forth the best robe and put it on him. Put a ring on his hand and shoes on his feet. Bring hither the fatted calf and kill it, and let us eat and be merry. For this my son was dead, and is alive again. He was lost and is found.'"

Jesus stopped again. No one stirred. Every eye was upon him. For a moment, Simeon thought the Master had finished, but then Jesus' chin lifted up. He turned and looked directly at Azariah and his group, then swung his gaze to the sour-faced Sadducees on the other side.

"And they began to be merry, rejoicing that the son had returned. But the father's elder son was in the field. As he came and drew nigh to the house, he heard music and dancing. So he called one of the servants over and asked what these things meant. And the servant said to him, 'Your brother is come and your father has killed the fatted calf because he has received him safe and sound.'"

Jesus' voice became heavy with sorrow. "And the older son was angry and would not go in. Therefore came his father out and entreated him to come in. But he, answering, said to his father, 'Lo, these many years have I served you, neither transgressed I at any time your commandments. Yet you never gave me a kid that I might make merry with my friends. But as soon as your son is come, which devoured your inheritance with harlots, you have killed for him the fatted calf.'"

Out of the corner of his eye, Simeon saw the Sadducees spin around and stomp away. Azariah's eyes were flashing indignantly. In another flash of insight, Simeon understood. Here, in the personalities of these pompous men, was epitomized the mentality of the older brother. Instead of rejoicing that the publicans, the "sinners," were returning to the family, were "coming home," they were angry and resentful.

Azariah mumbled something to his associates, and they too turned and flounced away.

Jesus watched them go, then turned back to the crowd. "And the father said unto his older son, 'Son, thou art ever with me, and all that I have is yours. But it was good that we should make merry and be glad. For your brother was dead and is alive again. He was lost and now he is found.'"

Chapter Notes

The three parables shared here are found in Luke 15. They were given by Jesus one after another in response to the criticism of the Pharisees that Jesus was mingling with publicans and sinners (vv. 1–2).

CHAPTER 22

WHY IS THIS NIGHT DIFFERENT FROM ALL OTHER NIGHTS?

—*Passover Haggadah, 9*

I

BETHLEHEM
10 APRIL, A.D. 31

Strictly speaking, *Pesach*, or Passover, actually consisted of two distinct feasts or festivals—the Feast of the Passover itself, in which the lambs were sacrificed at the temple and then taken to the homes of the people to be eaten that night, and the Feast of Unleavened Bread which followed it, wherein all leaven was purged from the home and only unleavened bread and cakes could be consumed. The first took place in a single day; the second lasted for the remainder of the week. In reality, the two festivals had become one and generally were what was meant by the Feast of the Passover. Since in the Jewish way of tracking time the new day began at sundown, the celebration of the festival began on Passover Eve.

In preparation for the event, and in keeping with the commandment given more than a thousand years previous, the house of Benjamin in Bethlehem had been thoroughly cleansed the night before. Benjamin the shepherd-priest, and his wife, Esther, along with the rest of the family, had made a careful search of every room in the house, using small candles. Every trace of leaven or yeast, including any products that might contain leaven, was removed. Since bread made with leaven spoiled quickly, leaven was a symbol of spiritual corruption and decay. Every home in Israel had to cleanse itself of even the tiniest hint of corruption in preparation for the Passover.

By the time Simeon arrived back in Bethlehem with two weary children that afternoon, the rest of the family were back as well. Deborah and Aunt Esther carefully washed the paschal lamb that Ephraim had received from the priests at the temple and put it on a spit over a bed of hot coals. Now, as the sun sank low in the sky, there was a general scurrying in the house to get everything ready. Leah and Simeon were given charge of the *seder* plate, with Esther and Boaz solemnly helping them. This was no ordinary meal they would be eating tonight. Everything about it was spelled out with great formality in the oral traditions, and the various items used as part of the meal were partaken of in a strictly prescribed order. *Seder* was the Hebrew word for order. The tradition of arranging things in perfect order had become such an important part of the meal that it was often called the Seder meal, and the evening of Passover was frequently referred to as Seder Eve.

Aunt Esther stuck her head through the door. "Hurry, children, the sun is almost down."

"It's ready," Leah said. "Everything is in place."

"Good. Simeon, go check with your father and Uncle Benjamin. See if the lamb is ready."

"They were taking it off the spit a few minutes ago," he answered with a smile. It was always like this—the last-minute urgency, the wild bustle to have everything ready, the breathless excitement as the moment drew near. Passover was a most solemn time and yet, simultaneously, it was a time of great joy and celebration.

Deborah and Rachel came out of the house. Deborah carried two pitchers of wine, which she sat on each end of the table. Rachel carried the plate of *matzos*, or unleavened bread, covered with a white cloth. She placed it near the center of the table. Deborah looked at her cousin-in-law. "Are you ready for Elijah's cup now, Esther?"

"I think so," Aunt Esther said. "Yes, go ahead and fill it."

Malachi the prophet, who lived some four hundred years before, had once given a very specific prophecy. He said that Elijah the prophet would return before the coming of the great and dreadful day of the Lord. It had become tradition, based on that prophecy, to assume that Elijah would appear to announce the coming of the Messiah and that he would do so on the eve of Passover. It would be a terrible embarrassment, one of the Rabbis had decided, if Elijah should happen to come to a family's Seder meal and there was no place for him. So in every home in Israel this night there would be an empty chair and a place set at the table. Typically, the chair was tipped up against the table so that no one would inadvertently take Elijah's place. Deborah carefully filled the wine cup so that if Elijah should choose this particular house as the one to which he would come, he would know that he had been expected and was welcome.

Aunt Esther looked around one last time. The other women held their breath, waiting. They were the guests. Aunt Esther was their hostess. Finally, she nodded with satisfaction. "Get the men," she said. "It's time."

II

11 APRIL, A.D. 31

Since Jerusalem was a city of steep hills and narrow valleys, the precise moment of sundown was not left to each person to decide. The last rays of the sun left the valley bottoms as much as fifteen or twenty minutes earlier than it did the tops of the ridges. Basing the start of Passover on such imprecision would not be seemly.

The official signal for sundown each Sabbath was given from the Temple Mount. One of the priests stood on the ramparts of the temple with a *shofar*, or ram's horn. Caiaphas, who was high priest at this time, stood nearby, one eye on the sinking sun. As it began to disappear behind the western hills, he raised an arm. The *shofar* was lifted to the trumpeter's lips. All around, everything became hushed. Slowly the glowing orb became thinner and thinner, and the shadows stole across the hills. It seemed to hesitate for one last, lingering moment; then it slipped behind the hills and the final rays faded away.

The high priest dropped his arm. A blast of the ram's horn sounded out across the great courtyards of the temple complex. It was a mournful but piercing sound. Instantly it was picked up by dozens more, priests with their own *shofars* stationed around the city. The sound rippled outward from the Temple Mount in every direction. Within no more than a minute, the shofars were sounding even in the villages surrounding Jerusalem.

Benjamin stood at the end of the table, his head turned toward the window. Everyone was in his or her place. They too looked at the open window in hushed expectation. When the sound of the ram's horn floated in through the window, there was a ripple of excitement; then Benjamin turned to face the family.

He lifted his eyes to heaven and began to recite in a low and solemn tone: "Blessed art thou, Lord, our God, King of the Universe, who dost create the fruit of the vine. Blessed art thou, Lord, our God, King of the Universe, who hast chosen us above all peoples, and hast exalted us above all tongues, and has hallowed us with thy command-ments. And thou hast given us, Lord, our God, with love, Sabbaths for rest and Seasons for gladness, Holy days and times for rejoicing. Blessed art thou, Lord, our God, King of the Universe, who dost sanc-tify the Sabbath, and Israel, and the Festivals. Amen."

"Amen!" Together all those present lifted their cups and drank the wine down. They were small cups used especially for the Seder meal.

Benjamin moved closer to the table. Before him sat a small laver of water and a folded towel beside it. Moving with slow deliberation, Benjamin washed his hands, then dried them with the towel. He moved around the table to where the plate of unleavened bread sat covered and waiting. He removed the cloth and set it aside, then lifted the *matzos* plate and held it high.

"This is the poor bread which our fathers ate in the land of Egypt. Let anyone who is hungry, come in and eat. Let anyone who is in need, come in and make Passover. This year we are here. Next year we shall be in the land of Israel. This year we are slaves. Next year we shall be freemen. Amen."

"Amen!"

Replacing the plate of bread on the table, he nodded at David and Ephraim. Both took a pitcher of wine and refilled the cups. When they were done, the family lifted their cups and waited. Benjamin looked down the table at Boaz and nodded. Boaz looked nervously at his mother. They had rehearsed this over and over. As the youngest male present, the next part was his.

Boaz got to his feet. He straightened to his full height, cleared his throat, and then asked, "Why is this night different from all other nights, Uncle Benjamin?"

III
ROME

Fifteen hundred miles to the northwest, in a spacious and luxurious apartment only a few blocks from the Roman Forum, Mordechai ben Uzziel raised his cup and nodded at Drusus Alexander Carlottus.

Livia's brother, freed from slavery just over a week before, looked around. His pale blue eyes were moist, and he suddenly found it difficult to speak.

When Livia had told him that the two of them were invited to celebrate a Passover feast with Miriam and her father, Drusus found the whole thing somewhat peculiar, and he said he didn't want to participate. At eighteen, he had determined he had no need for religion or ceremony. But at eighteen, he was the youngest male present, and by tradition it was his role to ask the crucial question. Livia had reminded him of the debt they both owed to the family of Mordechai and Miriam for their continuing kindness, and whether he found the whole tradition peculiar or not, they would be participating. Finally, he had reluctantly agreed. But when Mordechai had intoned those words—"This year we are slaves. Next year we shall be freeman"—Drusus was caught totally by surprise and found himself deeply moved.

"Go ahead, Drusus," Mordechai said gently.

He swallowed; then asked the question Miriam had taught him. "Why is this night different from all other nights?"

There were just the four of them. Rome had a significant number of Jews in the city, but many had gone to Jerusalem to celebrate the feast there, and Mordechai had not associated himself with the Jewish community in Rome, fearing that word of his whereabouts might somehow get back to Ya'abin. So he had declared that they would have their own Passover, simple and limited as it might be.

Mordechai raised the cup of wine high, and the others followed suit. "On all other nights, we eat leavened bread and matzos, or unleavened bread. On this night we eat only matzos. On all other nights, we eat all kinds of herbs. On this night we eat only bitter herbs to remind us of the bitterness of bondage. On all other nights, we eat reclining and in repose. On this night we eat with our feet shod and staff in hand, for tonight we shall flee our bondage and escape from Egypt."

IV

BETHLEHEM

They all drank together, then set their cups down again. Benjamin nodded at Boaz. Rachel hovered near his side to make sure he carried out his role properly.

More confident now, and clearly enjoying his central role, Boaz called out, "Then what mean ye by this service?"

Benjamin nodded his approval. "It is the sacrifice of the Lord's Passover, who passed over the houses of the children of Israel when he delivered them from bondage in Egypt, when he smote the Egyptians and delivered our houses."

All around the table bowed their heads. "Amen!" they intoned.

V

ROME

At a nod from her father, Miriam refilled their cups again. Mordechai picked up the plate of unleavened bread a second time and held it high.

Miriam and Livia asked the next question together. Traditionally, all others present were supposed to ask the questions of the one leading the service, but since Drusus didn't know the ceremony, just the two women led out while Drusus watched. "This *matzos* that we eat? What meaning has it?"

Mordechai answered, and as he did so Miriam wondered if this was the first time in history that the Seder feast had been performed in Latin. Livia would have been fine with the Hebrew ceremony, but Drusus, of course, spoke nothing but Latin and his native Greek.

"The dough of our forefathers," Mordechai said, his voice low and sonorous, "did not have sufficient time to be leavened, when the King of kings, the Holy One of Israel, blessed be his Name, revealed himself to our people and redeemed them."

VI
BETHLEHEM

Benjamin set the *matzos* down, then pointed at the seder plate. As one, the family asked the next question. "And the bitter herb that we eat? What meaning has it?"

"The Egyptians embittered the lives of our forefathers in Egypt," Benjamin answered. "As it is written, 'And they embittered their lives with hard labor in the brick pits and with all manner of labor in the fields.'"

"Amen!"

Deborah smiled as young Esther reached for the tiniest piece of the bitter herb she could see, already wrinkling her nose in anticipation. They used the roots of a leafy vegetable which were never eaten except at Passover. It was terribly bitter. Each took a piece and put it in their mouths, chewed quickly, then swallowed. Esther gave a little shudder as she got hers down.

Quickly now, they reached for the next bowl on the seder plates. This contained celery and parsnips. They dipped those vegetables in a small bowl of salt water, then turned again to Benjamin, poised to continue. He nodded, and they all spoke in unison again. "And the salt water that we see? What meaning has it?"

VII
ROME

Mordechai dipped his celery stick in the bowl of salt water and held it up. "The Israelites shed many tears during the years of their bondage in Egypt. The salt water reminds us of the bitter tears that were shed."

They ate the celery, this time not with haste, but savoring it. Miriam always liked this particular moment, for the salty celery helped purge the taste of the bitter herbs.

Finished, they looked up. Her father reached over. Leaning against the table beside him was a long walking stick he had purchased somewhere in the markets earlier that day. He grasped the walking stick and began to stand. That was the signal for each of them to stand as well. When they were up, Mordechai nodded and she and Livia again spoke together. "And why do we eat this supper with a girdle about our loins, our sandals on our feet, and a staff in our hands?"

Actually, only her father had a staff, but all four of them wore their sandals. This felt so strange to Miriam, because they always removed their outside footwear when they entered the home. They also had a sash tied around their waists, suggesting that they had girded up their loins in preparation for flight.

Once again, her father answered in a solemn voice. "The Lord God, the Holy One of Israel, blessed be his name, commanded ancient Israel, as it is written: 'And thus shall ye eat the Passover meal—with your loins girded, your shoes on your feet, and your staff in hand. And thus ye shall eat it in haste, for tonight is the Lord's Passover. I will pass through the land of Egypt this night, and I will smite all the first-born in the land of Egypt, and against all the gods of Egypt will I execute judgment this night.'"

"Amen!" all of them answered solemnly. They lifted their cups and held them up, turning to face Mordechai.

VIII
BETHLEHEM

The family members held their cups high, watching Benjamin with anticipation. This was the most solemn moment of all. Benjamin lifted his cup of wine heavenward. "In every generation," he exclaimed, his voice rich and low, "one ought to regard himself as though he had personally been delivered from bondage in Egypt. As it is said in the Torah: 'And this day shall be unto you for a memorial, and ye shall keep it a feast to the Lord throughout your generations.' Not only our forefathers did the Holy One, blessed is he, redeem, but also ourselves.

"Therefore it is our duty to thank, praise, laud, glorify, uplift, extol, bless, exalt, and adore Him who did all of these miracles for our fathers and for ourselves. He has brought us forth from slavery to freedom, from sorrow to joy, from mourning to festive day, from darkness unto great light, and from subjection to redemption. Let us then recite before Him a new song: *Hallelujah! Praise ye God! Hallelujah! Praise ye God!*"

As one, the family lifted their cups higher. "Amen!" they cried aloud. "Amen and Amen!"

IX

BETHLEHEM

13 APRIL, A.D. 31

Simeon was in the small courtyard, just buckling on the belt that held two scabbards, one for his dagger and one for the short Roman sword he preferred. The sky was just lightening, but it was nearly dark within the confined space. Above him, Uncle Benjamin's house was completely dark. Finished, he looked around, feeling a pang of sorrow. These past few days had been a wonderful break from the intensity of his quest in the wilderness of Judea. Now it was time to plunge back into that murky and dangerous world.

He turned as he heard a sound. His mother and father were there, standing at the entry. "You didn't need to get up," he said. "We said our farewells last night."

"I know," Deborah said, "but we were awake."

Bending down, he strapped his sandals on as they watched. Then he reached for his bow and quiver propped against the house. Only then did he move over to face them.

"You'll be careful?" Deborah said, trying not to sound too anxious.

"More than ever before."

The earnestness in his voice caused her to peer at him more closely. Before she could ask him what he meant by that, he spoke. "Do you realize that during this week we haven't seen Jesus perform one miracle or give one overt demonstration of his power?"

That came as a surprise to both of them. "I hadn't thought about that," David answered, "but you are right." Then he looked more closely at Simeon. "Is that a disappointment to you?"

"No. Actually, it's the other way around." He was thinking of what Yehuda had said to him that night while they waited for Issachar to come with the wine. "It's been good to just listen to him, to think about what he's trying to teach us. Sometimes, I think—at least this is true for me—the miracles are so powerful, they almost overshadow what he's saying. But it's his teachings that are really important, isn't it?"

His mother was nodding slowly. "Yes," she said. "No question about it."

"As I lay awake last night thinking about this last week, I realized that there has been one thread that has run through much of what he has said."

"Which is?" his mother asked.

"Well, for me, I think Jesus has been teaching us what it means to love as God loves. The story of the good Samaritan, that experience with Mary and Martha, the parables of the lost—the lost sheep, the lost coin, the prodigal son. It seems like all of those things are meant to teach us how to love both God and others better."

His father nodded slowly, obviously intrigued with the idea.

Simeon's face softened. "I'm learning that from you, Father. You ponder a lot about what Jesus has said; then you come up with these wonderful insights. So I've been trying to do that for myself."

"And what have you come up with, Son?" David asked.

"Well, here's one thing. It doesn't really matter *why* we are lost. Some of us are like sheep. It's not that we are rebellious. We've got our heads down, grazing along, looking for deeper grass and sweeter water, and the next thing you know we're lost in the wilderness. Other people get dropped through carelessness or neglect, like the coin. We get our feelings hurt. We kind of slip away and no one pays any attention. It's not that we're not valued, it is just that nobody seems to notice as we fall into a crack or roll under a piece of furniture."

He shook his head ruefully. "And some of us are determined that we don't need God, or at least that we don't need God telling us how we should live our lives. 'Give me my inheritance,' we demand. 'It's my life. Let me live it as I want.' We are rebellious and deliberately choose to leave the Father and go away to a 'far country,' as Jesus called it."

"The *lost* son," David said softly.

"Yes. Then it struck me that this story was different from the first two. The shepherd went after the sheep. The woman searched the house for the coin. But the father just waited. That seemed odd at first, but now I think I understand. This was the son's deliberate choice. He turned his back on his family and his heritage. So until he 'came to himself,' as Jesus put it, until he realized how stubborn he had been, how selfish and foolish, until he found himself sleeping with the swine and saw how far he had fallen, there was no way to convince him he needed to go back home. If the father had gone after him before that point, he would probably have told him the same thing. 'It's my life. Let me live it.'"

He looked at both of his parents. "Do you know what I thought was the most beautiful part of the parable about the two sons?" he asked.

"Let me guess," David said. "It was when Jesus said, '*And while he was yet a great way off,* his father saw him, and had compassion.'"

"Yes," Simeon said, his voice low. "Talk about a lesson in how God loves us. The father didn't make his son come all the way back before he would accept him. By every right, by every measure of justice, the father could have said, 'This was your choice. No one made you run off like you did. So once you have restored all that you squandered, once you have fully repaid me, then we'll talk about reconciliation and restoration.' But the father didn't say any of that."

Now Deborah spoke. "What occurred to me was this. For the father to see his son while he was still a long way away, he had to be watching for him, waiting and hoping that he would return."

"Yes," Simeon said eagerly, for he had come to the same conclusion. "And the moment he saw him returning, he *ran* out to meet him." His voice was tinged with reverent awe.

They fell silent, each contemplating that thought. Then Simeon sighed, grateful for the chance to express what had been on his mind. "It has been a remarkable week. I have learned much." He looked at his mother. "I can hardly believe this is coming from me, Mother, but all I want right now is to come home. I want to be with the family. I want to hold Boaz and have him go to sleep in my arms again. I want to watch Esther as one of those delightful smiles breaks out from behind her eyes and steals across her face. I want to be there when Leah gets betrothed and when Rachel has the new baby. I want to have time to think. I want to lay on my back and stare up at the clouds and ponder what Jesus is asking of us, of me."

"We would both like that very much too," Deborah whispered.

Simeon's eyes widened a little as a new thought struck him. "And I thought Jesus hadn't worked any miracles this week."

X

JERUSALEM

Simeon and Yehuda stood at the northernmost limits of the Court of the Gentiles. The walls of the Antonia Fortress, built by Herod the

Great and named in honor of his patron, Marc Antony, loomed over them. They were still early enough that only a few people moved here and there on the Temple Mount. Most were priests in their white robes, hurrying to enter the inner courts and begin their duties.

The crunch of metal-tipped sandals on stone brought them around. It was a young legionnaire, not much older than Simeon. "Follow me," he commanded. "And keep your hands away from your swords."

This time they did not object to entering the fortress. They followed the young man through the high, thick doors that stood open at the moment. The main court of the fortress was huge, large enough to assemble several hundred soldiers for review. It was far busier here than out on the Temple Mount. Men moved everywhere. Directly in front of them they could see the glow of a blacksmith's fire and hear the ringing blows as he prepared to shoe a horse. Workshops and storage areas and barracks filled the walls in every direction. Above them, an arched balcony ran all around the courtyard, and they could see doors leading into the upper chambers. At each corner, a soldier in full uniform, spear in hand, stood on sentry duty.

Yehuda nudged Simeon, and he turned to see where Yehuda was looking. Marcus Didius and Sextus Rubrius were just coming out of the main doors of the garrison. They walked down the broad stairway that joined the courtyard and started toward them.

Simeon started to move forward, but Yehuda hissed at him out of the corner of his mouth. "Make them come to us."

Simeon considered for a moment. There was some wisdom in that. The Romans looked for any sign of weakness. Then he shook his head and walked forward, ignoring Yehuda's soft grunt of frustration. "Good morning," he said easily.

Marcus nodded absently, eyeing them up and down, obviously noting the fact that they were both armed. "So," he said abruptly. "You're heading back to the wilderness?"

"Yes," Simeon said. "It's time."

"And what if Ya'abin doesn't return to this side of the Jordan for a while?" Marcus asked.

"What if summer doesn't come until December?" Simeon responded easily. "What if the rain falls upward? Those are not likely, but if it happens, then you change your plans accordingly."

Marcus felt a flash of anger, but he sensed that Simeon had not been trying to irritate him. It was a simple statement of fact. "I am returning to Caesarea tomorrow," he said. "I shall give Pilate a report of what I've learned. He may send me back, or he may keep me there until we receive further word from you. In the meantime, if you need anything, Sextus Rubrius here will be your contact as before."

Simeon nodded. That was how they preferred it. He looked at the centurion. "We'll let you know when we're ready for your help, but that could be several more weeks."

"Just remember—" Marcus started.

"Yes, yes," Yehuda cut in sharply. "Our time is almost gone, and Pilate is an impatient man. Do you think we are a couple of young boys who can't remember anything from one day to the next?"

Marcus stiffened at the insolent tone, but Simeon came in smoothly before he could react. "We are well aware of the limits your governor has put upon us, and we know when our year is up. If we were worried about keeping our agreement, I would have spoken to you about it sooner."

Still smarting a little, Marcus decided to put Simeon on the defensive. "I am told that you are a follower of this man they call Jesus of Nazareth."

Simeon was instantly wary. "And if I am?"

Marcus shrugged. "I find that curious for a man of your—" he smiled thinly—"of your inclination. Did you see him while you were here?"

Simeon fought the urge to look at Sextus. Sextus had seen him with Jesus in the Royal Portico. Was that what was triggering this line of questions? "Is this an interrogation or mere curiosity?" he finally said.

"Mostly curiosity," Marcus admitted. "Sextus was there the other day while he was teaching and reports that many people came to hear him."

Simeon felt himself relax. So Sextus had said nothing to Marcus.

Marcus continued: "Pilate has some concerns about the growing numbers of his followers, but we find his preaching quite harmless, almost quaint if you will. It is your own leaders who are alarmed about him, not Rome." That was not completely true. The swelling numbers this preacher drew was something Marcus wanted to keep a close eye on.

"They're not my leaders," Simeon said shortly.

Marcus laughed with a cold humor. So he had pricked a tender spot here, he thought. He decided to push a little more while he had Simeon off-balance. "By the way, Azariah the Pharisee told me something the other day that was a little disturbing."

Yehuda pulled a face. "It would be a rare thing to have Azariah say something that wasn't disturbing."

Marcus ignored him. Still looking at Simeon he asked, "Do you know if Miriam has any interest in this Jesus?"

Simeon went completely cold. Fortunately, he had turned his head to watch a squad of soldiers moving past them, so Marcus couldn't see his face. He turned back slowly, looking almost bored. "Miriam?"

"Yes. Azariah claims she was in the crowd one day when Jesus refused to condemn some woman for a violation of your law. According to Azariah, Miriam seemed quite sympathetic to Jesus. Do you think that is possible?"

Simeon's mind was racing. He didn't want to lie and yet . . . Then he had another thought. Did Sextus know that Miriam had been in Capernaum for the two weeks prior to her departure for Rome? Did he know of her interest in Jesus? If so, he obviously had not said anything to Marcus about that either.

"How could it have been her?" he finally said, as if it was only of passing interest. "Have she and Mordechai returned from Rome?"

"No, this was not a recent happening. It supposedly took place last summer before she left. Azariah swears it was her."

Simeon shrugged. "You've been here long enough to know how much it would please Azariah to find a way to embarrass Mordechai and the other Sadducees. I would be very careful about taking his word at face value."

"Don't tell me how to run my affairs," Marcus snapped. "I am well aware of what needs to happen."

Simeon laughed in open amusement. "You Romans! You're like children playing in a darkened room. You see shadows and strike out at them, but you have no idea of what is real or where the actual danger lies."

Before Marcus could respond, Simeon went on. "We have to go. Our men are waiting for us near the Dung Gate." He looked at Sextus. "We'll send you a report on what's happening at least once each week. Are the usual channels still in place?"

"They are," Sextus acknowledged.

Simeon started to turn away, but Marcus fired one last shot. "Don't dally too long, Ha'keedohn," he called mockingly. "Pilate would still love to put you on the rack and learn the name of the person who betrayed us that night at the Joknean Pass."

Simeon gave him a warm, open smile. "Like I said," he drawled, "children playing in the darkness."

CHAPTER NOTES

The Passover, along with the Seder meal, is still celebrated by Jews the world over more than three thousand years after Moses led the children of Israel out of

Egypt. What is depicted here in this chapter is shortened considerably from the full celebration, which takes a complete evening.

It is difficult to ascertain exactly how the Passover was celebrated at the time of Christ. There are two reasons for this. First, the traditions and rituals of the Jewish way of life were not written down and codified until many years after the destruction of the temple and the fall of Jerusalem in A.D. 70. How much changed between the time of Christ and when the Law was first systematically recorded about A.D. 200 is all but impossible to determine. In the second place, with the destruction of the temple and the cessation of the priestly sacrifices, the eating of the paschal lamb was no longer possible. That required several adjustments to the Seder meal. Today, it is traditional to place a roasted shank bone of a chicken on the seder plate to symbolize the sacrificial lambs of the past.

The author drew heavily on a "Passover Haggadah," or booklet outlining how the feast is celebrated in modern Judaism today (see Regelson, 1–64; see also Jacobs, 81–91). *Haggadah* means "telling" in Hebrew. However, knowing there were at least some differences at the time Christ was alive, I took the liberty of bringing in items from the biblical account (Exodus 12) that are additions or adjustments to the modern celebration. Thus the rituals described in this chapter are not a precise depiction of a modern Passover meal.

There is an obvious time difference between Rome and Jerusalem, so having the two families celebrating Passover at the exact same time involves some artistic license.

CHAPTER 23

AND A MAN'S FOES SHALL BE THEY OF HIS OWN HOUSEHOLD.

—*Matthew 10:36*

I

CAESAREA

25 APRIL, A.D. 31

FOR THE EYES OF MORDECHAI BEN UZZIEL ONLY

Greetings from Marcus Quadratus Didius, Tribune of the X Legion Fretensis. Salutations from myself and his excellency, Governor Pontius Pilatus.

I write briefly to inform you about the situation here and suggest a course of action you may wish to follow, though I realize it is not my place to counsel you. The matter with Moshe Ya'abin is not yet settled, but I feel assured it will be soon, perhaps even by the time you receive this epistle. Even as I write, Ya'abin is on the defensive, and the governor and I concur that it would be safe for you to return to Judea, though you may have to stay in Caesarea for a time. This would be advantageous not only to you—you could see to your personal affairs here, which I know are a concern to you— but there are also other reasons that would benefit both your country and the government of Rome.

The Great Council in Jerusalem grows more and more fractious and divided. Caiaphas functions well as high priest, with his father-in-law, Annas, pulling the strings behind the scenes, but your wise and steadying hand is sorely needed if we are to move forward in the directions we discussed before you left for Rome. The Zealot issue is still of great concern to us and needs resolution.

More pressing, however, is our growing concern about this man named Jesus of Nazareth. At Passover, the throngs around him swelled almost daily. His name was on everyone's lips. More and more there are rumors circulating about him claiming that he has miraculous powers. Some are even speaking of him as a Messiah. This causes the governor some anxiety. As you know, those leading rebellions against Rome in the past have often claimed to be your Messiah in order to convince the people to follow them. These rebellions were successfully put down, of course, but such outbreaks are always costly.

At this point, we are staying directly out of the matter because it is still a local concern, but Pilate is not happy with how the Great Council here in Jerusalem is dealing with the challenge. Jesus moves about at will, and your colleagues are so intimidated by his popularity that they do not act in any unified or effective way. Direct intervention is needed to squelch this movement before it gathers greater momentum. Pilate has asked me to express to you that it would be to your advantage and to ours if you could return on the first available sailing. We trust that will meet with your desires as well, for we know that you are eager to return home.

We realize that it is not our place to interfere in family matters, but Pilate asks that I at least suggest the following to you for your consideration. We feel it would not be wise to bring Miriam back with you at this time. Until Ya'abin is completely destroyed, there would be some risk to her. Also, and I hesitate to mention this at all, but there are some reports that Miriam may have come in contact with Jesus before you left Jerusalem and may even exhibit some sympathy for his cause. Your old nemesis, Azariah, reports that Miriam was present one day when Jesus was teaching and seemed intrigued with him. Do not construe that to mean that we think she is part of that movement, only that she may have some sympathy for it. For that reason too, it may be the wiser course to keep her in Rome until we are able to settle the situation here.

Since returning, I have been kept totally occupied in Jerusalem with the festival and so have not had a chance to formalize a proposal concerning betrothal to your daughter. I hope to have something for you by the time you arrive. My wish, if it concurs with your desires, would be to have things in order here (both with Ya'abin and Jesus of Nazareth) in time for you and me to return to Rome for the festival of Saturnalia (held in late December) and finalize the arrangements for the marriage then. If Miriam wishes, she could then return to Caesarea with me as my wife, or stay in Rome with my family until my assignment here is completed.

All of this, of course, assumes that this arrangement still meets with your approval. We can discuss this at length upon your return. May the gods speed your voyage. Your influence has been missed.

Written by the hand of Marcus Quadratus Didius this 25th day of April, in the seven hundred and eighty-seventh year since the founding of Rome.

Marcus set the quill pen down and blew on the last few lines. He carefully read through what he had written, then nodded in satisfaction. Using the candle and a stick of red wax, he sealed the letter, then called for one of the slaves. A ship was leaving for Rome later in the day, and his letter would be on it.

II

IN THE WILDERNESS OF JUDEA

18 MAY, A.D. 31

Moshe Ya'abin's men were tired. Earlier that day they had attacked what they thought was a small, isolated caravan moving north of Jericho. It had appeared to be an easy but lucrative afternoon. This part of the wilderness of Judea was desolate and bleak, and they badly needed a success. Ya'abin had created a problem for himself. His reputation had become so fearsome in the last several months that few travelers, other than those too poor to fear being robbed, came this way any longer. If they did, they waited at collecting points until they could form caravans too large and well-defended for the Desert Fox to jump. In the month since Passover, their successes had been few and their takings paltry. When word of this caravan reached them, it looked like something from earlier, better days and they swept in eagerly.

Then, just as they were ripping into the packs on the camels, a shout went up. Half a mile away, coming out of one of the dozens of narrow washes that were characteristic of this part of the country, what looked to be a full century of legionnaires appeared. Ya'abin couldn't believe it. It was as though they had sprung from the earth. Fortunately, only the officers were mounted, so Ya'abin had easily escaped. But he took nothing with him and they had ridden hard ever since.

They were fools, these Romans, but they were dogged fools. He knew they would track him until dark, then start again in the morning at first light. So they rode on now, three full hours after darkness had fallen. His goal had been to reach and then cross an area where the soil gave way to huge expanses of hardpan or rocky areas where no tracks would show. They had crossed that area, and in less than a quarter of an hour they would reach a small spring and camp for the night.

Ya'abin was tired. His body ached from a full twelve hours in the saddle. He was hungry. All of that combined to put him in a very foul mood. What should have been an evening of celebration had once again turned sour.

"*Ya'abin!*"

The voice echoed, bouncing off the steep hillsides.

He reined in sharply, throwing up his hand. Instantly, he was off his horse and using it as a shield. Behind him he heard his men dismounting and scrambling for cover as well.

The moon was high in the sky and nearly full again. The landscape was brightly illuminated wherever it shone, but in the canyon there were still deep patches of shadow. Ya'abin scanned the ridge top, then saw a single figure directly above him. He cursed softly. Eliab and Shaul, his second- and third-in-command, darted over to join him.

"I thought you had scouts out," Ya'abin hissed.

"We do," Eliab shot back. "We've got men out to the front and the rear."

"Well, where are they?"

"Ya'abin! I know you can hear me." The voice floated down to them clearly. "Stay where you are and no one will get hurt."

He grabbed Shaul and pulled him close. "Take ten men. Fall back. Keep to the shadows. Circle up and around him." He nodded and started to move. "Be careful. He won't be alone."

Then, even as Shaul scuttled away, Ya'abin stood, still keeping his horse between him and the figure above him. "Who are you? What do you want?"

"It's a mistake to try to send someone up here," the voice answered, almost amiable now. "Stand as you are. I only wish to talk."

Ya'abin heard the soft whir of arrows. Suddenly there was a cry, and something crashed in the bushes behind them. Then another man screamed. Ya'abin dropped to the ground, breathing hard. He heard someone moaning and writhing on the ground.

"Hold your men, or more will go down," the voice called. "We already have your six scouts. You can't afford to lose more."

He swung on Eliab. "How many scouts did you have out?"

There was a quick flick of the tongue, and Ya'abin saw his captain was pale. "Six."

There was another cry, and the sound of a body thudding to earth. "Shaul!" Ya'abin screamed. "Stay where you are." He looked around, assessing their position. Between the deep shadows, the few trees in the bottom of the draw, and dozens of rock outcroppings on the hillside, there were ample places for men to hide. They had walked right into an ambush.

"What do you want?" he called again.

"We want you to know what you're up against. We want you to know that you're finished. Your days are over."

Turning to Eliab, Ya'abin spoke in a low tone. "I know that voice."

"Who is it?"

He shook his head, trying to place it.

"You can't win. We know where you are. We know how to find you." There was an sarcastic laugh. "You need to pay your men more, Old Fox, for they are willing to tell us anything for a half-shekel or two."

Eliab shook his head as Ya'abin gave him a scathing look. "I don't think so," he said. But his voice didn't ring with confidence. The last few weeks had been lean ones, and his men often slipped into the villages to find food and other things.

"What do you want?" Ya'abin said again, the anger making him bolder.

"We want you to surrender."

He laughed raucously. "Come on down and I'll surrender."

"Do you think that Roman column this afternoon was just bad

luck?" the voice went on, ignoring the challenge. "We told them where you would be. Unfortunately, you struck the caravan just a little too soon, or they would have had you."

"Then the road would be littered with Roman dead right now."

"The lion roars," came the sardonic reply, "but it sounds more like the mew of a kitten."

Then he had it. Ya'abin stiffened visibly. "It's Simeon ben David."

Eliab gaped at him, going instantly cold. He still woke up in a sweat remembering that night when someone had shaken him in his sleep and told him he was the Javelin. "But he's dead!" he exclaimed.

A rich laugh pealed out above them. "Yes. That's right. I've come back from the dead, Ya'abin. I'm here to pay you for your treachery at the Joknean Pass."

Whatever else Moshe Ya'abin might be, he was not stupid. He had already come to the conclusion that Simeon had not been killed as reported. "I don't believe in ghosts," he shouted.

"Nor do I," came the reply. "Nor do I."

The figure on the ridge was suddenly no longer there. Ya'abin stepped out from behind his horse. "Simeon!"

There was no answer.

Ya'abin scanned the hillsides, looking for any shadow, any movement. There was nothing. Mind working furiously, he realized that he was still in an extremely vulnerable position. The bowmen who had dropped his men had not fired from the ridge; that was too far above them. That meant they were nearby and that he was still very much exposed. Yet the Javelin was not cutting him down. Why not?

He reached for his horse's reins. "Pass the word, Eliab. Mount up. We'll ride forward at a trot. Have the men stay close together."

He looked up one last time. "Simeon ben David! You can't frighten me. It isn't over."

From somewhere above him on the moonlit hillside he thought he heard a faint laugh. Other than that, there was nothing but silence.

III

ROME

22 MAY, A.D. 31

Livia and Miriam were strolling leisurely along the *Via Sacra*. It had become their daily habit. Each afternoon after the midday meal and the two hours of rest that followed it, Miriam would leave the large apartment where she and her father lived and descend to the street. There she would meet Livia and Drusus and together they would set out.

It was not a question of sightseeing any longer. After nine months in Rome, they were familiar with every building, every temple, every forum and plaza. It was their time to be alone, to be free to talk about Jesus or their longing to return home or whatever else was in their heart without fear of being overheard by the slaves or Miriam's father or having to retreat to Livia's apartment.

As they approached the *Rostra*, Drusus raised one hand in farewell. "I'll be back by suppertime."

"Where are you going?"

"Clodia wants to take me to see the Pantheon."

Livia started. "But that is a long ways from here. Do you think you can find your way back to our apartment block?"

He looked at her in disgust. "I'm eighteen, Livia. And I've lived in Rome longer than you have."

She smiled and touched his hand. "Sorry." But she was still some-what nervous. "You have your papers in case you are stopped?"

He patted his tunic. "I do."

With Miriam's help, Drusus had shed the simple dress of a slave and wore a cotton tunic and well-crafted sandals, so he did not look like a slave any longer. Fortunately, he had never posed the threat of running away, and his master was not one of those who branded all of his slaves, so Drusus carried no overt marks of his former life. But a lifetime of slavery had bred in him an air of subservience. When someone of the upper classes passed, he would automatically step back, bowing his head so he didn't have to meet their eyes. His behavior was almost as clear a mark as a brand in his forehead or in his hand. Twice he had been stopped and challenged by the city police, and Livia lived in mortal fear that he would be taken and she would lose him again.

"Will you be careful?" she murmured.

He sighed, feeling the weary burden common to all those in their teen years. "Yes." He gave a wave and disappeared into the crowds.

Livia watched him for a moment, then said, "He has found a friend, a son of one of the silversmiths in our building."

"That's wonderful. He's really changing, Livia. I can see it more every day." And that was really true. For a time, Drusus had gone with them on their walks but had hung back, not participating in the women's talk yet still wanting to be with them. The last few weeks, however, he had started to either stay home or go off on his own. That was not a surprise, really, Miriam thought. He was free. After long years of slavery, he was finally free to go where he wanted and do what he wanted.

As a young household servant he had often gone to the markets to purchase food for his master's villa, but usually that was early in the morning. The rest of the day was spent inside, meeting the needs of the family. When Marcus had brought him to Livia that night, his skin had been pale, almost fragile. Now it was tanned and firm. Where before he had been quiet and withdrawn, speaking only when directly spoken to, Drusus now showed greater confidence. He felt almost completely comfortable around Miriam now, though he still said little when Mordechai was around. Two nights ago he had startled Miriam when he laughed aloud at something she had said. That was an important first.

Livia gave Miriam a rueful look. "I've thought of him as a young boy for so long," she said, "it's hard to remember that he has grown up."

"But he has, hasn't he. He's a fine young man now."

"I'll be so glad to be out of Rome," Livia said. "I hate it that he has to carry proof that he is free to go where he wants, when he wants."

"I know, and hopefully—"

She stopped. To her surprise, Miriam saw Arcadius pushing his way through the crowds. When he saw her, he lifted a hand and waved. Arcadius was their chief household servant. He was one of the most trusted slaves from the estate of the family of Antonius Marcus Didius and had been assigned to attend to Mordechai and Miriam during their stay in Rome. He was a third-generation slave, a man in his forties, with a gentle manner and considerable practical wisdom. Miriam had come to like him very much and always treated him with courtesy and respect.

"Arcadius? What brings you here?"

"Your father sent me, Mistress Miriam. He requests your presence at home as soon as it is convenient for you."

Miriam looked at Livia. What was this about? She had breakfasted with her father this morning. Usually she did not see him again until just before the evening meal, which they usually took with Livia and Drusus as their guests. It surprised Miriam somewhat, but her father seemed to enjoy the company of the young lad, even though they said little directly to each other.

If Arcadius noticed her hestitation, he gave no sign. He just waited for a response. "All right," Miriam said. "We shall come immediately."

Knowing that she did not need an escort, he bowed, then turned and started back. In a moment, he was gone again.

IV

When Miriam stepped into the room her father used as his office and library, her heart fell. He was sitting at a small table, and there was a letter on the tabletop. Had he intercepted her mail? "Good afternoon, Father."

"*Shalom*, Miriam. Come in."

She did so, taking the nearest seat.

"Out walking?"

She nodded. That would hardly surprise him. His face was grave, and he seemed to be studying her. "Arcadius said you wished to see me."

"Yes. I received word from Caesarea yesterday."

Yesterday! She almost cried it out. He had heard a day ago and not said a word to her? Then she realized what he had said. From Caesarea, not from Jerusalem. "Marcus?" she finally asked.

"Yes."

She couldn't help it. Her excitement shot upward. "Have they caught Ya'abin?"

It was dashed instantly. "No. He is hopeful it will happen soon, but no."

"Oh, Father. Can't we go back anyway? I would even be willing to stay in Caesarea if you don't think it's safe in Jerusalem. Livia and I could—"

"I thought you loved Rome."

"Love it?" she cried. "No, Father. I find it fascinating. I have enjoyed being here in many ways. But this isn't home. I want to go home."

His eyes darkened a little at that, and she wasn't sure why. He seemed distracted, only partially present with her. She was searching for something to say that might change his mind when he spoke again, making her breath catch in her throat.

"Tell me about that day in Jerusalem when you saw Jesus of Nazareth."

She felt the blood drain from her face and feared that her expression would give her away. "Jesus?" she managed.

"Yes. It was about a woman or something, as I remember. You told me about it one day."

"Yes." She was fighting hard to maintain a calm demeanor. "The Pharisees brought a woman to Jesus. They were trying to trap him, make him look foolish to the people."

"Ah, yes. They had caught her in the act of adultery."

She realized then that her father remembered that day very well. Her heart began to pound within her chest. Had someone told Marcus about her baptism? What if her father asked her straight out? Some time ago she had determined that she would not lie to her father, not if he asked her directly.

His eyes were peering deeply into hers, probing, peeling back her defenses. "Was Azariah there that day?"

"Yes," she murmured, dropping her eyes to stare at her hands in her lap. "I told you that."

"Well," he said, his mouth tightening now, "Azariah's letting it be known that the daughter of Mordechai ben Uzziel may have some sympathy for this Jesus."

So that was it. In a way, it came as a tremendous relief. In another way, she knew she was on very dangerous ground. "Father," she said evenly, "I didn't hide that from you. I thought what Azariah and the others were doing to that woman was terrible. Jesus showed compassion towards her and made them look like fools. Yes, my sympathy was with Jesus that day."

Then she decided to forestall more questions. "If you remember, you demanded that I not speak of him again in your presence. I have honored that wish."

She bit her lip, instantly realizing her mistake. She had said "in your presence." Had he caught those words? Would he ask if she was speaking about Jesus outside of his presence?

But to her surprise, that seemed to satisfy him. He straightened and took a deep breath. "Miriam, things are not well in Jerusalem. There is trouble in the Great Council in Jerusalem."

"What kind of trouble?"

"Several things. Jesus, among others. The Romans are getting nervous. His following is growing every day, especially among the Galileans."

"They think Jesus is going to start a rebellion?" she asked incredulously.

He shook his head. "No, not yet. But anything in the Galilee is of concern to them. Those fanatics are like a sheaf of wheat. One spark and they explode into flame. If Jesus can provide that spark, then we have to extinguish it right now."

Miriam felt sick.

"Pilate and Marcus have asked that I return to Jerusalem immediately. I went to Ostia this morning to book passage. I leave the day after tomorrow."

She shot forward in her chair. "Really! That's wonderful." Then, at the look in his eyes, she realized what he had said. He had used the first-person singular. "No, Father!" she cried. "If you're going, I'm going."

"Marcus says it isn't safe for you yet. He's hoping by Saturnalia we can—"

She leaped up. "Saturnalia! But that's seven more months. No! I want to go now. Father, you can't leave me."

"It's too dangerous," he said, his voice hardening. "Sit down, Miriam."

"Father, please. Don't do this."

"Miriam! *Sit down!*"

She sank back in her chair, trembling with frustration.

"I know you want to return, but the time isn't right." He held up a hand as she stirred. "No, listen! I have no choice. The Council is in crisis. Marcus said that Simeon and Yehuda are closing in on Ya'abin. They should have this finished in the next few months. Then it will be safe again."

"I'll stay at the Praetorium. If—"

"Miriam!" His voice rose sharply in warning. "The matter is settled. I will hear no more of it."

She sat back, her eyes burning.

"I leave in two days. I'll have Livia and Drusus move in here with you. I've already talked to Antonius Didius. He has agreed to leave the household servants as long as you need them and will see that your needs are met."

"My needs are met?" she retorted, the anger flaring up in her. "If you are worried about my needs, then take me with you."

"There's another thing," he said, ignoring that. "I had hoped for a more auspicious time to speak with you about this, but . . . "

Something in his voice sent a prickle up her back. "What?" she asked softly.

"Tell me your feelings towards Marcus Didius."

She just stared at him.

His face darkened noticeably. He was not in a mood for her petulance. "Well?" he snapped.

"Why are you asking this, Father? What has that got to do with anything at this moment?"

"Because Marcus Quadratus Didius has asked for your hand in marriage," he shot back.

"*What?*"

"He has made a proposal of marriage, and I have agreed."

She could hardly catch her breath. It felt as though something terrible was squeezing her chest.

"He hopes to come back here for Saturnalia in December. I'll come with him. We'll make all the arrangements at that time. Then if you want to return to Caesarea, you can do so as his wife."

"And when did he first talk with you about this?" she whispered, already guessing the answer.

"Before he left here in March."

"How nice of you to finally tell me," she said bitterly.

"I'm telling you now."

She began to shake her head slowly, totally unable to believe what she was hearing.

"I know this comes as a shock, but you told me you find him intelligent, charming, and stimulating."

She looked up. "Were you even going to ask me? Were you even going to ask how I feel about this?"

"I'm asking you now."

"No, you're telling me."

His face flushed angrily. "Have it your way. It doesn't matter. I am your father and the decision is ultimately mine."

Something down deep inside Miriam solidified at that moment, and she knew they had just crossed a line from which there would be no retreating. "No, Father," she said quietly. "I'll stay in Rome for now if that is your wish, but I will not marry Marcus."

"You will!" he roared.

"No, I won't."

He got up slowly, his eyes glittering. "You dare to defy me on this? This is the daughter who betrayed her own father? You ran off to Capernaum and never gave a thought to what your disloyalty meant to me. And now you dare to defy me?"

She didn't look up at him. She was clutching at the edge of her chair to stop from screaming out, from leaping up and dashing from the room.

"You *will* do what I say in this, Miriam. Our law says, 'Honor your father and your mother.' Does that mean nothing to you?"

Her head snapped up. "*Honor?*" she cried in disbelief. "You used me, Father, to help you carry out an evil thing."

His face went a deep hue of purple. "*You call me evil?* I am trying to save our country from annihilation! I'll do whatever I have to do to accomplish that."

"Betrayal. Deceit. Treachery." She flung the words at him. "Nothing in our law says I have to honor that."

His voice was a low, menacing hiss. "Well, if our law means nothing to you, then consider this. We are in Rome now. Here, the authority of the *pater familias*, the father of the family, is absolute." He leaned forward, frightening her more than she thought was possible. "*Absolute*, Miriam. You think about that."

Just as suddenly as the darkness had swept across him, it was gone. "I know I've caught you off guard with this, but once you've had a chance to think about it, you will see this is a wonderful opportunity."

"For you or for me, Father?" she whispered.

If he heard, he gave no sign. It was almost as though he was alone in the room now. "The Didius family is one of the great families of Rome. They have the confidence of the emperor himself. This could prove to be highly beneficial to our people."

Miriam said nothing more. She simply stood, no longer meeting his gaze, then turned and left the room.

V

Miriam knocked on the door softly, then pushed it open. Her father looked up, then motioned her in. He didn't seem overly surprised it was her. The house was quiet. All of the servants were in their quarters, if not already asleep.

She moved across the room and stopped in front of him. He motioned toward a chair, but she didn't take it.

"Miriam, I'm sorry about this afternoon. I didn't handle it very well. I—It was just that Marcus's letter threw me in a turmoil. I wasn't thinking very clearly." His shoulders lifted and fell. "I'm sorry."

She only nodded.

"Sit down. Let's talk about it. I'm calmer now."

"Father, there's something I have to tell you."

"All right. Are you sure you won't sit down?"

She didn't move. "First, I want you to know that my decision to go to Capernaum and tell Simeon about the trap was not an easy one for me. They saved our lives, Father. But it meant going against you, you who have always loved me and given me everything I've ever wanted."

"Go on," he said. She saw wariness in his eyes.

"I understand why you did what you did. That doesn't mean I condone it, but I understand why you—"

"Now wait a minute," he said, his voice rising.

"That's not the main thing I came in to say."

His mouth clamped shut again. The calm she had seen when she entered was gone now. She took a deep breath and plunged. "When I went to Capernaum to tell Simeon and Yehuda, I talked a lot with Simeon's mother and father about Jesus."

There was a visible reaction in his eyes, but all he said was, "And?"

"They convinced me and Livia, and they convinced Ezra and Lilly, that Jesus is not just another preacher, not just another man trying to get people to follow him."

"I don't want to hear this, Miriam."

"And I didn't want to hear that you told Marcus I would marry him without even asking me," she shot right back at him. Then, before he could answer her, she went on, wanting it said. "Ezra and Lilly and I went back to Capernaum the last two weeks before we left for Rome. Ezra wasn't lying to you. He did need to go and look for a leather supplier, but we stayed in Capernaum with Simeon's parents most of the time."

He had gone very still now, and she felt the same flicker of fear that she had experienced when he had talked about the *pater familias* earlier that day.

"I went out to hear Jesus every chance I had. I listened to him, Father. I watched him work miracles. I came to believe in him. All of us did, actually."

"That is enough," he said, his voice very low. "I won't have this."

"I asked to be baptized," she went on. "So did Livia, and so did Ezra and Lilly. We are his disciples now. I believe he is the Messiah, Father. I believe he is more than that, but that is something you wouldn't understand. It doesn't matter what you and the Council try to do. You cannot stop him, Father. He *is* the Messiah. He is the Chosen One. I know that with all my heart."

He was on his feet, eyes blazing. "I said that is enough!" he roared.

"No, Father. It is not enough. I am going back home. Not with you. I can see that now. I don't expect you to accept any of this. I expect that you will disinherit me and perhaps even disown me. I understand, and I am prepared to live with those consequences. I should have told you sooner, and for that I am sorry."

"I'll have Ezra's head for this," he shouted.

"That's right, Father. Blame everyone else. Your ordered world of politics and power isn't working out quite like you planned is it? Your daughter has gone over to the enemy. So blame Ezra. Blame Simeon. Blame anyone but me. You can't stand that thought, can you? You can't stand to think that your daughter is ashamed of what her father has become and will have no part of it."

He started around the table, his fists clenching and unclenching, the rage mottling his face.

Tears welled up in her eyes. "Good-bye, Papa. Believe it or not, I do love you. I'm sorry it had to come to this."

He stopped, trembling with fury.

"I'll miss you terribly," she whispered, then turned and left the room, shutting the door quietly behind her.

CHAPTER NOTES

Reference has been made elsewhere in this novel to the concept of *pater familias*, or the authority of the father of the Roman family. To say it was absolute is not an exaggeration. At the birth of a child, it was traditional to bring the baby and lay it at the feet of the father. If he took it in his arms, it signified that he accepted it as his own, and the child was given all the rights and privileges belonging to the family. If he turned away, the child became an outcast, a pariah, without family in a society where family was everything. The child was not killed outright but was *exponere*, or "exposed." It would be taken out to a roadside by one of the slaves and abandoned. Sometimes families of the poor would take the babies as their own, but often such babies perished (see Johnston, 67).

CHAPTER 24

MAKE HASTE SLOWLY.

—*Suetonius*, Augustus, 25

I

IN THE WILDERNESS OF JUDEA
23 MAY, A.D. 31

Water in this part of Israel was not common, but a few springs could be found. The spring near Ya'abin's hideout was not in a place that lent itself to an ambush, and that was why Ya'abin had chosen it. It was near the base of a long row of hills. To the east, the land was flat and they could see anyone coming a long distance away. Behind the spring, to the west, the hills rose gently; Ya'abin had seven of his men patrolling those hills so that no one could surprise him from that direction. In the meantime, even though it was a hot day and the men were anxious to drink and to water their horses, Ya'abin held them back until he was absolutely sure no one was waiting there.

He knew that he was getting obsessive, but he would not be surprised again. More importantly, he wanted to find Simeon and his men. The morning after the confrontation in the canyon, they had ridden back to the site of the ambush and started tracking Simeon's band. Unfortunately, he had used the same trick Ya'abin had. Ya'abin's men were able to follow him easily—there were somewhere around fifteen to twenty-five horses, Eliab guessed—until they came to that same area where the rocky ground swallowed up any tracks.

Since then Ya'abin had doubled the guards and had been much more careful about where he camped. The pressure was getting on his nerves, and his temper was short. More critically, it was wearing on his men. Several did not believe that this was an ordinary man who was after them, and their morale was in shambles. At the ambush they had lost nine more men—the six scouts who disappeared without a trace, plus one dead and two more wounded severely enough that they had been taken to Hebron and would likely not be seen again.

Ya'abin realized that this was part of Simeon's strategy. He was trying to whittle his enemy down to size. Unfortunately, it was working. Ya'abin was down to little more than sixty men—still a powerful force, but just over half of what there had been a few months before. But he knew what he was facing now.

Up ahead, at the spring, Eliab was waving his arms, and Ya'abin came back to the present. About a mile farther on, the three forward scouts were waving a small flag, signaling that all was clear. He turned. Above him on the top of the hill, another man waved a similar flag. Ya'abin turned to Eliab. "All right. Let them drink. Ten at a time. First ones done get up on the ridge and relieve the others."

Eliab snapped out the commands and ten men dismounted. They led their horses forward. If Eliab had been paying closer attention to his men rather than watching the sentries to make sure nothing changed, he would have seen it sooner. The horses lowered their heads to the water, but then snorted and backed away. Terribly thirsty and tired of waiting, the men were not as careful. They threw themselves down and plunged their faces into the water, gulping deeply. Then their heads came up. There were cries of dismay. One man started to gag.

Eliab and Ya'abin whirled. Now all ten men were up, faces

contorted, bodies doubling over. Two suddenly began to retch. "The water!" one of them gasped. "It's poisoned!"

In three leaps, Ya'abin was to the spring. He dropped to one knee, sniffing. There was a faint odor, but he wasn't sure what it was. He dipped a finger in the water, then touched it to his tongue. He recoiled as though someone had slapped his face.

"What is it?" Eliab cried, coming to stand beside his leader. The noise of the ten men nearly drowned him out. All of them were twisted and bent. Several had fallen to their knees as violent spasms racked their bodies. The rest of Ya'abin's men shrank back, staring in horror.

"Not poison." Ya'abin stared grimly down at the spring. "It's spurge."

"Spurge!"

"Yes. My grandmother used to grind up the roots of the plant and give it to us to make us vomit when we were sick. It's a powerful emetic." He kicked savagely at the ground, sending dirt flying into the water. And then he began to swear softly and bitterly, frequently bringing in the name of Simeon the Javelin.

II

ROME

24 MAY, A.D. 31

"Arcadius?"

"Yes, Mistress Miriam?" Their chief servant looked up, then gave her a faint smile. It struck her as odd that it seemed more sad than happy.

"I can't find my father."

"He left last night, Mistress Miriam."

"But—" She was suddenly bewildered. "He wasn't supposed to sail until today."

"Yes, I know."

"He didn't even say good-bye?" she asked, a great sense of desolation sweeping over her. They had not spoken since she had told him about Jesus. He left early and ate alone when he returned. But she had thought he would at least say good-bye.

"I'm sorry, Mistress Miriam."

She tried to think. "He told me that Livia and Drusus—"

She stopped as he nodded. "They will be moved over this afternoon. Two of the servants are helping them pack their things right now."

She started to turn, still half-dazed. "Mistress Miriam?"

She turned back. "Yes?"

Arcadius sighed, and it was a sound of pain. "Your father asked that I inform you of several new circumstances."

That brought her out of her thoughts. "Such as?"

He couldn't meet her eyes. "Things will continue pretty much as before," he said. "You are free to go anywhere in the city. The same is true of Livia and the lad, Drusus."

Miriam suddenly went very still. "Why wouldn't we be?"

"You are," he answered. "Your escorts have been so instructed."

"Escorts?"

"Your father has left instructions that you are to have escorts at all times when you go out."

She peered at him, shocked deeply. "I don't understand." But she did. It was like someone had just snuffed out a candle inside of her. "Are we under house arrest, Arcadius?"

"That is a strong term, Mistress Miriam. The escorts' instructions are that you are free to go anywhere and do anything you wish, within certain limitations."

"Limitations such as not leaving the city?" she said woodenly.

"Except to visit the home of my master, Master Didius."

The breath went out of her in a long sound of despair.

"There's one other thing." His voice was filled with compassion.

Her head came up.

"Your father said to tell you that you should not try to get access to your funds. Even the accounts in your name in Jerusalem have been frozen. There will be a comfortable living allowance, and I have been instructed to let Master Didius know if you have any special needs."

Miriam groped blindly for the nearest bench. She had not worried about how she would pay for passage back to Israel. With what she had taken and invested with her father's help over the past two or three years, she personally was wealthier than many families in Jerusalem.

"Your father said to tell you that he and Master Marcus Didius will return before Saturnalia. You can discuss these matters with him then."

She rubbed slowly at her eyes, trying to make her mind work again.

Arcadius started to back away. "I'm sorry, Mistress Miriam. Those were my instructions."

"I understand, Arcadius. It's not your fault."

"Thank you."

As he started down the hallway, she had another thought. "I will be writing some letters today, Arcadius. Would you find someone who could see to their delivery?"

Arcadius stopped, not turning. His next words should have surprised her, but she was beyond that now. "I'm sorry, Mistress. The escorts have been strictly instructed. There will be no letters. Not coming in. Not going out."

III

The eyes of the shepherd woman were wide with terror, but her husband's were like flint, unbending, inscrutable. Even as Shaul held a knife to the man's throat, the shepherd showed no fear. Ya'abin walked around him, peering at the woman and her three children. The boy, about nine, was as defiant as his father. The two girls, both younger, had darted into the dark recesses of the black goatskin tent and had not shown their faces again.

Ya'abin moved easily, almost lazily, as he eyed the man. Then with the swiftness of a cobra striking, he lunged and caught the little boy. He swung him around to face his father. Finally, Ya'abin saw that he had the man's attention.

"We know the man they call Simeon came this way," he said, looking at the boy but speaking to his father. "We've been following their tracks all morning." He moved forward a step, so the boy's face was clearly visible to his father. "Now," Ya'abin went on. "I'm not interested in hurting your son. Just tell me which way they went from here and we'll be gone."

The woman babbled something in their Arabian dialect and finally the man lowered his eyes. "They took the wadi on the south."

"Wadi? What is that?"

"*Wadi* is our Arabic name for a canyon or wash."

"How many and how long ago?"

The man hesitated, but when Ya'abin tightened his grip on the little boy, he caved in. "About twenty. One hour ago, no more."

Ya'abin grunted and let the boy go. He darted to his mother, who gathered him in with a sob of relief. "That's better. Any Romans around?"

The man shook his head quickly.

"We know where you are," Ya'abin reminded him, his eyes going hard. "If you're lying, we'll be back. And this time, there won't be anything left of the boy, or your wife, or your two little girls for you to worry about. Understand?"

The man gave a quick nod, even though his eyes were filled with hate. "No, Romans," the man said. "There was a small patrol three days ago, east of Hebron, but that is all."

Eliab looked at his chief. They already knew about that group. The man was telling the truth, at least to that degree.

Ya'abin turned to his horse. It was as though the shepherd and his family no longer existed. "Mount up," he called.

IV

It was not a surprise that the wandering shepherds had come to this part of the wilderness at this time of year. They were seven or eight miles east of the Dead Sea and a few miles south of Jerusalem. Here the wilderness began to rise toward the central highlands that ran up and down the center of the country. Here the spring rains were always more generous than down in the lowlands. The grass, though little more than ankle high, was thick and mixed with the dead remains of the wildflowers that burst out in the desert in profusion each spring. Even up on the sides of the canyon there was considerable foliage. In the wadi itself, the grass was thicker and mixed in with thick patches of thorn bushes and a few trees. Now that summer had come in full force, everything was dry and brown, but it still provided excellent forage for sheep and goats.

Ya'abin's horses were taking advantage of the forage as well, grazing contentedly a few dozen paces below where the band waited for further word from the scouting party.

Ya'abin had about thirty men with him. They were scattered about beneath the trees just below the place where the wadi turned sharply to the north, narrowing rapidly. The turn was sharp enough that they could not be seen by anyone coming down the canyon until they rounded that bend. Ya'abin's strategy was simple. Eliab had taken fifteen men and swung around to the south. Shaul took fifteen more and went north. They were not to engage Simeon's men, but only let themselves be seen.

In the last two weeks, Ya'abin had finally realized that Simeon was trying hard to avoid a direct confrontation. Stupid fellow. That narrowed one's choices significantly. To the west, where the wadi finally petered out and joined the highlands, the terrain rose sharply. A man could negotiate those hills, but not on horseback. So the Javelin couldn't go west, and he could not outrun his flankers. That left only one option if he wasn't willing to stand and fight. He would have to drop back into the wadi and try to escape the way he had come an hour earlier. And that would bring him right into the arms of Moshe Ya'abin. Ya'abin was already savoring the various possibilities for extracting his revenge.

"Moshe, look!"

He turned. Instantly he saw what the man who had called out was seeing. Against the deep blue cloudless sky was a thin trail of smoke. His eyes followed in surprise as it rose higher and higher, then arched slowly and dropped toward them. Ya'abin's jaw dropped, and he shot to his feet. It was a flaming arrow. Before he could react, he saw three more appear from behind the top of the hill, then four more. All of them arched gracefully, then dropped into the canyon about three hundred paces below them, not far from where the horses grazed. For a moment he stood and stared. The archers weren't shooting at them. They weren't even close.

It was the horses that made him realize what was happening. Their heads came up and they turned to look down the canyon. There was a low nervous whinny from one of them; then they began to stamp the ground and shy back.

Then Ya'abin saw it. All day long the sun had been heating the air along the shores of the Dead Sea. Down there the temperature was nearing a hundred degrees. In contrast, the spine of the central highlands was almost four thousand feet above the Dead Sea. It was fifteen or twenty degrees cooler there. The difference in temperature was sucking the hot air upward, as it did each afternoon. It wasn't a strong wind yet, but it was stiff enough. The moment the flaming arrows struck the ground, the wind pushed the flames into the surrounding grass and brush. Billows of gray smoke were already beginning to rise.

"Fire!" Ya'abin gasped. "Get the horses." He grabbed his bow and sprinted away.

They were too late. The smoke was already rolling up the wadi and had reached the animals. Heads high, eyes wild, the horses were no longer milling around. They had started up the canyon to escape the smoke. They were already nervous, eyes rolling as they smelled the fire. To suddenly have thirty screeching men descend on them was not the wisest thing to do. The animals bolted, lunging forward with great leaps to race past their masters.

Moshe Ya'abin threw up his hands, jumping in front of his stallion. It reared up on its hind legs, pawing the air. He grabbed at the reins. He was quick enough, but not nearly strong enough. He screamed in pain as the full length of the leather straps pulled through his two hands, searing the flesh and leaving no skin behind. The animal came down, nearly knocking him over, then flashed past him and was gone.

"Run!"

He wasn't sure who had shouted it, but all around him men forgot about the horses and started running up the slopes of the canyon. He saw that some hadn't even bothered to grab their weapons.

"Not that way you fools!" he bellowed. "Follow me."

A few didn't hear him and continued on, but the rest stumbled to a stop and turned toward their commander. "Come on," he yelled. "The flames aren't that high." To prove his point, he threw an arm across his face and started running down the canyon. The smoke was thick, but he could easily see where the flames were. He chose a place where the fire was only knee high, took a deep breath and leaped over it. He ran on for another few steps, stamping hard in the smoking grass. In seconds, he reached the spot where the burning arrows protruded from the ground and stepped onto grass that wasn't burned.

He bent over, choking and coughing and wiping at his eyes. "Come on!" he shouted again. "It's all right. You can make it."

V

Near Bethany
4 June, A.D. 31

Simeon finished writing and set the quill pen down. He read quickly, then picked up the paper and blew on it. Yehuda, Barak, Samuel, and Issachar watched him in silence. Satisfied that the ink was dry, he folded it once and handed it to Issachar. "Make sure you wait for an answer."

"Sextus is going to want to send for the tribune," Yehuda said. "That could take another week, especially if he brings in more forces."

Simeon shrugged. "Ya'abin will probably still be looking for his horses." Then, smiling faintly at Issachar, he said again, "Wait for their answer."

Barak grinned. "One of the shepherd boys told me that Ya'abin has offered them one shekel for each horse they help them find." The smile spread to his eyes. "The boy said his father wants to know how long you think that will take them to do that."

Simeon smiled too. These wandering people who lived a life of simplicity and freedom had turned out to be loyal allies. "Tell them I would be surprised if those horses could be found in less than three or four days."

Barak nodded and backed out of the simple tent.

Samuel spoke up now. "Are you sure you want both me and Issachar to go? If Ya'abin finds you before we get back, you're going to need every hand you've got."

"He's not going to find us until we're ready for him to find us," Simeon said easily. "No, I need two of you to go—if something delays you, one of you can come back and let us know what's going on."

Issachar put the letter inside his tunic. "Anything else?"

Simeon shook his head. The two men went out, leaving Yehuda and Simeon alone. Yehuda moved over and took a rough, homemade stool the shepherd had let them borrow. "So," he said, "the time has finally come."

"Yes."

"I owe you an apology."

Simeon's eyes lifted. "For what?"

"For thinking you were crazy. That you had no heart."

Simeon was pleased to see there was no begrudging in his friend's eyes. "So you think it will work?" Simeon asked.

"When I was little, my father had a saying that I still remember."

"What was that?"

"'Do not stoke a furnace for your foe that is so hot that it consumes you as well.'"

Simeon laughed softly. "You think Ya'abin's temper is burning a little right now."

"I would guess he is smoking around the ears. He hasn't made a raid on anyone or anything now for almost two weeks. He wants one thing and one thing only, and that is to catch you and take the skin off your back one inch at a time. It's clear that he is so enraged he's not thinking clearly anymore."

"Good. That's exactly where we need him to be."

"I've decided that we need to change your name," Yehuda mused.

"Really? To what?"

"Instead of *Ha'keedohn*—the Javelin—I think we ought to call you *Malmahd*—the Ox Goad."

Simeon chuckled at the play on the imagery. *Ha'keedohn*, or the javelin, was a long shaft with an iron tip used in warfare. The *malmahd* was almost of equal length and also had an iron tip, though it was not barbed. Farmers and cart drivers used the ox goad to drive and control stubborn oxen. A few sharp jabs with the goad and even the most difficult animal could be made to obey. It was an appropriate metaphor for what they had been doing with Ya'abin these past few months.

"So what about you when we are finished?" Yehuda asked after a time. "Home again?"

Simeon looked surprised. "Of course. Isn't that what you want?"

"Oh, yes. For a time at least."

At the sharp look in Simeon's eyes, he laughed aloud. "You won't want to hear this, but did you ever consider that in your determined attempts to avoid shedding blood, you have taught your little band some new and very clever ways to fight? This strategy would drive the Romans as completely mad as it has Ya'abin."

Simeon just sighed. "You are incorrigible."

Now any humor in Yehuda's eyes died. "You may have forgotten what happened the last time the Romans marched into the Galilee.

Your mother's family lost as much as mine. My father, my mother, and younger brother. There are still many debts to pay."

For a moment Simeon was tempted to respond, but he knew that there was no point in it. He wasn't going to change Yehuda on this matter.

"Mooli talked to me about Shana at Passover," Yehuda suddenly said.

Simeon looked up. "He did? About the betrothal?"

"Yes."

"And?"

Yehuda was thoughtful. "I spoke to Shana. She would like a little more time. She thought it ought to be a least one full year since your betrothal was annulled before she does anything."

"But that will be—" he thought for a moment. "In a week or two."

"Yes."

"Shana is young and full of life, Yehuda. What she and I had together is past."

"She knows that now. I expect we shall begin the arrangements as soon as Mooli and I return."

"Samuel is a good man." Simeon realized that he had used those exact words before, but he didn't know what else to say.

To his surprise, Yehuda got up and came over to him. He laid a hand on Simeon's shoulder. "So are you, Simeon, son of David."

Touched, Simeon could only nod.

"It's too bad our paths have to diverge. We could raise some real havoc among those red-plumed helmets now."

Simeon looked up at his old friend. "Not for me." He hesitated. "You know, it's not too late for you to come down the path that I have chosen."

"It was too late for that once you went to Nazareth and talked with Jesus' mother."

CHAPTER 25

EVEN IF STRENGTH FAILS, BOLDNESS AT LEAST WILL DESERVE PRAISE;
IN GREAT ENDEAVORS EVEN TO HAVE HAD THE WILL IS ENOUGH.

—*Propertius*, Elegies, *II.i.43*

I

JERUSALEM
13 JUNE, A.D. 31

Tribune Marcus Quadratus Didius stepped to the heavy wooden door, searched the dark street in both directions one more time, then knocked softly. He was gratified to instantly hear the scrape of the heavy bar on the opposite side. In a moment, the door swung open and he stepped into the spacious courtyard of Mordechai ben Uzziel's palatial mansion in the Upper City of Jerusalem.

He pulled back the hood that covered his face, then removed the light cloak he wore to cover his uniform. Levi, Mordechai's steward and chief servant, took the cloak, pointed him toward the far end of the garden, then backed away without a word.

Marcus moved forward. There were no lamps lit, and the half-moon had not yet fully penetrated the courtyard, but he knew it well. He had been here several times since first coming to Jerusalem more than a year ago. A dark shadow moved near the fountain. "I'm over here."

In a moment, Marcus reached him. They shook hands firmly. "Your message came as a most pleasant surprise, Mordechai," Marcus said. "You made excellent time getting here from Rome."

"Your letter suggested the situation was of some urgency. I fully concurred in that assessment. I came as quickly as possible. The ship on which I took passage docked at Ptolemais. Under the circumstances, I came directly to Jerusalem. Would you convey my apologies to the governor for not stopping at Caesarea?"

"I will. And what of Miriam?"

Mordechai motioned to a spot near the fountain where two small stone benches had been placed facing each other. They sat down before he answered. "I concurred with your recommendation that it was best that Miriam stay in Rome for now."

Something in the way he said it made Marcus peer more closely at him, but in the soft moonlight it was difficult to read his expression, and he decided not to press him. "And what of the betrothal? Did you speak of that with her?"

"I did." There was a fleeting frown. "I would be less than honest if I told you that she welcomed that news. It caught her quite by surprise. It may take some time for her to become accustomed to the idea."

Marcus fought back his irritation. He had worried that Mordechai might handle the breaking of the news to Miriam with less than the finesse that was needed. Now those fears were only increased. But he finally smiled and nodded his head. "Excellent," Marcus said. "When I return from the wilderness, I shall present a proposal for the dowry and other arrangements."

Mordechai waved that away. "There will be time enough for that later. Tell me what is happening."

So Marcus did. He explained in some detail Simeon's strategy and his successes with the cunning Ya'abin. His report was not given without some admiration. Even Marcus had conceded that it had been a brilliant gambit. "Sextus and I leave in the morning with a full cohort, about six hundred men. It will take some time to get into position—we're heading due south out of Jerusalem and traveling nearly to Hebron before we turn into the wilderness; there, no one will be watching. Hopefully in a week we will return with the news you are looking for. The last threat to you will be eliminated. "

"What threat?"

The question surprised Marcus. "Moshe Ya'abin, of course."

"And what of Simeon the Javelin and the threat he poses?"

Marcus gave him a sharp look. "What of him? Pilate's agreement was that if he delivered Ya'abin to us within one year, he would go free. The year is not up for another month."

"And you concur with that?"

"It's not my decision. The agreement is set."

"And you concur with that?" Mordechai asked again.

Marcus, his irritation growing, started to respond, but the older man held up his hand. "Let me suggest something," he said. "I shall speak first in the interest of Rome. Then I shall speak in the interest of Marcus Didius."

Marcus sat back. This would partially explain the urgency of the message that had come to the Antonia Fortress. Mordechai had been insistent that Marcus come to his home this very night. "Say on," Marcus said with a wave of his hand.

"Simeon's band of Zealots are not anywhere near the largest rebel group in the Galilee. Gehazi of Sepphoris has triple the number of men. Amasa of Gamla at least ten times that number."

"So?"

"Simeon's group is one of the most effective. They are fast, cunning, highly skilled. Even their rival bands admit that none can equal them with the bow. What you have described just now proves my point. Your forces stumbled around for months out there just trying to find Ya'abin. Simeon has run him to ground. I'm not sure any other group could have done it."

"And your point?"

"Are you really sure you want to send them back to the Galilee?"

Marcus was too shrewd not to have already seen where Mordechai was going with this, but he decided to probe a little. "Sextus says that Simeon is through with the Zealots once this is over. He is a follower of Jesus now and wants no part of warfare anymore."

Mordechai laughed scornfully. "And you believe that?"

Marcus said nothing.

"Think about it," Mordechai said. "Instead of catching one vulture in the snare, you could take a second with little more effort. Ya'abin *and* Simeon. You and I have talked before about how to solve the problem of the Zealots in the Galilee. This would be an important start. Do you think Pilate would criticize you for that?"

He didn't wait for an answer. "But let me speak of the second aspect for a moment as well. There are some things I learned about Miriam before I left Rome."

"Oh?"

"Do you remember what Miriam did the two weeks before we sailed for Rome last summer?"

He thought for a moment. "Went with your cousin looking for leather goods in Gaulanitis."

"That's what I thought too." He was speaking carefully now. For all the anger that smoldered within him over Miriam's rebellion, he was not ready to let Marcus—and therefore Pilate—know that she was the one who had caused the Joknean Pass disaster. "But she was doing far more than that. They used that time to listen to Jesus of Nazareth."

One eyebrow lifted. "Oh?" Marcus said.

"Yes. I am sorry to say that Miriam decided to become one of his followers. She is quite adamant about it. She and I had a terrible battle over the whole thing."

Marcus thought he understood. "It matters not to me what she believes, or who she follows. I told you before. I don't put much stock in the gods, no matter whose they are."

"Let me put this bluntly, Marcus," Mordechai said, clearly irritated by that response. "Miriam says that she will not marry you."

"What?"

He held up his hands to soften the blow a little. "This Jesus is a major block between you. Another factor is the thought of leaving her native land. She loves her country. I think it will be important for you to bring her to Caesarea for a time."

"I told you already I was willing to do that." Marcus was annoyed. To all appearances, it looked like Mordechai had really aggravated the situation with Miriam.

"There's something else."

"What?" It had been a long day and it was now past midnight, and Marcus was feeling his temper shorten noticeably.

"It was Simeon's family that fostered all of this. Miriam stayed with them during those two weeks. They're the ones who introduced her to Jesus. They helped convince her he was a great prophet. They were there, encouraging her along."

"I thought you said it was your cousin's doing."

"My wife's cousin's husband, actually," Mordechai snapped. "And he has already been dealt with. But he just provided the transportation. It was Simeon and his family who converted Miriam."

Marcus began to nod. He saw exactly what Mordechai was doing. He would have to be careful. Mordechai could prove to be a formidable enemy. "Are you suggesting that there might be something between Miriam and Simeon?" he asked slowly.

Both hands came up in innocent protest. "I don't know that for sure. But I know she is determined to see him again. She's even talking about living in Capernaum when she returns." He gave Marcus a shrewd look. "I know that when she talks about Simeon, something happens in her eyes that I don't like."

Marcus said nothing. One part of him wanted to brush it aside. Something had happened between Mordechai and Miriam, and now Mordechai was trying to draw Marcus into it. On the other hand, down inside he feared that Mordechai had accurately perceived the situation. If that was so . . .

"I'm telling you, Marcus," Mordechai said, watching him closely. "Miriam has changed. I don't know how he's doing it, but Jesus is turning people into religious fanatics. I've never seen Miriam like this. I couldn't reason with her at all. That's why you can't just dismiss Simeon as no longer being a threat to Rome. All Jesus has to do is utter a single word, and his followers will rise up in arms and march against you. And Simeon will be at the forefront."

Marcus leaned forward, staring at the ground, his mind working rapidly.

"But if we were to eliminate Jesus," Mordechai went on smoothly, "take him completely out of the picture, as we need to do anyway, that would solve your problem as well as eliminate a huge potential headache for Rome. The Council will take the lead on this. Miriam doesn't have to know you had a part in it. Once Jesus is gone—really gone—she will come to her senses."

"But that is only one of my problems, according to you," Marcus said. "Right?"

"You said you'll have a cohort with you to take Ya'abin."

"Yes."

"And Simeon has only about twenty men?"

Marcus nodded again.

Mordechai held out his hands in feigned innocence. "That seems to suggest a solution to all of your problems, don't you think?"

II

IN THE WILDERNESS OF JUDEA
17 JUNE, A.D. 31

Eliab leaped off his horse, tossed the reins to the nearest man, and raced across the camp to where the men sat together in several groups. "We've got them!" he shouted as he reached Moshe Ya'abin.

The Fox of the Desert was on his feet in an instant. "Where?"

"They're camped just inside the canyon where the springs of Ein Gedi come out of the hills, maybe a half a mile from the shore of the Dead Sea."

"How many?"

"Twenty or twenty-one."

Ya'abin's ferret features were ecstatic. "So that's all of them."

Eliab was grinning. "Every one, Moshe. And they're exhausted. They came all the way from Jericho yesterday and didn't make camp until nearly midnight. Their mounts were moving pretty slowly."

"All right," Ya'abin shouted to his men, all of whom were on their feet now. "Mount up." He turned to Eliab. "Who's watching them?"

"Joktan. On the north ridge above their camp." His triumphant grin got even broader. "On his belly in some brush, last I saw him."

There was a curt nod. "You take a dozen men. Come in from above the springs. They'll see you before you can get close, which is what I want. I don't want them trying to escape up the canyon. We'll swing around and come in from the north. We'll drive him south, deeper into the wilderness." He grinned savagely. "Deeper into our country. We'll keep them running all day until they're ready to drop. Then we'll close in."

He jerked his head at Shaul, his third-in-command. "You stay back. Right now, Simeon's thinking that we outnumber him only about two to one. He may decide to stand and fight when he sees he can't outrun us." He clenched a fist and smacked it into his palm. "Let's save our little surprise until then."

"Yes." Shaul turned and ran back to a group of men who remained apart from the others. This was Ya'abin's "little surprise." Thirty-one additional men waited here. It had taken Shaul and two others a full week and most of what was left of his captain's gold, but they had come back from across the Jordan with enough men to raise their total to a few more than eighty. Now the odds would be more like four to one. And the Javelin knew none of that.

"Let's ride," Ya'abin said. "It's time to even the score."

III

THE WILDERNESS, SOUTHWEST OF EIN GEDI

18 JUNE, A.D. 31

Ya'abin reined up, squinting heavily in the blistering sunshine. About two miles ahead of them, a cluster of black dots were visible against the light brown of the hillsides that rose steadily from the western shores of the Dead Sea. He grunted in satisfaction. "He's turning inland. Looking for water, I'm sure." He swung around. "Joktan?"

A little brown man with twisted teeth and a pockmarked face trotted over. "You sure they weren't carrying water bags for their horses?"

The dark head, wrapped with a white cloth, bobbed sharply. "I'm sure. When they saw us up on the ridges, they scattered like chicks before the eagle. If they had bags for the horses, they didn't take time to fill them."

Ya'abin nodded, turning to Eliab. "Let's close it up a little. Let them feel the pressure."

"Yes, Moshe." Ya'abin had twenty-five additional horses, another of Shaul's purchases across the Jordan. They were trading off mounts on a regular basis, giving them some respite from the punishing pace they were keeping. Eliab knew that with the fresher mounts they could push hard and catch the Javelin at any time, but he agreed with Ya'abin. Push the enemy all day, then close in just before sundown when they were too exhausted to give much fight. Eliab felt a great sense of satisfaction. This was a day they had all been waiting for. Revenge would be sweet indeed.

IV

By the ninth hour of the day, with the sun about halfway down from its zenith, the temperature was deadly. It was like riding into the mouth of a furnace. The hot air was starting to rise again, blowing at their backs now, sucking the moisture from the body like a wick in an oil lamp.

Ya'abin reined up and waved at Eliab. As his captain came up to join him, he pointed to the mouth of the canyon about a half mile ahead of them. It was wide and beckoning, seeming to offer an easy route to the highlands further west. "Is that what I think it is?" he asked, his mouth drawn back into a wolfish smile.

"It is," Eliab crowed. "It's a blind canyon."

Ya'abin licked his lips, feeling the cracked dryness. "If I'm remembering right, once they get all the way in the walls are much too steep for horses. Even a man can't climb up without help."

"That's the one." Eliab had trapped a shepherd family in this canyon earlier in the spring and extracted twenty sheep before he would let them go. "We've got them."

The Fox stared at the canyon's mouth, picturing the man who had just ridden into it. "Simeon," he called softly, triumphantly, "only a fool runs when he doesn't know where he's going." Then to Eliab, he barked, "Signal Shaul. Bring everyone up. It's time."

V

Sextus Rubrius moved along the edge of the cliff, stopping at each coil of rope to make sure it was secure and had no tangles in it. Six of the ten coils were secured to large rocks along the edge of the escarpment. The other four were tied to stubby acacia trees that were thick enough to hold the weight of a man. From where Sextus stood, he looked almost straight down to where the canyon ended abruptly against the cliff face.

Satisfied, he stepped back, then walked to Marcus Didius, who waited in the sparse shade of one of the acacia trees, squatting on his haunches, staring moodily at the ground. "Everything is ready. Do you want me to have some men help pull them up?"

Marcus didn't answer, and for a moment Sextus thought he hadn't heard him. Then the tribune straightened slowly and stretched, rubbing at the backs of his calves. He turned, surveying the men who sat or knelt in a large U surrounding the canyon below them. He started counting by twos, then quit after a moment. He already knew what he had. There were close to a hundred that he could see from here. That was his first century. The second and third centuries—two hundred more—were out of sight, lining the ridge tops for another quarter of a mile down both sides of the narrow draw. The remaining three centuries, giving him a fully staffed maniple, were poised more than a mile down the canyon, completely hidden behind a huge rock outcropping. Once Ya'abin passed their position, they would drop down into the canyon and seal the trap.

Sextus wasn't sure why his commanding officer hadn't answered his question, but he decided not to push it. As he started to turn away, Marcus finally spoke. "Suppose we don't drop the ropes," he said in a low voice, not willing to have the other men hear this discussion.

Sextus turned back very slowly. "Pardon, sire?"

"Think about it," Marcus said, musing, not meeting Sextus's gaze. "Suppose we hadn't gotten here in time. Simeon's band is caught by Ya'abin before we can pull them out. That makes one less band of Zealots to worry about in the Galilee. Then we spring the trap and Ya'abin is ours as well."

Sextus watched him steadily, the disbelief heavy in his eyes.

"You don't approve?"

After a long silence, Sextus finally said, "Is this what it means to have a Roman's word of honor?"

Marcus's face flushed with anger. "Simeon is a thief and a rebel. His band has killed Romans in the past and will again. If we don't finish this today, someday we'll have to do it and it will cost us blood, possibly a lot of blood."

Sextus said nothing.

"Come on, Sextus," Marcus said hotly, "you know I'm right about that. Shouldn't we consider the greater good of Rome here?"

For a long moment their eyes held; then Sextus turned and spit over his shoulder. "Are you asking me these questions because you don't dare ask them of yourself?"

Marcus stiffened. "You dare to challenge my authority?" Several heads lifted and turned to watch the two officers.

"You haven't given me a command yet, sire."

Marcus dropped his voice, almost pleading now. He had come to feel great respect for this grizzled old veteran. They had stood back to back at the Joknean Pass and had barely avoided being massacred. "I know what we promised them. But this is too rich an opportunity to pass up. If we don't take Simeon now . . . " He let it trail off. He could hear how weak it sounded.

"Sire," Sextus said, his face like a rock, "Are you ordering me not to drop the ropes when Simeon and his band arrive?"

"In the name of Jupiter, Sextus! Think what this could mean for us."

"Not for *us*," Sextus said softly, as close to contempt as Marcus had ever seen him. "For you! And if that's what you want, you're going to have to give me a direct command." He whirled and started away, then stopped. "They saved our lives, Marcus," he said, calling him by his given name for the first time. "*Your* life. Why? Because Simeon gave his word." He spat again. "You almost make me wish I were a Jew."

Marcus could feel the heat in his face as he watched the broad back of the centurion as he stalked away. Marcus squatted back down, muttering angrily to himself.

It was almost ten minutes later when the runner came dashing up. All up and down the line, men reached for their swords and spears. "Report," Marcus barked.

"Two groups are moving rapidly up the canyon, sire. The first is a smaller group, about twenty men. Their horses are almost ready to drop."

"How far back is the second group? And how many?"

"The signal flags say somewhere around a hundred men. Judging from the dust cloud they're kicking up, they're not making any effort to hide themselves, and they're coming hard. Perhaps ten minutes behind the first ones."

"A hundred?" Marcus looked at Sextus. "I thought you said Ya'abin was down to fifty or fifty-five men."

"That was the last report we had, sire."

Marcus turned, looking over the rim of the canyon. The number wasn't a worry. He had six times that amount with him. Then he felt shame as he realized he was glad. Simeon's twenty wouldn't last for long against those numbers.

He turned as a low rumble sounded faintly. It was horses. He ran forward a few steps, then dropped to his stomach, crawling up behind a rock that secured one of the coils of rope. He peered over the edge down into the canyon. The sound was increasing rapidly, rolling up the narrow canyon as though in a barrel. He felt and heard Sextus drop down beside him, but didn't turn to look at him.

Two minutes later, the first two horsemen thundered around the bend and reined up short. Simeon was in the lead, with the big Galilean right behind him. They were off their horses even before they stopped, running forward toward the cliffs. Marcus saw that the horses' necks and flanks were white with lather. Foam dripped from their mouths. The animals stopped where they were, dropping their heads, bellies heaving.

As a dozen more came into the narrow defile, dismounting on the run, Marcus slid back, lowering his head so he couldn't be seen.

There was a hoarse cry from below. "Where are the ropes?" They could hear frantic footsteps running back and forth. Then someone bellowed out. "Sextus! Marcus!" It was Simeon's voice, filled with desperation.

He didn't want to, but he couldn't stop himself. Marcus turned his head and saw Sextus watching him steadily. His eyes were like two hooks, drawing him inexorably into the pit of Sextus's contempt.

"I have taken the *sacramentum*," Sextus said in a low voice, "the sacred oath taken by all legionnaires to be obedient under any and all circumstances. If I violate that oath, I am subject to death."

He stood up, and there was another hoarse cry from below as Simeon saw him. "*Sextus!*"

His eyes never left Marcus. "The last direct order I received from you was to ready the ropes to throw down to them. I am going to do that unless you give me a direct countermanding order."

He turned and darted to the nearest coil. He picked it up in one hand. His arm came back, poised to throw, then he turned to look at Marcus.

Marcus's mouth opened slightly as he too got slowly to his feet.

"*Sextus!*" It was Simeon. "Throw the ropes! Ya'abin's right behind us!"

For a long second the eyes of the two Roman soldiers locked. Marcus opened his mouth as though to speak, then suddenly clamped it shut again. He looked away. Sextus gave a mighty heave. The rope sailed outward, uncoiling as it dropped. "Get those ropes over the side," he bellowed. He darted to the next coil, snatched it up, and hurled it outward in one fluid movement. "Pull them up. Get those men up here."

VI

Moshe Ya'abin had his sword out as his horse raced around the last bend and into the blind canyon. Simeon was his. He had made that clear to all his men. But as he entered and saw the sheer walls, his ringing battle cry choked off into a strangled shout of dismay. He reined in sharply, gaping at the sight before him. Eliab and Shaul and the rest of his men poured in around him. They too reined up to stare. There were horses everywhere—soaked with sweat, heads down, totally beaten—but there was not a man to be seen.

The old familiar prickly sensation shot through Ya'abin as his head jerked back and forth, eyes searching. There were a few boulders here and there around them, and clumps of brush, but nothing was large enough to hide a man. And there was no one there. His head lifted and he scanned the cliff face. *Nothing!* Twenty-one men had magically vanished. Almost dizzy with heat and thirst and shock, he dismounted, sheathing his sword. He walked forward, still unwilling to believe what his eyes were telling him. There wasn't anything here large enough to hide a dog, let alone a man.

Shaul saw it first. "Look, Moshe!" he cried, pointing upwards.

Turning, Ya'abin saw it instantly. Fresh marks against the rock, deep gouges in places where there were patches of soil on the rock face.

"They had ropes," Shaul said.

Ya'abin swore savagely. They had done it again. But as quickly as the anger flared, his natural cunning kicked in. The canyon walls didn't smooth out enough to get a horse up them for almost half a mile back, but his enemy was on foot now. There was still another two hours before dark. They had gotten away, but they had not escaped.

He swore again, yelling at his men to mount. It wasn't over yet.

It was then that the last of his horsemen came pounding around the bend. They were Ya'abin's rear guard, told to lay back just in case someone escaped the slaughter. "Romans!" the lead man shouted.

"What?" Ya'abin roared. The shock rocked the men around him.

"Coming up the canyon on the run," the other confirmed. "Hundreds of them."

"Moshe Ya'abin!"

Every man whirled, their heads jerking up. Where before there had only been empty cliffs, now a hundred men stood in silhouette along the edge all around them. The sun was behind them, but that only sharpened Ya'abin's view of the plumed helmets, the drawn bows, the rigid spears. He shrank back, his knees suddenly weak.

"Recognize my voice, Ya'abin?"

He couldn't have answered even if all of heaven itself depended on it.

"You last heard it about a year ago. In the Joknean Pass. My name is Tribune Marcus Quadratus Didius." There was a short, mirthless laugh. "Welcome to Hades, my friend. We've been waiting a long time for you."

CHAPTER 26

GOD HATH DEALT GRACIOUSLY WITH ME.

—*Genesis 33:11*

I

THE WILDERNESS, SOUTHWEST OF EIN GEDI

18 JUNE, A.D. 31

Simeon stood off to one side watching quietly as the cohort moved into final formation. Sextus and another centurion were walking up and down the line, barking commands, rebuking soldiers for seeming too lax in guarding their prisoners. Simeon was pleased to see that while some of his men seemed to think that Ya'abin was completely subdued, Sextus did not. Each of the eighty-one prisoners was bound tightly at the wrists, hobbled at the ankles, and stood between two legionnaires. That number still shocked Simeon. The last count they had received from one of the clans of wandering shepherds was around fifty. That had seemed like an acceptable risk if something went wrong. But eighty-one? Four to one. It left Simeon cold to think what might have happened if those ropes hadn't come sailing down.

His eyes turned. Behind the column of prisoners and their guards, a group of mounted soldiers were keeping the herd of horses in a loose circle. It was obvious that several of these legionnaires were not cavalrymen, and it was almost comical to watch them try to manage their own horses while keeping more than a hundred others in check.

This was an unexpected boon for the Romans. Almost one hundred and thirty mounts had been taken. Simeon had asked for a share of those spoils—one additional horse for each of his men. He had received them from Marcus without comment. The rest of the animals would eventually be taken back to Caesarea and added to the governor's stables. At ten to twenty shekels apiece, that many horses represented a significant treasure.

One century of soldiers had already been dispatched to Ya'abin's main camp to see what other stolen booty they could find.

"Sextus?"

Simeon turned to see Marcus standing in his stirrups near the head of the column.

The centurion raised a hand. "Ready, sire."

"Then move them out."

Up and down the line, commands rang out. The lead soldiers, carrying the maniple's standards, moved out at four abreast, the flags flying majestically in the stiff afternoon breeze. Legionnaires prodded the prisoners, and one by one they began shuffling forward. As Ya'abin passed, he shot Simeon a murderous look. "It's not over, Ha'keedohn," he hissed. "We will meet again."

The soldier beside him cuffed him sharply, almost knocking him down, and his head turned back to the front. Simeon just watched him go by, his expression somber. He wasn't sure—Marcus had certainly not said anything to him—but Simeon suspected that Ya'abin and maybe his two chief captains would be executed, and the rest of these men would be sold as slaves, another welcome contribution to Pilate's treasury.

Behind him, Simeon's men were all on their feet watching the column leave. There were no friendly calls of farewell, no wishes for a speedy journey between Roman and Jew. An ironic twist of fate had made them allies this day, but none of that changed the fact that Rome was still the enemy. Nor had the Romans forgotten that these were Zealots and that there was a strong likelihood that some day they would meet again under decidely more antagonistic circumstances.

Sextus Rubrius left his place and came over to Simeon. Seeing that, Yehuda came up as well. "What now for you?" Sextus asked.

Simeon shrugged. "There's a small spring not far from here. We'll stay there for a day, maybe two. Our horses are badly in need of a rest. Then back to Capernaum. I haven't been much help to my father this past year, and there's the matter of three talents I need to help restore."

Sextus nodded. "My best regards to your parents."

"I'll tell them. And what about you? Will you be posted back to the Galilee?"

The leathery face turned toward his tribune, who sat on his horse, face inscrutable as the column moved by him. "It's hard to say," Sextus replied. "The tribune has suggested that I may be kept on here in Jerusalem for a time."

"What happened up there on the cliffs?" Yehuda asked Sextus. "Why weren't the ropes ready when we first came?"

There was a moment's hesitation; then Sextus just shook his head. "Something always seems to go wrong at the last minute."

A movement caught Simeon's eye, and he was surprised to see Marcus riding toward them. The three of them fell silent as he came up. Marcus looked down at Simeon, a thin smile on his face. "This ends it, then," he said.

Simeon nodded gravely. "Our year wasn't up for another few weeks."

There was a short laugh at that. "I'll remind Pilate."

"You could also remind him that he owes me three talents of gold."

Now the laugh was genuine. "You're welcome to come with us and tell him that yourself."

Simeon smiled. "It's not everyday you get invited to the palace of the governor. I'll give it some serious thought." Then after a moment he looked up at Marcus again. "I suppose you can write Mordechai now and tell him it's safe to come home."

"Mordechai is already here. He returned over a week ago."

Simeon noted that Sextus seemed as startled by that news as he was. "Oh?"

"And no, Miriam is not with him."

"I don't remember asking," Simeon said easily.

"Actually, Miriam has decided to stay in Rome until the wedding."

That had the desired effect. Simeon stared at him. "Wedding?"

"Yes, Mordechai and I will be drawing up the final papers when I return to Jerusalem. Miriam and I will be wed in December."

Suddenly Simeon began to laugh, soft and mocking. "Excellent try, Marcus. Very good."

"What is that supposed to mean?"

"I don't know why you've been trying to draw me into a fight since you returned from Rome, but I have to admit, that was a noble effort."

Marcus's eyes were glacial. "You don't believe me?"

Simeon shook his head. "No, Tribune. I don't believe you."

Marcus sneered, realizing what had just happened. Now it was Simeon trying to goad him. "Some things are just too painful to accept, is that it?"

Simeon's own voice went cold. "I don't know Miriam that well, but I know her well enough to know that if you are truly serious, then you are living a fantasy. That is something I would never have guessed about you."

Marcus sat stiffly in the saddle, glaring down at Simeon. "If I were you, Simeon ben David, I would return to your home and settle into the merchant business with your father. Pilate's pardon does not cover any further folly on your part."

"You won't believe this, Marcus Didius, but that is exactly my plan."

Marcus looked at Yehuda. "The same goes for you."

Yehuda smiled his bearish grin. "Oh, I am sure we shall meet again, Tribune. I am sincerely hoping that it shall be under circumstances that are—" A gleam lit his eyes. "How shall I say it? Less restrictive."

Wheeling his horse around, Marcus started away. "Sextus," he barked over his shoulder, "shouldn't you be with the column?"

The centurion jerked to attention and slapped his arm across his chest in salute. "Yes, sire." He glanced once more at Simeon, his expression unreadable, then trotted off to join the moving line of men.

They stood there for several minutes, Simeon and his men, watching them go. When the last of the horses had passed and the rear guard was disappearing in the distance, Yehuda turned to his friend. "Well, you did it."

"No," Simeon answered. "We did it." Suddenly, Simeon felt a great weariness come over him. He turned to look at the men around them.

Yehuda read his thoughts. "There are still twenty-one of us," he said softly.

"Yes," Simeon said, his eyes lingering on Samuel for a moment, thinking about him and Shana possibly being betrothed. "No tears in Beth Neelah this time," he said.

Yehuda was sardonic. "Except for those few moments when the ropes weren't there, the whole thing was almost boring."

Simeon chuckled softly. "Thank you. I know you didn't mean it that way, but I shall take that as a compliment."

II

"So you let him go."

Marcus nodded, a faint smile on his lips.

Mordechai exploded with disgust. "You had him in your grasp, and you let him escape."

"No," Marcus corrected him, "we *helped* him escape."

Mordechai stared at him balefully, shaking his head. "In the name of all reason, what possessed you?"

"I think it's called honor."

The Sadducee muttered something in Aramaic that Marcus didn't understand, but he suspected it was profane. "You didn't have to do anything," Mordechai exclaimed. "Ya'abin would have done it all for you. All you had to do was stand back."

"That's exactly right," Marcus admitted. "Ya'abin would have killed them all for us."

Mordechai's eyes narrowed as he realized that Marcus had shared the details of that day for a reason. He wanted Mordechai to know exactly what had happened. "Why have you told me all this? Why not just tell me that you couldn't make it work?"

"You know the answer to that without asking."

"You think I care about some childish sense of honor? I'm trying to save our country here. The Zealots are the single greatest threat to peace that we have."

"Do you feel nothing? Not even the tiniest hint of gratitude?"

"For what?"

"Simeon has done you a great service. Twice, in fact. Once in

Samaria he drove Ya'abin off. Now, Ya'abin can no longer threaten you or your family."

"I owe him nothing. He has turned my daughter against me."

Marcus didn't want to get into that. "Our agreement has been fulfilled. We kept our word. Now, if he so much as twitches his nose, Simeon will be back in that cell awaiting a cross."

Mordechai only grunted, and Marcus could tell he was still angry that the Romans had not done his work for him. Marcus stood. "I'd better go. We leave at first light to take our prisoners to Caesarea."

Mordechai didn't stir. Marcus watched him for a moment, wondering what was going on behind those shrewd but hooded eyes. Then he decided to see if he couldn't pull the curtain back a little and see for himself. "When Miriam learns that Ya'abin is captured, she's going to want to come home."

"Miriam isn't going to learn anything unless I tell her," Mordechai muttered. There was utter finality in his voice. "She is going to stay in Rome until you and I return for the wedding."

"Are you telling me that I shouldn't write and tell her that it is all over?"

"I'm telling you that she won't learn anything unless I tell her."

What is that supposed to mean? Word of Ya'abin's capture was already on the streets of Jerusalem. Simeon and his family would surely write and tell Miriam that it was safe to come now. Marcus moved back to his chair and sat down. "I've been thinking," he said carefully, his eyes never leaving Mordechai's face. "Maybe it's best if Miriam does come back. If she were here, then I would have a chance to spend some time with her and—" He took a quick breath at Mordechai's look. "I'm not going to marry her against her will," he said.

"She is staying in Rome until we get there," Mordechai said tightly. "And she *will* marry whomever I say that she will marry."

"Is this *your* daughter we're talking about?" Marcus asked incredulously. "Docile, submissive, compliant Miriam?"

Mordechai lashed out at him. "If you lose her, it will be because you didn't have the—" He caught himself. "Because you didn't eliminate Simeon when you had the chance."

For a long moment, Marcus didn't answer. He sat back, forcing himself to look faintly amused, fighting back his own anger. "That's an interesting perspective. It was your daughter who came up with the plan to free Simeon to begin with, remember? Now you're angry because the plan actually worked."

Mordechai's face darkened, but Marcus went on quickly, his tone still musing. "So think this through with me. Simeon delivers Ya'abin into our hands, as was our agreement—an agreement to which you were a party. Then, at your behest, I go back on my word and betray Simeon, let Ya'abin kill him. When word of all this reaches Miriam— as it surely will, those things always get out—she is so grateful to both of us that she falls into my arms and agrees to be my wife. Is that the way you see it unfolding?"

"What I am suggesting—"

"Or," Marcus cut in, his voice suddenly cold, "are you saying that if I lose her, it will be because I'm not willing to be the lackey of Mordechai ben Uzziel, because I won't let him goad me into breaking my word of honor?"

Mordechai realized his mistake and tried to back away. "No, what I am saying is that Miriam is confused right now. She's not sure of her own mind, let alone her own heart. Bringing her back here will only confuse her more."

"If I wanted a slave for a wife, I could have my pick of women, Mordechai."

For a long moment, the two men glared at each other, wills locked. Then Mordechai spoke. Any caution was now thrown to the wind. "It is true that I cannot force her to love you, but if you want her as your willing wife, Tribune, you're going to have to do more than simply show your handsome face and exercise your considerable charms."

Marcus stood slowly. "I know you are one of Jerusalem's most powerful men," he said softly, "but if you think you can use Rome—or any of its officers—as though we were your personal servants, I would advise you to carefully reconsider who and what you are."

He watched the blood drain from the older man's face; then, still seething, he turned and started for the door.

As he reached it, Mordechai called out to him. "Is Rome really your first concern?"

Marcus stopped and turned back. "Would you dare suggest otherwise?"

Mordechai's gaze was as cold as his own. "Then you had better give some careful thought to solving two problems. One is Simeon ben David. The other is Jesus of Nazareth. Do that, and you'll not only win Pilate's praise, but you will solve your problem with Miriam as well."

III

CAPERNAUM
25 JUNE, A.D. 31

Simeon sat on a long, high-backed wooden bench covered with blankets for padding. His mother was on one side of him, her arm slipped through his, sitting right up against him. Leah was on the other. Eleven-year-old Joseph sat at his feet, eyes wide, listening to every word as if it came from Moses himself. David sat on a chair across from them. Ephraim and Rachel were behind him, content to stand for now.

Simeon had not arrived back in Capernaum until after dark. By then Esther and Boaz were in bed, so Rachel had called one of the neighbors to come in and stay with them. Simeon would go see the children first thing in the morning.

He finished speaking, then leaned back, relieved to have the telling of it over. "So that was it. Ya'abin was so enraged after all of our harassment, he rode into that canyon without considering it might be a trap." He looked at his father. "We didn't lose a man, and neither did the Romans."

Pride shone brightly in David's eyes. "You did what you said you would do, Simeon. That's wonderful."

"Didn't you shoot anyone?" Joseph asked.

"Not a single one," Simeon replied, smiling at the boyish disappointment. "Actually, it wasn't very exciting."

"I'm glad," Leah said.

"Well, there won't be any more funerals in Beth Neelah," Ephraim noted.

"That's exactly what I told Yehuda. And that means a lot. Oh, by the way," he said, speaking to his mother again. "Yehuda thinks that Shana and Samuel may be betrothed in the fall."

"Really?" Deborah said, genuinely pleased.

"Wonderful!" Leah cried. "Oh, that is good news, Simeon. If I remember rightly which one Samuel is, he will be good for Shana."

"Samuel is one of the best. He'll make a good husband."

David nodded, but his face was grave. Seeing that, Simeon gave him a questioning look.

"There is some news that is not so good," his father said.

"What?"

"As you know, Ezra and Lilly are here in Capernaum."

"Yes, so?"

"If you're not too tired, I think it would be well if we went and talked with them."

IV

Ezra and Lilly lived in a small house about two streets over from David ben Joseph's main warehouse. The house was owned by David, as was the small shop behind it, which had been converted into a sandalmaker's shop. The furnishings were sparse, but comfortable. It was the first time Simeon had been there.

Watching Simeon look around, Ezra spoke up. "Mordechai got everything when we left Joppa, including our furniture."

"He is not a man who takes opposition lightly," Simeon observed.

"He's a powerful man," Lilly agreed. To Simeon's surprise, there was no bitterness in her tone. "Only a few of our closest friends and associates even dared help us. We decided that if we had to start over again, we would do it where we could be close to Jesus and to people we trusted." Her eyes became a little misty. "We didn't expect to have someone finance a new sandal shop for us."

"I'm delighted to help," David said, a little embarrassed. "Capernaum has needed a good sandalmaker for years. I've said that before, haven't I, Deborah?"

Deborah smiled. "He has. This worked out wonderfully."

"It certainly did for us," Ezra said. "What we thought was going to be a disaster is turning out to be a great blessing."

Simeon had waited patiently through the peripheral information. Now he jumped in with a direct question. "Father said there was bad news. Have you heard from Miriam?"

Both his parents and Ezra and Lilly shook their heads. "That's just it. We haven't heard. Not for months now," Lilly said. "In fact, when I wrote her about the baby I expected her to write back right away."

"The baby?" Simeon said, totally surprised.

Lilly blushed deeply and looked away.

"Yes," Ezra said, beaming. "Remember what Jesus said to her at the baptism, about her being like Sarah and Hannah? Well, it's happened. Lilly is with child."

"That is wonderful news," Simeon said. Then he sobered. "There's something you don't know. The tribune, Marcus Didius, claims that he and Miriam are to be married at the end of the year."

The shock hit them all hard. "No!" Deborah cried.

"I don't believe it," Leah exclaimed.

Lilly paled. "She would never—" she started, then stopped, unable to put it into words.

Suddenly Ezra was nodding. "So that is it."

"What?"

"We have a friend in Jerusalem. He wrote to tell us that Mordechai is back. He's telling people that there is a chance that Miriam may never return from Rome."

For a moment, Simeon was startled, then his face hardened. "Would that be such a great surprise?" he asked. "In that first letter she sent to Mother, Miriam talked as though she found Rome very pleasant and exciting."

Lilly was shocked by his suggestion. "Rome, yes, but marry a Roman tribune? Surely you can't believe that, Simeon."

Simeon turned to Deborah. "What did the letter say, Mother? Didn't Miriam talk in glowing terms about the family of Marcus Didius, about how wealthy and influential they are? And didn't she tell you what a wonderful host Marcus himself had been for her there? Weren't those her words?"

Deborah looked at her son for a long moment. She too was taken aback by the sudden harshness in his voice. "Simeon, I don't think she was—"

"Weren't those her exact words, Mother?"

"Yes, but—"

Again he cut in. "You tell me, Ezra. You know Mordechai as well as any of us. Do you think he would find an alliance between his family and that of one of the most influential families in Rome unacceptable?"

Ezra hesitated, but the answer was clear. "Mordechai is driven by one primary motive," he said softly, "and that is to maintain peace with Rome so that he and the Great Council can stay in power. I'm afraid he would find such a marriage of great importance to his overall goals."

Simeon shot his mother a triumphant look. "I'm not saying Miriam sought for this, but if Mordechai is pulling the strings, maybe she's agreed to accept his will."

"If you believe that, Simeon," Leah said, horrified by what she was hearing, "then you don't know Miriam like I do."

"Then why didn't she come home with Mordechai? Surely she must have heard that we had captured Ya'abin. Why did she stay in Rome?"

"I know what Mordechai is planning," Lilly came in, "but Miriam would never agree to marry this Marcus. Not ever."

Simeon was feeling a little badgered now, knowing he was the only one who felt Miriam might marry Marcus. And yet he couldn't let it go. "Then why would Marcus tell me that he and Miriam were betrothed? At first I thought he was just trying to goad me, to get me angry. But for all his faults, I don't think he would lie about something like that. And he didn't say that he merely *wanted* to marry her. He said that *they were betrothed!* They are to be married when he returns for Saturnalia in December."

David started to speak, but Simeon rode right over him. "It's been months now. Why hasn't Miriam written? Maybe she knows that we won't approve of all this. If she's decided to stay in Rome, it might just be easier not to communicate with us anymore."

"Something is wrong," David said. "I agree with Lilly. I won't believe this of Miriam until I hear it from her directly. And even if she did agree to the marriage, she would still write to us."

Deborah was watching her son sadly. More than any of the rest of them, she could see what was in his heart and understood his sharp disappointment. "We need to write Miriam first thing in the morning. We'll find someone to take the letter to Rome as quickly as possible. We need to hear about her plans from her, not from Marcus or Mordechai."

"It will take almost two months to get a letter there and an answer back," Lilly said.

Simeon nodded. "All the more reason to write immediately. Let's find out what is going on here."

CHAPTER 27

I

ROME
9 JULY, A.D. 31

It was not a knock. It was far more even than a sharp rapping sound. Miriam jumped in surprise as someone pounded on the door with what could only have been a closed fist. She looked at Livia, then got up quickly and moved across the room.

When she opened the door, she fell back, her mouth dropping open. Behind her, Miriam heard Livia gasp. Livia's brother, Drusus, stood before them, his wrists bound, a grim-faced Roman soldier on each side of him.

"Drusus?" Even as Miriam cried out his name, Livia was to her side. She started to push past Miriam, but both soldiers jerked their spears downward, crossing them in front of the boy and blocking her way.

Drusus had his head up, trying to look defiant, but Miriam saw that his face was as pale as a slab of marble and his eyes were deeply frightened. As all of this registered in her mind, another man stepped around from behind Drusus and his captors. He was the chief of Miriam's daily "escorts." He carried a paper in each hand. Miriam felt suddenly sick as she recognized one of them. It was the letter she had written just the night before to David and Deborah in Capernaum.

The man, who was probably in his late forties and who had a kind face, had always been friendly enough to her, almost amiable, but he had also never wavered one iota in his duty. He tried not to be too intrusive whenever she or Livia or Drusus went out, but "escort" was an apt description. He or one of his associates was always within eye-sight. She had once tried to learn his name, but he had just smiled and shook his head. This was not to become personal.

Now his face was grave, his eyes tinged with regret, but they were also filled with quiet determination. "Miriam, daughter of Mordechai ben Uzziel."

"Yes?" She was half-holding her breath.

He motioned with his head to the soldier nearest him. The man took out his dagger and sliced through the ropes that held Drusus. Then both soldiers turned and without a word started for the stairs, their duty finished. Drusus stumbled forward into Livia's arms.

The escort waved the letter at her. "This lad was caught trying to arrange for delivery of a letter to the province of Judea." With a deliberate flourish, the man tore the paper in half, repeated the action, then let it flutter to the floor. "As I have warned you before, this is in violation of the conditions under which you stay here in Rome."

"Conditions imposed by my father, not by Roman law," she answered, her voice much calmer than what she was feeling inside.

He ignored her. "It is clear that the letter was written by you and that the boy was only doing your bidding. If that were not so, he would be on his way to the slave markets as we speak."

Out of the corner of her eye, Miriam saw Livia's hand fly to her mouth.

He held up the second paper and shook it gently in her face. "As it is, I now hold the paper indicating that this boy is a freeman. I shall keep it in my possession until your father gives me further instructions." Now he looked directly at Drusus. "If you are out with Miriam or your sister, there will be no trouble. If we find you alone again in the streets, your freedom will be automatically revoked and you will not see either of these two again."

"Why?" Miriam cried. "He has nothing to do with this."

The escort continued to stare at Drusus. "Do you understand me, young man?"

Drusus, almost trembling, nodded numbly.

The man turned back to Miriam. "As for you, if you try to smuggle any other letters out of Rome, I will have no choice but to keep all three of you confined to the house until your father returns. That would be tragic for three so young, but make no mistake, this is not an idle threat."

Miriam stepped back, feeling as if she couldn't get her breath.

"Do *you* understand me?" he asked quietly.

"Yes," she murmured. She shut the door as he turned away. When she heard his footsteps going down the stairs, she turned to Drusus, her face stricken. "I'm sorry, Drusus." She went to Livia and threw her arms around her. "I am so sorry."

II

IN THE COUNTRYSIDE NEAR ROME
15 JULY, A.D. 31

The villa of Antonius Marcus Didius was seated on a low rise about two miles east of the city. Though it was one of the largest

Miriam had seen, like most other villas this was generally rectangular and quite drab in shape. Actually, in architectural terms, it was no more than two huge boxes butted up against each other. There were no windows on the outside walls, which gave it the look of a fortress as one approached it. Miriam found this a strange custom. She could understand the desire to close off the noise and smells of the city streets, and windows seemed superfluous when the only view was of another blank, drab wall. But out here in the country the views were pleasant and the breezes off the sea delightful, especially in the heat of the summer. It was strange that the Romans did not take advantage of both of these features of their environment.

The other odd thing about Roman architecture was that usually there was only one outside door that led into the entire villa. There might be other rooms around the outside of the building, such as the summer kitchen or storage rooms, but the outside doors to these didn't allow entry into the house itself. The main door led directly into the *atrium*, a large open area that formed the center of the first block of the villa. In the center of the second block, there was a garden court that was open to the sky. Unlike some of the smaller estates Miriam had visited, this garden court had a beautiful fountain in the center of it, fed by a spring from a nearby hillside. The courtyard provided the only natural light within the villa.

All of the rooms in the villa—bedrooms, eating rooms, rooms for daily activities—opened either onto the atrium or the courtyard. Here there were windows and doors, but they all faced the interior of the house.

As Miriam, Livia, and Drusus reached the main door of the villa, Miriam glanced over her shoulder. Cain and Abel had stopped beneath the shade of a trellis a short distance away. She smiled to herself. Their two escorts refused to give their names, obviously warned about developing any personal relationship with their wards, so Miriam had started calling them after the two famous sons of Adam and Eve. The larger one, a man who was mostly bald and who shaved his head to complete the effect, always took his responsibility with grim seriousness. He was Cain. A little harsh, Miriam thought, but it did seem to fit. The younger one, who would occasionally smile and nod when they came out of the apartment for the day, she called Abel.

Once the escorts knew the destination, they had visibly relaxed. Earlier, as it became obvious that the three of them were leaving the city, the two men had closed in within a few paces, poised to run them down should they try to escape. But once they realized the Didius estate was their intended goal, they fell back again. Since the Didius family were the ones who employed them, along with the four others who took turns guarding the apartment at night, they rightly assumed there was no need to worry.

Miriam lifted the brass knocker and rapped it sharply. Livia touched her arm. "We'll wait over there in the shade. I think it will be better that way."

Miriam nodded. Livia was probably right. As they moved away, one of the servants opened the door. There was an immediate smile of welcome when the girl saw who it was. "Is Mistress Cornelia at home?" Miriam asked.

"She is," the girl replied. "Let me take you into the courtyard, and then I'll let her know you are here."

"I know the way," Miriam said. The girl half bowed and backed away.

Miriam moved through the atrium and into the garden court. She stopped by the fountain, listening to the soft trickle of the water and drawing in the pleasant smells of mint, thyme, caraway, marjoram, and basil. In one corner of the court Marcus's mother kept a small herb garden, her personal hobby.

She turned at the sound of footsteps. Cornelia Alberatus Didius appeared from one of the rooms and came forward with a welcoming smile. "Good morning, Miriam. This is a pleasant surprise."

"Good morning, Cornelia. I'm sorry to come without announcement."

She took Miriam's hands, genuinely pleased. "You need no announcement, my dear. You are welcome in our home any time."

"Thank you. I wonder if you might have some time I could speak with you this morning."

"But of course." Cornelia half turned. "Let me tell the servants that we will be having company for dinner. You will stay?"

Miriam shook her head slowly. "Thank you very much, Cornelia, but I cannot today. Perhaps another time."

Cornelia's eyes showed her disappointment, but she immediately accepted Miriam's answer. Cornelia Didius, the *matrona* of the Didius household, was slightly plump, with long brown hair and the first sign of wrinkles around her eyes. Miriam guessed that she was nearing forty, which meant she had lived longer than many Roman women. Often girls in Roman society were married as soon as they reached puberty and could be a mother as early as twelve or thirteen years of age. Grandmothers who were thirty years old were common in Rome. Even for the upper classes, a woman's life was not one of gentle leisure, and many women never reached so called "middle-age." Cornelia was warm in spirit, generous in praise, and quick of wit—traits she had given to her eldest son. She represented all that was noble and good in Roman womanhood. She had a deep sense of *pietas*, or duty, to her family, and not only was accepting of her role, but was completely happy in fulfilling it.

She motioned to a stone bench near the fountain. "Come, let's sit down."

As they did so, Miriam looked into the woman's eyes and saw the steadiness and strength there. Surprisingly, that gave her a sinking feeling. Miriam remembered very clearly one of Marcus's stories about examples of Roman women and their commitment to duty. One of the noblemen of Rome had somehow offended the emperor. In such cases, ıt was customary for the man to be invited to commit suicide and thus spare his family the embarrassment of a public trial and execution. When the man faltered in his courage to do so, his wife took his sword from the scabbard and stabbed herself. Then, bleeding profusely, she handed the bloody sword back to her husband. "See," she told him, "it does not hurt. Now do your duty."

What Miriam was about to do could easily conflict directly with Cornelia's sense of *pietas*. If so, there was no question in Miriam's mind that duty would come before any emotional attachment Cornelia might feel toward her, strong as that might be.

"You are troubled," Cornelia said, reaching out and laying a hand on Miriam's. "It saddens me to see pain in your eyes. Are your needs not being met adequately by Arcadius?"

"No, no," Miriam said hastily, "Arcadius is wonderful. He is a most attentive servant and often runs to get us something before the request has even formed on our lips."

Cornelia relaxed a little. "That is why I told Antonius that we should send Arcadius to serve you. He is one of the best slaves in our household."

Miriam drew in a quick breath. "No, we have nothing but praise for his service. But I do have a matter that has created some difficulty for me. I have come to see if I might impose upon your good will for help."

"Tell me, and I shall speak of it to Antonius tonight. He will see that it is dealt with in whatever manner is required."

"No!" Miriam blurted. She forced a quick smile. "No," she said, more calmly now. "This is not a matter that your husband should be troubled with. It is a personal matter between my father and me."

"But your father has returned to Judea."

"Yes." Miriam looked away. On the walk out here from the city, Miriam had thought carefully about how much she should tell this woman. Cornelia and Miriam had grown close during this time—now almost a year—that Miriam had been in Rome. She decided that her only hope lay in complete honesty.

And so she began. She started with the day in Samaria, well over a year earlier, when Simeon and Yehuda strode into their camp and saved her from the viciousness of Moshe Ya'abin. She told Cornelia in great detail of the ambush at the Joknean Pass, emphasizing how Simeon's intervention had saved many Roman lives, including that of her own son's.

"Marcus never said anything about that," Cornelia said when Miriam paused for a moment. "I saw the scar on his arm. He just shrugged it off when I asked him about it. Is that when that happened?"

"No, I think that happened earlier. A minor skirmish is how Marcus described it to me." Miriam didn't see any relevance in going that far back. She continued, explaining about Moshe Ya'abin's escape and the danger that had created for her and her father. Cornelia nodded. This part she did know, and Miriam could see the anger in her eyes at such an outrage.

It took another ten minutes to explain what had taken place between Miriam and her father. She spent almost half of that time telling her about Jesus. She talked briefly about his miracles, told her about the woman taken in adultery, summarized some of his teachings. To her surprise, Cornelia was fascinated by this and asked several questions.

"If I tell you something," Cornelia said, interrupting her narrative, "you must promise not to speak of it when Antonius is present."

Surprised, Miriam nodded. This was good. A shared secret might be what was needed.

"Antonius knows of this, but he has little patience with it and gets irritated if I speak to him about it."

"About what?"

"I too have found a religion that has touched me in a special way."

"Really?" Miriam said, completely caught off guard.

"Yes, it is the worship of Mithras. It is just now becoming popular in the city."

"Isn't Mithras a Persian God?"

"Yes, he is the Sun King, or the Invincible Sun. According to the priests of Mithras, the Sun King fought a heroic struggle with a mighty bull. He finally killed the bull, whose blood flowed over the earth and fertilized it, bringing forth the plants that allowed men to live. So it is to Mithras that mankind is indebted for a multitude of blessings."

She looked around, then lowered her voice. "It is part of the worship of Mithras to believe that he is the only true god, that all other gods are but the creation of men's minds."

"But—" Miriam could hardly believe what she was hearing. She had thought her people were the only ones who held to a belief in one true god.

"Some of the teachings are secret and cannot be revealed except to those in the Mithraic fellowship, but they include the need for purity and righteousness, a belief that good shall triumph over evil, and that we must strive to live honorable and upright lives, serving the Sun King by how we live."

"Jesus also says that we serve him by following him, by accepting his teachings, by becoming like him."

"Then I understand the power he has upon you, Miriam. I always felt uncomfortable with the gods before—there are so many and they seem so different from each other. To think that there might be just one God is a remarkable concept to me, but I find myself growing more comfortable with it every day."

Miriam just stared at her. This had certainly not been part of the conversation she had rehearsed in her mind.

"I'm sorry," Cornelia said. "Go on. You say you father forbids you to follow after this Jesus?"

"Yes. He wants to destroy him because he thinks Jesus will stir up a rebellion against Rome."

Cornelia's eyes narrowed, and Miriam instantly saw her mistake. "Jesus isn't fostering rebellion," she said quickly. "Actually Jesus preaches that we change our hearts, not that we overthrow governments. He asks that we love our enemies and forgive those who wrong us."

Cornelia relaxed again. Her concern was not a surprise. Her son was in Judea. Any talk of rebellion there would understandably cause her anxiety.

Miriam moved on to recent events. She described the clash between her father when she told him about her baptism, and of his putting her under virtual house arrest.

Cornelia's eyes widened at that. "You are guarded each time you go out?"

"Yes. If you walk out with me when I leave, you shall see that there are two of them with me today."

"That is horrible. Antonius told me that Mordechai had asked that we see that you were safe and cared for, but not guarded, not restricted."

"In one sense," Miriam said glumly, "that's true. We can go anywhere within the city we wish, but we are always watched. Also, they have stopped all letters from coming in, and I can send no letters out."

The angry look on the older woman's face gave her heart. She went on, knowing she was coming to the hardest part. "Did Marcus tell you that he and I are betrothed?"

There was a brilliant smile. "Yes. We are so happy." Then as she saw Miriam's face, the smile instantly disappeared again. "Is that not true?"

"Oh, it's true all right. It's just that neither my father nor Marcus told me about it. Not until just before my father left to return to Judea."

Cornelia was shocked deeply. "No! You didn't know before then?"

Miriam shook her head. "Father said that the arrangements are all made, that Marcus and he will return in time for Saturnalia."

"But Marcus told us of his plans before he left to return to Judea the first time. He wanted to know how we felt." There was a momentary smile. "We were thrilled, of course. Even Antonius, who rarely shows much of what he is feeling, was pleased. He likes you, Miriam, as do I."

"Your family has been wonderful to me, Cornelia. And Marcus and I—" She hesitated, choosing her words with care. "We have become very close. I find him to be a man that I admire and respect greatly."

"But not love?"

Miriam didn't know of any way to soften her answer. "No. Especially now that I have found Jesus. I want to find someone with whom I can share my deepest feelings, my deepest convictions. Marcus wouldn't stop me from being a follower of Jesus. He told me I can believe whatever I want, but—"

There was a sudden wistfulness in Cornelia's eyes. "I understand. Antonius does not forbid me from participating with the Mithraites, but he finds the whole thing to be somewhat ridiculous." She looked away. "So I never speak with him about it."

Miriam felt a great wave of love for this good woman. "I would have considered it a great blessing to have you as my mother-in-law. I truly would."

"And I was so pleased when Marcus told us of his plans. He told me that it was not yet finalized, that he needed to speak with you of the details."

"I am sure that the decision not to tell me was my father's idea and not your son's."

Cornelia didn't answer immediatly, obviously deep in thought. Miriam was not sure what else to say about the betrothal. It was time to make her request.

But before she could speak, Cornelia's head came up. "You spoke of needing my help," she said slowly. "Miriam, in spite of my deep affection for you I cannot overturn anything my husband has set in place—the arrangements with Arcadius or the escorts or—"

"I know," Miriam answered quickly, "and I would not ask you to do so. I am coming to understand the depths of a woman's sense of duty to her family in your culture. It is something I respect and admire. I have not come to ask you to intervene in my behalf with Antonius in any way."

There was both relief and a touch of skepticism in Cornelia's eyes.

Miriam held her breath, knowing the critical moment had arrived. "I have accepted the loss of freedom. I have accepted the loss of privacy. But I have friends and family in Judea who do not know if I am even still alive. I have a cousin with whom I am very close. She and her husband were thrown out of their home by my father because they helped me warn Simeon of the trap. I cannot learn if all is well with her nor can I let her know all is well with me. I wrote a letter last week and tried to find someone to send it off for me. The guards learned of it and tore it up. They have threatened to restrict us to our apartment if I make any further attempts to write to anyone."

Cornelia's eyes darkened slightly. "That is not right."

Miriam reached into the folds of her dress and withdrew a piece of papyrus. "I have written another letter to my cousin Lilly to replace the one that was taken."

Cornelia was watching her closely, her eyes difficult to read.

"I know there are men in the city who for a fee will see that mail is taken to Ostia and put on the right ship. If you could have one of your servants do that for me, I would be deeply grateful."

For almost a full minute, Cornelia didn't answer. Finally, she straightened a little. "In this letter, have you asked your cousin to help you escape?"

Miriam shook her head, glad that she had foreseen this possible question. "I have not. I have not asked for any intervention, for I know that would compromise your honor and obligations to Antonius. I have done nothing more than explain my circumstances so they will understand why there has not and will not be any word from me until my father and Marcus return to Rome. I think I owe them that much."

"You give me your word on that?"

"I do." There was a momentary twinge of guilt at that, but it was true. Knowing Ezra and the family of David ben Joseph, she didn't think she specifically had to ask for help. Once they learned of her situation, she was confident they would take some kind of action. "And I also promise you that this will be the only letter I send out."

Cornelia's shoulders slumped a little as she considered the implications of the request. Then a faint smile softened the corners of her mouth. "I am tempted to say that I will do this if you would reconsider marrying my son."

Miriam smiled sadly. "And I am tempted to reconsider marrying your son so that I would finally have a mother I could love after being without one for all these years."

Making up her mind, Cornelia reached out and took the papyrus from between Miriam's fingers. She slid it quickly out of sight, then stood up. Miriam stood as well and put her arms around her. "Thank you, Cornelia," she whispered. "Thank you so much."

III

After letting Miriam out, Cornelia stood at the doorway and watched as Livia and her brother rejoined Miriam and started toward the road that led to Rome. Her eyes narrowed slightly as she saw the two men beneath the trellis who fell in behind them.

She went back inside the house, returning to the stone bench beside the fountain. She took out the letter and laid it on her lap, but made no effort to open it. For a long time she sat there, nearly motionless, her expression troubled. Finally, after almost ten minutes, she stood again. "Binicia!"

In a moment the young girl who had opened the door for Miriam came into the garden court. "Yes?"

She hesitated for a moment; then she held out the letter. "Would you take this around to the summer kitchen and see that it is put into the fire?"

The girl gave her a look of surprise, but immediately she bowed slightly. "Yes, m'lady." She started away.

"Binicia?"

"Yes, m'lady?"

"Be certain that it is totally consumed and that there are not even any ashes left."

The girl bowed again. "Yes, m'lady."

CHAPTER NOTES

The story of the woman who stabbed herself in order to bolster her husband's courage actually happened. However, it occurred during the reign of Claudius, about A.D. 42, eleven years after the time depicted in the novel (see Shelton, 294).

With the significant expansion of the Roman Empire around the time of Christ, huge numbers of Oriental, or Eastern, peoples were brought in as slaves. They brought with them various Eastern religions which, because of their mystical and exotic nature, gained increasing popularity among the Romans. Worship of the goddess Isis from Egypt and the god Mithras from Persia became especially popular and spread quickly in the capital. The worship of Mithras helped prepare the way for the eventual spread of Christianity because of the religion's belief in one God and the stark contrast between the forces of good and evil (see Grimal, 113–15).

Saturnalia is the Roman festival honoring Saturn, god of agriculture and the harvest. The festival, held in late December in the Roman calendar, was a time of unrestrained merriment and revelry. The festival often degenerated into wild orgies and riotous celebration. When Christianity became widely established in the Roman empire, it was decided to celebrate the birth of Christ in connection with Saturnalia, probably because it would receive wider acceptance that way. This was first done in A.D. 336. In northern Europe, similar festivals were held. The people prepared special foods, decorated their houses with greenery, and joined in singing and the giving of gifts. These practices gradually became part of the traditions of Christmas (*World Book*, 3:528).

CHAPTER 28

FREEDOM SUPPRESSED AND AGAIN REGAINED BITES WITH DEEPER
FANGS THAN FREEDOM NEVER ENDANGERED.

—*Marcus Tullius Cicero*, De Officiis, *bk. 2*

I

ROME
26 SEPTEMBER, A.D. 31

The skies over Rome were mostly cloudy and threatened rain, though it would probably not come until later in the day. A stiff breeze was blowing from the northwest. Flowing over the Alps some three hundred miles to the north, the wind had dropped in temperature sharply from the day before, and it was unseasonably cold. For the first time since March, Miriam and Livia exchanged light cotton *tunica interiors*, or undergarments, for heavier ones, and wore shawls over the *stola*, or outer dress, that was the standard attire for Roman women. Drusus had at first scoffed at this sign of feminine weakness, but once they stepped outside, Livia's younger brother quickly changed his mind and returned to the apartment to exchange his summer tunic for a woolen one. Both Livia and Miriam repressed a smile when he came out with cotton leggings as well.

They had briefly debated about staying indoors for the day, but that idea was quickly dismissed. Though there would surely be several more weeks of pleasant weather, the drop in temperature was the first reminder that winter was approaching. Miriam knew that once it arrived, their time out of doors would be greatly reduced, and she decided not to let this temporary change deter her. Fortunately, Livia and Drusus felt the same way.

With Cain and Abel trailing at a discreet distance, the three of them walked past the *Forum Romanum* and went to the Imperial Forum built by Julius Caesar. It was not only smaller in area and usually less crowded than the Roman Forum, but it also contained the Temple to Venus Genetrix, the goddess whom Caesar credited for his numerous successes in battle and politics. The temple had a columned portico that was open to the sun on the south side and provided considerable protection from the wind. That is where they had come on this blustery morning.

For the past two months, Miriam had been tutoring Livia and Drusus in Aramaic. Having lived with Miriam and her father in Jerusalem for five years, Livia could speak Miriam's native language quite well, but she had not learned to read or write much of it at all. As a lifelong slave in various Roman households, Drusus spoke only Latin and the Greek of his childhood. He could neither read nor write in any language. *Librarii*, or scribes, were the only slaves in a household allowed to be literate. If Drusus were to find any meaningful employment once they returned to Miriam's homeland, he would need to read, write, and speak Aramaic. So each day, the three friends used some of their time out of the apartment to pursue this study. They brought their writing slates and pieces of soapstone and spent about three hours together under Miriam's tutelage.

Miriam felt a momentary twinge of guilt as she looked up and let her eyes find their two guards. Though she could feel a little of the chill through her clothing, it was not unpleasant here beside the temple. But the escorts had taken up their station across the street about twenty-five or so paces away. They always stayed far enough back to avoid being intrusive, but close enough so they could quickly close the gap should their charges try to slip away. They stood where there was little protection from the wind, and she could see that both of them were hugging themselves and stamping their feet up and down to keep warm. One part of her wanted to take satisfaction in their discomfort, but another part of her knew that they were only doing what they were required to do. The real fault lay with her father.

"Would you like to stop for a while, Miriam?"

Miriam turned to Livia. She was watching her curiously, and Miriam realized that she was no longer thinking about Aramaic. Brother and sister sat with their slates on their laps waiting for further direction from her.

She sighed. "Sorry, I was just watching our two shepherds and wondering if they are getting cold."

"I hope so," Drusus snapped. "I hope their feet freeze and fall off."

"Drusus!" Livia gave him a chiding look.

"Well, I do. Maybe then they would leave us alone."

"They're just doing what they were hired to do," Miriam said, a little surprised that she felt like she had to defend them.

He snorted in disgust, then stood up abruptly. "It's too cold to study," he said. He rubbed out the lettering on his slate with his sleeve and started away. "I'm going to do some drawings," he said, not asking how the others felt about him leaving them. Glowering at the two men who had come to full alert when he stood, he moved across the street and started sketching the columned portico.

"I'm sorry," Livia said. "He's getting so petulant lately. But it's because he is restless. It's not good for an eighteen year old to be so restricted in his activities and to have nothing but the company of two women day after day."

Miriam sighed. "I know." She watched him lift his eyes and study the lines of the building, then start sketching with bold, even strokes. "He loves his drawing, doesn't he."

Livia nodded, pride evident in her eyes. Drusus had been a slave in the household of a wealthy Roman who built and rented out residential property in the city. One of the other slaves in the household had been a master builder and had taken Drusus under his wing and had begun to teach him some principles of design and construction. Drusus was fascinated and used every opportunity to learn how those principles were applied in real life.

"Perhaps when we return to the Galilee we can find him an apprenticeship in the building trades."

Livia gave her a quizzical look. "You don't even think about returning to Jerusalem any more, do you?"

Miriam looked away. "Return to what? My father? I still love him, Livia, but we both know that the only way he will ever accept me is if I am willing to marry Marcus and turn my back on Jesus."

"And what is he going to say when you move to Capernaum? I assume that's what you're thinking."

"I don't see any other options." A forlorn note crept into her voice. "We'll have to make a new life there. Father has taken all my funds. I'm not sure how we'll do it, to be honest. I have never worked a day in my life. We have no way to earn our bread. I'm sure David and Deborah will invite us to stay with them for a time, but that can't be a permanent solution. But I guess if that is what we have to face, I would rather do that in Capernaum than anywhere else."

Livia said nothing. One of the things that had been much on her mind of late was what Mordechai would do if Miriam refused to surrender to his will. She didn't picture him simply standing by while his daughter went her own way. That thought worried her, though she never expressed it to Miriam. "You can write and keep books," she finally said. "There is always a place for someone with those skills."

"If they are not a woman!" Miriam shot right back. The despair welled up like a surge of tide inside her. "Oh, Livia, no one is going to come. Ezra has no money, especially not now that Father has ruined his business. Simeon may still be in the wilderness of Judea hunting Ya'abin. David has a business to run. He can't just drop everything and come to Rome."

"We can't lose hope, Miriam. The Lord has heard our prayers before, he won't forsake us now."

"I know," she said, "but what if he doesn't want us to return? What if, for some reason, we are supposed to stay here in Rome?"

"For what purpose?" Livia said in surprise. That possibility had never once occurred to her.

Miriam had no answer. "What if Cornelia changed her mind?" she asked instead. "What if she never sent the letter?"

"It's been just ten weeks, Miriam. At the very least it takes three weeks for a letter to go from here to Judea. It would take at least another week for it to make its way to Capernaum. That's under the best of conditions. Bad weather can delay ships, sometimes for weeks on end. And you don't just walk up and find someone who will take a letter where you need it to go. It could have taken as much as two months before the letter even reached them. We can't give up hope."

Miriam listened, and let her natural resilience kick in. She hated it when she started into one of her self-pity phases. "I'm not giving up hope, Livia, but I don't think we can assume someone is coming. We have to make some alternate plans."

Livia's eyes widened slightly.

"Marcus and Father will be coming back here in less than three months. Once that happens, any chance we have to escape will be gone."

"Escape?"

Miriam lowered her voice a little, even though no one was close enough to overhear. "I've been carefully saving money from the allowance we receive each month."

"Really?"

"Well, if no one is coming, then we have to make some plans of our own. I have about sixty sesterces now. That's enough for our passage. But we need more than just sailing money. We'll need food and warm clothing."

Livia began to nod slowly. "I could hold out some of the money they give me to buy our food at the market."

"Good," Miriam said, pleased that Livia wasn't going to balk at the idea. "I don't think we dare sail from Ostia. That is the first place they will look for us. We'll have to go by land to another port, maybe Puteoli, to the south of here. That will take additional funds. I figure we need at least twenty or thirty more sesterces."

"And how do you plan to slip away from our two watchdogs?" Livia asked, glancing in their direction.

"I don't know. Maybe lure them into the apartment and tie them up."

Livia hooted.

"Well," Miriam said, miffed at that reaction. "There are three of us and only two of them. And Drusus is strong."

"I could wait behind the door and then hit Cain over the head with the big black skillet we have."

Miriam giggled at that image. "He's totally bald. With no hair to cushion it, it could ruin the skillet."

Livia chortled aloud.

"And we could stuff Abel into one of the chests in my bedroom and have you sit on it."

"Me!" Livia cried. "You weigh as much as I do."

"We could both sit on it," Miriam said, sniggering. "That would give us time to think about what to do with him after that."

They enjoyed the moment together, feeling an immense sense of relief to even be talking about alternatives. But both gradually sobered again as the difficulty of the challenge they faced settled in upon them.

"Drusus is my biggest concern," Miriam said. "And you too, Livia."

"Why? We can hold our own, and heaven knows that Drusus is ready to do something."

"Because if we fail, if we are caught, you know what they will do to Drusus. He'll be a slave again. And it could happen to you as well."

Livia didn't answer for several moments. Then she spoke slowly. "We'll not do anything without asking for God's help first. And then we'll put our trust in him."

"Yes," Miriam affirmed. "If no one else will help us, there is always the Lord."

II

It was well into the second watch of the night. Miriam was partially reclined on a padded *lectus*, or high-backed couch, reading one of the selections from the library of Cornelia Didius, which she had sent over for Miriam to enjoy. When Livia and Drusus had bid her goodnight and had gone to their rooms more than an hour earlier, Miriam had told them she wasn't tired and would read until she got sleepy. So far that had not happened. There was only one oil lamp burning just behind her, leaving the sitting room of the apartment filled with a soft, muted light.

Suddenly her head jerked around. There had been a whisper of sound from the direction of her bedroom, almost as if someone had spoken her name. She sat up, chills coursing up and down her back, staring at the door that led into the room where she slept. The door was partially ajar, but it was dark behind it and she could see nothing. She turned her head and looked at the doors of the other two bedrooms, but both of them were closed. No. It had come from the direction of her room. She was sure of that.

She listened intently for several seconds, then chided herself for her reaction. Every house creaked and groaned from time to time, especially at night as the air outside began to cool. Then she remembered something else and felt really foolish. When they had returned from their time in the city this afternoon, her bedroom had seemed stuffy and close, even though the day was unseasonably cold. So she had hooked the door to her balcony open to get some air and then had forgotten about it.

The *insula* or apartment complex in which they lived was three stories high. Because it was one of the more luxurious of the complexes, each bedroom had a small, private balcony. It was barely large enough for one person to stand on, but each balcony opened onto a narrow alley below. The view wasn't much—the windowless back of one of the numerous government buildings in Rome—but it was better than being totally enclosed. The sound she was hearing was probably nothing more than the shutters rattling softly in a breeze.

Deliberately taking in a deep breath to calm herself, she picked up the scroll again and started to read.

"*Miriam.*"

Again, it was only the barest of whispers, as if a voice from *Sheol*, the world of spirits, was calling to her from across a great void. But it was unmistakable. She flung the scroll aside and leaped to her feet. Crouching down, her eyes never leaving the door to her bedroom, she edged along the wall. For a moment she considered going for help, but their night guards were three floors down, stationed outside the entrance to the building. Near the small fireplace in the corner—which they hadn't used since the previous winter—there was an iron poker and a set of tongs. There was the scrape of a foot on tile and she froze. Every nerve in her body suddenly was tingling. Her mouth went instantly dry, and her heart raced like a runaway chariot. The door to her bedroom was slowly opening. In the dark was the shadow of a man.

Miriam gave a low cry and flung herself toward the fireplace. Her knee caught the corner of a table and she yelped with pain, but when she came up again, she had the poker in her hand.

"Miriam! It's all right. It's me."

She gasped, eyes flying wide open as Simeon stepped into the room. For several seconds she stood there gaping, heart pounding like a great hammer inside her chest, her knees nearly buckling as the relief hit her like a torrent. "Simeon?" She took a step forward, her mind still not believing what her eyes were telling it.

"I'm sorry I frightened you. I thought you were in your bedroom asleep. I called out a couple of times."

"But how—" She glanced at the open door, still dazed and bewildered.

"I have a rope. I came down from the roof." He grinned ruefully at her. "If you put down that poker, maybe we can talk."

Only then did Miriam realize that she still held the iron weapon tightly in her grip. She slowly lowered it to her side. Her mouth opened, but no words came out.

"Where is Livia?"

Miriam shook off the shock. "Asleep." She gestured with her free hand.

He started back toward the open door to her room. "Let's talk in here," he whispered. "I don't dare stay very long. Those guards of yours are very thorough."

She nodded, still half numb. She put the poker back in its holder, went to the couch and picked up the lamp, then followed him inside the bedroom. He shut the door softly behind her.

She set the lamp on her dressing table, then turned. "I can't believe it. You're here."

He smiled, but his eyes were somewhat hooded. "Yes. *We're* here. We've been here two days now."

"We?"

"Ezra's with me."

She let out a long breath and half-closed her eyes. "I knew you would come."

"We're here to help you, Miriam, but I have to ask you some questions first."

"Two days?" It was like her mind was moving at half-speed. The joy in her was pushing every other thought aside.

"Yes. We've been watching you, trying to find out what is going on. Ezra tried to get past the guards this afternoon. He told them he was your cousin, but like I say, your two watchdogs are pretty thorough." He shook his head. "Haven't you heard? Ya'abin is dead."

"Dead?"

"Yes. We finally captured him and his band about three months ago. Pilate sold most of them off into slavery, but he had Ya'abin and three or four of his chief lieutenants executed almost immediately. I learned that just before we left."

"And you and Yehuda are all right? You're free now?"

"Yes."

She moved to the bed and sank down on it to steady the trembling in her legs. "I didn't know. We haven't heard anything." Then her head raised. "So it is safe to go back now?"

There was a curt nod. "Yes. Is that what you want?"

Something in his voice made her hesitate. "Why would you ask that?"

"Is it true, then?" he demanded.

"Is what true?"

"That you and Marcus are engaged to be married." It came out cool and clipped.

It felt like she had just been struck a blow. "You know about that?" she asked softly.

"Only because Marcus flung it in my face," he said sarcastically. "He was crowing about it like the whole world knew."

"I—"

"So is it true?"

"You think I would do that?" she whispered. The joy in her was dashed completely.

"What other conclusion is there?" he shot right back. "In the only letter we ever got from you, it was Marcus this and Marcus that. Rome is so wonderful. Rome is so fascinating. The Didius family have been wonderful hosts."

She looked down at her hands, clasping them tightly together.

"Well?" He walked over and stood before her. "Why didn't you write, Miriam? We were all worried sick about you. Lilly and Ezra wrote. My mother wrote. Couldn't you have at least answered? Or were you afraid that you would be a disappointment to all of us?"

"So you never got my letter?"

That stopped him. "What letter?"

"About two months ago. We—" She shook her head, too hurt to want to explain. "It doesn't matter." Her voice was so low he barely heard her.

"How could you do this, Miriam?" he cried, throwing up his hands. "How could you turn your back on everything that happened with Jesus? I know your father probably set the whole betrothal up, but don't you realize that when we were baptized, we made a covenant with Jesus to always be faithful to him? To follow him no matter what circumstances confront us?"

"No," she said coldly, "I didn't realize that, Simeon. Thank you for reminding me."

He dropped to a crouch before her so he could look straight into her eyes. His voice was pleading. "Ezra and I came to find out what is going on, Miriam. To help you." There was a sigh of frustration. "Assuming you really want to be helped."

She looked up, her eyes flashing. "Sorry to frustrate such noble gallantry." Her anger took over now. "We don't need your help."

"So is it true? You still haven't answered my question."

She was fighting back tears. She would not let him see her weakness. "Is that really what you think?" she asked again.

"What am I supposed to think, Miriam! Why won't you just answer me? Are you going to marry Marcus or not?"

She stood, facing him squarely. She felt completely desolate inside. The euphoria she had felt when she saw who it was now tasted like bile in her mouth. "It sounds to me like you already have your answers, Simeon."

He stared at her. "And that's it? That's all you've got to say?"

"I think everything has been said that needs to be said." She was like stone. "Good-bye, Simeon. I am very sorry that you came this far for nothing." She bit her lip. "Tell Ezra I shall write to Lilly as soon as possible."

For a moment, she thought he was going to take her by the shoulders and shake her like a child, but then his mouth clamped shut and he spun away. He stalked to the window and stepped out onto the balcony. He turned and looked at her once more. His mouth opened; then he shook his head and turned away, reaching for the rope that hung down from the roof.

"Good-bye, Simeon," she murmured. "Give my love to your family."

III

27 September, a.d. 31

When Livia opened the door to the building and stepped outside, the two men there came quickly to attention. Their night guards had been replaced with the regular day watchers, a routine Mordechai had established. She nodded to them without speaking and shut the door behind her.

"Where are the others?" the big man said. This was the one Miriam called Cain. He was large and completely bald. His manner was always very cool and professional, almost curt.

"Miriam didn't sleep well last night. She's not going to go out until later. I have to go to the market and get some food."

"What about your brother?"

"He'll stay and get Miriam some breakfast when she wakes up." That wasn't completely true. Miriam always worked with the two of them in fixing the meals, but these two men would expect a subservient role for Drusus in this household.

As she pushed past them, the two of them conferred quickly. In a moment, Livia heard heavy footsteps behind her. Cain was following after her. Abel would stay back to make sure that no one else left without an escort.

She ignored the man as she walked swiftly down the street and onto the main thoroughfare that led to the vegetable market. *O Lord, please let Simeon still be watching.*

Ten minutes later, as she selected carrots and potatoes from the back of a small cart, she realized someone was standing beside her. "*Shalom*, Livia."

Though she was hoping he would appear, and half expected it, she still jumped a little. She glanced at the figure beside her, then smiled faintly. "*Shalom*, Simeon."

"I need to talk with you."

She glanced quickly in the other direction. Cain had already seen the exchange and had started moving toward her. "Play along with me," she said quickly, her voice low.

Simeon looked startled. "Why?"

They had been speaking in Aramaic. Now Livia switched to Latin.

"I can't believe this!" she exclaimed loudly. "Diomedes! What are you doing here in Rome?"

"What?" Simeon said, totally bewildered.

Suddenly Livia's guard pushed between them. "Who is this?" he demanded, glaring at Livia.

For a moment, she acted surprised at the interruption; then her face darkened. "This is someone I knew many years ago in Alexandria. Please excuse us." She stepped around him to look at Simeon again. "Tell me, Diomedes," she said, "are your parents still living?"

"They are," he said, catching on to what she was doing, though he wasn't sure why. "And what of your mother and father? I haven't heard anything about your family for many years."

Cain shouldered his way between them again. "Let me see into your bag," he commanded Livia.

Livia sighed wearily and held out the woven bag she used to carry her purchases. He pulled out two or three onions, rummaged around in the bottom for a moment, then dropped them back again. "Open the folds of your *stola*."

Livia looked annoyed, but complied. She turned out any part of her dress that might conceal something.

His face still as threatening as a storm cloud, the bald man swung around to Simeon. "You do the same," he said.

"What is this?"

"Just do it, Diomedes," Livia said wearily. "He is a very suspicious man."

Simeon complied, opening the folds of his tunic to show that he was hiding nothing.

"All right," the man said, "but I'll be watching." He glared at Simeon. "Stay at least three steps back from her at all times so that I can see you clearly. Do not try to exchange anything."

He moved away, stopping about ten or fifteen paces back, still watching them very closely.

"What was that all about?" Simeon asked, switching back to Aramaic.

"Please stay clear of me as he said, Simeon. Don't give him any reason to think we are more than old friends." Then before Simeon could answer, she said more loudly, again in Latin. "This is a great surprise, Diomedes. Come. Tell me all about your family."

She pointed toward the nearest building. "Let's go over there where he can see us clearly. Then maybe he'll leave us alone for a few minutes." She moved over to the steps and sat down. Simeon followed, careful to sit well clear of her.

"What is going on, Livia? What was he looking for? Did he think I might hurt you?"

"He was looking for letters, either from me to you, or the other way around."

"But—" Then his jaw dropped slightly as the realization of what she was saying hit him. "So they're not protecting you? They're actually guarding you?"

She gave him a strange look. "Miriam said you told her that Ezra tried to come to us yesterday and was stopped by the guards. Why does this surprise you?"

He was clearly reeling a little with this discovery. "Because we just assumed they were men hired by Miriam or her father because of Moshe Ya'abin. To protect you." Then he paled, looking sick. "I thought that seemed a little strange, this far away from Ya'abin's reach. So you are being confined? And that man is making sure you don't send out any letters?"

"Or receive them," she said, forcing a bright smile for Cain's benefit as she talked. "Mordechai's instructions to these escorts, as they call themselves, were very strict. We can have no communication in or out."

Simeon raised a hand and passed it across his eyes. The distress was evident now.

"Don't do that!" Livia hissed. "Look happy. Talk to me. We're pleased to see each other after so many years."

Simeon did so, tipping back his head and laughing for a moment. It sounded forced and hollow. He was clearly dazed. "Then . . . "

"Yes, Simeon. We are under virtual house arrest. We have been since Miriam's father left for Judea four months ago. We have received no letters in that time and can send none out. When we tried, we were threatened with serious consequences."

He was dumbfounded. "But why didn't Miriam tell me that last night?"

She gave him a sharp look. "The way she put it, you were not very open to anything she had to say."

"But—"

"Simeon, Miriam acted foolishly last night. She admits that now. But you hurt her terribly. You jumped to unwarranted conclusions. You questioned her integrity. You accused her of turning her back on Jesus—which couldn't be further from the truth. You wouldn't listen." Then she smiled, not only for Cain's benefit, but to soften her words. "Did I miss anything?"

He groaned softly. "Oh, Livia. No wonder. What have I done?"

"Listen to me, Simeon." She was very serious. "Our time is short. That man over there won't let us speak for very long. Miriam is not going to marry Marcus, and never had any intention of doing so. Mordechai and Marcus arranged it all. Mordechai didn't even tell Miriam what he had done until much later. When he did finally tell her, they had a terrible fight. Miriam told him about Jesus, about us being baptized. Mordechai was livid. He threatened to cut her off, to disinherit her, if she didn't renounce all of it. Miriam refused, of course, and told him we were going to leave. She said we would make our own way back to Judea."

He winced. "And that's when he put you under confinement?"

"Yes. He was in a towering rage, as you can imagine. At one point

Miriam actually thought he was going to strike her. The next morning Mordechai was gone and we had guards outside our door. We've been under guard twenty-four hours a day ever since."

He shook his head, each new revelation hitting him like a battering ram.

"We learned that Mordechai has seized all of Miriam's funds, so she has no money. All mail in and out was forbidden. When we tried to smuggle one out, we were stopped. Over two months ago, Miriam was so desperate she even tried to convince Marcus's mother to send off a letter Miriam had written to Lilly. It explained all of this. Evidently, it never reached Lilly."

Simeon felt physically ill. He shook his head. "We heard nothing. Ezra and I finally decided to come to Rome to find out what was going on. We—I!—thought you hadn't written because of the marriage, that Miriam was too embarrassed to tell us she was staying here." He blew out his breath. "I am such a fool!"

Livia cocked her head. "You weren't thinking I would contradict that, were you?" Then she forced a merry laugh. "Our friend is looking very suspicious, Simeon. We need to cheer up a little."

Simeon leaned back against the stone steps, as if relaxing. He smiled as happily as he could, casually looking in the man's direction. Livia was right. The man's expression was close to open hostility. Even as Simeon looked at him, the man started edging towards them.

"There's something else, Simeon." Livia was rushing the words now. "Did you know that it was Miriam who convinced Pilate to let you and Yehuda go free?"

He visibly jerked. "Ezra told us that you all had fasted and prayed about it."

"We did, but after Ezra and Lilly went on to Joppa, we learned that Pilate planned to torture you for the name of the person who betrayed them at the Joknean Pass."

He looked directly at her. "I would never have given them Miriam's name."

"She knew that, but she couldn't bear the thought of you facing the torture. She tried to convince both Marcus and Pilate to let you go because of what you had done for her and her father in Samaria. Pilate actually got a little impatient with her. That's when Miriam came up with the idea for the exchange—you, Yehuda, and your two friends for Ya'abin and his band. It was brilliant. It was the only thing that could have changed Pilate's mind."

"Father told me that Miriam had been part of getting us freed, but I had no idea," he said softly.

"She convinced her father to side with her in presenting the idea to Pilate. Do you know how?"

He shook his head.

"She told Mordechai that she was the one who betrayed the plan to you. That if you ever were forced to give up the name, it would be hers that you spoke."

He jerked forward. "She didn't!"

"Yes. Mordechai knows. Is it any wonder that he is so angry with her? I think the betrothal to Marcus is partly his way of punishing her. From his point of view, this was the ultimate betrayal."

Simeon looked away. Finally he turned back. "But if all of this is going on, why would she say you don't need our help?"

"She said that?" That was something Miriam had not told her this morning. She shook her head. "If it is any consolation, she called herself childish and petty."

"It was my fault, not hers." He was feeling very ashamed about what had happened.

Livia drew in a sharp breath. "Our man is coming back. We aren't acting like two childhood friends. Too grim, I think."

Simeon didn't turn. "Then listen carefully, Livia." He still spoke in Aramaic. He hoped that the guard would think they were speaking in Egyptian in case he overheard them. "Knowing you are being carefully guarded changes everything. It may take awhile for us to figure out how to do this, but we will be back. We'll get you out of here."

"I knew you would." Then she remembered something. "There are three of us. We found my brother Drusus. He's living with us."

Simeon nodded. "We saw the young man with you and wondered who he was." He thought for a moment. "No problem. We can take three."

He glanced over his shoulder. The bald man was moving closer, but slowly, still peering at the two of them. "One other thing. Will you not tell Miriam about today?"

That took her by surprise. "But why?"

"Tell her you saw me. That we're going to help. And by the way, you will all have to be very careful now. Act natural. You can't let them know that anything has changed. That will be critical. But don't tell her that you told me all of this."

She nodded slowly, not sure she understood why.

"She'll think the only reason I came back is because you told me all of this. I was coming back anyway, to tell her I am sorry."

"I know." She smiled, and this time it was full and genuine. "She knew you would. She always talked about Ezra coming, but it was you she expected."

"And then I acted like a complete dolt."

She laughed loudly, switching to Latin. "But you can always repent of that, can't you?"

Simeon glanced up and saw that the bald man was almost on them. He stood quickly, pretending nervousness. "Well, I must be going, Livia. This was a pleasant surprise to see you here."

"And for me as well."

Simeon looked sorrowful. "I am so sorry to hear that both of your parents are gone."

Livia only nodded, grateful to see the big man respond to that. They were talking about tragic things. That would explain Simeon's gravity. She felt a load lift from her shoulders. Simeon was quick, very quick. It was going to be all right.

Her guard stopped, close enough to hear, but his face relaxed somewhat. Simeon made as if to extend his hand toward her, then shot the guard a frightened look, and drew it back quickly. "Sorry," he murmured.

The man scowled at him, then turned to Livia. "I think your mistress is going to wonder why you are taking so long with the shopping."

Simeon was all formality now. "I'm off to Sicilia tomorrow. I'm in the wheat trade. If I am ever back in Rome, perhaps we could meet again."

"Perhaps," Livia said. "Farewell, Diomedes. It was good to see you after so long a time."

He smiled at her words. "May good fortune watch over us both until we meet again."

CHAPTER 29

WITHHOLD NOT GOOD FROM THEM TO WHOM IT IS DUE,

WHEN IT IS IN THE POWER OF THINE HAND TO DO IT.

—*Proverbs 3:27*

I

ROME

27 SEPTEMBER, A.D. 31

In the two hours Livia had been gone, Miriam's mood had gone from anger to self-condemnation to desolation. The moment Livia returned from shopping, Miriam began to berate herself again.

"I'm sorry for being such a fool, Livia. It was stupid of me to get angry."

Drusus glowered at Miriam from the far corner of the room, where he was once again sketching something on his slate. "I can't believe you told him we don't need any help. We can't even walk down the street without our two shadows peering down our necks."

"That's enough, Drusus."

"No," Miriam said. "He's right." Then the anger flared again. "But he was so infuriating."

"From what you told me," Livia suggested, "it sounds like Simeon was a little frustrated too."

"Are you taking his side in this?" Miriam demanded, rounding on her friend.

"No. But when Simeon told you that Marcus had told him that you and he were betrothed, you didn't say anything. Why shouldn't Simeon suppose that was true? They've not heard anything from us since your first letter, which was almost eight months ago." She hesitated, but decided some things needed to be said. "At that point, if you remember, even I was starting to wonder if you were falling in love with Marcus."

"I know," she said, instantly desolate once again. "I should never have written to them about how much I liked Rome."

Livia sat on a stool facing Miriam. Now she leaned forward, very serious. "Miriam, I think that what Simeon did last night was wrong. He jumped to unwarranted conclusions; he questioned your integrity; he accused you falsely; and he didn't take time to listen to you." There was a fleeting smile. "And if I get a chance to see him, I will tell him all of that to his face."

"But?" Miriam said, looking up.

She shrugged.

"No," Miriam said more forcefully, "I heard a 'but' in there. Go on, say it. I was too quick to react. I let my temper get the better of me. My pride was hurt and I lashed back at him without thinking." Her eyes dropped again. "And now I've sent them away when we need help so desperately."

Livia leaned back a little. "I would have to agree with all of that except for your last statement. I don't think you sent them away."

"He won't come back, Livia. He asked me directly if I was going to marry Marcus, and I didn't tell him no. If he thinks I'm getting married, there's no reason for him and Ezra to stay."

"Tell me, Miriam," Livia said gently. "What was it that Simeon did last night that hurt you the most?"

A little surprised by the question, Miriam thought for a moment.

"He said I had turned my back on Jesus and the covenants I had made with him."

"Is that the only thing?"

She looked down at her hands, shaking her head. "He actually believed that I could ever marry Marcus."

"And why does that hurt so much?"

"Because it's not true!" she cried.

"So he misjudged you."

"Yes!"

"And that hurts. It makes you angry."

Miriam blew out her breath in frustration. "All right, Livia. What are you getting at?"

"Do you really believe Simeon will just turn around and leave again?"

That set her back a little. "Well, I—After what I said, yes, I guess I do. He was pretty angry too."

"And what if *you* are misjudging him? Then doesn't he have the right to be hurt and angry as well?"

For a long moment, Miriam searched the face of this woman who was now the closest friend she had in the world. "I really don't like it when you are like that."

Livia's eyebrows raised. "Like what?"

"Absolutely right."

Drusus had set aside his sketching and was following the interchange very closely. "So you think they will be back?" he said eagerly.

"I do," Livia replied. Then she went on quickly. "But we can't act differently in any way. We have to go on as though nothing has happened. We'll go out every day as usual, but we can't be peering into every face that approaches us or look in every doorway we pass to see if they might be there. Simeon and Ezra know we're guarded now. That means they can't simply walk in and invite us to leave with them."

"Maybe they'll come down from the roof again." Drusus' eyes were shining with excitement. "We could all go out the same way. We could get past our escorts."

"Drusus," Livia said, trying not to smile. "It could be many days before anything happens. So don't be searching the rooftops every time we go out."

He looked disgusted. "I'm not a child anymore, Livia."

"You really think they'll come?" Miriam asked softly.

"I do. You still don't understand what happened last night, do you?"

"What do you mean?"

"Why do you think Simeon reacted the way he did?"

"Because he's a stubborn, hardheaded fool!"

"A stubborn, hardheaded, *jealous* fool," Livia corrected her.

Miriam's expression registered momentary astonishment.

"But then, perhaps that is just as well, because he's dealing with a stubborn, hardheaded woman." Then Livia's eyes softened. "A woman who wants very desperately for this man to understand that she could never consider marrying a man by the name of Marcus Quadratus Didius."

II

30 September, a.d. 31

They had returned to the Roman Forum; the crowds were thickening quickly. Drusus was a few steps ahead of them, carrying both slates beneath one arm. As they passed the *Rostra*, where the orators were already gathering, he dropped back. "Where do you want to study today?" he asked.

Miriam shrugged. The cold days had gone again, and they were back in the pleasant fall weather for which Rome was renowned. "It doesn't matter to me."

"Let's go up on the Palatine Hill," Livia suggested. "There's that place you like up there. It's usually quiet."

"Fine."

Drusus led out again as they threaded their way through the throngs. The return of good weather seemed to have brought everyone out on this day. They had come to conduct business with the government or worship the various gods or pontificate on philosophy and ethics or sell their wares or simply walk around gawking, dazzled by the splendor and opulence that lay at every hand.

Miriam glanced back. Cain and Abel were there, close enough to remind them of their presence, but not enough to be too intrusive. For one wild moment, Miriam was tempted to break and run, dart into a side street, or duck into one of the temples, just to see what they would do. But she pushed the urge aside. She knew where the feeling came from. Three days had passed since Simeon had stepped out of her bedroom doorway. Nothing had happened in that time. Not even the slightest hint that he and Ezra were still in Rome. In spite of Livia's warning, every time they were out Miriam's eyes scanned the faces of the crowd. Each day that passed chipped away at her confidence. Livia had been so sure they were coming. Well, Livia just might be wrong. Her heart heavy, Miriam was once again turning her mind to how they might escape on their own.

The bleakness she felt was even more of a prison than their constricted existence. Whether it was because she had withdrawn into herself, or because her former Roman friends were aware of the restrictions her father had set up, Miriam's social interaction had fallen off to nothing in the last few months. The women who had once frequently visited no longer came. If she saw them on the streets, they were still cordial, but their friendship now seemed strained to Miriam.

Each day, they rose in the morning, had breakfast together, and read for an hour or two; then they went out for half a day to study or walk or anything else that helped pass the time. Every third day, usually while they were out, Arcadius, the slave the Didius family had assigned to them, came in and thoroughly cleaned the apartment. When they returned late in the afternoon, they spent the rest of the day reading, talking or, for Miriam, writing her feelings on papyrus sheets so she would have a record of these dreary days. Any charm and excitement she felt for Rome had long since vanished. It had become a prison, a stockade, a tomb.

She realized with a start that Livia was watching her curiously. She forced a smile. "I'm all right. Just wallowing in self-pity again."

They moved slowly along the *Via Sacra*, and the crowd thickened even more. As they passed by the temple of Divus Romulus, approaching the point where they would turn off for the Palatine Hill, one of the many street hawkers veered directly in front of them. He was an old man who carried a basket of candles in front of him. His tunic was filthy. His hands and face were smeared with dirt. Beneath a ragged hood, his hair was a rat's nest of matted, greasy black. In the midst of the stubble of whiskers Miriam saw a dark gap where one tooth was missing. The only thing that seemed at all normal about him were the light brown eyes, which were both alert and intelligent.

"Candles, m'lady?" he cried, stepping directly in front of her. A whiff of something that smelled suspiciously like dead dog assaulted her nostrils. Then she realized it was the odor of animal tallow used in candlemaking.

"No, thank you." She averted her eyes and stepped around him.

"Excellent quality," he cawed, falling in behind her. His voice was high and warbled, as though coming from a dried reed. Livia moved closer to Miriam to prevent him from pushing in between them.

"No," Miriam said, more firmly. "Not today."

"Not even for Hanukkah?" the man asked.

Miriam stopped dead and turned. "Hanukkah?"

A smile split the dirty lips, and she saw that what she thought was a missing tooth was actually only a blackened tooth. "Aye, m'lady. You know about Hanukkah then?"

She did, but she was astounded to find someone in the Roman Forum who also knew of the holiday.

Drusus moved closer to look in the basket. Wrinkling his nose at the smell of the man, he looked at Miriam. "What's Ha—Hanna—?"

"Hanukkah," Livia answered. "It's a Jewish holiday."

Miriam was still staring at the man in disbelief. There was something about him. . . . "It's a holiday that celebrates our independence from Greek tyranny," she explained to Drusus, still peering at the man.

The man turned his head away to look at Drusus. "Aye," he said in a rough voice, "and it requires candles to celebrate it."

They had stopped in the middle of the Sacred Way, and the crowds were swirling around them. Several people shot angry looks in their direction. "Get out of the way," an older man in an expensive toga snarled at them. Another man pulling a small cart bumped roughly into Miriam and swore at her.

"Perhaps we should move over there," the vendor suggested, gesturing toward the side of the busy thoroughfare. He took her elbow and started forward.

Miriam jerked her arm free. She had looked into his basket and had seen only cheap household candles. "These aren't Hanukkah candles," she said sharply, wanting to be done with him.

"Aye, m'lady," the man answered with another quick grin. His voice had suddenly lost its reedy, nasal quality. "But if you celebrate Hanukkah in Capernaum, that won't be a problem, will it?"

Miriam gasped, gaping at him. The man reached out and took her arm again, pulling her forward gently. "Don't stop, Miriam!" he commanded, his voice low and urgent.

"Simeon?"

"Keep walking!" he hissed. "Your escorts are watching you."

"You came back!" Livia exclaimed.

Still moving, keeping his head down, Simeon chuckled at Miriam's expression. "I know this is asking a lot, but try to look natural. You too, Livia. You can't let them suspect there's anything unusual happening." He squeezed Miriam's arm gently. "I'm very sorry about the other night."

They reached the side of the nearest building, and Simeon lowered the basket to the ground. He knelt beside it, speaking quickly to the three of them. "Listen carefully. Do exactly what I say."

Miriam couldn't have spoken if she wanted to. The shock was giving way to joy and immense relief, and she felt a little light-headed.

"Move around in front of me, Miriam," Simeon commanded. "Pretend you are examining my wares. Don't look directly at the men, but tell me, are there only two men guarding you this morning?"

"Yes."

Simeon picked up a candle and stood again, holding it up for Miriam to see. "Hold this up to the light and pretend to study it." When she did so, he went on. "I know the bald man. Is the shorter man in the dark tunic the other guard?"

"Yes," she murmured. "Those are the two."

"Good." Simeon half turned, lifted one hand, and scratched his nose. Miriam realized that it was a signal of some kind. Then he looked back at her. "Take a look at another," he suggested, handing her a second candle.

Tears sprang to her eyes as she obeyed. "You came back," she whispered.

"Yes, but if you could hold off punching me in the nose until we get this worked through, I would appreciate it." He looked at Drusus. "This must be your brother, Livia. The resemblance is strong."

"Yes. This is Drusus."

Simeon smiled at the young man. "I'd shake hands, but now is not the time." He turned back to Miriam. "Good. I'm glad you are all three together." He became deadly serious. "Is there anything at your apartment that you absolutely cannot leave behind?"

Miriam gave him a sharp look.

"We can go back there if we must, but it will make it much more difficult if we do. It will be safer if we can leave from here right now."

"Now?" Livia said. "What about clothes and food and—?"

"We have some money hidden there," Miriam added.

He brushed that aside. "We'll take care of all that. Your two friends are starting to look suspicious. Think! Do you have to go back there?"

Simeon picked up another of the candles and thrust it at Drusus as the three of them looked at each other. Miriam handed her candle back to Simeon and picked up another. "This is too much money!" she exclaimed loudly. "And the quality is poor." Then her voice dropped again as she looked at Livia and Drusus. "Can we, Livia? Can we just leave?"

Livia turned to her brother, who was already bobbing his head. "There's nothing there that matters to me," he said.

Livia looked at Miriam. "We can go easily. You're the one with the most things."

That was true. Miriam and her father had brought numerous trunks filled with Miriam's clothing, books, and the personal items needed for an extended stay. But instantly she knew that none of that mattered. She turned back to Simeon, her heart soaring. "Tell us what you want us to do."

Pleased, Simeon turned and again his hand came up and scratched at his nose. Even as he did, he spoke to the three of them. "Be ready.

The moment I say *go*, we're going to duck between those buildings. Just stay with me."

III

Ezra started moving the moment he saw Simeon scratch his nose again. It was just in time. The two men he was following had started to drift slowly toward where Miriam and the others stood. He cut directly in front of them, then stopped, blocking their way. The bald man started to step around him, but Ezra confronted him, placing himself so that the man had to turn his head away from Miriam and the others to speak with him. "Excuse me, sir," he said in halting, heavily accented Latin. "Where is the House of Vestal Virgins?"

The man gave him a sharp look, then ignored him. He tried to thrust his way past Ezra but again found his way blocked. "I speak very poor Latin," Ezra said apologetically. He withdrew a leather pouch and shook it. Coins rattled distinctly. "I wish to make donation to famous priestesses of Vesta—"

"Ask someone else, fool!" the man snarled. He put an arm against Ezra's chest, prepared to shove him aside. Suddenly his eyes narrowed. "Wait! Aren't you the one who came to the apartment the other day?"

Ezra was not as tall as the older guard, but he was solidly built and a lifetime of making sandals had left him with powerful arms. He grabbed the man by the wrist. "Help! Help!" he screamed. "This man steals my money!"

Many in the crowd turned toward them. Common thieves were plentiful in Rome, and there was considerable resentment against them. Instantly people started moving in toward them, dark scowls on their faces. Ezra felt someone grab at his arm. He turned to see the man in the dark tunic. "We don't want your money. Get out of here."

The man gave him a half shove. Ezra let go of the bald man's arm and stumbled forward. He snapped his pouch open sharply and coins shot outward. The clatter of money sent everyone scrambling. "Thief! Robber!" Ezra screamed. "My money! They're taking my money!"

Behind him a man threw himself at the bigger guard, putting a headlock on him. Two more grabbed the smaller man and pinned his arms back.

"We didn't take his money," the bald one raged. "Let go!"

Ezra stood there for a moment. The people had swarmed in now, and there was no way the guards could see where Simeon and Miriam were. With a tiny smile, Ezra lowered his head and ducked into the crowd.

IV

"Are you all right?" the big man with the shaved head asked his partner.

The younger and smaller man rubbed at his throat where someone had punched him. "Stupid oaf," he muttered. The two of them had been in serious trouble until someone came up with the empty leather pouch and held it up to show that it wasn't missing. When the people realized that the accuser had disappeared as well, they quickly lost interest and turned away.

The man turned, then suddenly stiffened. Where before Miriam and her two companions had been standing with a candle vendor, now there was no one. He gave a low cry and started in the direction where he had last seen them, thrusting his way roughly through the crowds. The second man registered shock, then broke into a trot behind his partner. A minute later they reached the spot close to the large building. There they found a basket of cheaply made candles and two writing slates, but nothing else.

V

"Where are we going?" Miriam asked. They were walking briskly, but not fast enough to draw attention to themselves. They were in one of the narrow back streets, now a good three blocks from the Forum.

Simeon didn't answer, but just then took a quick turn into a recessed doorway. There on the step were four folded robes. He grabbed the top one and handed it to Miriam. "Here. Put this on. Put the hood up." He grabbed another and handed it to Livia. The third went to Drusus. As they started putting them on, Simeon shrugged out of his smelly tunic. Then he rubbed quickly at the blackened tooth, and it became as normal as the others. He reached up and tugged at his head. The greasy thatch of black hair pulled away, and he flung it aside. Miriam saw that he had smeared soot around the edges of his own hair so it would blend into the wig. She had to smile. In the dim light of the narrow street, Simeon looked like a Roman dandy who had dyed his hair yellow but had forgotten the edges.

As Simeon pulled his robe on, Miriam realized these were the robes worn by initiates of Isis. The temple of the Egyptian goddess was just a few blocks from where they were. The mystical religion was making remarkable inroads in Rome and such initiates were a common sight in the city.

Simeon looked at the three of them, then grinned. "Good. You look appropriately humble. Keep your heads covered until we're out of the city."

"What about Ezra?" Miriam wanted to know.

"We'll link up with him in a couple of hours." He slowed the pace a little, more in keeping with the office they supposedly represented. "Our hope is that your guards will spend the next hour trying to find out what happened to you. Then, if all goes as planned, they'll return to your apartment, thinking that maybe they just lost you. By tonight, they'll realize you're gone, but by then we'll be well on our way east."

"East?" Livia said in surprise. She had expected west or south, the closest way to the coast.

"Once the guards realize you've disappeared, they'll alert Marcus's father. He's a wealthy and powerful man. After promising Mordechai to keep you guarded, he'll see this as a blot on the family's honor. By tomorrow I'm sure he'll have searchers along every main road, at every port, especially Ostia. They'll assume we're trying to get a ship out of there."

"We thought maybe we'd have to go to Puteoli," Miriam said.

"Still too obvious," Simeon answered. "We'll go east, over the mountains. There are no major roads between here and the coast of the Adriatic Sea. We'll travel only by night until we are well away from here. In a few days, maybe as much as a week, we'll reach the coast. There's a major highway between Ravenna and Brundisium." He stopped. "Do you know where that is?"

Surprisingly, it was Drusus who answered. "Italia is like a great boot, with the heel and toe far to the south of us. Brundisium is on the heel of the boot."

Simeon was impressed. "That's right. They'll never think to look for us in that direction. From Brundisium it's a short sail over to Greece. Then we'll continue overland to Athens. From Athens we'll take passage on a ship to Tyre or Sidon. By then, I'm sure the Didius family will have alerted Marcus and your father to what has happened. They may be watching the ports in Israel, so we'll again go by land over that final leg to Capernaum." Simeon knew that Mordechai would suspect that Miriam might go to the Galilee and send someone there too, but he didn't say that. The Galilee was Simeon's territory, and his father and Ephriam would be alert.

His mouth pulled down with concern. "It's a long way to walk, but we think it is the safest way."

Miriam felt her eyes start to burn again. "We'll walk the entire way if you say," she exclaimed softly. "You came. We're free. That's all that matters."

VI

EAST OF ROME

They stopped briefly at a tavern, where Simeon washed the soot out of his hair, shaved off the heavy stubble of his beard, and changed into a fresh tunic. Two hours later they shed their novitiates' robes just inside the east gate of the city, then walked through it without anyone taking any particular notice of them. A mile into the countryside, a figure suddenly stepped out from a grove of trees.

"Ezra!" Miriam cried. She broke into a run and threw herself into his arms. He picked her up and swung her around joyously. Finally he set her down again. "I am so glad you're safe, Ezra. Simeon told us what you were doing."

"Any trouble?" Simeon asked.

"None," came the answer. "I'm sure they were two very surprised guards when they finally saw that you had all disappeared, but I was long gone by then." He turned to Miriam again. "Are you all right?"

"Yes. Now we are. Thank you, Ezra. I knew you would come."

He turned and disappeared into the trees and a few moments later returned with a small carriage pulled by a pair of average looking horses. There were two traveling cases in the carriage. As Ezra pulled the carriage onto the road, he looked at Miriam and Livia. "I wish I had Lilly here to help me buy some clothes for you, but hopefully they'll be close to your size. We also have some personal items for you. If I've missed anything, I'll slip into the first village and purchase what you need."

"We'll take whatever you have," Livia said.

Miriam nodded her agreement, then asked him, "How is Lilly, Ezra?"

A huge grin split Ezra's face. "We have a baby girl."

"But—" Then she cried out for joy. "Of a truth, Ezra? I didn't even know Lilly was—"

"I know," Ezra said, taking her hand. "Simeon told me that none of our letters got through to you."

"A baby. After all these years." She shook her head in wonder. "Lilly must be ecstatic."

"Much more than that. She positively glows." Ezra was beaming too. "We named her Miriam, in honor of a courageous and wonderful woman we both know."

"Really!" She felt like crying and laughing and cheering all at once. It was as though a blast of wind had blown away the clouds of noxious fumes that had hung over them for months. "I can't believe it. It is all just too wonderful."

She turned to Simeon to express her thanks, but he cut her off before she could speak. "We have to keep moving now. Perhaps in the next few days there will be time to talk and make things right between us again."

"What you have done today is enough."

He shook his head. "There is much that needs righting," he murmured. "But it must wait for now. We must be far from the city by the time night falls."

CHAPTER NOTES

Though officially only a minor festival in the Jewish calendar, Hanukkah (which was still about two and half months away at this point in the story), was one of the most popular of the holidays. Hanukkah, which means "dedication," celebrated the successful revolt of the Jews in 168 B.C. against the Greek kings who had ruled Israel. One of those kings, Antiochus Epiphanes, decided to stamp out the religion of the Jews. He forced the worship of the Greek gods on his subjects and made any observance of the Mosaic Law punishable by death. He even went so far as to have his soldiers force their way into the temple in Jerusalem. They set up an idol and had apostate priests sacrifice pigs to it, an unbelievable abomination to the faithful. That had sparked the revolt. Led by a priest named Judas Maccabaeus, the Jews fought back and eventually drove the Greeks out.

Therein lay the beginnings of Hanukkah. When Judas Maccabaeus recaptured the Temple Mount, he immediately set about to purify the temple so that once again the worship of Jehovah could resume. The purification ritual took eight full days, and a significant part of the ritual involved the great *menorah*, or sacred candelabra, that provided the only light inside the temple. It was massive, taller than a man, and on the top of each of its seven branches was a large cup for specially purified olive oil. However, when Judas entered the temple on the twenty-fifth of Kislev, 165 B.C. (which occurs in early December on our calendar) he found only one jar of oil that had not been desecrated by the Greeks. It was enough to burn for only one day. Purifying more oil also involved an eight-day process. Rather than waiting an additional week to rededicate the temple, Judas Maccabaeus lit the sacred menorah anyway. Miraculously, the one-day supply of oil continued to burn for the entire eight days until the new supply was prepared.

Because of that, Hanukkah was also called the Feast of Lights. Part of the commemoration of that miracle involved lighting eight candles or small oil lamps, one each day for eight days in remembrance of the eight days of purification.

Hanukkah (the Feast of Dedication, or the Feast of Lights) is still celebrated by the Jewish community today, almost twenty-two hundred years after the one-day supply of oil miraculously burned for eight continuous days (see Jacobs, 118–21; Wouk, 75–76).

CHAPTER 30

BE GLAD IN THE LORD, AND REJOICE, YE RIGHTEOUS:
AND SHOUT FOR JOY, ALL YE THAT ARE UPRIGHT IN HEART.

—*Psalm 32:11*

I

ON THE ADRIATIC COAST OF ITALIA
7 OCTOBER, A.D. 31

Crossing the rocky spine of Italia proved to be far more difficult than Simeon had expected. For the first two days, they followed well-traveled roads eastward, laying over in the woods by day and moving forward only by night. With all of the walking Miriam, Livia, and Drusus had done everyday in the city, they were able to hold up quite well. The carriage was large enough to carry only two people—the driver and one passenger—so they took turns walking. As they continued eastward, the roads began to peter out. Main roads became narrow farm roads and narrow farm roads gave way to barely discernible wagon tracks. Finally the carriage was abandoned. They were tempted to keep the horses, but finally decided it would make them too conspicuous. They took only what they could carry and moved deeper into the mountains. By then, they felt safe enough to start traveling by day, sleeping out in the open by night. The climb became

556

steeper, and eventually even the few shepherds' paths ended and they had nothing but open wilderness.

It was roughly a hundred miles from Rome up and over the mountains to the eastern coast. That took them almost a week. As they descended toward the eastern coast, they found people again, but far fewer than before. The highway that ran along the eastern coast of Italia was a typical Roman road, well maintained and graded to drain off heavy rainfall, even though this part of the province was for the most part sparsely settled. Once they reached the road, the first mile marker they came to showed that they were still one hundred sixty-eight miles from Brundisium, the port that was their destination.

For the first time in almost a week, they stopped at an isolated, rustic roadside inn and took lodging for the night. Never had Miriam reveled in such luxury. She and Livia shared a simple straw mattress, probably crawling with fleas and ticks. There was a dinner of roast venison; hard, round loaves of bread; and as many vegetables as they could eat. There was a roaring fire in the huge fireplace in the dining room. And for five sesterces, the innkeeper's wife kept a rusted iron tub filled with tepid water so that one by one they each had a private bath. After a week of sleeping on the ground in the open, rain, cold, or sunshine, it was heaven itself. Most importantly, the innkeeper agreed to sell them a small rickety cart to carry their belongings and a horse to pull it.

II

Miriam stood up from the table. That brought Ezra's eyes open with a start. He had fallen asleep three different times during dinner. At the look Miriam gave him, he grinned sheepishly. "I give up. I'm going to bed."

He and Simeon and Drusus shared one room behind the quarters of the innkeeper. Livia and Miriam shared a small bedroom in the loft above. Yawning mightily, Ezra stood and stretched, then stumbled away.

Livia looked at Miriam for a moment, then stood as well. "Come, Drusus. It's time for us to retire too."

He started to say something, but a look from his sister cut him off. He got up and the two of them left the room. Miriam looked at Simeon, who was staring into the fire. As the door shut, he turned to her. "What about you?" he asked. "Are you tired yet?"

She shook her head. "Actually, I was thinking of stepping outside for a little while. It's a beautiful night."

"Do you mind if I join you?"

She gave him a fleeting smile. "We have been studiously avoiding any opportunity to talk. It's probably time we did, don't you think?"

"I do. I've thought about it several times, but . . . " He shrugged. "It's time."

She stood, wrapping a shawl around her shoulders. He watched her for a moment, then stood and followed her out.

The quarter moon would not be up for at least another hour, but there were no clouds, and as they walked slowly down the short path that led to the Roman road, their eyes adjusted to the starlight. When they had arrived earlier that evening, Miriam had noted a huge old oak tree near where the entrance to the inn joined the road. She moved beneath its generous branches, found a round rock that was partially buried, and sat down. Simeon dropped to a crouch facing her. He smoothed a place in the dirt with his hand and then sat down as well.

Both were quiet for almost a minute, staring out into the darkness, lost in their own thoughts. Finally, Miriam stirred. "Simeon?"

He turned his head.

"I don't want you to think that you have to say anything about that night you came to see me. That's over. You don't have to explain."

He grunted softly, and she couldn't tell if it was from relief or frustration.

"I'm sorry I reacted the way I did. I shouldn't have gotten angry with you."

"Really?" he said with a sardonic smile. "What should you have done? Whacked me with that poker?"

"You had no way of knowing everything that had happened."

"True, and one of the gifts I have developed in my life is charging ahead full speed when I am not hampered with an overabundance of knowledge."

She laughed. "A gift, huh?"

"Greatly perfected."

"So," she went on after a moment. "It's over. There's nothing to be gained by talking about it now."

"That's another of my gifts," he drawled. "Talking about things when there's nothing to be gained by it."

"Really, Simeon. I wish we could go back and hold that conversation over again, but we can't." She had thought a lot about this and feared that the result of talking about that night would only be more pain, more awkwardness, more feeling like a fool. "I would really rather not."

He took a deep breath, then finally nodded. "All right, I'll respect that. Can I speak with you about something else?"

"If it really is something else."

"Miriam, I would like to say something. Actually, three things. I am tempted to ask you not to say anything until I finish, but that wouldn't be fair to you. So you can break in and disagree with me at any time."

She almost said something glib, but the somberness in his face stopped her. "I'm listening."

He took another deep breath, looking directly at her now. "Let me do the most unpleasant one first."

"Oh, dear." She found herself tensing for what he might say next.

"I'm afraid this is not over for you, Miriam. Your father is a powerful, wealthy man, with enormous influence both with our own people and with the Romans. He's not going to take your disappearance lightly."

"I know," she whispered. "I've thought about little else since we left."

"He'll eventually figure out that you are with us and headed for Capernaum."

"Yes."

"I don't think he'll try to do anything to hurt you. At least not physically. Despite all that has happened, I still think he loves you as his daughter."

"I'm not so sure." Then she shook her head. "No, that's not true. For all he has done, I still love him as my father, so I suppose he still loves me too."

"He will send someone to try to bring you back. He will definitely take action to see if he can't stop Jesus, so that you have nothing to follow anymore. In his mind, that would solve at least one of his problems."

"It makes me sick to think that I might bring some kind of retaliation down on Jesus."

"Miriam," Simeon said, almost sternly. "Jesus is the Christ. He is the Promised Messiah. He is the Son of God. Your father cannot do anything that Jesus is not capable of dealing with."

That almost startled her. She had been so consumed with worry about what her father might do, she hadn't considered that. "You're right, of course." But her concern didn't disappear. "My other worry is that he will try to do something to Lilly and Ezra." She looked away. "Or to your family."

Simeon started to wave that away, but she went on quickly. "I've almost decided it isn't wise for me to stay in Capernaum. I will—"

He cut her off. "That is a problem, Miriam, and we have to face it. But I think there is a solution to it, and it's not running away or hiding. Eventually, he'll find you. He has too many resources at his disposal."

"What is your solution then?"

"I would like to hold that answer for a moment, if I may, and talk to you about the second thing."

"Can I ask you a question first?"

"Of course."

"One of the Ten Commandments says that we are to honor our father and our mother that our days may be long upon the earth."

"Yes," he said slowly, suspecting what might be coming next.

"How do I honor a father who is not himself honorable? Am I still obligated to keep that commandment? I wish it said, 'Honor your father when he does what is right; otherwise, you can ignore the requirement,' but it doesn't."

"No, it doesn't," Simeon agreed.

"You know now, I think, that it was Father who arranged the betrothal between me and Marcus." It wasn't a question.

"I do."

"Am I under obligation to accept my father's will in this matter? Normally, the father has a say about whom his daughter should marry."

"True, but not without the consent of the daughter."

"He's angry with me for a host of things I've done. He doesn't care whether I give my consent or not." She took a breath, glad to finally be saying all of this to Simeon. "I refused to accept his will in this. I have run away from him in order to escape it. Am I honoring my father, as God commands me to?"

She drew her knees up and laid her head on her arms. Simeon

watched her for a long time and then spoke quietly. "Do you believe God has infinite power, Miriam?"

She answered without looking up. "Of course."

"And yet he doesn't use that power to force his children to do his will. Why not?"

Her head came up. "Because he wants us to come to him of our own choice."

"But if following him is what is best for us, wouldn't it be better if he did force us to be obedient?"

She knew he was pressing her because he wanted to make a point, but she was curious what the point was. "No."

"Why not?"

"I'm not sure. If he forced us . . . " She thought about it more carefully. "If he forced us to be good, then it wouldn't really be good, would it?"

He was obviously pleased. "Exactly! If there is no choice, how can you impute good or evil to an act? For example, if a man forces a woman to submit to him physically, he has committed a great evil, *but she has not*. She had no choice."

"I agree."

He leaned forward, ready to make his point. "So do you think God would say that it is all right for his children to do what he himself will not do?"

"No, of course not."

"Then that's your answer. If God himself won't force you to do something, why would he grant that right to your father?"

She began to nod slowly, a glimmer of hope showing in her eyes.

"We bring honor to our parents by doing what is right, no matter what they think about it," he said. "We always dishonor our parents when we do evil, even though they may approve of that evil."

His eyes softened as he looked at her. "What you have done, Miriam, brings honor to the house of Mordechai ben Uzziel, even though your father doesn't believe that. I think you can be at peace about whether or not you have violated that commandment."

"Thank you," she whispered. "It means a lot to me to hear you say that." Then she straightened. "What else did you have to say to me?"

Simeon took a quick breath. To Miriam's surprise, he was suddenly nervous. He began to pluck at something unseen on his tunic. "Have you ever considered that our relationship is somewhat odd?"

She stared at him incredulously. "Did it ever occur to *you* that there is not one thing about our relationship that *isn't* odd?"

He chuckled. "Agreed. Every time we have met or had time together, it has been in some kind of crisis."

She tipped her head to one side. She hadn't considered that.

"Think about it. The first time we ever saw each other was that terrible morning with Moshe Ya'abin. Next was when your father had Yehuda and me come to Jerusalem. Another time, you slipped away from Jerusalem and came to Capernaum to warn me about your father's trap. I raced off to save the world while you and Livia and my mother sat off in the distance waiting to see what happened."

"Then there's you in prison in Caesarea," she broke in, "and me a prisoner in Rome." She suppressed a sudden, wild urge to laugh. "And how about you dropping into my bedroom from a rope in the middle of the night or putting on a wig and selling candles? I don't see anything odd about that."

He smiled briefly; then his voice became wistful. "That's exactly what I mean. Look at us even now. Here we are out in some desolate corner of the Roman Empire, on the run from people who would put you back in confinement and probably hang me from a cross if they could catch us."

She wished that she could see his eyes, read what was behind them, but in the darkness they were mostly in shadow. "I won't argue with any of that. The past year and a half have been one long crisis for both of us. So why are you saying all of this?"

"I don't know. I can't help but wonder what it would be like for us to get back to Capernaum and settle into something even close to a normal life."

"That's not going to come easily," she responded gloomily. "I have no money. The only thing I can do to earn a living is peel vegetables, and I picked up that skill only in the last few months." In spite of herself, her shoulders sagged a little. "It will be a long time before my life is normal again, Simeon."

"If you're looking for sympathy from me, woman," he growled roughly, "you've come to the wrong place. You're talking to a has-been Zealot chieftain who is so worried about loving his enemies and treating the Romans as if they were really people, he can't even pick up a bow anymore."

She tossed back her head and laughed. He watched, fully smiling now, seeing the starlight reflecting off the blackness of her hair. Simeon continued, "I also thought about a career in diplomacy, but my first attempt at that a few days ago didn't go so well."

She hooted softly. "I definitely would recommend something other than diplomacy."

He kept his face completely sober. "See what I mean? Even my friends mock my efforts to make an honest living."

Miriam thought back to the first day she had met Simeon. She had never met a man more aloof and cutting. His tongue bit like acid on the flesh. He was infuriating. Then moments later he would be gentle and considerate, filled with quiet, subtle humor. Now here it was again. The night he had come to rescue her he had hurt her more deeply than anything she could ever remember. She suddenly started at that thought. *He hurt me even more than Father did.* That filled her with wonder. Why was that so?

And here he was again—teasing, witty, droll, and utterly charming. One part of her wanted to curl up here with him beneath this oak tree and never leave. At the same time, another part of her was shouting, "Warning! Warning! Intense pain ahead!"

She realized that he had stopped talking and was watching her steadily. "You said there were three things you wanted to say," she reminded him. "The first was my father and what he'll try to do. The second was the strangeness of our relationship. What is the third?"

There was a deep sigh, tinged with pain.

"Simeon, you promised. I don't want to talk about the other night. I mean it."

"It's not about the other night."

"All right. Go on."

He paused for a long time; then he began, speaking quietly. "The first time you saw Jesus, you believed in him, didn't you?"

That question was the last one she had expected, and she had to shift her thoughts into a completely different direction. "I think 'believe' might be too strong a word," she finally answered. "I didn't know him at all. I don't think he said anything that day other than telling the moneychangers they had turned his Father's house into a den of thieves." Then she shook her head, remembering back. "But even then, there was something about him. Yes, I guess I did believe in a way."

"It wasn't that way for me."

"I know. Your mother told me how you struggled at first."

"Even after I was convinced he was the Messiah, I couldn't reconcile Jesus' teachings with what I expected him to be. I grew angry. Why couldn't he just be what I expected him to be?"

She said nothing, for she sensed that he was peeling back a layer of his soul that she had not seen before.

"Then something started happening inside me. I reached the point where I could not not believe. I watched with my own eyes as he worked some incredible miracles. I went to Nazareth and spoke with his mother. When I came away, I knew that he was far more than just the Messiah. I knew he was the Son of God."

He stopped, looking past her, seeing back into the past, sifting through the memories as though they were single sheets of paper. Then he laughed in soft self-condemnation. "That should have changed everything, but in a way it only made things more difficult. I told Yehuda that I couldn't lead our band anymore. Then came the situation at the Joknean Pass. Because I asked Yehuda and others to help me, Daniel ended up dead and Yehuda landed in prison awaiting a sentence of death. It seemed like everything I tried to do to be a more faithful follower of Jesus only led to deeper complications.

"Then I began to notice a pattern developing. I was trying to stay faithful to Jesus, and yet I couldn't seem to get the sword out of my hand."

"Sometimes we have no choice but to fight against evil," she suggested.

He didn't seem to hear. "I began to develop these elaborate schemes that I thought would allow me to fulfill my duty and still be true to my discipleship. Every one of them turned out to be disasters."

"Like what?" Miriam asked, moved by the depths of emotion she could feel in him now.

He uttered a short, bitter laugh. "Did you hear about my clever plan to purchase Roman uniforms so I could break into the prison at Caesarea?"

"Yes. Ephraim told me all about it one night."

"It was cunning, brilliantly planned, and would have been flawlessly executed. It had only one small problem. It was insane. Everyone could see that but me."

"Simeon, you—"

He went right on. "Or how about my next idea? Just saddle up a horse and ride straight into the Praetorium in Caesarea. Dangle three talents of gold in front of the nose of the governor and ride out again.

I planned it all so carefully. I thought I had even made allowance for possible treachery. So what happened? Marcus sprang the trap so neatly, all I could do was stand there and stare at him." He waved an arm in the air. "Again, it was brilliant strategy, immaculate planning. And utterly stupid. Even a child should have seen what was coming."

"You were trying, Simeon."

"That's my point. I *was* trying. My motives were good. My desire was sincere. It was my execution that was flawed. I charged ahead like a blinded bull, knocking over fences, trampling on people, breaking every vase and pot in the village as I went through."

"You got Ya'abin. That worked. Ezra says your plan *was* brilliant. You didn't lose a single man, and yet you met Pilate's demands. You are free, and I don't have to worry anymore about whether or not the governor will find out that it was me that betrayed him. Surely you can take satisfaction in that."

"Yes," Simeon said, again surprising her. "I came home from the wilderness of Judea feeling like at last I had learned something, that at last I was making it work."

"So why can't you accept that you did something right?"

"Because within a month of that, what am I doing? I'm brooding about this woman in Rome who has promised to follow Jesus too, but now she seems to have turned her back on him. I'm sitting there getting angrier and angrier when I think about her marrying some pompous Roman tribune, the very man who once nearly killed me, who almost sold my mother and sister into slavery, and who betrayed his word to me and clapped me in chains."

"Simeon, don't. You promised."

He swung on her. "I'm not talking about the other night, Miriam. I'm talking about me." Then his voice softened. "There are some things that very badly need to be said. Do you really want me to stop?"

She lowered her head. "No."

"Oh," he went on, more softly now, his voice heavy with irony, "my motives were good. My desires were sincere. My planning was impeccable. I was going to charge in and save Miriam bat Mordechai, the woman who had saved my life. But what did I do?" There was a mocking laugh. "Like I said, I was an angry bull, swinging around at every sound, charging at every movement, smashing every decent thing I had supposedly come to save. That's when I realized I hadn't changed at all."

For a very long time they sat there, not looking at each other, enveloped in their own thoughts and emotions. Finally Simeon turned to her. "I am so sorry, Miriam. How could I have been so blind? How could I have thought that you, you who accepted Jesus the first time you saw him, could turn away? I knew that you could never marry Marcus, and yet I wouldn't believe it."

For a moment, she wasn't going to answer; then she smiled slightly. "That next morning, I told Livia that you were a stubborn, hardheaded fool."

He shook his head. "You were always far too generous with me."

"I thought so at the time too," she said, teasing him just a little. Then she was serious again. "But Livia added one word to my assessment."

His eyes lifted to meet hers. "What?"

"She said you were a stubborn, hardheaded, *jealous* fool." Her eyes lowered, the dark lashes covering them from his view. "Is that true, Simeon?"

He stared at her for a moment; then he nodded very slowly. "Yes."

She felt her heart skip a beat and her breath catch in her throat. "Go on," she said.

"I was sick when Marcus told me he was going to marry you. Once Ya'abin was caught, I had dreams of coming back to Capernaum, of you coming back from Rome." There was a sigh of pain. "Of perhaps having a time when life was normal and we could walk along the Sea of Galilee and just talk."

"Why didn't you tell me *that*, Simeon?" she whispered.

"Because all I could think of was Marcus and you. I kept saying over and over to myself, 'What if it's true?'"

She slid off the rock and moved over to sit beside him. After a moment, she reached for his hand. He grasped it as though he were sinking in deep water. "Thank you for telling me now, Simeon."

He nodded. "There's one last thing."

She laid her head against his shoulder. "I'll say this, Simeon, son of David, when you finally decide to talk, it is a wonder to behold."

He laughed, loving the feel of her against him.

"Don't stop. I wasn't suggesting that. Say on."

"All right. I told you that I have a possible solution to this problem with your father."

She lifted her head. "Yes?"

"If you had married Marcus, or even if you had gone ahead with the betrothal, at the moment it was finalized, your father's legal hold on you would have ended."

They were close enough that he could see that her eyes were wide. "But—" she started.

He put a finger to her lips. "A husband, even a betrothed husband, has first claim on his wife, not the father. You are of legal age now. You don't absolutely have to have his permission to marry now." He drew in a deep breath. "I know I have no right to say this, no right to hope that it could ever possibly be, and I won't speak of it again until we reach Capernaum and things settle down."

She jabbed him sharply in the arm. "Simeon! Just say it!"

"I had thought that if I could ever convince you to forgive me, I might, when the time is right—"

She briefly clamped her hand over his mouth. "*Tell me!*" She was barely breathing now. "What do you plan to do?"

He stood and pulled her up to face him. He reached out and touched her cheek, brushing it with the tips of his fingers. "I plan to ask you if you would ever consider accepting another offer of betrothal. That would still give you a year before the marriage to see if there is any hope of taking this old has-been Zealot in tow and—"

She cut him off again by going up on her toes and kissing him soundly. "Yes, Simeon," she whispered exultantly. "The answer is yes. But please, don't wait too long to ask. A girl might lose hope."

His countenance changed to awe and wonder. Slowly and with great gentleness, he took her face in both hands. She closed her eyes as he bent down and kissed her softly. When he finally pulled back, she didn't move, nor did she open her eyes.

"Hanukkah candles, m'lady?" he asked.

Her eyes flew open. He laughed at her expression.

"Are you saying . . . ?"

He nodded gravely. "I think Hanukkah would be a perfect time for a betrothal. The slowest portion of our journey is behind us. If we keep moving, we can reach Capernaum by then. Assuming, of course, I could find a woman who was willing."

"Willing to marry a hardheaded, stubborn fool?" she whispered contentedly.

"A hardheaded, stubborn, *jealous* fool. Do you think that is possible?"

"Of course," she said. She pulled his arms around her, closed her eyes and went up on her tiptoes again.

CHAPTER NOTES

It is commonly thought that in the Jewish culture at the time of Jesus, all marriages were arranged by the parents, especially the father, and the woman had no say in who her husband would be. Some modern writers, both popular and scholarly, would have us believe that women were traded and sold like livestock with no choice in the matter. While this was likely the case in some instances, evidence suggests that the woman had significant rights and that romance between the sexes was not uncommon. Though Abraham sent his servant to find a bride for Isaac, and the arrangements were made with Rebekah's father,

Rebekah was asked for her consent (see Genesis 24, especially vv. 8, 58). Ruth, who was a widow, deliberately sought out Boaz and took action that told him clearly she wanted to be his wife (see Ruth 3–4).

Two selections from modern scholars should serve to dispel the idea that women had no rights whatsoever in the marriage decision:

"The father as head of the household usually instituted the plans for marriage on behalf of his son. This included the selection of the bride. On her part, she was more or less a passive participant in the transaction. . . . The place of the father in arranging marriage is consistent with the concept of the family in the Bible. *It does not rule out some activity on this stage on the part of the potential bridegroom and bride. There is some indication of romance.* We are told, e.g., that Michal loved David (1 Sam. 18:20). At harvest festivals and at the village well the sexes met and mingled freely. . . . Certainly Rebekah [in the Genesis 24 account] is not chattel to be bought in the market. The conception of the status of a wife found in Prov. 31 further supports the view that marriage by purchase is an untenable interpretation" (Buttrick, 3:283–84; emphasis added).

"The arranging of a marriage was normally in the hands of the parents . . . ; there are, in fact, few nations or periods where the children have a free choice. But (a) infant or child marriages were unknown; (b) *the consent of the parties was, sometimes at least, sought* (Gn 24:8); (c) the rule [of the parents] was not absolute; it might be broken wilfully, or under stress of circumstances; (d) *natural feeling will always make itself felt in spite of the restrictions of custom; the sexes met freely, and romantic attachments were not unknown* (Gn 29:10; 34:3; Jg 14:1; 1 Sam 18:20); *in these cases initiative was taken by the parties*" (Hastings, 584–85; emphasis added. Not all references cited by the author of this passage were included here).

BIBLIOGRAPHY

Alexander, David, and Pat Alexander, eds. *Eerdmans' Handbook to the Bible*. Grand Rapids, Mich.: Wm. B. Eerdmans Publishing Co., 1973.

Bahat, Dan. *Carta's Historical Atlas of Jerusalem: A Brief Illustrated Survey*. Jerusalem: Carta, the Israel Map and Publishing Co., 1973.

Berrett, LaMar C. *Discovering the World of the Bible*. Provo, Utah: Young House, 1973.

Bloch, Abraham C. *The Biblical and Historical Background of Jewish Customs and Ceremonies*. New York: Ktav Publishing House, 1980.

Buttrick, George Arthur, ed. *The Interpreter's Dictionary of the Bible: An Illustrated Encyclopedia*. Nashville: Abingdon Press, 1962.

Carcopina, Jerome. *Daily Life in Ancient Rome: The People and the City at the Height of the Empire*. New Haven, Conn.: Yale University Press, 1940.

Casson, Lionel. *Travel in the Ancient World*. Baltimore: The John Hopkins University Press, 1994.

Clarke, Adam. *Clarke's Commentary*. 3 vols. Nashville: Abingdon, 1977.

Collins Gem Latin Dictionary. New York: HarperCollins Publishers, 1996.

Cornell, Tim, and John Matthews. *Atlas of the Roman World*. New York: Facts on File, 1982.

Dummelow, J. R. *The One Volume Bible Commentary*. New York: Macmillan Publishing Co., 1908.

Edersheim, Alfred. *Sketches of Jewish Social Life in the Days of Christ*. 1876. Reprint, Grand Rapids, Mich.: Wm. B. Eerdmans Publishing Co., 1979.

———. *The Temple: Its Ministry and Services as They Were at the Time of Christ*. 1874. Reprint, Grand Rapids, Mich.: Wm. B. Eerdmans Publishing Co., 1958.

Fallows, Samuel, ed. *The Popular and Critical Bible Encyclopædia and Scriptural Dictionary*. 3 vols. Chicago: The Howard-Severance Co., 1911.

Farrar, Frederic. *The Life of Christ*. Portland, Ore.: Fountain Publications, 1964.

Grimal, Pierre. *The Civilization of Rome*. New York: Simon and Schuster, 1963.

A Guide to the Monumental Centre of Ancient Rome, with Reconstructions of the Monuments. Rome: Vision S.R.L., 1962.

Guthrie, D., J. A. Motyer, A. M. Stibbs, and D. J. Wiseman, eds. *The New Bible*

Commentary: Revised. Grand Rapids, Mich.: Wm. B. Eerdmans Publishing Co., 1970.

Hastings, James, ed. *Dictionary of the Bible.* New York: Charles Scribner's Sons, 1909.

Jacobs, Louis. *The Book of Jewish Practice.* West Orange, N.J.: Behrman House Publishers, 1987.

Johnston, Harold Whetstone. *The Private Life of the Romans.* Chicago: Scott, Foresman and Co., 1903.

Josephus, Flavius. *Antiquities of the Jews.* In *Josephus: Complete Works.* William Whiston, trans. Grand Rapids, Mich.: Kregel Publications, 1960.

Keil, C. F. and F. Delitzsch. *Commentary on the Old Testament in Ten Volumes.* 1878–89. Reprint, Grand Rapids, Mich.: Wm. B. Eerdmans Publishing Co., 1975.

Mackie, George M. *Bible Manners and Customs.* 1898. Reprint, New York: Fleming H. Revell Co., n.d.

Regelson, Abraham. *The Passover Haggadah.* New York: Shulsinger Brothers, 1965.

Schürer, Emil. *The Jewish People in the Time of Jesus.* Nahum Glatzer, ed. New York: Shocken Books, 1961.

Shelton, Jo-Ann. *As the Romans Did: A Sourcebook in Roman Social History.* 2d ed. New York: Oxford University Press, 1998.

Vincent, Marvin R. *Word Studies in the New Testament.* 4 vols. New York: C. Scribner's Sons, 1887–1900.

Vine, W. E. *Vine's Expository Dictionary of Old and New Testament Words.* Old Tappan, N.J.: Fleming H. Revell Co. 1981.

Who's Who in the Bible: An Illustrated Biographical Dictionary. Pleasantville, N.Y.: Reader's Digest Association, 1994.

Wight, Fred H. *Manners and Customs of Bible Lands.* Chicago: Moody Press, 1953.

World Book Encyclopedia. 22 vols. Chicago: World Book, 2000. S.v. "Christmas."

Wouk, Herman. *This Is My God: The Jewish Way of Life.* Rev. ed. New York: Pocket Books, 1974.

Wright, George Ernest, and Floyd Vivian Filson, eds. *The Westminster Historical Atlas to the Bible.* Rev. ed. Philadelphia: The Westminster Press, 1956.

ABOUT THE AUTHOR

Gerald N. Lund received his B.A. and M.S. degrees in sociology from Brigham Young University. While in southern California, he also did extensive graduate work in New Testament studies at Pepperdine University in Los Angeles and studied Hebrew at the University of Judaism in Hollywood. His love for the Middle East and its people has taken him to the Holy Land more than a dozen times as a tour director and lecturer.

He was a religious educator for more than thirty-five years in the Church Educational System for The Church of Jesus Christ of Latter-day Saints, where he taught students both on the high school and college levels. During his career, he also wrote and developed curriculum materials, including numerous media presentations on the Old and New Testaments.

He is the author of more than nineteen books. In addition to the nine volumes in the bestselling *The Work and the Glory* series, he has written five other novels: *One in Thine Hand*, *The Alliance*, *Leverage Point*, *The Freedom Factor*, and *Fire of the Covenant*. He has also written several books on gospel studies, including *The Coming of the Lord*, a study of the Second Coming of Jesus Christ. His books have won several honors, including twice winning the Independent Booksellers "Book of the Year" award.

He and his wife, Lynn, have seven children and live in Alpine, Utah.

THE ROMAN WORLD AT THE TIME OF CHRIST

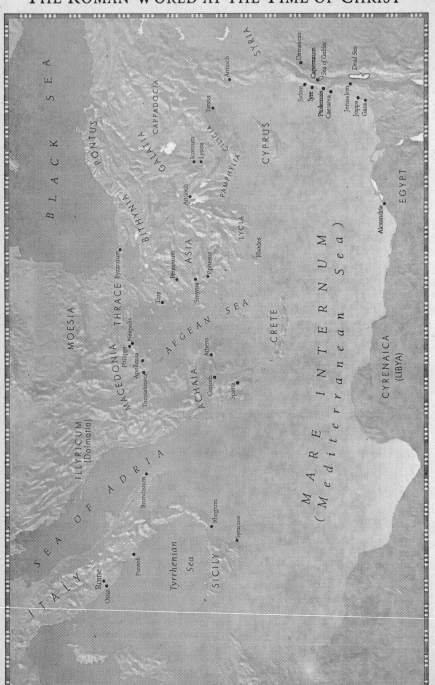

THE HOLY LAND AT THE TIME OF CHRIST

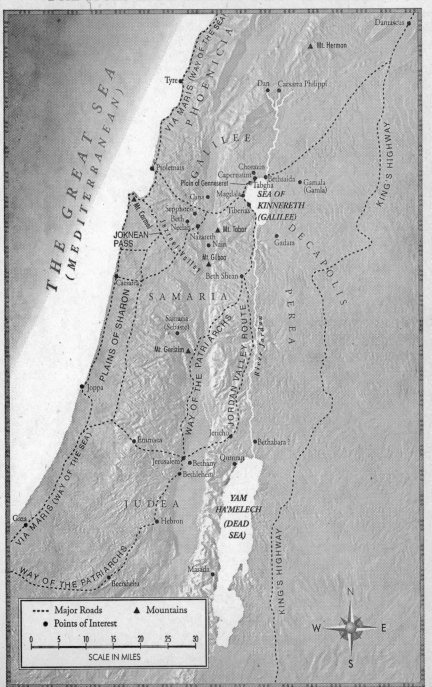

Damascus

▲ Mt. Hermon

Tyre

Dan Caesarea Philippi

PHOENICIA

VIA MARIS (WAY OF THE SEA)

GALILEE

KING'S HIGHWAY

Ptolemais

Chorazin
Capernaum Bethsaida
Plain of Gennesaret Tabgha Gamala
Cana Magdala (Gamla)
Sepphoris **SEA OF**
Beth Tiberias **KINNERETH**
Neelah **(GALILEE)**
Nazareth ▲ Mt. Tabor
Nain Gadara

THE GREAT SEA (MEDITERRANEAN)

▲ Mt. Carmel

JOKNEAN
PASS

Jezreel Valley

DECAPOLIS

▲ Mt. Gilboa

Beth Shean

PEREA

Caesarea

SAMARIA

PLAINS OF SHARON

Samaria
(Sebaste)

▲ Mt. Gerizim

WAY OF THE PATRIARCHS

JORDAN VALLEY ROUTE

River Jordan

Joppa

Emmaus

Jericho

Bethabara ?

Jerusalem Bethany
Bethlehem Qumran

VIA MARIS (WAY OF THE SEA)

J U D E A

**YAM
HA'MELECH
(DEAD
SEA)**

Gaza

Hebron

KING'S HIGHWAY

WAY OF THE PATRIARCHS

Masada

Beersheba

- - - - Major Roads   ▲ Mountains
● Points of Interest

0   5   10   15   20   25   30

SCALE IN MILES

N
W   E
S

Note: Beth Neelah is a fictional village. All other sites are authentic.